A Dance of Storms and Shadows

S.L. Green

Copyright © S.L. Green
All rights reserved.

No part of this publication may be reproduced, distributed, or transmitted in any form or by any means without written permission from the author, except as permitted by U.S. copyright law.

The story, all names, characters, and incidents portrayed in this production are fictitious. No identification with actual persons (living or deceased), places, building, and products is intended or should be inferred.

Book Cover by MiBlart

Map Illustration by MiBlart

Edited and formatted by Scott Editorial

To everyone who thought maybe you were a little strange,
Or who thought maybe you just didn't belong.
To anyone who has ever scrawled hundreds of story ideas into a notebook,
Or has been planning out the same story for a lifetime.
We're all a little strange.
You belong here.
Here's the invitation to your story.

A Dance of Storms and Shadows is a fantastical adventure with dark themes. Some elements included are death, kidnapping, attempted murder, murder, poisoning, gore, grief, graphic violence, torture, sex, sexual violence, weaponry, and isolation. Readers who may be sensitive to any of these themes please take note.

Table of Contents

Prologue- Tobyn
Chapter 1- Allanora
Chapter 2- Allanora
Chapter 3- Lysan
Chapter 4- Allanora
Chapter 5- Henrie
Chapter 6- Allanora
Chapter 7- Allanora
Chapter 8- Allanora
Chapter 9- Allanora
Chapter 10- Allanora
Chapter 11- Henrie
Chapter 12- Henrie
Chapter 13- Allanora
Chapter 14- Allanora
Chapter 15- Henrie
Chapter 16- Henrie
Chapter 17- Allanora
Chapter 18- Allanora
Chapter 19- Henrie
Chapter 20- Allanora
Chapter 21- Aros
Chapter 22- Allanora
Chapter 23- Aros
Chapter 24- Allanora
Chapter 25- Rylan
Chapter 26- Allanora
Chapter 27- Allanora
Chapter 28- Allanora
Chapter 29- Rylan
Chapter 30- Allanora
Chapter 31- Allanora

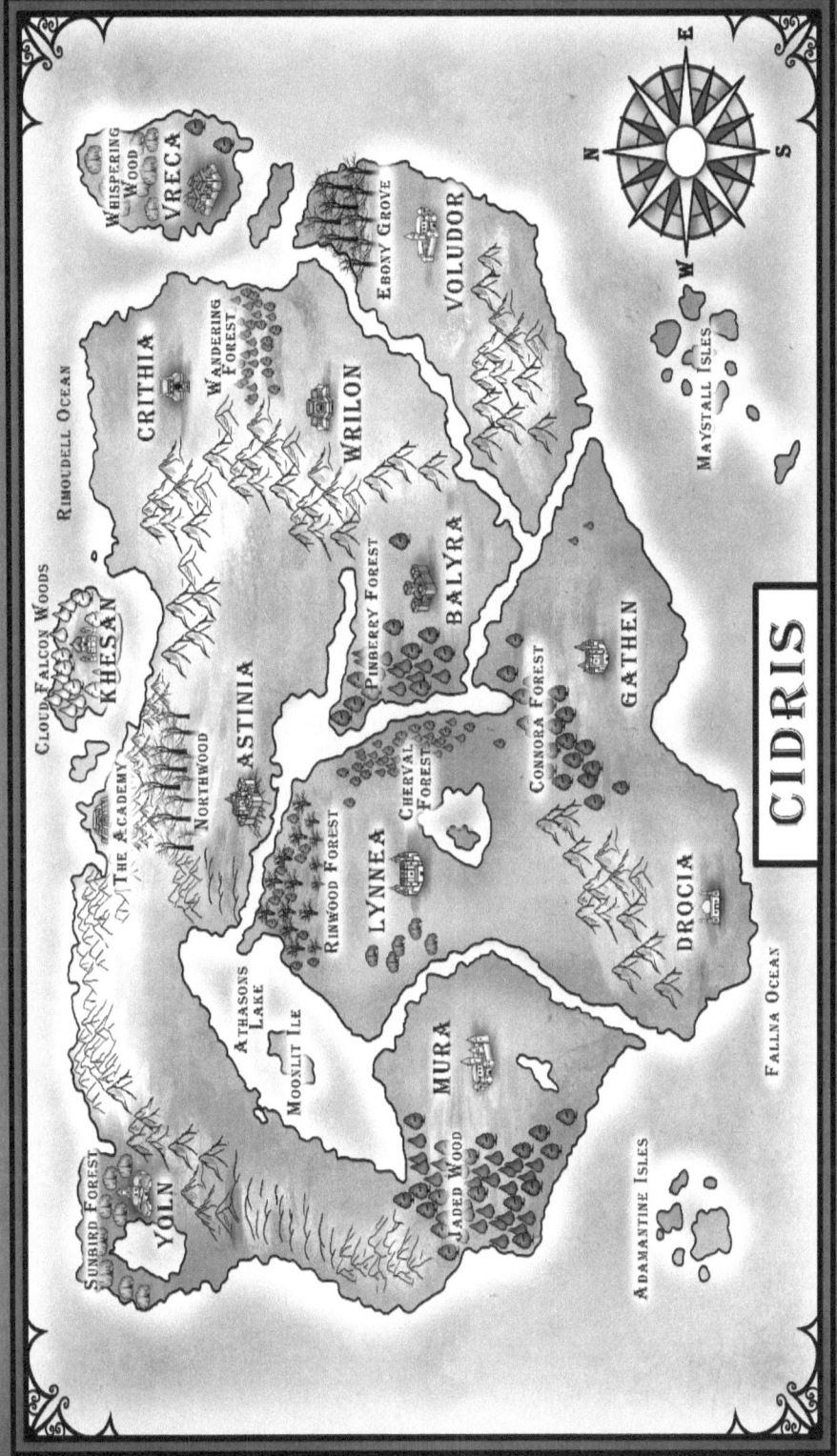

Prologue

Tobyn

Outside Violet's chamber door, the suns had both long gone, and the marble halls of the Lynnean palace grew quiet. Pharon, Queen Violet's mage, had been trying to cast a spell to help her sleep, soothe her dreams. He had the silver eyes of a mage and long gray hair that he kept tied back with a gray ribbon. His robes were a deep blue, embroidered with small flecks of silver thread. Pharon exuded power; he was considered one of the most powerful mages to have lived.

"Tobyn," he crooked a finger at me, his voice no higher than a whisper, "I would speak with you."

I gulped, my skin prickled under an unexplainable heat. Mages always made me uncomfortable, even though Pharon had been in Violet's trusted circle almost as long as I had, but he held a very mysterious air around him like a cloak. "Pharon, what news of the Queen?"

"Her mind is weak. I've placed a series of light dreams into her mind to soothe her, but I'm not sure they'll take. There's something there, a wall around her that I am struggling to break through." He let out a breath, and the air around us chilled.

"I don't know why the King even went to this ceremony in Astinia. They haven't openly pledged their allegiance to the Deities or the Triini of the Golden Dawn in this war. Our King, a King whose Lynnean kingdom has aligned itself with the Deities, shouldn't put himself at risk that way. Especially when it leaves his Queen in such disarray, not to mention what that does to Lynnea." My anger boiled. I rubbed the scar that had been carved into my face, but Pharon was unphased, a marble statue of patience.

"It is not for those of us in service to the crown to question their choices, Tobyn," he said softly. His velvet tone was meant to soothe, but it only pushed me to infuriation.

"It's my job to protect the Queen," I snarled through my teeth.

"And you are doing that, Tobyn, by standing guard outside her chamber and protecting her from outsiders. It isn't your job to guard her mind, make her decisions, or question her as your monarch." His expression iced, and he drew his shoulders back, squaring up, but kept his hands folded in front of him.

The clapping of footsteps echoed through the empty halls then. I drew my sword, facing the dim emptiness, while Pharon braced with his hands out in front of him.

A young guard came racing toward us out of the darkness, out of breath as he fell to his knees on the ground, clutching his chest and wincing. "Sir Hawkham, please, it's the Princess, send for healers. Pharon, help her." He collapsed with another breath. I turned my head toward Pharon, and he pulsed from the room in a puff of smoke to tend to Allanora. I rolled my eyes. *Must be nice to be able to pulse from one room to another without a second thought.* I scoffed, with no one to hear me but the unconscious guard and the empty air. *Mages...*

Remembering myself, I dashed a few paces down the hall to ring the bell, alerting the castle to danger before storming into the Queen's chamber to check on her.

The sight of her had me rushing to her bedside. She was convulsing; her eyes were wide and glazed over. Her jaw hung open in an impossible position, and foam had gathered in her throat. Frantically, I ran to ring her bell for Pharon. Another puff of smoke had him back in the room, immediately joining me at her side.

"The Princess?" I asked him feverishly. My hands braced on the Queen's shoulders. I tried to hold her still while he looked her over.

"The same," he replied hurriedly. He placed one hand on her forehead and the other on her abdomen. She settled, taking in a shaky breath. "That will hold her for now. I have to return to the Princess." And in another maddening puff, he was gone.

"What is happening?" I muttered to myself. Outside, I heard the clatter of armor and the rush of shuffling feet. Before I stood, I checked that Violet was still breathing steadily.

Out in the hallway, I couldn't remember why I went out there. For a moment, I stood in dumb silence before a servant running past bumped me back into reality. The motion jarred me, and looking around, I realized that everyone in the castle seemed to be frantically running around or pacing as if they were unsure what to do or where they were going.

I broke into a run toward my sons' chambers. Henrie's was empty, and when I peeked into Julian's room, I found him with a servant girl bent over his bed, enjoying her company without any worry about anything going on outside. *No honor—I'll deal with him later.*

"MOVE!" An older guard carrying a crumpled-up Allanora came soaring down the hall straight at me. We collided, and darkness blanketed me.

My eyes were so heavy that I could barely get them open. The light that flooded through felt like something I hadn't ever experienced before, burning to the point I had to close them again. I clapped my hand over my eyes and tried again, letting just a little light through the cracks between my fingers.

"Sir Hawkham?" An elderly voice cut through the silence of my mind.

"Yes?" I managed to groan out. My throat felt as if it had hardened into stone, the word barely clawed itself through my teeth.

"Are you all right?"

Keeping my eyes guarded, I did a survey of my body and didn't find pain or any strange feelings. I nodded slightly. "What happened?"

My eyes finally focused, just enough to see the face before me. He was dressed in a scarlet cloak, with the hood pulled over his brow. He was pale underneath and seemed to have an inhuman snake-like look to him, but I couldn't quite put my finger on why. His eyes were brown and worn with age. I studied him with guarded apprehension—a Brother of the Triini if the rumors were to be believed.

He spoke in a honey-coated tone. "You've been delivered, along with your Queen, your Princess, and the rest of Lynnea, to the safety of the arms of the Unnamed God."

The Unnamed God. The Triini have taken the kingdom.
Violet.

"Where is she?" I forced as much authoritative demand into my voice as I could muster to the stranger.

"Your Queen is well. She is being seen to by our healers, along with the little Princess."

"What happened?" I demanded again, this time more powerfully.

"The Deities have fallen, retreated into the ether from whence they came. You are all safe now, safe from their tyranny. Your true God has delivered you." Gently, he placed a hand on my shoulder, and I sat up. The world around me spun, and I was sure I would vomit, but I kept swallowing to keep it down. "Your Queen now has free reign to rule as she pleases, and your people will be blessed by the prosperity of the Unnamed God."

All I could do was nod. His words confused me. Deities, Unnamed God... My memories swam in and out. My mind reached for them, but I couldn't grasp them.

"Why don't I remember?"

"The Triini want your people to feel peace, not unrest. We've helped heal your minds by pushing memories of the war away. You'll find you remember a war but not much about it. You'll know your friends died, your family, but you won't remember what you saw, the grating sights of mangled bodies strewn about a bloody battlefield." He spoke in a sickly-sweet tone as if soothing a child.

"The King—I—what happened to the King?" I stuttered, my brain fumbling around, tripping over itself, trying to find the words, the memories.

"Your King has disappeared; we haven't been able to find him in the wreckage of the madness in Astinia."

Astinia. The King had gone to Astinia. The memory danced on the barriers of my mind, taunting me.

"But we—Violet—she pledged our soldiers to fight for the Deities."

The Triini Brother's face hardened just slightly, and he pursed his pale, dry lips. "Your kingdom has been forgiven, as now Queen Violet's eyes have been opened to the Golden Dawn, and she's vowed to loyally praise the Unnamed God."

My head started to spin again. Everything in the room became a blur. "Can I—can I see her?"

"Not just yet. You're still unwell, but don't worry, the Queen is cared for." He laid me back down on the overstuffed mattress, and I was enveloped in a cold blanket of darkness once more.

Chapter 1

Allanora

Thin fingers dragged gently through my hair, brushing and styling. My eyes stayed closed, pretending I was anywhere but here in my bedroom. I'd grown tired of hearing how important today was from everyone who cared to tell me. I knew how important it was, I'd spent my whole life preparing for today. My nails dug themselves into the etched mahogany in front of me.

"Princess Allanora?" My handmaid Lyra's voice hummed from behind me. I snapped back to attention; I had been slumping down in the chair of the vanity in my bedchamber. She was fussing with my long chestnut hair for what had felt like hours now, twirling each piece into place. Her gray eyes met mine in the mirror. I took a deep and frustrated breath, and she turned her face back down, pursing her lips as she worked.

I looked out the window. The second sun was slowly surpassing the first, symbolizing mid-afternoon. My heart skipped a beat, then started to pound in my chest. Evening was drawing near. I longed for the night. When all the fuss would be over and the Lynnean sky would be painted in silence and darkness, the only light being the cascades of stars millions of miles away shining brilliantly with the light from the fallen suns. It felt like this ball would take a lifetime before that reprieve.

"Sorry, Lyra, I guess I was lost in thought," I relented, forcing myself to stay fully upright.

"It's a big day for you, Your Highness. Your choosing ball is one of the most important days of your life. You get to choose your husband today." Her voice was giddy, and she giggled, an innocent, sweet sound that didn't match how I felt at all.

"Get to'?" I tutted. "*Have to*, more like. Her Majesty the Queen insists on it." I waved my hands around, mocking my mother.

Lyra's cheeks flushed pink.

"Come now, Princess, Queen Violet just wants what's best for you. You know that." I sighed.

"I do know that. But, of course, my grandmother Cressida allowed her to wait *four years* after her eighteenth birthday to have her choosing ball. Four years, Lyra. Could you imagine what I could do with four years? I could see the other eleven kingdoms, ride my horse through all the forests of Cidris, maybe even see a dragon!" My sapphire eyes lit up at the thought, *a dragon in the flesh.* Of course, I'd been to most of the other kingdoms, but I had only been inside their castles or seen the lands from the safety of my guarded carriage. The thought of seeing all of Cidris entranced me.

"A dragon, Your Highness, really. No one has seen a dragon since the Deities went into hiding after the Great War. Even then, they were scarce. You certainly wouldn't remember, you were just a babe. I myself was not much older, of course. No, no, the Triini Brothers and Sisters of the Golden Dawn are working to put an end to all the magical foolishness of our realm." She rolled her eyes at my folly, and I slumped again slightly in the chair. Of course, she was right. Magic had been all but prohibited, save for a few sacred healing practices and things of that nature. The Unnamed God was meant to be an all-powerful being who protected and provided for us, making magic almost wholly unnecessary for the people of Cidris. Kings and Queens were given the freedom to rule as they saw fit, without interference, as long as we continued to pray to and follow the teachings of our God, practicing his way for our ceremonies and gatherings.

Like weddings. A chill ran down my arms when my mind returned to what today was meant for. I cast another glance out my window. Dark and menacing storm clouds gathered over my beautiful kingdom of Lynnea, a perfect mirror of what I was feeling deep inside.

"Well, at least it would give me time to maybe fall in love on my own. I'm supposed to decide this evening, and I've barely gotten to spend any time with any of the eligible men of the kingdom, Lyra. Let alone the few attending from neighboring kingdoms. She keeps me so close under her watch, I've barely gotten to know anyone my whole life, except you and the other servants, of course. I don't even know many of the other noble inhabitants of the castle. My whole world revolves around her."

"Sometimes love finds a way to break through the surface, even in political marriages such as yours." Goosebumps covered my arms at the sound of my mother's voice, and I cringed, knowing she had been listening. Lyra dipped into a hasty curtsy.

"Your Majesty," Lyra greeted my mother as she entered the room.

My mother waved her off with a kind smile. She was the picture of grace, as always. Her golden hair was pulled up in a neat and regal bun underneath her crown; her hands were folded neatly in front of her enchanting lavender ballgown that was embroidered with delicate gold stitching. She placed her hands on my shoulders, and I felt them relax slightly under the kind pressure. "She's a pretty little thing. Skinny. Quiet. And seems to understand your royal duties a little better than you do."

I groaned and rolled my eyes.

"It's much easier to understand when you're not the one doing it." I pouted. "Everyone expects me to live up to you. The beautiful, graceful, *perfect* Queen Violet of Lynnea. You don't have a King ruling beside you, and you're the most beloved Queen Lynnea has ever had." I crossed my arms over my chest. She brought her face next to mine, and I saw us together in the reflection of my mirror. I'd always been told I looked just like her, aside from her blonde hair, high cheekbones, and dimples. I couldn't always, but in that moment, I could see it. I felt my anxiety bubbling below the surface, storm clouds gathering in my stomach.

"You'll be perfect, my darling. You are *my* daughter, the future of this kingdom, and your people love you. Any man who you might choose tonight will love you." I looked down into my lap and laced my fingers together as she spoke; her voice was calm and soothing in my ear. She tipped my head back up to the mirror. "I remember my choosing ball. It was perfect. I was surrounded by all the people that I would one day rule. And I was twirled around the dance floor by all the eligible men in the room—" She shook her head and let the thought drop to the floor. The weight of it hung between us.

She rarely ever talked about her choosing ball or my father. I'd tried asking about my father when I was little, but she had always just told me that he had gone far away and it was for the best. It didn't take me long to realize that she wasn't going to talk about it, and it took me even less time to decide that she was all I needed anyway.

"Brysa—my dear, please join us," she said, turning toward the door.

Her handmaid, Brysa, who had apparently been outside the door this whole time, stepped in and made her way over to us. She was holding an old and beautifully ornate silver box, perfectly polished. Tiny little flowers covered the entirety of the box, all beautifully welded into the metal.

Brysa was plain but pretty and youthful, a couple of years younger than me. A blond ringlet fell in front of her face while she bowed to my mother. She hurriedly brushed her hair aside and held the box toward me. I reached out and ran my fingers over the lid. Brysa's little fingers were trembling; she was new to her position, as my mother's previous handmaid had just gotten married and moved from the palace into her husband's family home.

My mother took the box from Brysa and waved her off, as she had done to Lyra. Little Brysa scurried off, leaving us alone once more. My mother placed the box in front of me and turned the little elaborate rose key that rested in the lock. The key had the same tiny, opulent flowers decorating its handle as the box. She raised the lid, and I saw the loveliest glittering tiara lying on a purple velvet pillow. It was silver and glistened with diamonds and sapphires.

"Oh—Mother, it's stunning," I crooned. I felt my eyes spring open with more excitement than I had felt the entire day.

She smiled, took it carefully from the box, and placed it on my head. It was a perfect fit. I saw myself in the mirror. I had worn tiaras before, but this one was bigger, closer to the look of a crown. For the first time, I looked at myself and saw a Queen. I turned my face back and forth in the mirror, admiring the beautiful tiara.

She smiled at me while I admired myself.

"This was the tiara my grandmother Fiona wore for her choosing ball. My mother gave it to me for my choosing ball, and now I am giving it to you, my darling, and one day, you will give it to your own daughter." The thought of having my own child turned my stomach, and the excitement I had felt wearing her beautiful tiara washed away with the sudden reminder of what I was meant to do that day.

Wincing, I opened my mouth to reply, but before I could, there was a hurried knock on the door. The door opened, and Tobyn, my mother's closest and most trusted adviser and longtime friend to the crown, entered the room. My mother looked annoyed but held her composure as she always did, staring at him, waiting.

"My apologies, Your Majesties, but your guests have gathered, and it is time for your announcement." I stood, and he bowed to both of us. I curtsied in return, and my mother held out her hand. He kissed it gently, as most did when they greeted her. He returned to his full height, towering over both of us. His presence was intimidating, his eyes dark brown and piercing, and he had the strength and build of a well-learned knight. He carried a mysterious air about him, though I had known him my whole life. He was the closest thing I had to a father since mine disappeared. His hair was peppered gray, and he bore a long scar down his right eye—a mark he received while protecting my mother as the head of her royal guard. This feat had earned him the title of General of the Lynnean army. It was an extremely high honor for a man who had not been born to one of the Great Houses of Lynnea, though he was still from a noble family.

"Tobyn," she greeted through gritted teeth. "Thank you for escorting us. Very kind of your family to spare you. Are both of your sons in attendance this evening? Henrie and Julian?" I cringed as she shot a pointed look at me from the corner of her eye.

"Oh, yes, Henrie and his wife, Eleanore, are in attendance, and Julian will be there, hoping for a dance with our lovely Princess, of course." I tried to hide my disgust at the thought of Tobyn's oldest son being one of my suitors. I opened my mouth to reply, but my mother answered for me.

"Allanora will, of course, be considering *every* option presented to her tonight. Though I do believe the stubborn thing plans to choose a match on her own without either of our input." She smirked at me from the side, and Tobyn held his hand out for us to walk ahead of him. I followed behind my mother, and Tobyn put his hand between my shoulder blades to guide me in his fatherly way.

Lyra and Brysa were waiting for us in the hallway. The light had grown steadily dimmer. The second sun had fully set, leaving the first to slowly creep down the horizon behind it. I tried to focus on anything besides where we were going and found myself looking sidelong at Brysa, who was studying Tobyn carefully, and the color drained from her face.

He grinned a wide, toothy grin. "You admiring my scar, girl?" Both my mother and I groaned. *Here we go.*

Brysa's eyes went wide; she was lost for words but shook her head.

"I got it protecting your lovely Queen here." He chuckled. "She wasn't much older than you lot, and her carriage was attacked by an Astinian soldier on the way back from Balyra. You know those brutish Astinians. Always out for blood, they are." He tapped his finger on his scar. "This one had a taste for royal blood, or he was paid to. He put up a good fight, but I bested him. Put a nice sharp spear right through his chest," he made a spear-throwing motion with his hands, "but he left me this so I'd never forget." He ran his finger over the scar. "Our Queen doesn't have much to do with those bloodthirsty Astinians anymore anyway."

"That's quite enough of that, Tobyn." My mother silenced him with a steady hand. I let out a relieved breath. I couldn't even count how many times I'd heard the story. She ushered him in front of her. "You're the one that told us the guests had been gathered, and it was time for the ball. Here you are dilly-dallying in the hallway, preening for the maids." She shooed him down the hall, following a few paces behind him.

My breath caught in my throat when we approached the double doors leading down to the main ballroom. They opened for Tobyn, and a footman stood waiting to make his announcement. They locked eyes, and Tobyn nodded to him.

The footman hit his staff on the floor to gather the attention of the guests. "Sir Tobyn, son of Tygrin of House Hawkham." Smiling and waving proudly, he descended the steps into the ballroom.

For being a man from a lesser noble house, he was known by everyone in the kingdom, and in other kingdoms, as well. He carried himself with as much pride and self-assuredness as any of the Great Lords did and was a strong and highly dignified General.

I watched my mother step to the top of the stairs behind him and nod to the footman. He tapped his staff once again. "Her Majesty, Queen Violet of Lynnea, daughter of Late Queen Cressida of House Harthope." The room erupted in joyous clapping, lit up by the presence of the Queen. She glided effortlessly down the steps, the sea of beautiful subjects parting. She turned around in the center of the ballroom dance floor, focusing her attention, and therefore everyone else's, on me.

Nerves clenched my stomach, and I focused on her. She was my safety, my joy, my family. She was in her mid-40s, but she glowed with the youthful glory of a woman half her age. She showed not even a trace of a wrinkle, and her light skin was as smooth and beautiful as a young child's. I could only hope that I would age as gracefully as she did.

With a hard swallow, I took a step forward, feeling the pressure of their collective gazes on me. I made wary eye contact with the footman who tapped his staff on the ground, this time for me. "Her Royal Highness, Princess Allanora of Lynnea, daughter of Queen Violet of House Harthope." I reminded myself to breathe; I was tied so tightly into the ballgown that it was easier to simply hold my breath. My nerves exploded, and I became uncomfortably aware that everyone's eyes were fixated on me. The footman cleared his throat with the slightest sound, and I finally stepped forward, gliding down the steps, hoping I was half as graceful-looking as my mother.

The music switched to an upbeat waltz, and a man appeared in front of me, Brendan Cypra. He held his hand out for me to take. *Eager.*

"Sir Brendan, how lovely to see you again." He smiled a haughty smile. I looked into his eyes; they were a dark but pretty brown, almost the same shade as his hair. He had dark skin and a square jaw, a desirable and manly set of qualities. He was clean-shaven, as most of the men in the room were. Brendan stood taller than me but not towering, as many men were, considering I was of short stature. His attire was gold and white and adorned with the winged horse emblem of House Cypra, a favorite house of my mother's.

"Princess Allanora, might I have this dance?" He bowed and kissed my hand.

"Oh, just Princess Nora, please; Allanora was my great-great-grandmother," I said softly, flustered.

He twisted his face a little at my apparent informality, but he spun me into the dancefloor nonetheless. He was a good dancer, not pushy as he led, though I could tell he had a "take charge" attitude about him. His hand on my hip made me feel uncomfortably electric, a sensation I had not felt much before. I had practiced dancing many times, most of which with my mother or dancing instructor, an older woman named Gretchen. Dancing with a man, a suitor, felt different, sensual, though I didn't find Brendan Cypra himself particularly exciting.

"I suppose I should thank you for the aid House Cypra is always providing to the crown."

His proud smile said it all; it was important to him that I knew his family was wealthy. The Cypra family was one of the richest in Lynnea, and they always flaunted it so everyone knew just how full their coffers were.

"House Cypra is proud to provide the crown with anything it needs. Lynnea is a strong kingdom backed by many powerful houses. I hope that you consider House Cypra among them." His voice was arrogant and powerful. "I'm sure it helps that House Cypra has deep pockets."

I'm sure you're going to be dangling that money over my head all night. I felt more disinterested the more he spoke. He spoke only a little of his family, his father, who was older, his mother and sister, but mostly about the family money. Evidently, it was endless. I listened as intently as I could, but money was not all that interested me.

The song ended. *Finally.* I felt a hand clasp mine, guiding me away from Brendan of House Cypra. Feeling a sense of relief but also anxiety, I was whisked off by my next dance partner before I could give Brendan Cypra another thought.

My next suitor was tall, easy on the eyes, which were a stunning sky blue, like the ocean. With my hand resting on his arm, I once again felt that spark of sensual desire. He was warm to the touch and breathtakingly handsome, looking younger than Brendan but still older than me. He was built like a knight, broad-chested with a chiseled jaw. His blond hair was tousled beautifully atop his head. It looked so soft, and I fought the growing urge to run my fingers through it. He was dressed in baby blue and the oak tree emblem of House Blackwood.

"Princess Allanora," he addressed me formally as he kissed my hand. I sighed as I realized I would be hearing my full name quite often tonight. I smiled and nodded my head.

"Just Princess Nora is fine, Sir Arthur." He beamed with humble pride, almost looking surprised that I knew his name. House Blackwood was another very well-known noble family. Lord Horst Blackwood was a generous man, always at the aid of others without expecting much in return, whether providing monetary aid or fighting in battle. The crown could always count on House Blackwood. I recalled a story my mother told me about Horst Blackwood helping to solve a dispute between two Lynnean families. My mother offered to repay him, and he had refused, asking only to be recognized as a friend and ally by the crown.

"I recall your father helping my mother with a particularly difficult exchange. The Blackwoods have always held a special place in her heart."

He smiled, his cheeks flushing pink.

"The Blackwoods are forever at the aid of the crown, my dear Princess. You can call on my sword anytime, and I shall serve you justly."

His humility was almost as attractive to me as his face. Hundreds of butterflies fluttered in my stomach. We exchanged a few niceties, and I thought he had some real potential, though I knew I had to complete this political song and dance of meeting with every eligible bachelor. We didn't want any of the noble families feeling cheated. My mind raced back to Arthur throughout every introduction. Every time I thought of him, the flutter returned. From the corner of my eye, I saw Arthur dutifully take the hand of another young woman, and my cheeks flushed with jealousy. *It doesn't matter. If I choose him, he's mine.* The thought shot through my mind like an angry arrow flying toward its mark.

I eventually found myself in the arms of Tobyn's oldest son, Julian, and a shudder crept down my spine. Julian was tall and not attractive; at least, not my type. He was quite well known to be popular among servant girls if Lyra was to be believed. His face was round, and he was weathered and much older than I was. I would have much preferred his younger brother Henrie if I had been forced to wed one of them, though I understood Henrie to be happily married. I winced as Julian's large hand trailed down my back while we danced clumsily.

"I'm glad you could be here tonight, Julian," I croaked out. The discomfort in my voice was thick, but I pasted on my best smile. He grinned and picked me up off the floor, the skirt of my gown flaring out around me as he set me back down. I stumbled but kept myself upright.

"My father insisted I be here; our family has served the crown faithfully for a great many years. He feels I should put my best foot forward."

"Happy to have your best foot," I said shortly.

I curtsied to him when the song came to an end and turned quickly on my heel, running directly into an extraordinarily handsome but strange man. I turned back just in time to see Julian scowl and walk away, giving the mystery man enough time to take my hand and twirl me into him at the beginning of the next song.

    His clothing was noble but odd, not a usual style for Lynnea, but perhaps a neighboring kingdom. Quickly, I went through the list in my mind of suitors attending from other kingdoms, trying to figure out if he could be one of them. He was wearing mostly black with just a few details in green and gold, accentuating his piercingly striking green eyes. He did not speak or try to exchange names but merely spun me around elegantly throughout the waltz while I stared into those captivating emerald eyes. He had an arrogant and mysterious air about him, the way he led me around was so powerful yet graceful. I found myself letting my eyes wander all over him, from his broad shoulders and chest to his chiseled jaw. He was muscular but lean, like he had been well-trained for battle. Perhaps he was a knight, though he surely wasn't dressed as one. One hand trailed almost delicately down my waist, and I noticed the calloused fingers of an archer. *A soldier?* I thought to myself, *but he held himself almost like royalty.* I was enticed even by his scent, cypress and vetiver, nothing I had been particularly drawn to before, but now I couldn't seem to get enough of it. A strange pull tugged at me, and I felt a peculiar almost familiarity about him, as if I'd met him before. Surely, though, I'd have remembered.

    My palms were sweating, though he didn't seem to notice. I wondered if he could feel my heart pounding in my chest pressed up against his. He bent me backward, and I was relieved that he hadn't spoken, as my tongue had gone completely numb, my mouth dried, and I was lost for words. My breath shortened, and he kept me dipped down for what felt like an eternity before bringing me back up, his hand fixed on the small of my back. *He has to be the one.* I smiled at the thought. I just as quickly shook it from my mind, dismissing it entirely. *Foolish girl, you don't even know who he is. Control these carnal notions.* I pursed my lips, feeling scolded by my own mind, knowing that these would be the opinions of my mother. He twirled me out and back in, our faces so close together I thought he'd lean in and kiss me. *Do I want him to?* He took a step back, and I finally let my breath out, feeling cooled off and empty all at once. He reached out and took my hand, kissing it as he bowed, sending goosebumps up my arm and making me start to sweat all over again. My other hand fluttered involuntarily to my chest.

I looked around and took my hand back from him, realizing suddenly that some of those around us had begun to whisper among themselves. My cheeks blushed pink.

Much to my relief, the footman hit his staff on the floor, calling everyone to attention once more.

"Who—" I started to ask the man who he was, but he had vanished from my side.

"Dinner is served," the footman announced, sending the guests to find their seats as servants poured between the tables with platters piled high with roasted pig, quail, exotic fruits and vegetables, endless loaves of fresh bread, and my personal favorite, braised beef. The mixed scents of my kingdom's most delicious foods captured my immediate attention. I scurried off to my table, where my mother was already seated.

A plate had been made for me, and I took a liberal pat of butter and smeared it on a thick slice of hot bread.

"You still have time, sweet girl, but how are you feeling?" she inquired, trying to mask her own excitement.

I swallowed the huge bite of bread I had just greedily taken and found my voice. "Well, I'm sure you saw Brendon of House Cypra."

She tried to hide a smile at my bringing him up.

"He's quite handsome, but I got the feeling he has a large ego. I'm just not sure he's going to be my first choice."

Her face fell slightly with disappointment.

"Arthur of House Blackwood seems to be a very fine man and so gallant." I blushed again as the excitement returned to her face.

"Oh, yes, House Blackwood is a very old house and a very close friend of the crown." Her face glowed with anticipation and pride. "Arthur is quite alluring as well."

She dropped her voice to a whisper so quiet that I almost couldn't hear, resting her chin on her hand. "Now, who was that last man? He seems familiar. You seemed quite taken with him."

My heart raced. "I have no idea, Mother, but when he took me to dance, I felt that spark, you know, the one people talk about when they're instantly attracted to someone." Without even thinking, I was looking around the ballroom full of faces, trying to land my eyes on him again. Finally, I saw him, standing nonchalantly near the back of the ballroom, seeming to watch everyone around him. Careful that no one seemed to be paying attention, I quickly pointed him out to my mother. "He's so mysterious. And handsome. But I don't even know his name, nor if he's even eligible. I didn't recognize his clothing or any identifying emblem. I was hoping you'd know who he was or where he's from."

Her violet eyes followed where I had pointed, and she shook her head slightly.

"I'm sorry, my darling, I don't recognize him either." She sounded wary, concerned that even she did not know who he was. She watched him intensely for a moment, as did I, to see if there was anyone he talked to who could introduce us, but he remained alone, watching the crowd and lazily eating an apple.

It was my turn to be disappointed, my heart in my feet, as the mysterious man seemed a far less likely candidate. I sighed, despite myself. I knew there were many other choices, handsome Arthur being at the top of the list. Yet my need for excitement and adventure seemed to be drawing my mind over to the mysterious nobleman again and again. Excitement and adventure weren't what my mother wanted for me, and they certainly weren't what the kingdom needed. The kingdom needed a man like Arthur—strong, kind, fair, and stable. At least, that's how he seemed to me.

Once everyone was seated, my mother stood up, raising her glass of wine to the room of glittering subjects. Everyone fell silent when she spoke; her voice was warm and captivating.

"Today is a celebration, not only of my beloved daughter, Allanora, but of every son and daughter of our beloved kingdom, Lynnea; every one of you here. I have been proud to be your Queen, and I will be proud, one day, to put this kingdom in the hands of my daughter, your Queen-to-be. Tonight, she will choose her husband, witnessed by every one of you, and soon, their union will be blessed in front of the entire kingdom in a royal celebration. Raise your glasses and honor your future Queen."

It seemed almost everyone was smiling as they lifted their chalices high and sipped their wine.

As I touched my lips to my glass, I heard shocked gasps around the ballroom. To my right, I saw only a glimmer of the Queen's golden cup as it clattered to the floor. Her eyes widened in pain, and her face twisted inexplicably as she cried out, clutching at her throat. She ripped a string of pearls from her neck as she clawed and attempted a couple of breaths before her eyes rolled back into her head.

I knocked my chair to the floor when I stood, throwing myself toward her in a panic. Frozen, I watched my mother fall before me onto the cold stone of the ballroom floor. Everything around me blurred. I could only feel that I was screaming as I knelt beside her, guards whirling around us, carrying her and escorting me out as quickly as they could. The last I saw of the ballroom was other guards surrounding my subjects as the doors to the hallway leading to my mother's rooms slammed behind us.

We were rushed to her bedchamber. I knocked over a small table that clattered to the ground in front of me, earning me a glare from one of the guards trying to get her to the bed. I forced my trembling hands out in front of me and propped the table back up on its legs. The massive room suddenly felt small, the walls and ceiling pressing into me as my whole world crumbled and shrank. I clutched her ice-cold hand in mine.

"Out of my way, out of my way!" Healer Tolland Brightwood pushed through the guards, his face pale with worry. Tolland was a Triini healer, practiced in the way of medicine using herbs and poultices, occasionally potions. Practical healers were what they were called, and it was the only kind of healing allowed under the eyes of the Triini.

"Violet, my dear!" His forehead wrinkled while he looked her over, his aged eyes scanning her up and down. He pulled a few vials from his sleeve and mixed them together in a bowl next to the bed. He was moving so quickly he spilled a little bit, which he wiped up with his sleeve.

"Healer Brightwood, please, what is that? What is happening to her?" My mind clung to her. She was the only family I had left; my whole world was wrapped up in her. Rocks in my chest dragged me down into the abyss of panic, my breaths coming closer and closer together, hot tears stinging my eyes.

He looked up at me in surprise as if he didn't know I was there.

"Allanora, my dear," he grumbled. "It seems she may have been poisoned. I don't know what with, but I am trying to make an antidote." He took my hands carefully in his. They were trembling just like mine.

"Poisoned? I don't understand."

He returned to hastily mixing. My nose filled with aromas of strong herbs as he ground and mixed, the paste turning to liquid. Sometimes, I wondered if things had been easier when mages were allowed to practice properly. Magical healing seemed so much more efficient.

Pushing the thoughts from my mind, I focused on my mother, knowing healer Brightwood would do everything he could for her. "Everything was wonderful... I was going to choose my husband. She was so happy... Who would want to poison her? Why?" I asked him frantically; he tensed up but started trying to get her to drink his antidote.

"Your Highness," he finally turned back toward me, "I think it would be best if you returned to your chambers for the time being. I need to keep a close eye on your mother, and you'll be safe there with a guard posted at your door if whoever tried to hurt her is after you as well. I promise I will take good care of her. Please." His eyes were tired, droopy, solemn, and I knew he was right. He motioned for two of the guards to escort me back to my rooms. I took one more glance at my mother, who had been so vibrant and lively only a short time ago, now drained of all color. She lay so still on her bed. *Why,* I wondered to myself, *would anyone want to hurt her?*

Chapter 2

Allanora

I was no more than an empty shell on my bed. I did not know how much time passed; I did not care, didn't even look out the window at the suns to craft a guess. Lyra had come just to get me into bedclothes and put my hair in a braid. Neither of us spoke. My body was tired. The weight of drowsiness tried to pull me into its warm abyss, but I didn't sleep; my mind was too busy worrying. *What happened to her? Who did this to her? Why did they make me leave when I only want to be with her?*

Walking would be a good way to clear my head. I slid off my bed, tucked my arms into one of my robes, and pulled my braid from beneath the silky fabric. It was dark, and the hallway was cold and lifeless, almost eerie. Both suns had set, and with them had gone all my hope. I had never felt uncomfortable in my own castle until now; the only home I had ever known was strange to me.

I passed by a few Brothers of the Triini, our religious leaders who resided in the castle for ceremonies and religious proceedings. They wore scarlet robes tied at the waist with a corded rope, the emblem of the Unnamed God hanging from the bind. It was the shape of a kite, surrounding three intersecting arrows. Claws clutched the shape from the outside.

"Good evening, Your Highness," the leader, Brother Sol, greeted me. The Triini had always seemed other-worldly to me, though I couldn't exactly put my finger on why. They just gave me an eerie feeling. The Triini were humans who had transcended into the light of the Golden Dawn. No one outside of their sanction knew what it was exactly that happened when they took on their role as a disciple of the Unnamed God. But they had convinced millions of Cidrins to fight and win a war against the Deities to free us from their tyrannical reign, so it must be something miraculous.

"Good evening, Your Excellency," I croaked out, sweeping down into a curtsy. I realized I had barely spoken a word since my mother had fallen ill.

"I only wish to greet you under happier circumstances." He looked up from underneath his red hood. His face was very pale, and his skin was worn and leathery, as if he were elderly, though he didn't seem to be of advanced age. He smiled at me, a less-than-sincere smile, and I nodded back. Even though he was a religious leader, meant to guide us, there was something about him that made me uneasy. He crossed the few steps to my side of the hallway, the other two cloaked figures shadowing him. A shudder crawled down my spine. "Your mother has not always been a steady follower of the faith, my Princess. She always held on to the beliefs of the twelve, even after they were long gone. I should hope that when you ascend the throne, you better understand the mercy and power of the Unnamed God." All the liquid seemed to drain simultaneously from my lips, forming an unquenched desert in my mouth, leaving me speechless.

Is he threatening me? Admitting to harming my mother because she was not a great follower of the Golden Dawn? I gulped and forced another nod. He squinted at me, awaiting me to say something. I stared at him silently, then forced myself to speak.

"I have always considered myself to be an avid follower of the Golden Dawn. The Unnamed God is my light and my truth," I recited carefully, as I had always been taught to do. Brother Sol regarded me with a satisfied smile and continued his slow stride down the hall.

Though he gave me the creeps, he was a holy man, and part of me believed he had been put in my way tonight to remind me of the power of our God.

Once I was back in my room again, I started to pray to the Unnamed God as I had done before, this time to spare the life of my mother. I lay back down in my bed, feeling a hungry blanket of sleep start to engulf me.

As I drifted between realities, a woman appeared in front of me. I tried to blink her away, thinking she couldn't be real. She looked strangely familiar, but I couldn't figure out why. She was middle-aged and strikingly beautiful, with a familiar gleam in her purple eyes.

"Who are you?" My voice sounded as if it were coming from a different room. She smiled and took my hand.

"I was like you once, my dear. Young, full of life, so many choices ahead of me. I wanted everything my way and damned the consequences. Your mother is dying, my dear Allanora, and someone ordered her death. You must trust no one, fear everyone. *You,* my darling girl, are the future of Lynnea, of Cidris. You will be very loved but very coveted, and that may prove to be very difficult for you." Her voice was grave but warm and somehow calming, even with such strong words on her tongue.

"I—I don't understand." My lips quivered. I heard my voice, still distant. I wondered if she could even hear me. My mother couldn't be dying, not now; I had so much to learn.

She turned her head as if she heard something in the distance.

"I must go now, dear girl. Listen to me. They may be after you, too. You are your strongest ally. Take the reins, find out who killed her." She disappeared in a soft *pop,* and I was left rubbing my eyes in disbelief, trying to figure out if it was all just a dream.

The door flung open, and Lyra entered my room in a fuss. I wasn't sure if she had woken me up or if I was already awake; I was in such a fog. My head was heavy along with my eyelids, and my stomach was churning endlessly. Lyra sat quietly and twirled her hair around her fingers; she was uneasy. There was a knock at my door, and she jumped.

"Come in," I called coldly. I sighed in relief when it was Tobyn who entered the room. But when he lifted his face to look at me, my eyes started to fill with tears once again.

"She is not well, my lady, but she is still breathing. The healers have tried everything they can think of. They've said at this point, only time will be able to tell if she will be well again," he said hurriedly. He looked tired and defeated. His already wrinkled skin looked like it was sagging, his eyes were downcast and weary, and he looked as if he hadn't slept in weeks. It felt like the wind was being knocked out of me again, but I kept my composure; at least she was still alive. That meant there was hope.

"Where are my guests? What happened to them?" I asked. I was hoping he had some information as to what was going on outside and if he had any idea who'd done this. *Tobyn always seems to have insight into everything.*

"All guests have been kept for questioning; any suspects will be locked up for further interrogation, my lady. I have asked the guards to report to me—"

Trust no one. The voice of the strange woman rang in my mind; I held my hand up and cut him off. His jaw snapped shut, and I felt a sense of satisfaction that came with giving orders.

"Any problems or information will be reported directly to me, no one else." I took a deep breath, realizing the gravity of my situation. Thrown into responsibility I wasn't ready for, not knowing who to turn to. "In my mother's absence, I will rule." Determined, I hardened my mind against the instinct to flee, knowing I must fight. "That is final." I sealed my words with a cold stare. He tensed up at my demand, but I did not care; I was the Princess. That dark cloud crawled back through my thoughts again, casting its gloomy shadow on my mind. *Fear everyone,* the voice warned. *But who can I trust if not my mother's most dependable advisor?*

"But my lady, you are—" I cut him off again with a wave of my hand, feeling strangely like my mother.

"Take me to her immediately, Tobyn. Tell the guards to report directly to me if they have any information." He looked defeated once again, and the scar on his eye curved downward as he frowned. He bowed to me and opened the door to escort me out. I followed him through the hallways to my mother's bedroom. As we approached, I stepped ahead of him and threw the door open, slammed it before he could enter, and rushed to her side. Three healers scattered out of the room, leaving us in peace.

She looked even paler than before. Her once sun-kissed golden hair had turned white and lay strewn about her pillow. The color was slowly fading from her once vivid violet eyes. She held her hand out to me, and I grasped it gently.

"My love." Her voice was weak and raspy, barely a croak breaking through the silence. The floodgates of tears opened, and I began to cry. She looked so fragile when, just hours ago, she was so strong, so graceful, and full of life. She smiled at me. She had never been afraid of anything, even in our darkest moments. I admired that about her.

"You look just like your father, my flower," she said softly. The hair on the back of my neck prickled, as it did every time I considered the man who had left us behind. That feeling of sadness clutched my heart. I climbed up on her bed just as I did when I was a child, woken in the night by nightmares.

"My father doesn't matter, Mother, only you." I started to sob, and she reached out to take me in her arms. She hushed me and continued, despite my protests, while she ran her fingers weakly through my hair.

"Before you came along, your father was everything to me; he made me everything, and he gave me you," she began, and I stilled in her arms. "I fell for him instantly at my choosing ball. He was handsome and charming. A true King. Any woman would have been thrilled to have him. Many had tried, yet he was always mine." Her eyes filled with tears also, and I continued to sob.

"His name is Aros," she continued, every word hanging painfully on her lips. "I am sorry that I never told you. After he left, I just wanted to be everything that you ever needed, and now I know that I was wrong. That I have been selfish. I loved your father so much. As husband and wife, we could not be together, but you, you, my darling, can be with him. Find him, my flower, and you will understand." I heard what she said, but it didn't matter. I didn't care about my father; I never had. All I ever needed was my mother, and now I could feel her very soul dying, withering away into the unknown, and there was nothing I could do. I was helpless. The door creaked open again, and Tobyn entered, two guards in tow. I glared at him; his presence, once more, irritated me.

"What do you want now, Tobyn?" I asked him angrily.

"My apologies, Your Highness, um—these guards have information for you," Tobyn said curtly. He seemed to shrink a little bit beneath my words. I nodded and squeezed my mother's hand before standing and composing myself by smoothing my dress and tucking my hair behind my ears. Then, I followed the guards down the hall. I didn't want to be separated from my mother, not even for a moment, but I knew I had to learn everything I could about what had happened to her if I had any hope of making things any better. I followed the guards into the library. In the corner, I saw Henrie, Tobyn's quiet younger son, the palace bookkeeper, seated at his desk. He noticed us and hurriedly took off to a different part of the library. I sat in a chair in the corner and motioned for them to sit as well. They shook their heads no.

"No, ma'am. We are not permitted to sit in the presence of a monarch," the first guard sputtered out uncomfortably. I stared into his eyes. I could tell he was afraid, possibly afraid of me. Not many guards or servants were ever directly spoken to by royalty. I tried to soften my gaze to make him more comfortable, but I was on edge, just as he was. I sighed.

"If you have any information to share, please share it, sir..." I hesitated; I had not been given the name of either guard. The first spoke up again.

"I am Micah. This is, uh, Orin. We were both stationed near the, er, kitchen during the ball, m'lady, and we 'ave some information that might, uh, help with the Queens...situation. Miss, uh, I mean, 'Yer Highness." He fidgeted with his hands as he spoke, and I felt myself getting more annoyed with him. He elbowed the second guard, Orin, and he jumped. I let my hand drop into my other palm in frustration, hoping this was worth it. I rubbed my temples, and the second guard started speaking.

"Yes, uh, 'Yer Highness, there was a man in the kitchen, but 'e wasn't wearing servant clothes, so, uh, we figured 'e wasn't supposed to be there."

I started tapping my fingers on my cheek as I listened. He stuttered a few more syllables before I interrupted him.

"So, did you see who he was or what he looked like?" I asked in a hurried tone. I knew I was coming off as irritable towards these poor, scared guards. I just wanted to get back to my mother, but I also wanted to know what happened to her. I tried to draw patience as I knew she would.

"Well, uh, 'e was tall. Oh, and 'e dressed in all black, Princess Allanora," the first guard said. *Tall? Most of the men in the kingdom are 'tall.' I can't go storming through the city looking for a 'tall' man in black.* I stood up from my chair. Both guards towered over me, but still, they both took a slight step back. I opened my mouth but was interrupted by the door flying open and Tobyn rushing in. His eyes were blazing, and he looked like he had been running. Both guards let out a relieved sigh and hurried from the room, quickly bowing to me before exiting. At this point, I was angry; my cheeks were flushed hot, and I felt my heart racing in my chest.

"Tobyn! You've interrupted every single significant moment of my night. You just chased away the only two men who had any information that might help me. They'll probably never speak in front of me again! Whose side are you on, anyway? Because it certainly doesn't feel like you're on mine!" I let out an exasperated breath and waited for an explanation. He was out of breath himself, looking stunned, gasping, but finally mustered up some words before I was able to unleash any more on him.

"You must come, my lady," he gasped. "She's leaving us, she's barely breathing, and the healers have exhausted all of their options." My heart fell through the floor; I brushed him to the side and ran down the hallway. I felt like my feet couldn't move fast enough. *Why is this palace so big?* I saw room after room fly by me: Tobyn and his sons' rooms, servants' quarters, my room... Salty tears stung my face. My lungs were struggling for air. I was running out of breath. I reached my mother's room and flung the doors open without waiting for the guards to open them for me.

A Dance of Storms and Shadows

There were still two healers in the room; a mage had joined them, along with two Triini Brothers who were praying quietly at her side. I hadn't seen a mage in many years; we were not permitted to allow them on castle grounds anymore by order of the Triini. I wondered what deals Tobyn had made with Brother Sol to allow this to happen and how he had even gotten a mage here so quickly.

The mage was quietly casting a spell over my mother's closed eyes and met my gaze upon my entrance. It was bizarre to watch. His fingers danced in the air as if playing an invisible harp, and I found myself inexplicably drawn to the thrum of energy being emitted by him. It was not unlike the way I was drawn to the unexpected man at the ball, something strange and unspoken drew me in. Immediately, I was sobered when he shook his head, lowering his hand. I didn't think it was possible, but my heart sank further as I looked at my poor, frail mother lying in her bed. Her once beautiful blonde hair was now completely white, drained of all life. Some had fallen out of her scalp and lay strewn upon her bed. Her hands were trembling, her lips a mawkish shade of purple. She tried to give me a warm smile but started to cough instead. The mage wiped her mouth, and I saw a streak of scarlet blood. I felt dizzy at the sight. An older healer was sitting beside her, opposite the mage, with a cloth pressed to her forehead. He looked up at me with a tear dripping down his face. He stood and bowed to me, gathered the cloth and his bag, motioned for the mage and the others to follow, and left me there, alone with my dying mother. I lay in her bed with her and held her hand. I felt so much overwhelming love and sorrow washing over me. Her face was a pale, sickly green, and her eyes were still open, but I could feel her heart weaken with every beat. I wept harder than I ever had, and her hand squeezed mine tightly.

Her lips quivered, parting slightly. A hoarse sound came from her throat, and I realized she was trying to speak. My fingers flew to her lips to stop her, calm her. "Don't, Mother," I said through a curtain of tears drowning my eyes.

My mother took a shaky but determined breath. "No number of tears will ever heal the sick, my love." Her words came out in a forced whisper. Every word was hurting her, but I knew trying to silence her would be useless. She'd be a Queen till the end. She'd be heard. I brought my ear closer to her lips to help ease her strain. "My heart is always with you. Rule your people, my beloved flower. I will smile down on you always." Fresh sobs escaped my tight chest. Fear was taking me over, the darkness dragging me into an abyss of storm clouds, my chest constricted, barely allowing me to take a breath. "Remember me as I was, not as I am." I nodded shakily. How could I ever forget the willful, determined, just, and fair Queen she had always been? My loving mother would not be reduced to this moment, not so long as I drew breath. "Never let anyone make you feel small. You are a Queen. Don't let them forget it." I watched her through blurry eyes, not being able to promise that I wouldn't let her down but needing her to know I'd try. Her breaths were coming in quicker now, as if she wasn't getting enough air. I felt my own air depleting as well, as if my life force was entwined with hers. I squeezed her hand tight, willing her to stay with me.

"Please," I begged, "please don't leave me." I dropped my head down, burying it in her chest.

She stroked my hair sleepily, and I could feel her slipping away. "Lynnean Queens fear no one," she continued, fighting the drowsiness of death, "bow to no one, and rise above. Be strong, my flower. No blade can cut a golden stem." Finally, a look of peace washed over her face, but I could feel no peace of my own as she closed her eyes, her last breath leaving her body. I screamed so loudly that five guards rushed into the room.

I lifted my head enough to peer at them through angry eyes. "Get out. *Get out!* GET OUT!" I shouted, letting my head fall on her chest in a fit of sobs once more. I would not allow her subjects, none of them, to see her in this state. I screamed again, but this time it was an angry scream, and when the door flew open once more, it was Tobyn. The room shook as I wailed, or perhaps I was just imagining that. Tobyn was nothing but a blur behind the angry tears in my eyes.

"Stop it, my lady, you must stop!" he shouted at me. "You can't let them see you break, whoever did this. You must overcome it." He grabbed me from behind and squeezed my arms tightly to my sides to restrain me.

"I don't care!" I yelled at him, trying to pull away. "I don't care about any of them, and I don't care about a worthless, spineless murderer!" I spat the last words and cried out, pulling and kicking at him before I felt him cup his hand over my mouth, muttering under his breath. I felt him squeeze me tightly around my stomach before I went limp in his arms. Then everything went black.

A dark-lit castle, the walls lined with years of dust and crumbling bricks. A single torch at the end of a hallway. A masked figure outlined in the light of the torch. The figure moved closer. I tried to step away, but I was paralyzed. I tried to shout, but no words came. The figure was almost upon me. My eyes stayed open, unable to shut to escape the fear. The figure became a face in front of me, cold and ruthless but familiar. Why familiar? A hand gripped my neck, and once more, I tried to shout, but only silence emerged from my throat. Tears welled up as fingers tightened around my neck, nails biting into my delicate skin. "Be strong, my flower, no blade can cut a golden stem." I heard my mother's voice softly spinning around me. Another voice echoed hers, a man's voice I did not know.

"No blade can cut a golden stem." I shut my eyes tightly and, with my mind, reached for my mother, her face shining in the darkness behind my eyelids.

Chapter 3

Lysan

The news of the death of Queen Violet had spread through the castle like wildfire. The whole kingdom was in mourning an hour after her death. All tapestries of her crest had been brought down and replaced with black silk. New tapestries with the crest of Princess Allanora would have to be made and put in place once the mourning period had passed. Poor Allanora, I thought. Already 18 but still so young to lose her mother and have to take on the crown. All the servants felt sorry for her. Brysa had said to all of us that she could hear her screams the moment her mother died even from the next wing over, where she and Lyra had been waiting to hear news of the Queen's health. She said, in that moment, she knew the Queen had died, and the hearts of all the people of Lynnea had shattered.

"Lysan!" I heard the gruff shout from inside my grandfather's room. Tobyn had been acting Regent since the Queen's death 3 days ago, as Princess Allanora had not been seen since. I grabbed my silver tray and dashed into his room as quickly as I could. He had taken quite a liking to wine since the Queen passed. My job as his cupbearer had never been so busy. I approached him and filled his cup. His room smelled strongly of alcohol, and he took a large sip and let out a sigh. His room was dark; the curtains were all drawn over the windows. He looked around as if just noticing the darkness and flung the dandelion-yellow silk curtains open. He winced as the brightness of the suns flooded his eyes and seemed to knock him back a step. I snorted, covering my mouth with my hand quickly. He cast an irritated glance my way, and I straightened up immediately.

"Lysan, have you heard of any movement of the Princess from Lyra? I know all the servant-types talk," he asked me gruffly. His eyes looked tired as he rubbed his brows with his fingers.

"Lyra hasn't been down to the servants' quarters since the Princess shut herself in her room, sir," I told him. I could tell my eyes were wide; him speaking to me made me uneasy. He stood up and threw his cup to the side in frustration.

"It's been days," he shouted to no one in particular. "Where is she?" I gulped and shuffled over to pick up the cup, putting more distance between myself and my grandfather. His nostrils were flared out, and he looked like he was going to start shouting when a guard burst into the room, panting and clutching his chest.

"Micah? You have news?" Tobyn asked him hurriedly. The guard collected himself and nodded.

"Yes, sir. Lyra gave word the Princess has woken." Tobyn's eyes were wild, and he looked between the guard and me. He quickly waved me off. *Woken?* I thought as I quickly ran from the room. *She's been asleep? I thought she was mourning.* Confusion racked me as I stood outside my grandfather's doors. *Father isn't going to like this. He told me to keep an eye on the Princess. She's been asleep for three days, and I had no idea. My father will be furious.*

I stood in the hallway for a moment to gather my thoughts, the rise and fall of my chest quickening as anxiety bit into me. I didn't like to disappoint my father. I heard the Regent and the guard going back and forth a little inside the room, but I couldn't make out what they'd been saying. They sounded hurried, agitated. I started making my way toward the palace library, knowing I'd find my father there waiting. He was the palace bookkeeper and younger son of the now Regent of Lynnea, my grandfather, Tobyn. I passed the doors to the Princess' room and hesitated, thinking I should check before I made my way to the library, but I shook my head and kept walking, heading to the staircase leading to the library.

As I approached the top of the steps, I heard angry footsteps coming behind me. I turned slightly and saw my grandfather thundering down the hallway toward the Princess' room. He threw the door open and stormed in in a hurry. Knowing I had to alert my father before my grandfather caused more ruckus, I quickly rushed down the winding marble steps, hoping he hadn't seen me.

Breathless, I found my father, Henrie, writing on a scroll in the library. He was deep in thought as I approached him; he didn't even notice me at first. Finally, he looked up from the scroll. He was fairly young; we celebrated his mid-thirtieth year recently, but at this moment, his eyes looked old and tired.

"Father?" His eyes finally met mine. He rolled up his scroll and focused his eyes on me.

"Yes, my son? What is it?"

"Well, I—" I hesitated, afraid of his disappointment.

"Spit it out, son." He sighed. "I have work to do."

"It's the Princess. She's been asleep for three days. I just heard word that she has awoken. I'm sorry, Father, Lyra's been with her the whole time. We all thought she was just mourning. We didn't know she'd been asleep this whole time. The Regent—Grandfather—is with her now. I'm sorry, Father, I'm sorry." My father's eyes softened, and he rested a hand gently on my shoulder. My body relaxed, and it was comforting to know I had an understanding father who always put everyone else's needs above his own.

"It's all right, son. You came as soon as you knew anything. Please, go now. Your grandfather will be readying a coronation, I am sure. Say nothing to anyone. I have something I must do." He sighed and set his stack of books aside, making his way toward the staircase. He motioned me to go down the other staircase to the servants' quarters. I quickly obeyed and dashed off down the steps.

As I ran down the stairs, I noticed a gathering of other servants by the entry to the kitchen. I joined in the huddle, hoping to gather some more information.

"I saw him—I saw him in the East Wing of the castle not far from the Princess' rooms. Do you think he's the one? Maybe he's why she hasn't emerged from her rooms. She's been having a secret affair!" Brysa was saying to them as I approached.

"Who?" I asked. They all turned and looked at me.

"The mystery man from the ball? Don't you remember? Before the Queen fell sick, the Princess was dancing with that man no one knew. I saw him late last night near her rooms. I think they've been having an affair!" she said excitedly.

"What's an affair?" I asked. She brushed me off with her hand, shushing me.

"You're too young to know," another girl said, turning up her nose at me. My face flushed at her calling me too young. I was eleven. They were both only four years older than me!

"I thought the Princess has been sleeping?" I blurted out.

"Shouldn't you all be getting the Queen's coronation prepared?" a dark and intimidating voice bellowed from behind me. My shoulders bent in, and a shiver crawled down my spine. I slowly turned and saw Uncle Julian, my father's older brother, towering over me, looking directly at Brysa. The huddle of servants scattered, and Brysa shrunk back and tried to go into the kitchen. Her reaction didn't surprise me. My uncle was not friendly; he had never had much to say to me, nor did he ever exchange pleasantries or even remember my birthday. I scrunched my nose in his direction.

"Brysa," he crooned in a sickeningly velvety tone and crooked his finger at her, a devilish sneer painted across his face, "Come with me, please." He took her upper arm tightly in his grip and led her away from the other servants. I watched them disappear and crept closer, hoping to hear what he had to say. I liked to know everything going on in the castle. I had spent much time listening to lots of conversations. This time, though, I wanted to be able to help my father with any information I could possibly give.

"You think you saw the Princess' *mystery man* here in the castle last night?" he asked her. His voice was almost a whisper but chilling, nonetheless. His tone was raspy and intimidating; he was trying to scare her. I peeked around the wall; I could see them not too far from me.

"Yes, yes, he was in the hall not far from her rooms. I thought maybe he had been in there. I'm sorry—I was probably mistaken. I get overexcited sometimes. You know how I feel about a good piece of gossip." Her voice was shaking and trailed off, her eyes darting everywhere but his face. He took her face in his hands and turned it up toward him so she had to look him in the eye.

"Don't tell anyone else you saw him, you understand me? If I ever hear you mention it again... I'll make you sorry." He pushed her back against the wall, her face still clasped in his hand, and kissed her hard on the mouth. *Ew,* I thought, *he's way too old for her. Gross.* Uncle Julian backed away and dropped his hand. Brysa quickly scampered off toward the kitchen again. As she ran past me, I could hear her start to cry. Then she disappeared.

I hurried to the kitchen behind her, hoping not to have a run-in with my uncle myself. He was a frightening man. Most others avoided him, though he always seemed to have a girl he toted around like an accessory. He was the opposite of my father. Julian had not yet married, though he was pushing his 40th year. My father and mother were married very young; they were only 17. My father was kind, caring, and intellectual, while his older brother was a cold and brutish man. Two sons that couldn't be any more different. I remembered when my father was proudly introducing the family to my youngest sister, Lily, with his eyes full of pride and love. Uncle Julian had said, "Ew."

The servant bell rang from my grandfather's room, and one of the footmen yelled, "Lysan!" from down the hall, interrupting my thoughts, and I dashed off back up the stairs to bring him his wine.

"LYSAN!" I heard Tobyn calling from down the hall as I ran into his room. "There you are. Where's my wine?" I hurriedly poured him a cup, and he gulped the whole thing down. I hesitated, waiting for an order. My mind was spinning; there was just so much going on.

"What are you waiting for? Pour another cup and go help the other servants get ready for the Princess' coronation!" he shouted at me. I poured him another cup and dashed out of the room as fast as I could. As I was closing the door behind me, I noticed a scary-looking woman poised in his sitting area. She was blonde, her hair pulled tightly in a bun, with high and painted cheekbones. Her face angled in such a way she seemed inhuman. I peeked out from behind the door curiously to get a better look. Her eyes met mine, and she flashed a sinister smile as I closed the door behind me. I let out a heavy breath. *What is going on around here?*

Chapter 4

Allanora

I woke up in my own bed, shaking and sweating. *It was just a dream,* I thought, blinking my eyes. Rubbing my neck, I felt a strange phantom pain where I had been strangled in my dream. *It was just a dream, so why does it hurt?*

Lyra was sitting over me; her eyes were big and wide. I could tell she hadn't slept because the skin underneath her eyes was dark and baggy—poor thing. I sat up slowly, feeling as if I had been asleep forever. My eyelids threatened to close again; they were so heavy. My mouth was dry; I looked around, hoping to see a pitcher of water, and locked eyes with Lyra. As if she could read my mind, she brought me a cup of water. I gulped it down, the first swallow stinging my dry throat.

"How long have I been sleeping, Lyra? All night?" I asked her quietly; my head was throbbing immensely. Subconsciously, my hands flew to my temples to try to massage the pain away. She fiddled with her hair, wrapping her thin golden locks around her fingers, then dropped her hands into her lap and took a deep breath.

"Three days, my lady. I didn't think you would ever wake up. I was so afraid." Her large grey eyes filled with stormy tears. I looked at her in disbelief. *No one sleeps for three days.* My eyes glanced over to the window; the first sun had just come up over the horizon, the second one barely coming out of its hibernation behind it, and early morning dew was glistening on the glass.

"There must be some mistake." I shook my head at her. "You look like you haven't slept either, you must be delusional." Her face remained grave and serious, and I got the feeling she was not wrong at all, but she said nothing.

"Well, what happened? I have no idea what's going on." I remembered a little bit; I remembered speaking to the guards and arguing with Tobyn... Something about my mother—*Oh, no. My mother.* Lyra opened her mouth to speak, but I interrupted her again.

"Lyra, please, what has been done with my mother's body?" I implored. Lyra bit her lip and twirled her hair some more. She was clearly upset, but I needed information. Instead, she sighed to herself, walked over to the door, and opened it. She whispered something to one of the guards outside before dismissing him and returning to my bedside. As if I hadn't just asked her about my dead mother's body, her fingers flew to my hair and began working to take my braid out. I swatted her hand away.

"What are you doing, Lyra? I need to know what you know! What is going on?" I demanded. She looked terrified; her grey eyes were huge and dilated, but she just shook her head again. She took a deep breath and composed herself, painting on a smile.

"I have to get you ready for your coronation, my lady," she said in a measured tone. My mouth dropped open. *My coronation? My mother just died!* I looked around frantically when I spotted a purple satin gown draped on a chair on the other side of the room. My skin began to prickle with heat, anger bubbling deep inside me. I was shaking, not from the cold anymore, but from pure rage. My whole body tightened, fists clenched so hard my nails were slicing through the skin. The pressure built, and I opened my mouth to start yelling when a flustered Tobyn burst in. My wild eyes flew to his. He looked confused, but it was too late. Lyra would be spared my fury, for Tobyn had volunteered as tribute. I unleashed.

"What exactly do you think you're doing in here? This is my bedchamber; don't you ever knock?"

"I'm sorry, Your Highness. I, just... Well, you've been asleep for three days. When I heard you had woken, I had to see for myself. We were starting to think the worst, my Princess," he explained, dropping to his knees clumsily. He stood up straight and folded one of his hands into the other, hiding his fidgeting fingers.

I waved away his concern, not that it sounded very genuine to begin with. "What is this about a coronation, and where is my mother's body?!" Someone was going to give me answers. Tobyn exchanged what seemed like a knowing look with Lyra, which only drove me deeper into my rage. I could feel it in every inch of my body. I pointed to the ground, and Tobyn rushed into a bow, kneeling before me once again.

"Well, Nora—" I held my hand up to cut him off.

"You are to address me as Your Highness, Tobyn." I looked back and forth between him and Lyra. "Unless someone is finally going to start giving me answers, none of you are to think that you will get away with being anything but formal in my presence." I could see that my words hurt them, but that was exactly what I wanted. I especially wanted *him* to hurt as I was hurting. He was my mother's most trusted friend, and he was just carrying on, business as usual. Tobyn sighed and paused, seeming to gather himself before trying to speak again.

"Your Highness, my deepest apologies. The law states that in the event of the death of a monarch, the next in line must assume the throne as soon as possible. You are of age now, my lady; you must follow the law and choose your husband to accept your crown, and it needs to happen today. The kingdom has been restless, and the people must be put at ease." He kept his head down, refusing to meet my eyes.

I took in his words for a moment, let him believe I was considering them. Finally, when he dared to lift his gaze, I gave him my answer.

"You want me to marry and be crowned Queen *today,* Tobyn? Because of the law? My mother is *dead!* And you would have me rush into my own coronation to claim her crown without properly burying her first?" I shouted back at him. He stared at me, looking guilty and sheepish. An awkward laugh escaped his lips, and I noticed the faintest pearls of sweat beginning to form on his forehead. My eyes narrowed at him, willing him to spit it out.

"Well, Your Highness, you were unconscious, and I—I had to act. I had her buried in the gardens as per her wishes and—" Before he could finish his sentence, whatever burning rage had kept me up gave out, and I crumpled to the floor.

He buried her. I didn't get one last goodbye. I watched her die, and they buried her without me. How will I even know if they gave her proper burial rites? How will I know that the Unnamed God will welcome her in the everlife? With my heart hollow, I remembered my grandmother Cressida's burial just before the end of the war. The memories were distant; I was only four. With tears in her eyes, my mother had placed rose petals over the eyes of her mother and read a passage she had chosen to honor her. So vividly, I remembered my mother fussing over the burial robes, which passage to read, and the flowers to surround her with that would decorate the fields of the eternal life beyond this one. I didn't get to choose that for her, and the thought made me want to vomit. *This was my duty, and I failed. I let them take it from me. Another way I'd never live up to my mother.* I felt empty, betrayed, defeated, and knelt there on the floor, silently, with nothing left, no further reason to move, quaking like the frightened child I was. My world was spinning, and I felt like I couldn't breathe.

Then it washed over me, the cold nothingness I had felt before. I reached my hand up for Lyra to help me stand and dusted myself off, gathering my mind and wits. Then I turned to Tobyn.

"Leave me. Have the castle prepared for the coronation, but let it be known to the people that *Queen* Allanora will *not* be choosing her husband today." He held his hand up and opened his mouth to protest, but I glared at him. He shrunk beneath my stare, excused himself, and left my bedroom.

I turned my stare to Lyra, who immediately began to shuffle around, preparing me for my coronation. She brushed and washed three days of sleep from my hair and pulled it into a regal braid that wrapped into a bun- -just like my mother used to wear. My heart sank a little as she set the silver tiara box in front of me, but I kept my composure, fighting back tears. Tobyn had been right about something. My people needed me. Today would be for the people, not for me. That's how my mother would have done it, and it was the only way left to honor her now. They needed to know that they had a strong leader, no matter the circumstance, and I would do everything in my power to do that for them.

Lyra placed the tiara on top of my head, and I looked once more into the mirror. I started to see a little more of my mother in myself, and the thought left a wave of confusing emotions in its tracks. The door opened behind me, and I rose from my chair. Tobyn stood before me, much calmer and more collected than he had been before.

"My dear Nora," he started. I held myself back, allowing him the informality. "I know your mother wanted to be here for this moment to watch you cross the bridge from being Princess to Queen of Lynnea, and she would be so proud to see that even in this moment of true darkness, you will stand before your people and vow to be a fair, true, and compassionate Queen. You've always been like a daughter to me, and I will be proud to act as a regent and father figure to such a beautiful ruler." He bowed low, with a fist placed over his heart. I nodded and curtsied to him. "I would like to offer to you in this time the hand of my eldest son in marriage. Julian would make a fine King, and I know in such haste, the kingdom will be happy to have a strong hand at the back of the Lynnean Queen." My lips pursed together. I had already let myself fly off the handle plenty today. *What would my mother do?* I knew I wouldn't be marrying today, I had made that much clear, but I wasn't sure adding insult was going to improve my relationship with the advisor to the crown.

"I appreciate your offer, Tobyn, but my mind is made up. I will have my own choice in this. I won't make this choice today, and just to be clear, it won't be your son. I do hope you understand; I just fear he is much too old for me. I hope you don't think me foolish, but I am still hoping to make my own choice, perhaps even based on love." My voice was as gentle as I could make it, not wanting to crack the thin glass of the fragile vase that was our current relationship. He nodded thoughtfully, pondering my answer, knowing that this was not something he could force me into. Finally, he held his hand out to guide me out of the room. I exited, this time knowing my life would change drastically once more, and this time, I was entering this new life without my mother, my best friend, my safe haven. The darkness I had felt before my ball returned, a black thundering cloud hanging over me. I stepped into the throne room filled with golden sunlight and was once again surrounded by my glittering subjects.

Quickly, I realized that the thin glass vase was not only the relationship I had with my advisor but the rest of the kingdom as well. Behind the smiling facades of Lynnea were worried eyes; a million unspoken questions hung in the thick air of the throne room. These faces that had been woven through my memories, people I had come to know throughout my life, suddenly seemed strangers to me, or I to them. This child that had grown up before their eyes, suddenly crowned in the cruel wake of the death of their beloved Queen. It was like I could hear their voices in my mind, feel their emotions mixing and becoming my own. Pinning my shoulders back, head held high, I started down toward my destiny, as I had been taught to do.

The throne room was a sea of beautiful gowns, suits, and a rainbow of jewels. Selfishly, I stole a moment to look around for Arthur. Finally, I saw him, looking just as dashing as he had at the ball, this time dressed in royal blue. His family was with him: his father, mother, and younger sister, Valeria. He wasn't looking at me, but I secretly relished the thought that his eyes would be focused on me for the entire event. Perhaps I'd be able to dance with him after the dinner.

Reluctantly, I returned my thoughts to the aisle before me and forced myself forward. Each subject smiled and curtsied in turn, forming a synchronized wave as I walked. I felt a twinge in my stomach as my nerves took hold. At the end of the aisle, I saw the Presiding Brother, Sol, poised perfectly still with the cushion holding my orb and scepter. He was completely hidden, except for his face peeking through the hooded scarlet cloak marking his place in the Triini. He nodded sternly as I broke from Tobyn and knelt before him, ready to begin the ceremony with my head bowed to the floor.

I heard the words being said as I knelt: *The Unnamed God blesses you, Your Majesty, Queen Allanora of Lynnea, as you embark on the sacred journey of Queenship.* His mind connected with mine, allowing only me to hear his voice. Telepathic connection between the ruler and religious leaders of the kingdoms of Cidris had been one of the only forms of magic not frowned upon by the Triini. My mother had always considered it a way for them to take control, but she allowed it, nevertheless. His voice in my head became a muffle, and my tiara was removed to make room for my mother's crown. I held the golden orb and scepter of the great Queens of Lynnea in my hands and fought back tears as I knelt where my mother had knelt, alone. I imagined what my father must have looked like, kneeling next to his Queen to be crowned. The absence of my King didn't go unnoticed, and I could feel the discomfort in Brother Sol's voice as he anointed me, skipping over the parts of the ceremony that would've mentioned my husband.

Finally, I felt him touch my forehead and then lower the golden crown onto my head. The weight of it made me feel small, but I kept my shoulders straight; I would not let Brother Sol or my people see me falter. I turned to them, keeping the perfect composure that I'd always been taught, and raised the orb and scepter to the sky, as I had practiced doing so many times before. The crowd cheered, and a small involuntary smile slipped from beneath my dark cloud.

As I turned to set the orb and scepter back on their sacred pillow, I heard a strange, high-pitched ringing sound. An explosion of stained glass rained to the floor. Before I could understand what was happening, an arrow sprouted through my left shoulder, already dripping with my scarlet blood. Gripped with excruciating pain like nothing I'd felt before, I let out an ungodly wail. A black shadow danced out of sight in the corner of my left eye as I fell to the floor and heard my subjects screaming and gasping around me. Drenched in a pool of blood, it was cold, suddenly, so cold. The blood drained from my face as it rushed to my wound like a stampede. The darkness enveloped me.

Around me was a cascading green field painted with golden light, but I found myself cold and alone. A crimson river flowed from my shoulder. I let my head drop back to the ground, defeated, and closed my eyes, feeling warmth in my toes where they had been cold. Suddenly, I felt eyes on me. Figures loomed over me, adorned in all white. Their faces were blank, veiled by the golden light surrounding them. I surrendered to them, 11 angels, here to welcome me home.

Only they didn't. One figure stepped forward and held their hand over my wounded body. His motions were distorted, and I couldn't focus my attention on anything he was doing. Before I could register anything, relief washed over me. "No blade can cut a golden stem," I heard the voice in my mind. When I sat up and looked around, there was nothing and no one for miles. A wave of exhaustion hit me, and I fell to the ground in a deep sleep.

Chapter 5

Henrie

Everyone was gathered in the throne room for the coronation. I knew if I made it quickly to the raven's tower, I could send a message just in time to get back for the ceremony. I hoped my son had gotten me the information in time to pass it along; Aros was a good man but impatient. I hadn't sent him news of his daughter for quite some time. *The Rose has grown beautiful and strong, the Violet has pruned it beautifully, it will be ready for display at the choosing ball in a week's time.* That was the last message I had sent to him. How things had changed.

The tower steps were small, narrow, and winding. I was winded just making my way up them, the empty scroll and ink clutched in my hands. The top was up so high that I felt the air thin around me. The room was large and airy, full of ravens destined for all different areas throughout the land. The ravens were just starting to rustle as the morning suns rose. Hastily, I scribbled my note. I usually had significantly better handwriting, but, of course, I also usually had more time to write neatly. I shook my head at myself, *he's not going to care what your handwriting looks like.*

The message read: *The Violet has wilted; the Rose fell into hibernation but now has bloomed. Hoping to reveal the snake in the garden soon. The Rose will take root today.* I attached the scroll to the bird I kept here specifically to communicate with Aros. Very few came up here anyway, but to be safe, I had a mage who resided in the outskirts of the kingdom secretly create an invisibility potion for the cage. My father would've been furious, not to mention Brother Sol. I had told him it was to hide communication with my mistress, and he had agreed almost too quickly, enclosing the bottle in my hand with a knowing wink. I shuddered to think about it. *As if I would ever have a mistress.* I freed the bird and sent him on his way, hoping the message would reach Aros sooner than later.

I made my way back down the staircase, relieved that no one else was lingering around to ask questions. My wife would be waiting for me to escort her to the coronation. I turned down the hallway toward my and my brother's rooms when I encountered my older brother, Julian, entangled with one of the servants. He had her pressed against the wall, his hands clenched around her waist, kissing her. He backed away from her as I walked by, and she turned her beet-red face toward the wall, embarrassed. She pushed him away quickly, receiving an irritated growl from the power-hungry throat of my brother.

"Julian, please not here, let's go to your room," her mousy voice squeaked. She turned her face from me, but I recognized her instantly as the Queen's new handmaid, Brysa. She was young and beautiful, hardly 15. He was pushing 40, and while he did have somewhat rugged good looks, she was much too pretty for him. I rolled my eyes at them both and kept walking. *She's old enough to make her own mistakes,* I thought to myself, choosing not to get involved any further. My brother hadn't settled down, but he sure knew how to whore his way around the castle. Very few of the young female servants walked through these halls without being enticed by my brother. It made me sick. Julian was strong-featured, with thick facial hair and thicker eyebrows. His chin was pointed, and his hair was thinning a little along the sides. He wasn't the most handsome man and surely wasn't the most powerful; I had always wondered what all these young ladies saw in him. Allanora assuredly hadn't fallen for whatever spell he had cast on the other women in his life, much to my father's dismay.

Poor Brysa, unlike Allanora, was exactly what he was looking for: young, naïve, and dumb to his brutish ways.

My brother nodded to me curtly.

"Henrie."

"Julian." I kept walking past him and toward my own rooms, where I knew my wife would be waiting for me. I heard Brysa giggle behind me, a shuffle of feet, and I presumed they had disappeared into his room. I shook the thought out of my head as I opened my door, greeted by my beautiful wife, Eleanore. A smile lit up my face when I saw her. She was all ready for the coronation in a lovely baby blue gown, my late mother's sapphire necklace gracing her neck. She was not as young as all the little girls my brother spent his nights with, but she was the most stunning woman I had ever laid eyes on. She had carried for me five children to date: Lysan, Lucian, Lance, Luna, and Lily, with one more coming in the next few months. She was the definition of classically beautiful, with high cheekbones and long, light brown hair. Her skin was porcelain and glowed with her pregnancy. Aside from her swollen belly, she was slender; everything about her was small and graceful. She was perfect in every way and always had been to me. I kissed her softly and touched my hands to her small pregnant belly. She smiled and blushed.

"Were you in the library today, my love? I went to look for you, but I didn't see you." She sat down at her vanity and started fixing her silver diamond earrings onto her ears. I sighed. I knew I had to lie to her, and I couldn't stand that.

"I was, dearest, but I left to help my father with a couple of coronation details. I hope I didn't worry you." I felt the lump form in my stomach that I always felt when I had to tell a lie, and I felt even sicker that I was lying to Eleanore.

"No, I wasn't worried--just curious is all." She smiled and stood back up, looking into my eyes. "You should get ready; we are going to have to leave any moment. You know your father won't forgive you if you're late to Princess Allanora's coronation. She's like a daughter to him, you know." She said it sweetly. I started to pull on my best suit and sapphire cufflinks to match my lovely wife, watching her busy herself trying on different shoes to see what would look best. *Does she know how perfect she is? No matter what shoes she wears.* I adored her with every fiber of my being. She had held such poise, even through her mother's death when she was a young teenager. The thought reminded me of the Princess.

"After the coronation, maybe you should visit Princess Allanora. You lost your mother young, too, so maybe you could comfort her in her mourning period. I'm sure she'd find solace in your words. She probably feels estranged and alone. You could be a companion for her," I said to her. She smiled softly and looked down at the ground.

"Maybe I could. If she'd have me. Of course, I'd be happy to advise her in any way I could. Although, I don't know if my situation is the same. I didn't have to rule a whole kingdom after my mother's death." Her voice trailed off into a whisper. I could tell she was thinking about her mother. She had taken on a mysterious illness shortly before Eleanore and I were due to be married. It had crushed Eleanore to her core, but she had come out so strong in the end, and I was so proud of her. I held her face in my hands.

"The Princess has a gentle heart. I'm sure she is crushed, just as you were. She'd be thrilled to have someone to talk to. Trust me," I said as I kissed her forehead. "Let's head down to the coronation. I don't want to be running late and have you hurrying in your condition." Her hand moved protectively to her belly. I offered her my arm, and she linked hers to mine.

We made our way down to the throne room and positioned ourselves near the center of the crowd, where we'd be able to see the ceremony without being right at the front. We always preferred to keep our distance from all the pomp and circumstance that tended to ignite in these sorts of events. My brother, on the other hand, positioned himself front and center, and I'm sure my father would take his place right beside him after escorting the Princess to the throne. Julian was eyeballing Brysa, seeming to try to undress her with his gaze. She was in a back corner with a small group of servants, my son Lysan included, craning their necks, hoping to catch a glimpse of the festivities.

The throne room was cheerful despite the recent death of Queen Violet. Festive gatherings, such as coronations, always brought out the best in the people of Lynnea. There was happy chatter among the guests, but everything fell silent as Princess Allanora appeared in the large doorway.

She was a beautiful sight, the picture of royal perfection in an elegant purple satin gown. Aside from her dark brown hair and dark blue eyes, the Princess was the mirror image of Queen Violet. She was beautiful, poised, and elegant.

After pausing for a moment and scanning the room, she floated through the sea of her subjects as they each bowed or curtsied to her in turn. Each person smiled at her, the outpouring of love for the beloved Princess of Lynnea tangible in the air.

She reached the end of the long aisle, and the ceremony continued. My wife leaned against me as we stood and watched. My father joined my brother at the front of the crowd, as expected. They whispered to each other before turning their attention to the Princess. The whole room beamed with pride as the Presiding Brother, Sol, of the Triini, lowered Queen Violet's crown onto the Princess' head. She turned to face her people as their Queen when the room filled with the sound of shattered glass. It all happened so fast that it took me a moment to realize an arrow had sprung from Queen Allanora's chest, only missing her heart by a few inches. I froze, my body in a state of shock. I felt like I needed to move, but my body was rooted, unmoving.

A blood-curdling scream ripped through the throne room as Allanora fell to the ground. Gasps and shouts filled the air while guards started to surround the Queen and close all the doors to the room. Eleanore slumped against me, unconscious; she had fainted at the sight. I caught her and lifted her easily in my arms, then ran with her quickly to my father. He would need help keeping everyone back from the Queen. He was knelt next to Allanora, clasping her hand in his. Shifting Eleanore in my grip, I tried to put my hands up to signal for the crowds of people to stay back, then turned to look at her. All color had drained from her lovely young face, and she lay in a pool of scarlet blood that drenched her coronation gown. I couldn't tell if she was breathing, how she could survive this. There was a hole in her shoulder that was gushing blood; her skin hung like ripped parchment inhumanly off her body. My heart shattered and dropped to my feet. I thought of her father but quickly shook the thought out of my head and focused on Eleanore, who had come to slightly but was breathing so quickly that she was losing color and starting to panic.

"I have to get her out of here, Father, but is there anything I can do to help?" I asked, out of breath. He shook his head and waved me away. The guards were now trying to hold back the people trying to swarm the Queen's body; my father and Julian were calling frantically for healers to aid her. Lyra had rushed to Allanora's side, bending over her hysterically and drenching herself in Allanora's blood.

I walked quickly to the nearest door with Eleanore but was blocked by two guards.

"No one leaves," one said shortly. My body stiffened angrily, and I clenched my fists, holding my wife tighter.

"My wife is pregnant; she fainted. I need to get her some fresh air and to see a healer. Do you want her death and the death of my unborn child on your hands? Do you know who I am? Tobyn Hawkham is my father. He won't be happy about you endangering his grandchild." Normally, I wouldn't use my father's name that way, but I needed to get Eleanore to safety. The guards exchanged glances and silently let me pass. I rushed with her through the corridors and back into our room. Laying her gently on our bed, I rang our bell for a servant, but no one appeared. Irritated, I rang again and waited for a moment. Still, no one came. The color had returned to Eleanore's face, though, and a sigh of relief rushed from my chest.

"Henrie? I think I had a nightmare." She held her hand to her forehead and winced. I shook my head and took her hands in mine. I studied her beautiful face, tears filling my eyes. Moments like this reminded me how fleeting and precious life was.

"It wasn't a nightmare, my love. The Queen was shot by an arrow. It ripped open her chest. I don't know how she could survive that. The healers are with her body now." Her face twisted in anguish, dropped into her hands, and she let out a sob. I sat next to her and held her in my arms to comfort her.

"I just don't understand," she said softly. "First, Queen Violet, now Princess—I mean Queen Allanora? What is happening?"

"Try not to worry about it, my sweet, I don't want any harm to come to the baby. Please, try to rest; I'm going to go see my father and get some more information." I kissed her lightly on the forehead as I laid her back down. She nodded and closed her eyes. Tears stained her perfectly painted cheeks, and I could see the worry carved into her face.

I returned to the throne room, where the guards had rounded up all the guests and servants. Only my father, Julian, Brother Sol, Lyra, and two castle healers were gathered around her body, mixing concoctions and examining her carefully.

"Father." I caught his attention, and he turned to me; he shook his head gravely. His age showed in that moment; he looked old and tired, drained by years of service to the crown.

"You have to get the Queen out of here. This scene is too shocking, and the guards need to start questioning people about what happened here today." My father nodded as I spoke, a grave and ponderous expression on his face. "I'll carry her back to her rooms with the healers—"

"No, I'll take her," my brother interrupted. The hair on the back of my neck stood up as he spoke. He didn't even look saddened at the death of yet another monarch. He looked satisfied and determined, his self-serving air like a thick cloud hanging around him.

"Don't you have a servant to go seduce?" I bristled.

"Sounds like you care a little bit too much for the Princess, brother. Is there something you need to tell us? Or Eleanore?"

My father shot me a questioning glare. I had no choice but to back off, my mouth gaped open in shock. Otherwise, I might reveal my connection to the girl's father or make them think I was having an affair, neither of which would end well for me. I digressed, stepping out of my brother's way, my hands in the air. Julian smirked at me as he picked up the Queen's small body and carried her off. Lyra let out a sob as more blood dripped down onto the floor. She was white as a sheet, as if she had seen a ghost or become one herself. Her entire body was trembling. Gently, I sent her off to the servant's quarters to clean up and decompress.

"Father, do you need anything?"

My father was looking around the room anxiously, as if he didn't know where to start. "Maybe you need to go lie down. I can help out here..."

"I think the guards have it handled. I have work to do," he said coldly and pushed past me. He never handled emotions well. He didn't speak to anyone for a month after my mother died, and with both Violet and Allanora gone in just a few days, it would be a lot for him to handle. I watched him walk out, slouched forward, the years of protecting the Queen and the realm held heavy on his shoulders.

My son was huddled amongst the group of servants, and I made my way over to him. Some were crying, and some were just pale and wide-eyed in shock. My son looked drained and anxious. I pulled him away from the group.

"Did you see anything?" I whispered to him. He shook his head but gestured toward Brysa.

"She said she saw the mystery man the Princess was dancing with outside. She said she saw him last night, too, near the Princess' rooms... Thought they were having *an affair...*" His voice trailed off. I shot him a glare.

"Where'd you learn that word?!"

"That's just what she said. I don't know what it means." He shrugged his shoulders, and I sighed.

"Please go check on your siblings in the nursery, then go tend to your mother, Lysan. Get her a healer as soon as one is available. Don't talk to anyone else for the rest of the night until you and I have another chance to speak," I warned him. He darted off out of the throne room and down the hall. *Apparently, the guards aren't too concerned about the comings and goings of an eleven-year-old cupbearer.* I rolled my eyes and made my way over to Brysa, who was crying hysterically at the center of the group of servants. I gestured for her to come see me. She walked over sheepishly, her pale face turning red. She tucked in her shoulders and wound her hands together uncomfortably. She was very pretty; her untamed blonde ringlets were pulled into a messy bun behind her head, her face was blotchy, and her eyes were puffy. Cringing, it hit me that this girl, who was only a little older than my son, was mixed up in some physical relationship with my brother, poor thing.

"Brysa—Lysan told me you saw the mystery man that Allanora was dancing with. Last night and today, during the coronation. Do you know what he was doing? Or who he is?" I asked her softly. All the remaining color drained from her face, and her eyes widened like a bug.

"I—don't know what you're talking about," she choked. "I didn't see anything. Last night or today. All I saw was the Princess..." She trailed off as fresh sobs filled her chest.

"Brysa—I'm trying to help. Please, tell me the truth." She shook her head and scampered off. I turned to see where she was headed when I saw my brother had returned. She went to him, and he gestured carelessly for the guards to let her leave the throne room. They were taking orders from him without question, which I found very odd.

He hovered over a few guards who were questioning subjects. Someone must have said something he didn't like because he had a man by the throat, turning his chin back and forth in his meaty hand. I sighed and stepped up to him.

"Julian." He paused, his cheeks puffing out with each breath. "What exactly are you doing?" I asked him calmly. I could feel the rage pouring from every part of his body.

"This doesn't concern you, bookkeeper." The words were bitten out between his gritted teeth. I nodded curtly and looked at the middle-aged man locked in his grip. I recognized him as a retired knight, Sir Warren. His skin had begun to turn purple underneath Julian's thick fingers.

"Am I not to be concerned, sir?" I asked him. The man shook his head, as much as he could, anyway, and Julian released him. Sir Warren gripped his neck absently and took a labored breath in. "Do you have information pertaining to this attempt on the Queen's life, sir?"

"I just—" He met Julian's eyes, which were icy daggers staring into the poor man's soul. "No, I don't think I do."

I glared at Julian, who gave me a satisfied smile and folded his arms over his broad chest.

I'm clearly not going to get anywhere with this.

I remembered the message I had sent earlier and hung my head. *How am I going to tell Aros this?*

Julian started to oversee other conversations with guards, suddenly taken up by responsibility he had never shown in his life. I scanned the throne room and realized it was the perfect time to slip away. The guards were distracted, keeping people away from the Queen, and my father was preoccupied with the healers. Wringing my hands uncomfortably, I knew I had to get a message to Aros as soon as possible. Slipping out the side door of the throne room, I found myself back in the empty hallway. The servants seemed to scatter back to their duties or their rooms, and some were obviously helping tend to the Queen. I was sure that no one would even notice my additional trip to the raven's tower.

My feet dragged more slowly even than they had before. I trailed my fingers lazily along the old stone walls of the staircase. I was in no hurry to let the mysterious King Aros know that his only daughter was likely dead. I cringed at the thought, thinking of my own daughters, hoping no one would ever have to write me such horrid news.

The suns had begun to set on the horizon. It was dark by the time I made it up the winding tower steps. I hesitated at the window, looking out at the beautiful kingdom of Lynnea, gardens and fields that went on for miles, beautiful rivers and brooks winding through the terrain... I wondered what was in store for all of it and sighed, turning toward the writing desk just as the raven I had sent off earlier flew through the window. A small scroll was attached to his leg. I unrolled it hesitantly.

Henrie, thank you for keeping a watchful eye on my beautiful garden all these years. While I loved my Violet flower, the Rose is my pride and joy. Knowing it has blossomed and grown all these years without me tending to it is my greatest sadness but also my greatest satisfaction. I plan to return soon. Just to see how beautifully it has grown in my absence. Forever in your debt- A.

Tears filled my eyes as I read his words, knowing his daughter was gone and he would never get to see her fully grown. I thought of my own children and imagined what it would be like not being a part of their life, seeing them become adults and make their own way without me. I scribbled one short note. *The Rose has wilted.*

With a heavy heart, I attached it to the leg of the bird and returned to the window as I let it take off into the horizon, wondering what would be in store for me when the message was received. The raven's wings were a black knife against the largest of the four Lynnean moons, set to tear out the heart of an unsuspecting father. I let a tear slip from my eyes as the thought stung me in the chest. Feeling dense with emotion, I made my way back to my bedchamber, feeling more tired than I had in a long time.

Chapter 6

Allanora

I awoke in the darkness. My body was moving, and I could wiggle my fingers and toes. As my senses slowly returned to me, I could feel cloth fastened around my face and bindings around my legs and arms. Quickly, I realized I had a cloth tied over my mouth as well. I squirmed my body as much as I could, but I was tied down to something. My nose gave me a hint of something familiar. I focused my pounding head on it. *Stables, I must be on a horse.* With my hair hanging down toward the ground, it occurred to me I must have been thrown over the back like an animal. *Ugh, what a way to treat a Queen.* I started to slide backward when I felt strong hands wrap around my arms and right me. A gruff "Woah" filled my ears, and the horse came to a stop beneath me. I felt myself being lifted down to the ground and the cloth removed from around my face. The sunlight flooded into my eyes, and I winced as if I were seeing the brightness for the first time. The suns were blazing, so close they almost looked like one sun in the sky; it was nearly midday. Almost an entire day had passed since my coronation. *It could even be more than that.* Twinges of guilt filled my mind. The Lynnean castle must have been in disarray. So much chaos in so little time. As bile rose in my throat, I felt like I would vomit right there.

My vision finally focused, and I saw a man dressed in an entirely black tunic standing before me. The tightness of the dark fabric outlined the toned muscle on his chest and arms. A handsome and terrifying specimen.

His arms were crossed over his chest, and there was a familiar devilish gleam in his eyes. That's when it hit me; he was the mystery man from the ball on the night my mother died. A tornado of emotions blew through my mind all at once. Anger, sadness, confusion, more anger. My body quaked, and all the memories of what happened that night flooded through my mind, a tidal wave crashing into my skull. I tried to throw myself at him in a fit of fury, but I was still bound tightly, and he avoided me easily. He seemed amused...had that diabolical smirk and a relaxed posture, which only irritated me more. Finally, he untied the gag from my mouth, let it fall to the ground, and stepped back from me.

"Who on earth are you?" I yelled at him loudly. He looked me up and down, still amused, but he did not answer.

I started to take in the scene around me now that I could finally focus again. We were deep in the woods. Where exactly? I wasn't sure. I could see no buildings or landmarks nearby. The trees had thick, rough trunks and had grown close together, all of them covered with menacing, invasive vines, an old wood for certain. I imagined this was the Rinwood forest north of the castle. No one ever came this way as it had been said to be home to all manner of dangerous and mysterious people. Murderers, thieves, vagabonds... I was sure this mystery man was among its dangerous inhabitants.

"I guess I could tell you," the handsome, strange man interrupted my thoughts. "It won't matter too soon, anyway. The name's Rylan, third son of Rhonan of House Thorne," he said matter-of-factly, puffing up his chest, emphasizing his muscles and broad shoulders even more. *House Thorne,* my mind wandered. *I don't remember a House Thorne from Lynnea.* I thought hard, then remembered something. House Thorne wasn't a Lynnean house; it was an Astinian house and the ruling house, no less. Astinia was our neighboring kingdom to the north, though we hadn't had much to do with them since the end of the war. I had never even met the Royal Astinians. Until now, I guess. This would mean war, one kingdom kidnapping a Queen. Anger hit me again, and I wrenched against my bindings.

"Release me, *Rylan of House Thorne,*" I said mockingly, "and I'll not have you beheaded, or you'll face the wrath of the warriors of Lynnea."

"Oh, don't you worry, my little Princess. Your *magnificent* knights of Lynnea won't be thinking about you or looking for you at all," he sneered.

My stomach dropped into my feet. Why wouldn't my soldiers be looking for me? Why wouldn't they be fighting for me?

"What—what do you mean?" I sputtered. His eyes darkened with amusement.

"Well, it turns out you're not that easy to kill." He picked at the edge of a dagger he had pulled from his belt. "I've tried twice now. Never fear, though; your whole kingdom is mourning your death as we speak. I made quite sure of that with the arrow to your chest." He tapped his own chest.

Then I remembered. The coronation, the arrow, my people in distress. It all came flooding back like water out of a broken dam. Collapsing, I knelt at his feet, eyes downcast; I was crushed by the weight of my failure. My breaths came short and close together. I could feel my face start to numb as the trees around me began to shake and whip with a sudden wind. Thoughts of my mother, of Tobyn, of all the people that I needed to be strong for at that moment flooded my mind. Taking a deep breath, everything began to still around me. The wind calmed, and I took steady hold of my emotions. I had so many questions. *Would he even answer them?* I looked at my shoulder where the arrow had ripped through me. The fabric of my wisteria dress was torn, but the skin underneath was clean and seemed to be unscarred; it didn't even hurt.

"What do you mean, I'm not that easy to kill? You missed my heart. Maybe you're just a bad shot," I spat. For a split second, he looked offended, but then the mask of darkness returned to his face.

"A blow to the heart is too quick. Too painless. An instant kill. Too easy. I tried to strangle you first while you were asleep. A quiet, clean, suffering death. Your little handmaiden came back too soon. Then I thought, how much more fun would it be if all your people had to watch you die, too? A public assassination." He spoke calmly, arrogantly. I remembered the dream I had of being strangled while I had apparently been asleep for three days. My blood ran cold with the realization. *Who does that? Who thinks like that?* This was far from the enticing dance partner I'd twirled across the floor with a mere few nights ago. Disgust shot through me; I'd even considered making him King, however briefly.

"An assassin prince. There's a first." A flash of anger streaked across his face at my words. His mesmerizing green eyes narrowed to slits.

"Only the first son is Prince in Astinia. That title goes to my oldest brother, Raysh. Not me," he spat back at me. I fought back a smile, *a weak spot.*

"One gets the glory; the rest are cold-blooded murderers. Astinia sounds like a fairytale. I would assume the second son, your other brother, is just another hired hitman just like you," I teased, trying to expose the wound in his pride further. His face twisted, and he turned to grab something from his horse's saddlebag. He walked toward me, and I realized what was happening; I just couldn't stop it while I was bound. He jabbed my arm, and I felt a stinging pain shoot through my entire body. I crumpled on the ground, completely unable to move or speak. My eyes were open, and I could close them, but that was all; everything else was nonresponsive. *Dragonshade*, I thought. A paralyzing poison that allows the victim to stay awake but leaves them unable to use their body. A nasty poison and exceedingly rare. I had only heard about it from one of the mages who would pass through the castle from time to time. The Triini had kept a lid on most magical doings and knowledge in Lynnea.

"Dragonshade, my dear. You talk too much." He lifted me easily and set me back on the horse, tying the reins around my hands and strapping me down on the saddle. He scribbled something down on a piece of parchment from his saddlebag, swung himself up into the saddle behind me, and tucked it back into the bag.

"Your fairytale awaits," he sneered. "Don't get too excited. My father and brother won't be entirely pleased with your...unexpected visit. There won't be cheering and beautiful balls to greet you there." I felt a tear roll down my cheek as the saddle started to shift back and forth beneath me.

My kingdom lay behind me, and I didn't dare to look back. Couldn't, even if I wanted to. They didn't even know I was alive. How much power did a Queen have without her people? I couldn't imagine what awaited me in Astinia. I had never been there, but I knew it was a cold, dark, and rough land, and the same could be said for its people. My heart sunk into my paralyzed toes. With my eyes closed, I brought myself back to the coronation, looking out to all the smiling faces of Lynnea, so proud to be their Queen even when my heart had felt so empty. I'd remembered in that moment that, even without my mother, I had a family, people to protect and love, rule and serve. In less than five breaths of being their Queen, I had already failed them.

With no heir to the throne and me not having a husband, it would be left to Tobyn to protect Lynnea. Tobyn would be a wise and fair ruler, but he was older, and the throne then would pass to his son, Julian, whom I had turned down for marriage. His son was a cruel and selfish man. Even my mother had briefly wished for me to marry him. I had finally squashed the idea of Julian ever sitting on the throne just before my coronation, and now he'd be King anyway. The thought made me shudder. *Shudder.* My body moved... The Dragonshade was wearing off. I wiggled my toes ever so slightly in my boots to make sure.

"*Help!*" I screamed as loud as I could, knowing it was my only chance. "*Please, someone help me!*" I threw my body off the horse, which took off, startled by my outburst. I hit the ground hard, and a stinging pain shot through my shoulder. The impact dazed me, and I needed a moment to collect my thoughts, my mind swirling. Mistake.

I had given assassin-prince Rylan enough time to throw himself onto me and stab me with another dose of Dragonshade. I wasn't stupid-- there was no way I was escaping. I had just hoped my outburst was enough to capture the attention of someone, anyone, in the forest nearby.

"Pain in the ass, Princess," he spat at me as he lifted me back up from the ground, rubbing his own shoulder.

"I'm the *Queen!*" I spat back as I felt the Dragonshade take over my body once again. I heard a few twigs snap nearby and smirked to myself. Maybe my outburst had worked. Rylan heard it, too; I felt his body tense up beneath me as he looked around, one arm holding me tightly in place and the hand of the other around his sword hilt on his belt. Another twig snapped behind a tree, and he quickly set me on the ground and drew his sword in one fluid motion. All at once, a blur of four figures ran toward him, armor gleaming and swords outstretched. Relief washed over me as I saw the Lynnean crest on the armor of one of the men. *Lynnean guards! They must have been on a patrol.* Swords drawn valiantly, they descended on Rylan.

"It's the Queen! He has the Queen!" The sound of metal clanging against metal rang in my ears as I watched helplessly from the ground. Rylan took down one guard, then a second; he looked as if he wasn't even trying. He whirled around and leaned toward the other two, tucking one arm behind his back. He was toying with them. I stifled a sob in my paralyzed state as one lunged for him, and he plunged his sword through the guard's chest. When the other came swinging at him, Rylan dropped to his knee, pulled out a dagger, and maneuvered to slit his throat. The light left the guard's eyes as blood spurted, and his skin fell away from his body. More tears filled my eyes as I watched him wipe the blood of my guards off his weapons. *Gone,* I thought, *just like that.* Their lives and my chances of survival disappeared in the blink of an eye. I had been defeated. I was helpless in the woods, with no chance now of anyone even knowing I was still alive.

Rylan sat down in front of me, his breathtaking, deadly, emerald-green eyes fixated on mine. He took a breath to speak, then got up quickly-- someone had snuck up behind him. He moved swiftly and silently, had them pinned against a tree with his sword to their neck before I knew it. They wore an all-tan tunic like his black one, no markings or crest on their clothing. Their face was covered in tan wrappings, which he ripped off, revealing a woman. Her long blonde hair tumbled down over her shoulders. Rylan let out an agitated breath and lowered his sword. She had sharp, menacing features, furious brown eyes, pin-straight blonde hair, and a belt of pouches and weapons wrapped around her slender waist.

"Gen," he growled. "What on earth are you doing back here? I thought you'd left." She smiled at him, and he released her from his grasp. She came over to me and touched my face with the back of her fingers, then looked back at him.

"Your father asked me to stick around," she said coldly, clicking her tongue. "He wanted to make sure you carried out your duties, and I didn't want to miss the fun anyway." She smirked at me. He sat back on the ground and started sharpening his blade absently with a rock he'd picked up.

"And why exactly did he send *you*?" Rylan threw an annoyed look her way. She smiled again, a sweet but dark smile.

"I volunteered." She shrugged and sat down next to him, and both started staring at me. Gen squinted her eyes.

"The Princess, I take it?" I tried to retort, but I couldn't. *Not yet.*

"*The Queen*," he responded carelessly, mocking me. She came back over to me and pulled my dress away from where the arrow had hit me. She gave Rylan a confused look, and he shrugged back.

"You're a quiet one." She sneered at me.

"Dragonshade," he explained.

"How fun for you." He gave her a shadowy look when she said that, and she backed away from me.

"So—why isn't she dead then?" she asked. *Maybe this will get me some answers,* I thought, but he just shook his head and didn't reply to her. *This is getting me nowhere.* I focused on restoring my ability to move and speak again and opened my mouth.

"Who—are—you?" I asked weakly. The Dragonshade was definitely wearing off even faster than before, but my body was tired, and I was putting everything I had into fighting the paralysis. They both looked at me with wide eyes and shocked expressions.

"How long ago did you dose her?" she asked him, ignoring my question and pinching my chin in her hand to study me closely.

"Not long. Second dose, too," he said, but he made no motion to attempt another dose. I started to steady my breathing and slowly regained some strength. Gen looked me all over, then, taking my hands in hers, she drew a small dagger from her pocket and made a small cut in my palm. I winced as the blood started to flow freely from the laceration. Rylan moved behind me and began tying me up even tighter with more ropes. The hatred I harbored for him simmered just below the surface of my hot skin. He tied another cloth around my mouth so I wouldn't be able to shout again when I regained my full strength. Gen started looking closely at my blood on her dagger. She gave him an odd look, and he walked over to her. They whispered to each other for a few moments before returning to me.

"We need to get her to your father as soon as possible, Rylan," Gen said urgently. He rounded on her.

"You think I don't already know that?" he shouted back. "She took an arrow through the shoulder, and look—" He ripped the fabric from my chest, exposing it completely, "not even a scratch on her." I looked at my shoulder again. My skin was smooth where it should have been scarred. I didn't understand it, and apparently, neither did they. He regained his composure and took a breath. "I took her because I didn't know what else to do, but it doesn't matter. The Lynneans think she's dead, and there's no reason for them to suspect otherwise. She took an arrow and bled out on the floor of her coronation. That's all they needed. She's dead to them."

"But she's *not* dead, Rylan. There's not even a scar on her, and she's ripping through Dragonshade like it's *nothing*."

"That's *enough*, Gen," he warned. "She can *hear* you," he said more quietly, gesturing to me. She put her hands on her hips and looked back and forth between us.

"Well, it's a good thing for you that I showed up then," she said and made her way over to him, wrapping her small arms around his neck. He looked annoyed and rolled his eyes. "Oh, come on," she said, "you know you missed me." She leaned in to kiss him as he grabbed her arms and pushed her away just enough to keep her at bay. She huffed at him with annoyance.

"What exactly do you plan to do with them?" She pointed a narrow, calloused finger at the dead bodies of the guards.

He shrugged. Disgust ripped through me at his indifference.

"We can't just leave them here," she growled at him.

"Of course not, Gen. Don't be stupid," he bit back at her. He threw one guard over his shoulder. I gagged at the sight of his body hanging so limp and dripping blood onto the ground.

She watched him with curious fascination. "What are you doing with him?"

He fastened the guard to the back of his horse. "There's a small lake not far from here," Rylan said and motioned to a smaller brown horse that I hadn't noticed before—must have been Gen's. Rylan started to walk back toward the next guard he had brutalized.

Gen rolled her eyes and started dragging another one by his feet toward the second horse, a trail of blood dripping over the fallen leaves that crunched beneath his mangled body.

With two men strapped to each of their horses, Rylan came back to me and scooped me up in his arms. I willed myself to be heavy, to make him strain, weaken him, but he didn't bat an eye and carried me easily back to his horse. He sat me in front of him, with my head propped against his muscular shoulder so I had to look at the poor dead men behind him. Swallowing a bit of vomit at the sight of them, I promised myself I'd find their families when I got out of this and see to it that they were taken care of. They sacrificed their lives for me; it wouldn't be in vain.

The second sun had well passed the first when we reached the clearing with a small lake tucked amidst the trees. Evening had come so quickly. Rylan dropped me to the ground with a thud and went about removing the men from his horse and Gen's. With a gruesome disinterest, he threw each man's body into the water, watching as they sank below the surface. A tear slipped from my eye, and I swallowed back more vomit, horrified and disgusted at the knowledge that they wouldn't receive proper burial rites.

"He's so strong, isn't he?" Gen commented to no one in particular. Another reason for me to gag. He pushed past her wordlessly once he had let the lake swallow the last man without a hint of remorse for what he had done.

"Well then, we will need to make camp for the night anyway." She swung a small pack from her back to the ground and sat down on the ground next to him. *They better not start going at it the second they think I'm asleep.*

"Oh great," he said, annoyed. "So you're staying?"

"Of course I am. Your father sent me to make sure nothing goes wrong, and that's what I'm going to do. The way it's going right now, he'd have your head on a platter, so you're going to need all the help you can get." He ignored her, brought his own bag down from one of the two horse's saddles, and started to unpack. He rolled out a mat behind me and laid me on my side. I felt so helpless lying there, all tied up with these strangers. I closed my eyes and willed myself to drift off, to dream of anything but what I was dealing with now. Maybe a dream would help me to escape.

After what felt like hours, I felt myself finally starting to doze off. The darkness wrapped around me like a blanket. I wondered how many others in this forest were as bad as these two... Or worse. I heard Rylan and Gen whispering, but I couldn't make out what they were saying. Sleep engulfed me as I wondered how I would ever get out of this mess and what lay ahead of me in Astinia.

Chapter 7

Allanora

I woke in the night shivering uncontrollably, a cold enveloping me that I'd never felt before. There was immense pressure on my abdomen and hand. I opened my eyes. Gen was holding me down by the stomach, gripping my hand where she had cut it. Her eyes were wild but focused on me, watching me intently as my body writhed beneath her. I forced myself to lash out at her, and she momentarily lost her hold on me. I threw my head at hers with everything I had. The blow knocked me back to the ground and made a cracking sound. She was stunned, only for a second, then had me back in her hold. The cold sensation started to turn into a burning pain, ripping through my entire body as if each of my veins was on fire. I tried to scream, but I couldn't. Tears flowed from my burning eyes. Off to the side, I saw Rylan jolt awake. He looked over, eyes blinking, saw us, and threw himself at Gen, knocking her to the ground. The pain didn't stop; it was overwhelming, taking over my mind and body like a fire engulfing a forest. I was being torn apart from the inside. Thousands of knives ripped into my stomach, accompanied by an extreme pressure that made me sure I'd explode any second.

"Gen, *what did you do?*" he shouted at her, keeping her pinned to the ground. She turned her head calmly toward me, a menacing coolness about her.

"I had to see for myself," she said unemotionally, keeping her eyes fixated on me. Rylan turned and studied me as well.

"See *what* for yourself?" he asked hurriedly. "What did you give her?"

"Hemlock," she said matter-of-factly. "She will either die or she won't." They both looked at me, watching carefully. I felt everything in my body shutting down. I could feel liquid dripping from my mouth; what exactly it was, I wasn't sure. The pain burned through me as my vision started to darken. My eyes rolled up to the sky and then closed.

"I guess she's not so special after all." I heard Gen laughing. They both felt so far away.

Blinding light filled my eyelids as the pain disappeared from my body. *This is it*, I thought; *this is death.*

"No blade can cut a golden stem." That same voice, now familiar but still unrecognizable, called through the abyss of my mind.

I opened my eyes, expecting to see my mother and Lynnea's past Queens lined up to greet me in the everlife. Instead, I saw darkness. I was alone. I could smell the faint burning of coals and feel the hard bedroll underneath me. *I'm alive,* I thought, *but how?* I wiggled my fingers easily. My toes moved as well. I rolled to my stomach and pushed myself up from the ground. *My ropes are gone. They must have thought I was dead.* I took off running, not even sure which way to go. It didn't matter. I was elated; I was free and could go back to my people and promise to lead them as fairly as I knew how. Everything was going to be okay, finally.

I heard a familiar ringing sound behind me as I felt the sleeve of my dress rip. An arrow pinned my sleeve to a tree next to me. I ripped the fabric and started to run again but was suddenly thrown backward before being slammed into a tree. I felt a body holding me there, and warm breath filled my ears from behind. My elation came crashing down around me. It had to be Rylan.

"Not so fast, Princess," he breathed into my ear. I couldn't see him, but I could feel his smug smirk behind me. His very air exuded arrogance. He turned me around to face him. I could barely see him in the darkness, but his pride exuded from him. "Maybe it's a good thing you're not dead—you're clearly something special. Quite a prize to bring to my father, I would think. Who knows, maybe he will even crown me prince." His voice was thick with sarcasm. He pushed the whole weight of his body against me. I was enveloped in him; his hard chest pushed firmly against my face.

He brought my arms behind the tree, and I felt him tie something around my wrists to keep me there. I pushed back against him to free myself, but he held me still, securing my arms.

"Trying to squeeze in another dance, Princess?" He looked down at me, backing away momentarily to admire his work.

"*Queen!*" I shouted at him angrily, remembering my mother's words. *I must not let anyone make me feel small, I am the Queen.* I pulled at the ties on my wrists and pushed myself as hard as I could away from the tree, but it was no use. He smirked and stepped back to me, bringing his face close to mine. I was sure he could feel the heat of my hatred on his skin; I hoped he could.

"Yes, Your Highness," he said, so close to my face that his lips almost touched mine. I shrank back desperately. Then he let out a menacing laugh. He started tying another rope around my ankles, then another around my waist, completely securing me to the tree. "I like it when you're feisty, makes this all the more fun for me, Your Majesty." He stood back again and glanced over the bindings. "Well, you're not going anywhere."

Out of the shadows, I saw a second figure appear: Gen. She stalked up to me and studied me closely.

"Fascinating," she noted as if she was commenting on some exotic new species she'd captured and was studying. "What are you going to do now, Ry? You can't very well take the tree with you. Astinia is still a day away, maybe two, even three, at this rate. Do you even have enough Dragonshade to keep dosing her all the way?" Rylan tensed up as she turned toward him and let out an annoyed sigh.

"No," he said, defeated. "I have another plan, though." She narrowed her eyes at him.

"And what might that be?"

"I guess you'll just have to wait and see, Gen. *Do not* touch her, or any agreement you have with my father will be null and void, I'll see to it myself. Or I'll just save myself the headache and cut to the chase." She looked at him curiously and turned her head to the side.

"Well, you can't collect on an agreement if you don't have a head," he clarified. Her face twisted in annoyance and maybe just the slightest bit of fear. He buckled his sword belt around his waist and took off running behind me.

Once we were well and truly alone, Gen sat down near me and started building the base of a new fire.

"Best get comfortable, sweetheart. I don't know what he's up to, but we might be here for a while." She lit the fire easily with a couple of flints and started poking at it to get all the wood to catch. We stayed like that in silence for a while before she finally turned to look at me.

"*What* are you exactly?" It was the most genuine I had heard her sound so far.

"I don't know what you mean," I said softly.

"A dose that big of Hemlock should've killed you, like right away. Yet here you are, getting pinned to a tree by Rylan, kicking and screaming only a day later." I shrugged at her.

"You know as much as I do, maybe more. You were the one over there studying my blood," I said coldly. It sounded like I was hiding something, but my words were true. I didn't know why the Hemlock didn't kill me, or the arrow, or the strangling. In fact, my sheer hatred for my captor should've killed me by now. She stood up and got in my face again.

"You must know something. No one can survive that. No one. Not only the Hemlock, but Rylan has *never* missed a mark. Not once, not even in training. How did *you* survive?" She was angry now. I pursed my lips into a line; I didn't answer her. I couldn't, I didn't know. She pulled out a dagger and pressed it to my neck. I felt just a little blood drip down from where the blade had broken the skin and drew a sharp breath.

"*Tell me*," she shouted. I stayed silent. "Fine." She sat back down in a huff and started poking the fire again.

"Who are you, anyway?" I asked her stiffly. Her head snapped in my direction. She laughed.

"Rylan's fiancée," she said. "Or, at least, I will be when your head is hanging on Rhonan's gate." *Fiancée,* I thought, *they don't seem particularly in love. He doesn't, anyway.* I thought about the way he'd twirled me around the dance floor. The way I'd foolishly thought he'd be the one before even learning his name. Before my mother died and before I knew he was a cold-blooded murderer. Damn my carnal senses. Heat rose from my stomach and flushed my face; I had almost forgotten that I'd found him attractive then. I guess I wasn't the only one who thought he was handsome.

"So that's the agreement you have with his father? You want to marry *him?*" I asked. I started to wiggle my wrists back and forth behind my back, trying to pull the knots loose. If I could buy myself some time and distract her, I might just have been able to escape.

"Of course I do. Have you seen him? Those beautiful eyes, his perfect hair, his body the Gods carved themselves..." Her breathing sped up a little as she spoke about him. "All the Thorne's are handsome, but Rylan..."

"Well, sure, if you can get past the trail of dead bodies he has lined up behind him." She smiled at me ominously.

"It's okay, sweetheart; I've left my own trail." Her eyes were almost black as she said it. She twirled a dagger between her fingers, and a smirk ran across her face. I continued pulling at the ropes. One knot had come loose, and I started working on another.

"So, you're just like him, then."

"Well, not *just* like him. I kill with more *finesse,*" she said, almost sweetly. "Rylan has his sword, his arrows, his dagger. I have my potions. I carry weapons, too, but I prefer a slow, suffering death." She pulled a small bottle from the pouch on her belt and displayed it proudly in the palm of her hand. "Sometimes, you just need a softer hand. Right, Violet? I mean, *Allanora.*" Her smile spread even wider across her face, and her menacing eyes delighted as they watched the realization settle on my face. *She poisoned my mother.* An angry shriek escaped my mouth as I finally loosened the last knot. I was careful not to bring my arms forward even though the devastation was ripping through me. Gen stood up and moved toward me.

"Poor little orphan Princess." She imitated a pout and drew her hand mockingly across my face. I screamed at her as loud as I could, and the ground beneath us shook. She braced herself and drew her dagger back out from her pocket, grasping it in her hand. She looked at me with confusion and held her hands up by her head. I brought my hands forward, finally grabbed for the dagger, and threw myself against her, knocking her to the ground. I hurried to cut my feet and torso loose and started to run in the opposite direction from where Rylan had taken off. A hand reached out and grabbed my collar, pulling me back and bringing me hard to the ground. A body swung down on top of me, leaving me unable to get back up. I looked and saw that it was Rylan, holding me down and panting. Angrily, he stabbed my arm with what I assumed was another dose of Dragonshade and then lunged himself at Gen.

"How'd you let her escape? I had her tied up. All you had to do was *watch her!*" he yelled. Gen looked away from him, embarrassed and afraid. He sighed.

"It's fine, Gen. She won't be so difficult anymore. He motioned to one side; Gen looked in that direction, and so did I. A small figure was crumpled up on the ground, motionless. Gen walked over and turned them over with her foot. The body rolled to its back, and a small groan came from its lips. A pair of familiar grey eyes met mine. *Lyra.* I tried to move, shout, something, but nothing was happening. Rylan crouched down next to me and pulled me up so I was sitting in front of him.

"So, here's the deal. If you try one more thing, Princess, I'll kill her. You might not be so easy, but my blade will cut through her pretty little neck like butter. Try me, and you'll see." His voice was soft, almost a whisper in my ear. Little Lyra was completely motionless; he had obviously dosed her with the Dragonshade, too. Her figure was small, and her pale blonde hair was in tangles. I wondered if she had put up a fight when he took her. He propped her up on a tree and crouched back down next to me. His hand came around my neck from behind to grasp my chin.

"There are more ways than death to punish you," he whispered in my ear. Gen was watching us from across the firepit.

"I forget how exciting it is when you've got your prey," she said breathlessly to him. He let out an annoyed sigh and ignored her. I couldn't laugh out loud, but I was laughing in my mind. I wasn't sure exactly what deal she made with Rylan's father, but it didn't seem like he was pleased about it. *Hopefully, he just kills her.* The dark thought crossed my mind, and I shocked myself with the careless malevolence. I shook my head and focused again on Lyra. It looked as if she had fallen asleep with her eyes open. I looked her over; there were bruises and scrapes where she had tried to defend herself.

The clouds looming low in the night sky above us threatened rain. The scent of an impending storm filled my nose, and I breathed in the familiar and somehow comforting smell. I had always loved the rain; it was cleansing, calming, and powerful.

"Let's get a move on, Gen," Rylan said to her. He picked Lyra up, laid her across the front of the horse's saddle, and gestured for Gen to get on. She huffed and rolled her eyes. He pulled me up, sat me in the front of his saddle, and jumped up easily behind me. With his arms wrapped around me, he grabbed the reins, and the horse took off galloping. I could hear Gen's horse thundering not far behind.

I knew I was stuck. There was no way for me to escape without letting them harm Lyra. Once again, I felt helpless. Had my people already accepted my death? Had they already moved on and accepted Tobyn as King? Slowly, sensation returned to my body, and Rylan slowed his horse down to a walk as we came into a more densely wooded area. Even with my feeling back, there was nothing I could do. One wrong move and Gen would plunge her deadly little dagger right into poor Lyra's heart, and her blood would be on my hands.

After what seemed to be hours, judging by the first golden sunlight peeking over the horizon, Rylan slowed to a stop. He brought me down to the ground, my legs trembling beneath me. Gen came up next to us. Poor Lyra was still paralyzed; her eyes were wide, nearly void of life, and saliva was dripping from the corner of her open mouth. Clumsily, Gen dragged her to the ground with a thud. Rylan shoved a wad of fabric at me from his bag and gestured to a small pond near where we were standing.

"Wash and dress yourself," he said coldly. "You look ridiculous in that tattered rag." I looked at him in disbelief, my jaw practically hitting the floor.

"You can't be serious." I scoffed at him. He stared at me, flicking his eyes to Lyra, *a threat*. "I'm not going to undress in front of you, let alone *bathe*," I said incredulously. He shrugged.

He ran an arrogant hand down my face and over my chest. "I can do it for you." The devilish gleam returned to his eyes. I snatched the clothes from his other hand and stalked off toward the small pond. Quickly, I peeled my dirty and tattered coronation dress off behind a tree and lowered myself into the water to wash off. I let down my hair, letting it tumble around my shoulders. The water was shallow and cold. I had to crouch down to immerse myself, but I felt Rylan's eyes on me, so I did my best to stay hidden. Even though the water was cold, I felt refreshed, washing the pain and suffering caused by the trauma of the last few days off my porcelain skin. Closing my eyes, I imagined myself back at my choosing ball, back in Arthur's arms. Thinking of him holding me had my heartbeat quickening, with my mother smiling down on me from her perch in the ballroom. Everything was right in the world.

"If you don't hurry up, I'm going to come help you." Rylan's deep voice cut through my warm memory. Disgusted, I washed quickly and tied my hair into a messy braid; Lyra braided much better, of course. Stumbling out of the water, I grabbed the clothes hurriedly and pulled them on. They were obviously Rylan's. A too-big black shirt and pants that I tried to tie up a little to fit more snugly, though I was sure I still looked like a man. *Gross.*

As uncomfortable as the experience was, it did feel good to be somewhat clean and out of the destroyed gown that had too many tainted memories of the last few days wrapped up in it. I walked sheepishly back over to them and let my gown fall to the ground behind me. No seamstress would be able to save it now, anyway. I wished I could burn it. Rylan clapped his hands together and turned to Gen.

"Gen, I'm going to wash. Are you capable of handling her, or do I need to dose her with the Dragonshade?" he taunted, flashing the Dragonshade pin at her. Gen just rolled her eyes and held her dagger to little Lyra's neck to send a message. I stood in front of her silently, defeated. I saw her eyes drift over to the pond where Rylan was undressing, then she snapped her attention back to me. I let out a small laugh, just enough to make her tense up and hold the dagger harder on Lyra. Her unreciprocated desire for Rylan was so obvious. So pathetic.

"*A match made in heaven,*" I said under my breath. She glared at me but didn't let go of Lyra. I had gotten under her skin.

Admittedly, I had stolen a glance at him when he started to undress. He noticed me quickly, and I turned my attention elsewhere. *Foolish.* The glance lasted long enough for me to notice he was covered in tattoos and what looked like scars. When I started to wonder what other secrets he had hiding under his tunic, I was disgusted with myself and focused on anything else I could while he bathed in the shallow pond.

"What are you up to, Princess?" I felt Rylan's hot breath in my ear as he appeared behind me. Gen's nostrils flared out, but she looked at him sweetly. I turned around to face him and backed away, uncomfortable with his proximity. He had changed into a black short-sleeved shirt and pants that were even more revealing of his muscles. I could see his toned chest and bulging tattoo-covered arms very clearly now and started to feel much smaller and more intimidated. The green of his eyes pierced against the olive tones of his skin and black clothes. She was looking him over just as I was, and I swore I saw a little drool pool at the corner of her lips.

"Just talking about what a perfect match we'd be, Ry." Gen flashed him a beautiful smile. He let out a long sigh as he studied her up and down. They really were a match made in heaven—beautiful, cold-blooded killers.

"We'd better get a move on. We are still a half a day's ride away." I gave him a puzzled look.

"She said we were still days away from Astinia," I said, confused.

"We have a stop to make," Rylan said as he fastened his bags back onto his saddle. Gen gave him the same puzzled look. Rylan lifted me quickly back into his saddle.

"Enjoy your comfort while it lasts, Princess. We're headed to Griddick's." Gen's eyes widened, and she reluctantly hopped back into her saddle.

"Are you sure that's a good idea, Ry?" she asked him hesitantly. He ignored her, eased into the saddle behind me, and took off at a gallop.

Chapter 8

Allanora

I closed my eyes. The wind whipped through my hair, pulling strands of my loose braid out as we tore through the forest. I stole a glance over at poor Lyra, still slumped in stunned silence. Even though she was almost completely unconscious, her presence made me feel slightly less alone in the hands of the two assassins I'd found myself with. I let out a long sigh. My right leg was beginning to feel numb, so I leaned a little to my left. The moment I shifted, I felt a dagger blade press against my left thigh, and my entire body tensed up. *One wrong move and that's going into my stomach. Whatever is keeping me from dying doesn't protect me from the pain that comes with these wounds.*

"Don't even think about it, Princess," Rylan huffed behind me. His voice was low and almost soothing. *A good way for a predator to lure in his prey,* I thought.

"I'm the Queen! And I'm not going anywhere, murderer. My leg just hurts!" I rolled my eyes instinctively, even though he couldn't see them. I felt the blade of the dagger push a little harder into my leg. I whirled my head around to pierce him with my angry gaze.

"I'm not the only murderer here, you know," he gestured over to Gen, "One signal from me and your pretty little ladies' maid will be greeting the Gods—er, the Unnamed God you've all been so quick to worship. Helpless sheep." He looked around us uneasily. I bit my lip and held my breath when I looked at Lyra. Her once glossy hair looked dry and stringy, her face twisted in paralyzed pain. *What a mess,* I thought to myself, settling back into the saddle, defeated. I felt his grip loosen on me and let out my breath in slight relief.

"What exactly is it that you have planned for me?" I turned my body again as much as I could and asked him. I saw his mouth twitch into what looked like a wince. His eyes were cold.

"I don't make the plans. Rhonan is King. You'll answer to him. Or Raysh, the Crown Prince, and he has his own...proclivities." He set his jaw, and the chilling sound of bone on bone gave me goosebumps as he ground his teeth together.

"Queens don't answer to Kings in Lynnea. And I most definitely won't be answering to any *Astinian* King or Prince." I straightened my back and turned my face up toward the skyline; the suns had begun to set over the horizon, a gradient of beautiful color between them.

"You'll want to try a different tactic when you face Rhonan, *Your Majesty*. He isn't as patient and kind as I am." It sounded like it was supposed to be a joke, but I had turned enough to see his face from the corner of my eye, and he was serious. If Rylan was tame compared to his father, I might have truly been in trouble. *Lynnean Queens fear no one, bow to no one, and rise above.* My mother's words rang in my ears. I wouldn't let Rhonan or his murdering brat of a son get the better of me. I couldn't disgrace my beloved Lynnea or my mother that way; I just couldn't.

"If you're patient and kind, I'm a horse's ass," I muttered under my breath. Rylan fought back a laugh, but I still heard it. Gen must have heard it, too, because she looked over at us. If eyes could kill, I would have been dead on the spot.

"Rylan, we won't make it to Griddick's before dark," she pleaded with him. He pretended not to hear her and kept thundering forward. "*Rylan*," she shouted, annoyed.

"You afraid of the dark, Gen?" he called back mockingly. She scowled and refocused her eyes on the horizon.

It wasn't long before the suns disappeared, and the sky was speckled with stars. The vast expanse of sparkling diamonds sprinkled across a sea of midnight blue was dazzling. My heart sunk into my stomach, thinking my mother was one of those beautiful diamonds, forever a light in the darkness, guiding my way. My stomach churned, and I wondered if she was guiding me now, even in my darkest moment.

I hadn't realized that I had started to drift off to sleep until I found myself slumping backward against Rylan; I was too exhausted, constantly worrying about what fresh hell would be meeting me next. I immediately sat myself up in disgust and straightened my shoulders, praying silently to the Unnamed God to spare me. I opened my eyes and saw that we were on the verge of entering a small town nestled in between where a canal split in two. Most of the buildings were small homes, with a few larger buildings sprinkled throughout. The ground was mostly unkempt grass and dirt paths; a poor town, to be sure, stuck between Lynnea and Astinia. Very few lights were on, and only a few chimneys had smoke coming from them. *Not a very well-inhabited town, either.* I felt a wave of fear slither over my skin as we approached the town's gate. The gate was tall, but the hinges were rusted to their last leg. A tall man in a dark cloak greeted us there. I couldn't see much of his face, but he seemed to have a significant amount of moles and only a couple of teeth.

"Where to?" he croaked, an eerie, nearly toothless grin pasted on his pale face. Gen pointed at Rylan, who brought down the hood he had been wearing. His face shone in the glow of the largest of the four moons of Cidris; he looked menacing and authoritative in the light, and the gatekeeper retreated into the shadows as the gate opened for us.

"I still don't think this is a good idea, Ry," Gen whispered as we descended a dirt path toward the only lit building in sight. There were boards over most of the windows, and the windows that were uncovered had been overgrown with spiderwebs and dust.

"No one asked you to be here, Gen. You're more than welcome to leave any time you want." They both scowled, refusing to look at each other. We slowed to a stop outside the tavern-looking building, and I felt Rylan's hand clench around my arm. "If you try anything funny, Princess—"

I cut him off. "I know, I know, you'll kill her," I said, rolling my eyes. He slid off his horse easily and yanked me down next to him. Gen poked at Lyra until she sat up sleepily; her eyes widened with shock when she started to take in her surroundings. Rylan, Gen, the tavern, eventually landing her eyes on me. The realization finally hit her that I was alive. She opened her mouth, and I held up my hand. Her jaw clicked shut. Rylan pulled a heavy and dark cloak over my head and tied it.

"Do not remove this cloak if you know what's good for you," he growled at me. I scowled back and held my head high. Even when I was straightened to full height, he towered over me. Gen was pushing Lyra forward into the tavern when he grabbed my arm and started pushing me as well. I shook off his hand irritably.

"I can walk myself, thank you." I pivoted on my heel and turned to start walking on my own. He yanked me back by the arm and pulled me against him, pressing his face to my ear, feeling the heat of my anger burning against him.

"Listen up, Princess. You might think that you're invincible and that *I'm* the worst thing you've ever encountered. I don't know what it is that keeps helping you cheat death, but let me tell you, there are men in there that will try a hundred different ways just to make you suffer, and they'll do it for pleasure." He pondered his own words for a moment, probably imagining how fun it would have been to watch me be tortured. "Keep it up, and I'll let them. Rhonan will be just as happy, I'd imagine, if I tell him I left you here with them to be tortured till the end of your life, however long that may be. But if I were you, I'd take my chances with Rhonan over that. Your choice." He released me with a shove, and I stumbled into his horse. He stalked off into the dark through the door, leaving me alone to contemplate my choices. The thought of Lyra drew me begrudgingly into the tavern behind him. The light was dim, and the stench of alcohol and testosterone-fueled body odor was strong; thick enough to feel dense on my tongue and make me gag. I caught a glimpse of Gen's hair and made my way in that direction. I had taken barely two steps when I felt a hand grasp the hood of my cloak and yank it back. I felt a blade at my throat and an arm wrapped tightly around my waist. Fear shot down my spine like an urgent bolt of lightning when I heard a voice in my ear.

"You look like quite the pretty prize to take home," the man's voice said. His breath stunk of heavy alcohol and sour, rotting flesh, forcing me to gag. Tears welled up in my eyes as he grasped and pulled my braid. I tried to remember the self-defense tactics Tobyn had taught me when I was young, but my mind was blank with fear. I had never needed to practice what he taught me; no man in Lynnea would ever dare to handle a woman this way. Two more men turned toward us and started to come closer. I felt myself being pulled backward and choked, and I coughed as the cold blade threatened to draw blood.

"She's mine, boys," the man holding me captive growled at the others. The tears flowed freely from my eyes. I started to breathe more quickly as panic filled my lungs, restricting me like a tight corset. A feeling I knew all too well. *What would my mother do, what would my mother do?* I heard my own panicked voice in my head and raised my foot to stomp down when I heard a familiar ringing sound. A split second later, an arrow followed, launching into the left eye of my captor. I let out a spine-chilling scream as the blade fell away from my neck, and I stumbled from the man's body. He collapsed to the floor, twitching and gushing blood from his obliterated eye socket. I gagged and forced myself not to vomit right there on the tavern floor. Rylan stepped forward over the man's body and yanked me toward him by the braid in my hair, forcing me to kneel next to him so I wouldn't fall. The tears kept coming as sobs started to escape my lips. I saw Gen across the way, holding Lyra down in a chair and glaring at me.

"Who's next? Go ahead, give it a shot," Rylan barked at the nearby men with their eyes still fixated on me. He drew his sword from its sheath and waited, staring them down.

"It's Rylan, the God-killer," I heard a man whisper nearby. I saw the corner of Rylan's mouth twist into an almost evil grin. *God-killer,* I thought, *what does that even mean?*

"Anyone?" he taunted. The two men near me withdrew from him with their hands behind their heads. He stuck his sword into the floor right next to the still-twitching assailant. He kicked the body over, allowing the blood from his eye socket to drip freely onto the wooden floor. I forced back a gag. "Didn't think so." He pulled me to my feet, still by my hair, and pushed me up a flight of nearby steps. Gen was not far behind, dragging Lyra mercilessly by her cloak. She threw Lyra against the wall at the top of the steps and rounded on Rylan as Lyra stumbled and fell.

"Way to 'not attract attention', Rylan. Really smart. As soon as you take your eyes off her, you know they'll come for her. Then what? I don't really feel like beating down a bunch of thugs all night, Ry." She threw her hands up in the air. "Let's just go."

"They were going to come for her anyway. Look at her, those irritatingly innocent doe eyes she's got," he said. Gen rolled her eyes, her face flushing red. "At least, this way, I've sent a message. Plus, I don't intend to take my eyes off her." He puffed up his chest, daring her to continue arguing.

"Yeah, or posed a challenge." She scowled at him and stormed off. I rushed to Lyra and helped her up.

"Lyra, are you all right?" Her body was shaking, and her stony grey eyes met mine. She nodded her head yes, still too weak to speak. I brushed the hair from her pale face. I looked up at Rylan and pleaded with him.

"Please, she needs water and food. Your Dragonshade has weakened her. Please."

He scoffed. "I have no reason to help you, either of you," he remarked.

"If she dies, you have no leverage over me. It's the whole reason you took her. You said so yourself." He rolled his eyes and disappeared back down the stairs, taking multiple bounding steps at a time. I sat Lyra back down in the poorly lit hallway and brought her head into my lap. I brushed her hair gently with my fingers as she had done with mine so many times before. Rylan returned after just a moment with a small tray of dried fruit, bread, and a dirty ceramic cup of water. I helped Lyra drink, and she took a few bites of food before dropping her head back onto my lap. While I fed her, I heard him open a door in the hallway with a heavy creak. He returned and swung Lyra over his shoulder while grabbing me by the arm. I immediately yanked away from his grip.

"You don't have to force me; I'm coming with you. I won't leave her alone with *you*." I swept his heavy cloak around myself and stomped into the room with the open door. The room was dusty and dark, the furniture well-worn, and there was only a small bed in one corner and a small table in another. The room smelled of sweaty men, sour milk, and mold. I wrinkled my nose and gagged, swallowing a little bit of vomit. He tossed the small tray of food on the table, letting it clatter loudly. *He acts like such a troll.*

"Eat," he said to me, his voice thick with irritation, and gestured toward the table. Seeing the food, I realized I was rather hungry, and he hadn't given me much to eat during our travels. The thought of eating turned my stomach, though, and I shook my head. He shrugged and sat down on the floor, propping himself up against a wall by the door, drew his sword, and placed it in his lap.

"You're *that* afraid that I'm going to try to escape? I couldn't get very far with her in this state. I think we both know that."

He winked an eye. "Oh, Princess, I'm not worried about keeping you in," he nodded toward the door. "I have to keep others out." A cold shudder ran down my spine as I remembered the man in the tavern who had taken hold of me. I swallowed hard.

"A pretty face like yours gets a lot of attention around here. Not to mention the rest of you." He gestured up and down my body with an outstretched hand, "Your head would catch a hefty price—attached to your neck or not." He winked again and rested his head back on the wall. I rubbed my neck softly, the thought of beheading hanging in my mind. "And, trust me, they'd have more creative things to do with your pretty little neck than just trying to slice it open. I promise you that." I shuddered. I couldn't see myself surviving even that. The door opened, and my body jumped involuntarily in fear. I never thought I'd be relieved to see Gen reappear. She scowled at the sight in front of her.

"You'd think the son of a King could afford two rooms." She glared at him. He laughed.

"You're more than welcome to take the serving girl wherever you'd please, Gen. The Princess stays with me." He closed his eyes and leaned back against the wall, and she shot daggers at me again.

"They won't go anywhere if you lock them in here," she said, her voice sickeningly sweet, a quite obvious show she was putting on for him. "We can be alone next door if we want. There's no one in there." She sat herself down on his lap, trailing her fingers up his chest. He opened his eyes and brushed her easily off to the side. I choked back another gag.

"I'm not going anywhere with you, Gen. I don't even know why you're here."

Her face twisted in disappointment. "Your father and I have a deal."

He opened one eye and looked at her with slight interest.

"Oh yeah? And what's that, Gen? You want to be head of his guards? My mother's lady-in-waiting? Land? A title?" He laughed again; her face started to burn red. I wasn't sure if it was from anger or embarrassment. Discomfort ran through me. They seemed to be on the brink of an all-out fight, and I was not in the mood to be right in the middle of it.

"He promised me your hand if I helped you finish your mission," she blurted. Rylan stopped laughing immediately.

"He promised you what?" His already angry face twisted in rage.

"Your—"

"*I heard you, Gen.*"

A heavy silence hung in the air between them. He was seething, his fists clenched.

"Well, I—"

"Just to be very clear, I will never marry you. I will never marry anyone. You know that." His tone was dark and intimidating; his eyes could have burned holes through her. She looked defeated, but only for a moment before determination took over. She opened her mouth to speak but closed it again just as quickly. She turned to kneel next to him and whispered something in his ear that I couldn't hear. He grimaced before answering her.

"That was one time, and I was in a bad place. You have to stop. I don't care what my father told you. You're not getting what you want here, so you'd better think of something else you want from him, anything else. Or better yet—just leave." Her expression made no attempt to hide her hurt, but I could tell she wasn't going to give up. She threw her leg over him, straddling him, and angrily took his face in her hands before crushing her lips to his. My mouth fell open in shock, and even Lyra's previously expressionless eyes widened. For a moment, he kissed her back, but only long enough to bring his hand up to her neck and clench it between his fingers. His eyes were harsh and dark. His hand squeezed her neck. I let out a gasp as she started to choke beneath his grip. Her hands clawed at his. Part of me, and not a small part, wanted him to kill her. She'd admitted to poisoning my mother; she deserved to die. A tiny part of me felt guilty about my excitement at the thought of watching her die.

He released her from his grip, and she slid down onto the floor, gasping for air. She turned toward him, but he was already up and out the door, slamming it behind him. Gen threw her head back against the wall and started to cry. I almost felt bad for her, but then I remembered my poor mother, dead by this woman's hand. She turned and seemed to realize I was still there, so she quickly wiped the tears from her face.

"Not all of us are Princesses who can be with whoever we want," she said coldly. I rolled my eyes.

"First of all, I'm the Queen. You people keep forgetting I was crowned before you took my whole life away. Secondly, I am *not* going to feel bad for you here. Your 'boyfriend' kidnapped and tried to kill me. He drugged Lyra and is holding her hostage. He's put my entire kingdom at risk. So he doesn't want to marry you? Get over yourself. Some of us have real problems." I crossed my arms over my chest and turned away from her. I moved Lyra from the floor to the small bed and covered her with the thin blanket, turning to sit at the foot of the bed when my head was yanked backward. Gen's eyes were feral, and her nostrils flared. I twisted myself back up into a standing position and pulled my hair from her grip.

"Spoiled Princess bitch!" she shouted at me. "You have everything! Your own kingdom, people who love you, people who miss you, men fighting over you. You don't even care!" My mind shot back to a mere few moments ago, those disgusting men fighting over their claim of me. Gen made it sound like such an honor. I would've done anything to be free of the memory. His sharp blade against my neck, his garbage breath on my skin...

"Rhonan will probably marry you off to one of his sons if he can't kill you. You'll still have everything!" Tears streamed down her face as she shouted. I stood in stunned silence. *Marry me off to one of his sons? An Astinian King on the Lynnean throne?* The thought of it made me gag, my stomach churning, enraged and afraid. The ground started to shake violently below my feet. My heart dropped, and I knew I was going to vomit. Black patches filled my vision, and before I could right myself, my body hit the floor.

An unfamiliar room in an unfamiliar castle. Swirling faces and glistening ballgowns surrounded me. Cheery music filled the large room. I walked forward down a long aisle toward a man I did not know, but he smiled at me and took my hand. We glided forward together, toward a smiling Brother of the Triini dressed in ceremonial wedding robes. I tried to focus on the face of the man next to me, but I couldn't. Panic started to set in. Terror filled me. I tried to pull away and run, but his grip on my hand was like steel.

I awoke to the sound of Gen and Rylan arguing again.

"What's wrong with you, Gen? What did you do to her?" He stood over me but looked at her.

"I didn't *do* anything. It was another one of those earthquakes, they keep coming out of nowhere. She fainted like the wimpy Princess she is."

"There was no earthquake, Gen. I would've felt it downstairs."

"You're too drunk to know the difference. I know what happened. I don't care what you think anymore." She crossed her arms over her chest, her right hip jutting out to the side. I started to try and sit up but collapsed back on the ground; my head was spinning violently. With my face flat on the floor, pine and vinegar filled my nose. My ears filled with a high-pitched ringing, and everything around me seemed to be pulsing, or maybe that was just my head. I looked toward the door, trying to regain my vision. A boy was standing there, staring at me wide-eyed; he was no more than 13, a small, dark-skinned boy with tattoos down both arms. Rylan motioned for him to leave.

"Get a move on, boy, and get that message to my father *immediately*." The boy looked terrified. He clutched a piece of paper in his hands and darted off through the doorway, closing the door behind him. Rylan rounded back on Gen.

"My father sent you to help, Gen, stop making everything more difficult. You just keep getting in my way."

I tried once again to sit up, but I was unsuccessful and let my head fall back to the ground. Rylan's gaze landed on me, and he crouched down quickly, squinting at me with his menacing eyes.

"My father wants you in Astinia tomorrow. Now's not a good time to die," he growled.

"I'm not marrying your brother," I said weakly. "I'd rather die than sit an Astinian on the Lynnean throne." He laughed and dropped himself into a sitting position, resting his arms on his knees.

"You just keep telling yourself whatever you want, Princess. Whatever my father desires, he gets. Apparently, now, he wants *you*." He glared angrily at Gen, who turned away, embarrassed.

A sharp, pounding noise came from the other side of the door. Rylan stood up straight, tensed, and drew his sword. The door opened slowly, and Rylan started forward, stopping mid-lunge when a large man entered the room with his hands up. He was a tall, heavy-set, intimidating man; he had to bow his head to come through the doorway. He was missing almost as many teeth as the guard at the gate, and he smelled of old garlic and bitter alcohol. His clothes were stained and tattered, and he wore the apron of a barkeep. Rylan straightened himself, relaxing slightly, and nodded his head toward the man, who nodded back.

"Griddick," Rylan said shortly.

"Rylan. I came to see if it was true." He jutted his chin toward me. "A living mark after the kill. I heard the little strumpet was dead. The Lynneans are devastated." He smiled and turned back toward Rylan. "I've never seen any of your marks without an arrow through their hearts." He made the motion of shooting an arrow from a bow. He gargled a deep and sinister laugh. Rylan scowled at him and clenched his fist around his sword, his face flushed. It was like his blood was boiling just beneath the surface of his skin; I could almost feel the heat from his anger.

"Are you just here to taunt me, Griddick? I have this one here for that." He pointed his sword toward Gen, then put it back in its sheath.

"Like I said. I wanted to see if it was true. *They're* all talking about it. The others come through here a lot. The God-killer's lost his touch, apparently." His grin was so off-putting I felt bile rising in my throat; his crooked teeth were bared in a smile for the world to see, an evil glint in his dark eyes.

"I'd tell you to give it a shot yourself, but it seems my father wants this pretty face intact. He left a messenger boy here for me. I just sent him off, back to Astinia." Rylan gestured toward the door. Griddick cracked his knuckles. His hands were inhumanly large. I imagined he could crush my skull like a berry between them. I quaked, buried beneath that thought.

"Don't worry, I'll leave her face intact," he said, his mouth curling into a more devious smile, sizing me up. He seemed to undress me with his eyes, looking me up and down. My heart started to pound as he took a step forward, his fists still poised in front of his chest. He didn't seem to have any weapons on him, but I also wasn't sure if he even needed any with hands like that. Rylan sighed an agitated sigh, drew his bow, and set an arrow.

"Do you really want to see if I've lost my touch? I'd be happy to test that theory for you." Rylan's own lethal snarl spread across his face as he fingered the bowstring and pulled the arrow's end to his cheek. Griddick put his hands back up.

"No, no, it's fine. But I did come to warn you. They're talking. Steele sent out a message saying you're to return to The Academy. Some are saying you've gone soft."

This is soft?

"I don't care what *they're* saying, Griddick. I'm not going back to The Academy, and I am not seeing Steele. You can let whoever you want know that. I'm taking this *Princess* to my father, and then I'm done. Steele will just have to deal with it."

Gen let out a huff of air in the corner and approached the two men, hands on her hips. "If Steele wants you, Ry, you know the others will be coming for you. Your Princess, too."

He scoffed and glared at her. "*My Princess?* Back off, Gen, or I'll tie you up here and leave you to answer to Steele yourself. You haven't exactly been in the good graces of the others with that last mess you made." Gen's face dropped, defeat in her eyes, and she took a step back. I looked between them all with confusion. *Steele? The Academy? The others? What are they even talking about?* I took a deep breath and calmed myself. I'd be kidding myself if I thought any of them would answer the questions I had.

"You can't stay here, Ry." Griddick sighed. "I've already got folks taking off since you showed up. They've heard the talk, too; they know the others will be coming for you. Maybe Steele, as well. No one wants to be around for that. Look, you're just bad for business." Eyes downcast, and finally off me, he ran his hand through his matted brown hair sheepishly.

"It's the middle of the night, Grid. The horses need rest, and so do I if they're coming for me. We will leave at the light of the first sun rising, I promise," Rylan pleaded with him. Gen rolled her eyes.

"I'm going down and getting a drink," Gen announced. "If they're coming, I don't need to be ready. I need to be happy." She stomped through the doorway and slammed the door behind her. Both men cringed.

"She's a feisty one, eh?" Griddick smiled and clapped Rylan on the shoulder. "Loads of fun for you, if you know what I mean." Rylan pushed his hand off his shoulder and scowled.

"It's not like that, Grid. You know I'm not with Gen, not after everything—well, you know." His gaze darted between me and the man-monster who seemed to take up the majority of the room.

"All right, all right." He took a step back and put his hands back up. "Well, I guess if you're all staying through the night, maybe I'll take a shot at her myself." He laughed and punched Rylan's arm. Rylan rolled his eyes as Griddick turned and left the room. *Gross,* I thought to myself. I could hear the floor creak under his tremendous weight with each step he took down the hall until he disappeared down the stairs. I let out a sigh of relief.

"Who's Steele?" I asked before I could stop myself. Rylan glared at me and slid his bow back over his shoulder.

"None of your business. Now lay down and go to sleep. I need some rest, and I won't get any with you yapping at me all night." He huffed and moved back into his position by the door. I sighed and crawled in next to Lyra. The bed was hard and lumpy. I tried not to imagine what kind of creatures had occupied this room or, worse, had slept in this bed. As I drifted off, I started to wonder what was happening in my beloved Lynnea and how I would ever get myself out of this mess. Get everything back to the way it was. Not that I knew what that even looked like anymore. Maybe it would start with Arthur Blackwood. A fleeting smile graced my lips, followed by another dark cloud in my mind. When I'd been crowned, Lynnea was already on the precipice of unwelcomed change, of a new era.

Mine. Even if I returned, I'd be alone. More than anything, though, I just wanted to go home. A tear slipped down my cheek as I drifted off into a troubled sleep.

Chapter 9

Allanora

Lyra was tossing and twitching in the bed next to me. I opened my eyes and tried to wake her, shaking her shoulder and shouting her name, but she wasn't snapping out of it.

"Lyra! *Lyra!* LYRA!" I saw Rylan open his eyes and look over at us; he looked tired and agitated.

"Side effect of the Dragonshade," he said, disinterested. He closed his eyes and let his head rest against the wall again. I huffed at him and kept shaking her.

"This didn't happen to me, and you dosed me way more times. Why?" I demanded. He just shrugged and rested his head back on the wall.

Finally, Lyra started to wake. Her eyes fluttered open, and her body relaxed. She took a deep breath and sat up. Suddenly, she snapped to attention and frantically looked around the room, terrified. She breathed in and out, taking short, shallow breaths, and the color drained from her face.

"You—you died!" she shouted at me. Rylan turned toward us, a lick of anger gracing his face.

"Be quiet, or you'll be sorry," he hissed at us between gritted teeth. I rolled my eyes. I wanted this to be over. I needed it to be over. He'd become a thorn in my side more than a threat, knowing he wasn't able to kill me, for whatever reason that was. His father wanted me alive in Astinia now. Rylan wouldn't try to kill me himself.

"I didn't die. I guess everyone thinks I did," I explained to her.

"I feel like I'm seeing a ghost," she whispered. "What happened to you?"

I glared over at Rylan. "He happened," I accused. "He shot me with an arrow. I was 'supposed to' die, apparently, but he sucks at being an assassin." I shot him a pointed glare. I'd poked the bear; his brows furrowed, and a vein popped out of his forehead. "Then he kidnapped me, and now we're both here because he couldn't kill me, so he is using you as leverage to keep me from trying to run." My emotions started to get the better of me, and I could feel the tears welling up. Lyra finally turned and looked at Rylan very carefully. She squinted her eyes at him, seeming to think very hard.

"I know you," she said. "You were at the ball." She gasped. "And you were outside her room when she fell into that sleep!" His face darkened. In a heartbeat, Rylan flew across the room and clapped his hand over her mouth.

"I should've just killed you," he hissed. "Shut your mouth, or I'll dose you with the Dragonshade again, and by the looks of it, that might actually kill you." He released her, and her mouth snapped shut, and I released the breath I'd been involuntarily holding.

"What does she mean you were outside my room when I fell into that sleep?" I asked him angrily. I remembered what he had said about trying to strangle me; it must've happened then, after my mother had died.

"I don't answer to you," he said sharply. Before I could think better of myself, I reached out and slapped him across the face. He looked stunned but grabbed my wrist before I could retract and pushed me down onto the floor, positioning himself on top of me so I couldn't move. Lyra let out a gasp.

"I would think *very* carefully, Princess, before you ever lay a hand on me again. I'm the only thing standing between you and all those brutes downstairs who want to get their hands on you." A chill ran down my spine and drew goosebumps on my arms. The fear of him I had started to lose was creeping back in. He leaned down, entirely filling my space, and whispered in my ear. "I'd be happy to let them." His warm breath on my face made me wince, and he sat back just as Gen burst into the room. She was clearly drunk, stumbling in and slurring her words, and once she'd taken in the scene before her, she threw her half-empty cup across the room over Lyra's head. Lyra screamed.

"Oh, I see. You don't want me, you want her." She pointed at me, nostrils flaring. "I'm not good enough now that you've had a taste for royalty," she stammered, choking out the last word. Rylan rolled his eyes and stood up. I stayed put.

"I don't want any of you. I had to teach *that* one a lesson." He pointed down at me, shoving his finger toward my face. "Go sleep it off, Gen. We have to leave in a couple of hours, or we might be facing off against the others. Or Griddick and his goons. Either way, I'm not in the mood for it." He tried to push past her, but she grabbed him by the shirt and pushed him against the wall, forcing his hands to his sides and sticking her tongue down his throat. Lyra grimaced. I gagged and looked away. It was starting to get pathetic. I heard a thud and warily looked back toward them. Gen was on the ground, looking stunned. Maybe he pushed her. Maybe she was so wasted she fell. I stifled a laugh, a snort coming out of my nose. She glared at me. Embarrassment and anger entwined themselves in the air, snaking around me.

"That's it, Gen. I'm done." He picked her up, opened the door, and dropped her on the other side of it. "We leave at daybreak. I don't care if you join us or not." He slammed the door in her face and locked it, then rounded on us and gave us a look that could've burned our very souls into ash. "Anyone else think it's a good idea to stick their tongue in my mouth?" We shook our heads slowly, fear settling back in fully. "No? Good. Sleep or don't, I don't care. We leave first thing. I can't wait to get rid of every single one of you." He huffed and slid back down into his guarding position by the door. "Next person who speaks a word gets an arrow to the foot." Lyra and I exchanged fearful looks and laid back down on the small mattress, closing our eyes and hoping for sleep.

I must have drifted off because I dreamed of Arthur before I was woken by my legs being pulled down off the mattress. It was Rylan.

"Rise and shine, Princess. You meet your fate today." His voice was sinister, and I gulped. He went to grab Lyra, but I held up my hand and used the other to grip her shoulder. She woke immediately with a start. Rylan threw his one bag over his shoulder and grabbed Lyra by the arm.

"You going to come quietly, or do I need to tie you up and drag you?" he threatened me, a dark playfulness lacing his tone. I let out an exasperated breath.

"I'll come." He pushed his way out of the room and down into the tavern's main space, with Lyra stumbling in front of him. Along the way out, Gen came running down the staircase, dark circles under her eyes and hair tousled all around her face. She looked like a mess. Rylan didn't acknowledge her. Down the stairs, not far behind her, came Griddick's heavy footsteps.

"Last night wasn't good enough for you?" he called out to her, laughing. She grimaced as Rylan looked her up and down and rolled his eyes. *Ew*, I thought. Gen cringed and kept walking, falling in behind me.

"You slept with *him?*" Lyra said loudly. Gen grimaced and glared at both of us, fire in her eyes. Rylan tensed and smacked Lyra on the mouth, silencing her. She reeled backward, but he dragged her outside by the hair to where our horses had been resting.

"Listen, I'm really not in the mood to have to skewer Griddick or deal with all his grimy goons," he relented. Gen's cheeks flushed with embarrassment.

"Rylan, I—"

He cut her off, looking exasperated. "I don't care, Gen. I really don't. You can roll around with whoever you damn well please." Lyra giggled, and I pretended I didn't hear them. He said he didn't care, but I wondered if he really did. Obviously, the two of them had history.

"I just—"

"Shut up and get on the horse, Gen." His face was cold, his stern expression frozen on his face as if it had been carved that way. I climbed up on the horse, and he swung up behind me. Gen sighed and got on behind Lyra, who shifted uncomfortably. She shot me a pleading look. I held my hands up helplessly. Rylan took off in a huff.

Even under such awful circumstances, I could appreciate how stunning the countryside was between the two kingdoms and how much I enjoyed horseback riding. I took a deep breath and filled my lungs with clean, fresh air. The trees were lush and green, wildflowers peppered thick grasses, and the air was warm and welcoming. I closed my eyes and remembered riding through the grounds of Lynnea with my mother at my side, learning the names of all the plants and watching the animals run carelessly and freely through the forest. Everything was simpler then; my path was planned and set out before me, and I had my mother to guide me. I always knew what was coming. I didn't know that now, and she wasn't here to guide me anymore. A tear slipped from my eye down my cheek as the skies above started to darken with incoming clouds. I shook my head. I had to stay strong; that was the only way I'd ever be able to get myself back to where I needed to be, I told myself. With my eyes closed, I was starting to wonder how I'd even gotten here and how I was ever going to make it back home.

"Can I ask you something?" I blurted out.

"No," he responded shortly.

"Why were you even at my choosing ball?" I persisted.

"I don't answer to you, Princess."

"Queen."

"Whatever."

"If Gen poisoned my mother, why were *you* at my choosing ball?" He rolled his eyes and glared at Gen. I couldn't tell if she was ignoring us or not close enough to hear. "And why did you dance with me?" He ignored me again. But I wanted answers. I yanked back on the reins, and his midnight black horse knickered and started to back up, tossing its head. Fury bubbled through me, shutting out any self-preserving instincts. "Tell me something," I shouted. The sky above us darkened even more, and rain began to drizzle from thick and thundering clouds. "Why are you doing this to me?" I screamed.

Gen stopped her horse and started looking around her; Lyra shrunk into her cloak and pulled her hood over her head to shield herself from the coming downpour. Angrily, I slipped myself out of the saddle and out of his grip. "You're not an assassin; you can't even kill me. You're barely an envoy delivering me from one kingdom to another." I stomped my foot on the dampened ground. Lightning struck in the distance, and a boom of thunder followed it. Gen shot Rylan a concerned look. He let out an irritated breath and slid off the horse, gripping my shoulders in his strong hands. I shrunk back just a little.

"You need to calm down," was all he said, looking warily around at the skies. My jaw dropped. Gen slid off of her horse and moved a few steps behind him.

"*Calm down*? You want me to calm down? You appear in my life for no reason, hang around my castle while I am sleeping, shoot me with an arrow during my coronation, kidnap me, drag me across the kingdom, blackmail me by enslaving my handmaiden, and you don't even have the decency to tell me why you, or whoever assigned you to me, wanted me dead? And I'm supposed to calm down? You may be great with a bow and arrow, but there's nothing but mushroom dust between those ears of yours!" He took a deep breath and looked at Gen, who held her hands up and shrugged. The initial drizzle turned to heavy drops, and a huge thundercloud appeared over us. Lightning was striking the trees, and branches began flying about. Gen took a step back, and Rylan looked back and forth between the sky and me, unsure of what to do next. The thunder rumbled in my chest as more lightning cracked in the sky. A strange tingle made its way up and down my fingers, almost like strong static sizzling at my fingertips.

Lyra reached out toward me from the horse. "Um, not to interrupt, but can we go somewhere, I don't know...dry?" she squeaked.

Rylan glared at her. "What, are you made of sugar?" Lyra stuck her bottom lip out in a defeated pout. The rain began to drench us all. Lyra pulled her hair back into the hood of her cloak in hopes of keeping it dry. She flung herself clumsily off the horse and stumbled to the nearest tree, plopping herself down stubbornly. Gen jumped down and started after her. Lyra held her hands up in defense.

"I'm just sitting down; I'm tired of getting drenched, and if you're both arguing, I might as well be at least a little comfortable." Lyra's words were licked with sarcasm and irritation. "I'm not that stupid to try to run away from 'the poison queen' and 'arrow happy' over there." She crossed her arms over her chest and pulled the hood down over her face. I fought back a giggle. The rain lightened just a little, and a tiny bit of sunshine peeked out beneath the curtain of clouds. Strange.

"Listen," Rylan said, his cold eyes meeting mine. "I do the job I'm hired to do. I don't ask questions."

"Why were you assigned to kill me? What did my mother and I do to slight the King of Astinia so?" I set my jaw, and the clouds seemed to be sewn back together, casting an eerie shadow over us.

Rylan looked around uncomfortably. "I can't tell you that."

"What *can* you tell me?" He put one hand under my chin and focused his eyes on mine. My breath caught in my throat, and the rain started to pound on the ground.

"My brother, the Crown Prince, is not a gentle man. If my father does force you to marry Raysh, you won't be having your sweet, comfortable life anymore, I can tell you that." A shudder crawled down my spine. He laughed.

The rain had gotten so heavy that I could barely see Lyra and Gen at the nearby tree. I started to shiver, and my boots filled with water.

"We're leaving, are you coming?" he barked at Gen.

He mounted his horse without waiting for her to answer and held his arm out to me to pull me up. I scoffed but got in the saddle in front of him.

A Dance of Storms and Shadows

The rain pelted down in thick bullets, making it hard for the horses to run, so they trotted along slowly, carrying us through the downpour. I was soaked to the bone, the water sloshing around inside Rylan's boots on my feet. *Maybe this rain will buy me some time. I need to stay out of Astinia and away from the hands of...the brother.* My body quaked at the thought. If Rylan, the assassin, thought his brother was terrible, I couldn't even imagine what kind of person he must be.

We traveled most of the day with the rain pouring on, no end in sight. It didn't even look like we had gone anywhere; everything looked the same. The same trees sagged under the weight of the raindrops, and there were no buildings or houses to mark where we might have been. As the suns moved across the sky, I hoped we were still far away from the Astinian King's castle; I hadn't come up with a plan yet.

Lyra's voice brought my mind back from where it had been wandering. "Your Majesty?" Her voice was soft and fearful. I looked over at her, and she was pointing off into the distance. I followed the path and saw a man on a horse, quite some distance from us but close enough to be seen. The rain had lightened enough that we could see a little further ahead, but it was still drizzling. Rylan's grip on me tightened, and Gen pushed her dagger against Lyra's waist; both stopped the horses. The stranger slowly made his way forward until he was directly in front of us. His horse was a beautiful white, and he wore a knight's armor; the unmistakable Lynnean emblem adorned his breast. He wore no helmet, and his face was vaguely familiar, but I couldn't place it. I'd been so tired, so much had happened in such a short time, I wasn't sure I'd recognize my mother even if she stood in front of me.

"What's a Lynnean knight doing all the way out here?" Rylan grumbled at him. The knight looked taken aback and stayed silent for a moment. I kept my eyes trained on him, willing myself to recognize him; I was sure I knew him from somewhere.

"I am Arthur of House Blackwood. The Lynnean King has sent knights far and wide to look for the assassin that murdered both the Queens of

Lynnea," he declared boldly while resting his hand over his chest. It came flooding back, and I felt foolish for not immediately recognizing the man who I'd been daydreaming of this whole time. *Arthur, thank goodness, we're saved!* "I would ask what an unmarked man such as yourself is doing out in the middle of nowhere with these three lovely ladies." He looked at me, Lyra, and Gen in turn. When his eyes reached mine, they blazed and lingered for a moment, and I held my breath, but then he moved on. Lyra opened her mouth to speak, but Gen's dagger pushed further into her waist, cutting through the fabric of her dress. I pursed my lips tightly as I saw Lyra shift uncomfortably.

"I am Justyn, these are my three sisters; I am escorting them to Astinia to be presented to the King before they are wed," he said smugly. The lie rolled off his tongue like butter. *What a disgusting, egregious excuse for a human being.*

"Quite a job for one man alone." He searched our small party with his eyes, landing on Rylan with a wary gaze. "Let us build a fire and take a meal together. I am sure you'd be anxious to have a more gentlemanly conversation with three women in tow." He swung down from his horse and gestured for Rylan to do the same. Lyra fought back a laugh at his words; 'gentlemanly conversation' was not something we would've imagined Rylan to take part in.

I focused all my attention on Arthur, willing him to recognize me. I looked down at myself, dressed in Rylan's tunic clothing, my hair in a messy braid that hung down past my chest. He'd only seen me dressed in an evening gown with a crown on my head.

"That's quite all right," Rylan said. His hands were tightened. The kindness in his voice was forced. "I need to get my sisters to the King as quickly as possible."

"I'll hear no more of it, come now," Arthur persisted, "they must be tired from a long ride. I have extra food in my bag. This one looks like she's half-starved anyway." He pointed at Lyra. Rylan sighed and swung down, offering his hand for me to get down as well. His being forced to have some manners was comical, but I kept a straight face. I couldn't risk Lyra's life by giving anything away. Rylan allowed Arthur to lead Lyra and sit her down near a tree. He pulled me close and whispered in my ear.

"Don't forget how easily I can kill her, Princess. Him, too." He squeezed my waist hard. "If you try to say anything to your Lynnean knight, I'll have her head and his before you can say coronation." When he noticed Arthur staring at him, he swiftly kissed my cheek. It took all my willpower to stop myself from vigorously wiping at my face.

"I understand you don't want to marry him, sweet sister, but in Father's stead, I am the man of our House, and he is the best match for you," he continued loudly. Arthur turned his attention back to Lyra and Gen. Rylan gave me a cold wink before leading me to where Arthur was gathering wood for a fire.

"Having cold feet before your wedding?" Arthur asked, his eyes focused curiously on me. I hesitated.

"Our sister thinks she should be able to do whatever she wants and marry whoever she wants. You'd think she was some kind of Queen, the way she acts," Gen provided before I could choke. Lyra bit back another laugh. I glared at her; she had never been good at lying. She laughed when she was uncomfortable, something I had never understood. It's like she didn't realize our lives were in danger and Arthur Blackwood might be the only man out there that could help us.

"Perhaps she should be able to marry whoever she wants. Love does conquer all, doesn't it?" I saw a twinkle in his eye that reminded me of how we had connected at the ball. *Please, please, recognize me. I'll marry you a hundred times if you would just recognize my face. I'll crown you King, give you children, please.* Rylan noticed him staring a little too long.

"Arthur, how about we walk a moment? Have some of that gentlemanly conversation, eh?" Arthur opened his mouth to speak. I thought my lungs would burst as I held my breath, waiting. I willed him to stay, to trust that gut feeling. Any moment now, it would click; I could feel it. But so could Rylan, who urged the knight along. They walked not far from us, just a little further past Lyra, but too far for me to hear what they were saying. I leaned in that direction but could hear nothing and sighed, defeated.

"They're talking about you, Your Majesty," Lyra whispered. Gen glared at her but made no move. "Arthur asked what price was offered for your hand." My heart skipped a beat, and hope dared to hold its breath. Maybe he'd finally remembered his Queen, and this was his attempt at rescue.

"Oh no..." Lyra's voice trailed off.

"What is it?" I begged. Gen stared at me, letting her eyes flick for just a moment toward the men, with her hand gripped firmly on the dagger in her waistband.

Lyra continued, more warily, "He told Arthur he lied about you being his sister, that your hand is actually promised to him," her face twisted, "and that you've already, well, you know." I scrunched my face up in disgust. Gen's face looked equally disgusted. She turned her eyes toward Rylan again and drew the dagger from her belt. *Silent and deadly,* I thought.

Gen's focus was trained on Rylan. I turned back to Lyra. "He can't believe that!" I whispered loudly. "I think he recognized me. I know he did. He'd be stupid not to; I thought we had a real connection at the ball." Gen rolled her eyes and made a fake gag sound.

"Wait, wait," Lyra shushed me. "Arthur is asking about your bloodline."

"How do you even hear them?" I asked. "I can't hear a thing!"

"Servant's ears," she said casually. "Lots of practice."

"Well, what are they saying now?" Both Gen and I leaned in, listening attentively. I narrowed my eyes at Gen, who raised the dagger up just a little higher, reminding me what she was capable of.

Lyra's face dropped. "Arthur admitted he found you very attractive but yields to an already binding engagement." She sounded defeated. My heart fell into my chest, a mix of anger at him for not knowing me and despair, knowing that I'd soon face an unknown fate in Astinia. Arthur had been my last chance.

Gen stood up in a huff and stomped over to the men impatiently. "I'm hungry, aren't we going to eat?" she demanded.

"The least mannerly of my sisters, the toughest for me to find a match for," Rylan chided, brushing her off. *The lies just never end.* Arthur eyed her and nodded.

"As I said, I have lots of food in my saddlebag. Come sit with me and have a meal." Rylan moved to refuse, but Gen interrupted.

"We'd love to break bread with a knight," she cooed, batting her eyes at him. "Especially a handsome one." She brushed his chest with one hand. Lyra and I exchanged confused looks. She was either trying to make Rylan jealous, trying to distract Arthur, or just trying to erase Griddick from her mind. Arthur looked her up and down again and gestured for them both to follow him.

He sat close to me, and I could feel his gaze on me constantly. I couldn't tell what he was thinking. *Is he second-guessing Rylan's story? Or is he just appreciating what he can't have?* My hopes of any rescue were fading fast. Rylan sat even closer to me on my other side, so I was sandwiched between them. Gen pushed me aside and slid herself right between me and Arthur, distancing me from him once again. I started to consider simply revealing myself. *Would Arthur be able to defeat both Rylan and Gen? Would I even be willing to risk his life that way? Or Lyra's life?* I remembered the four Lynnean guards that Rylan had taken down so easily and buried in the lake without a second thought. It wasn't worth the risk; I couldn't allow any more blood to be spilled on my behalf. Especially Arthur's. It was too much already.

Arthur knelt down with some kindling and logs. He started spinning a piece of kindling between his palms into a hole he had carved in the log. I watched him with fascination as, after a moment, sparks flew from the wood, igniting the rest of the kindling around it. I found myself admiring his strong arms and chiseled jaw, which were perfectly outlined against the firelight.

"What's your name?" Arthur turned and asked me kindly. His voice was soft and reassuring. Part of me wondered if I would have indeed chosen him had I carried out the rest of my choosing ball. *My name,* I thought.

What is my name? My eyes went wide, and my mind went blank. As the thoughts turned and turned in my mind, all of a sudden, I felt lips crash into mine. Static shot through my body when Rylan's hand clasped behind my head. Before I could react, he had pulled away, leaving us all in a stunned silence.

"Her name is Summer." Rylan shot me an arrogant look, knowing he had sealed the story he'd spun to Arthur with that hateful kiss. Arthur narrowed his eyes a little and opened his mouth to speak.

Gen interrupted him, capturing his attention. "My name is Lily," she said flirtatiously. She nestled into his side when he sat back down from igniting the fire and caressed his arm, playing coy and interested. He looked past her, unphased.

"Summer's a pretty name," he said with a smile. "I'm Arthur." He held his hand out for mine. I offered it to him as I did for everyone, and he kissed the back of my hand, just as he had at the ball. I looked down at him, and our eyes met. In that moment, I knew he knew me; it was the same genuine, caring smile I had seen before. Gen scowled, and Rylan's face turned red. Lyra giggled. Arthur carefully turned his attention toward her.

"And you are?"

Her eyes grew large; she'd been caught off guard, and she swallowed hard.

"Nora," she coughed out before Rylan or Gen could speak for her. A stunned silence fell over our little camp again as everyone awaited his reaction. The campfire itself seemed to stop breathing.

He leaned toward her with sharp intention. "Is that...short for something? Honora, Eleanora, Allanora?" he prodded, flicking his eyes to me for just a moment.

"Uh...no," she squeaked. Her stormy eyes drifted carefully to Gen's sheathed dagger. Lyra had let her mouth fall open, and her eyes were wide, shocked at his apparent stupidity. He narrowed his eyes at Lyra but shrugged and went back to eating his meal. *How are you not catching on?*

Are you catching on? You said my name. I was starting to wonder if they'd cast some sort of spell on me to hide my identity. Though neither of them struck me as a magic user.

"We'll be making camp here for the night," Gen told him hurriedly, regaining his attention. "Maybe you should come with us, you know, to keep us safe." Gen smirked at Rylan, who rolled his eyes angrily at her.

"I'd be happy to provide protection for you for the night. First thing in the morning, though, I must return to my hunt. The Lynnean kingdom will not rest until the murderer has been brought to justice." He placed his fist back over his chest as he spoke.

"What makes you think it's the same person?" I asked him slyly. Rylan's hand gripped my forearm. Rugged fingernails dug into me, and I bit my lip.

Arthur stuttered, "Well—I can't imagine more than one person wanting to kill our beloved Queen or Princess, I mean, Queen. They were both kind and beautiful and very much loved by the whole kingdom. Their deaths have brought a darkness upon Lynnea that we have never felt." His voice was so sad as he hung his head. My heart broke thinking of the devastation all this brought to my kingdom.

"I think everyone needs to get some rest. We all have a lot of traveling to do first thing," Rylan urged. Arthur nodded and started to set up his bedroll. Gen's eyes brightened as she unrolled hers not far from his. Lyra set herself up a little farther from the tree to avoid being dripped on by the leftover rain. I started to set myself up near her when Rylan picked me up by the waist.

"It's all right, my dear," stubborn sarcasm dripped from his hardened tone, "he knows about us, you'll be right next to me." Pretending to be his betrothed made me want to vomit. I opened my mouth to protest, but he shushed me. "Don't worry, I'll keep my hands mostly to myself," he crooned and set out a bedroll. My nose twitched with repulsion. '*He knows about us.*' Ha. *If only he actually knew.* I glanced longingly at the poor dumb knight who had no idea what he'd run into. Rylan laid down first and then dragged me down to him, gently but firmly, keeping his façade intact while still reminding me who was in charge. I tried my best to fight the anger ripping through me and settled in beside him. I felt trapped and caged next to him, especially when he tucked his arm securely around my waist and bent his head around to my ear.

"I know you thought you could escape with your silver knight and your little servant girl and ride off into the sunset, but you're not going anywhere." He pressed his body firmly against mine, locking me in. He was so close I could feel his heart beating against my back. If I didn't hate or fear him so much, I might've been comfortable. I'd never had anyone sleep so close to me. Hopefully, Arthur would still want me after seeing me in another man's arms like this. I closed my eyes. I could hear the chatter of noisy bugs and the very slight pitter-patter of distant rain. The air around our camp was warm and damp, the smell of rain mixed with the smell of Arthur's comforting campfire. Arthur Blackwood had sealed my fate; I'd be going to Astinia tomorrow. Rylan's body was warm despite his ice-cold heart, and after a few moments, I had no choice but to let myself drift off to sleep in his firm grip.

Chapter 10

Allanora

I opened my eyes and realized I had turned toward him in my sleep. He was right in my face, his beautiful green eyes hidden behind closed lids. His arms were still locked around me. A chill like a spider crawled down my spine, realizing I had felt warm and comfortable waking up in his arms. The thought terrified me. I tried to push myself backward out of his grip, but he pulled me tighter to him, engulfing me in an embrace. Finally, he opened his eyes, and I was electrocuted by the invitation into his soul through those emerald doors. A devilish grin spread across his face, and he pulled me in and kissed my lips, then my neck, holding me tighter, a dominating yet tender hold. Everything around us faded into a blur. He was everywhere. He must have taken his shirt off in the night because he was bare-chested, with his hot skin pressed firmly against me. The need to get away from him echoed through my whole body. Run, RUN! My heart started to race as I struggled to free myself, but a strange desire ignited in me. The two feelings mixed and battled within me, and suddenly, I gave in to him, going soft in his arms. He leaned in to kiss me again, covering my lips with his.

My eyes flew open, and I gasped loudly, breathing heavily. Relief poured through me when I realized it had just been a dream, followed by disgust. Taking in my surroundings, I realized that I was facing him like I had been in the dream. He was desperately, menacingly handsome. *No,* I shoved the thought from my mind. He was a murderer. I had broken into a cold sweat, and I began to hyperventilate, reeling from my hyper-realistic dream. The rising and falling of my chest felt strangely tight. I looked at him a little differently, just for a moment. A strange heat engulfed me, and I reached out wonderingly toward his face. *What does his skin feel like under his rock-hard façade? Does he feel as rough around the edges as he acts?* My curiosity got the better of me, and I touched his face ever so gently with the palm of my hand. Rylan woke with a start, gripping my arm in his hand, thinking I was going to run off or attack him, maybe. Lyra woke next, used to listening for me in her sleep, and rushed over to me.

"Are you all right, Your Majesty?" Her eyes searched mine. I gulped and nodded, allowing my breathing to return to normal.

"Bad dream," I whispered to her, casting my eyes over to Rylan. She nodded and sat down beside me. He released his grip and closed his eyes. I watched him breathe for a moment, trying to remind myself that he was still a human with thoughts, feelings, and desires, just like me. I wondered what it was like in his mind, his soul, so full of torment.

"Don't even think about trying to leave. I'll put an arrow in both of you," he grumbled. I snapped back to reality with his cold threat. He was still an assassin, and he was supposed to be my assassin. The thought infuriated me, dousing out any pity I had felt for him.

Rylan looked quickly over to Arthur, who was still sound asleep, it seemed. I sat up and wrapped my arms around my knees uncomfortably. Lyra put her arm around me. I had slid off his bedroll, and the damp grass kissed with morning dew was soaking through the clothes Rylan had given me to dress in. After a moment, Rylan began to snore slightly, but his hand was wrapped firmly around a handful of my clothing, ensuring he'd wake if I tried to leave.

We kept our voices in the lowest whisper we could.

"It'll be all right, Your Majesty," Lyra comforted. "Maybe, once we get to Astinia, we can find a way to get a message to Tobyn. He can send the Lynnean army to come for you. Astinia is large, but they've never been able to overcome us in war. You'll see." I could barely hear her myself, but checked to make sure our captor was still snoring away.

I sighed, glancing back at Rylan sleeping again and taking a quick survey of Gen and Arthur, who were still asleep as well. "I don't want war over me, Lyra. So much has been lost already. Once we get to Astinia, I plan to try to come to a diplomatic agreement with the King. Perhaps make them an offer of a—match." I winced, the words sour on my tongue. Her eyes enlarged at my words.

"You can't mean that? Put one of those brutish Astinian princes on the Lynnean throne? Your mother would—"

"My mother isn't here, Lyra," I snapped. I was Queen now; everything fell on my shoulders. She shrank back, realizing her mistake. We sat in silence after that, watching the suns rise slowly over the horizon. Golden light kissed the trees around us, light glimmering off the condensation of yesterday's storm. As the warm light spread over the ground, the others started to rise. Gen had made her way closer to Arthur through the night, whether by accident or intentionally, I wasn't sure. When he woke, realizing she had come so close, he jumped and scooted over, making eye contact with me right away.

"You look...familiar," he said, rubbing sleep from his eyes. I looked at Rylan, not quite awake next to me, but I chose my next words carefully.

"I don't think we've had the pleasure, Arthur of House Blackwood. Please do give my kindest regards to King Tobyn, though, when you return safely to Lynnea. I was so sorry to hear of the news of what happened at Princess Allanora's choosing ball and the coronation, of course." I begged him with my eyes to recognize me from our short dance, from the coronation, though he'd been far away. His eyes narrowed, and I drew in a sharp breath, holding it, waiting.

"Oh, Arthur, you're awake." Gen was miraculously awake at the perfect time. She yawned and leaned close to him. He got up quickly and dusted himself off. He looked at me briefly and winked. *He knows. Where is he going?*

"It is time for me to return to my travels; I, uh—the assassin that took the Queen and Princess from us must be brought to justice before the King." He hurriedly gathered his things and mounted his horse. *He's going to get help. He has to.* My heart was racing; every beat carried the weight of my crumbling kingdom, calling out for help against my chest.

"You don't have to leave so soon!" Gen called after him. He shuddered. Lyra giggled. By now, Rylan had risen and watched Arthur turn his horse and take off in the opposite direction of where we were headed. I watched him disappear down the path, carrying all of my hopes of survival on his back.

"Pack it up, ladies. We arrive at Astinia today. No more delays. The King is not going to be happy we weren't there yesterday as he demanded." He gave me a dark look. Now that Arthur was gone, he didn't have to attempt chivalry or decency anymore. Hopefully, that also meant he wouldn't be so close to me either. In a few long strides, he walked toward me, grabbed my arm with one hand, and pulled me close.

"Sweet dreams, Princess?" he whispered.

I winced, and my whole body shuddered, thinking of my unsettling dream. It was as if he knew, as if he were reveling in it. The thought of him knowing that I thought of him that way... even subconsciously, sickened me.

"Queen," I whispered back. He pointed in the direction Arthur had gone.

"Looks like your knight in shining armor didn't rescue you from the dragon after all," he sneered. I straightened myself, ignoring him. He dropped his face to my ear, "You know what I dreamed of, Princess?" I shook my head. "I dreamed that I ran my sword right through the heart of that pretty knight while you watched and screamed." His voice was a deadly hiss.

He was just playing at a show of force. If he really wanted to kill him, he would have. "Why didn't you kill him then?" I bit back at him.

He shrugged carelessly. "Too messy. If there's one knight out looking, there are bound to be more. I didn't need anyone thinking there was someone to look for, and I surely wasn't going to slow us down by having to drag a body all the way to Astinia." I shuddered, annoyed.

The small camp was packed up quickly. It was much tamer outside today than it had been yesterday. As if the world had picked up on the glimmer of hope that Arthur may be able to help us yet.

"You're quiet, Gen," Rylan prodded her.

"You didn't have to mention it," Lyra muttered under her breath. I let out a small laugh, quickly covering my mouth. Gen's icy gaze met mine.

"I'm just sick of all of you," Gen snarled. "Stupid Princess. He didn't even know who you were and was still obsessed with you." She groaned.

"I guess he picked up on which one of us is actually a nice person and who's a Queen-killing murderer," I said simply. I swung myself up easily on Rylan's horse and took the reins.

"I don't think so, Princess." He swung up behind me and snatched the reins out of my hands, but I saw the beginning of a smile in the corner of his mouth.

"Was that a smile? Do you have a slightly pleasant side? You know, besides the cold, cruel killer?"

"Nope," he said, his face resuming its usual hard mask.

"He's telling the truth," Gen said with a shrug. "I've never even seen him smile."

"Then what do you even see in him?" Lyra asked curiously.

She shrugged again. "The heart wants what it wants."

Lyra looked Rylan up and down, admiring him despite herself, "Yeah, 'the heart'," she chided, masking a laugh.

"All of you—shut up," Rylan growled, and we rode on through the forest in silence.

What seemed like hours passed; we had seen thousands of trees, thickly entwined with each other, creating a boundary between us and the rest of the world. The sky was painted blue with thick billowing clouds, the suns casting their beautiful golden light in rays through the trees. An opening formed where the tree line stopped to give way to a quiet river, winding through the forest and out of sight. I closed my eyes and bathed in the sunlight as the horses stepped onto the riverbank. I took a deep breath of the fresh air and smiled for the first time I could remember since being forced to leave the palace.

I opened my eyes just in time to come face to face with three men mounted on horses, all dressed entirely in black, masks hiding their faces from us. They were dressed just as Rylan and Gen had been. *Great, more assassins.* Rylan tensed his grip around me. I hadn't even realized his arm had been holding onto me the entire time. Gen was the only one who didn't look uneased; she looked wholly pleased. She slipped down from her horse, leaving Lyra alone, and met the man in the middle, firmly placing her hands on her hips and taking a sturdy stance before him.

"Do. Not. Move," Rylan whispered in my ear. The urgency in his voice made the hair on the back of my neck stand, and chills crawled down my spine. He slid down, hitting the ground hard but bouncing forward intentionally into his next step. He swung his bow from around his shoulder in one fluid motion and drew an arrow from his quiver.

"Brother," he sneered. The man in the middle smiled an icy smile; only his mouth and black eyes could be seen through the mask. His eyes bounced from Gen to Rylan and then to Lyra before finally landing on me.

"Your Majesty," he said sarcastically through a smirk. His voice was raspy and deep sounding. "Even in my baby brother's rags, you look absolutely ravishing and positively alive." He dismounted easily, drawing no weapons, but approached me with his hands tucked behind his back. He removed his mask; his gaze was menacing. His hair was short and dark, like Rylan's, but he let his fall just above his eyes where Rylan's was swept to the side. He was built like Rylan, with slightly broader shoulders and smaller arms. My breath caught in my throat at the sight of him; he had a weapon on what seemed like every part of his body. Daggers were strapped at his chest, two swords on his belt, bow and quiver poking out from behind him, and even more daggers were tied to his legs. I found myself trailing my eyes over every inch of him, trying to see exactly how many there were. I imagined they must have made riding a horse uncomfortable. Rylan followed him with his arrow as he approached me. My heart pounded in my chest fearfully, and his eyes scanned every inch of me. When he took a deep breath, he seemed to take me with it.

"She's my mark, Rowan. You know the rules," Rylan growled at him, tapping on his own chest. *Rowan? I thought the Crown Prince was Raysh.* Rowan seemed unphased. He closed his eyes and took another breath. When he opened them again, they briefly looked reptilian. The pupils formed into black almond slits standing in a yellow sea. Lyra let out an audible gasp next to me, but I tried to keep my composure. I pursed my lips and locked my knees, keeping myself still.

"Come now, baby brother. No reason to ruin all the fun with your rules. Raysh is the Crown Prince, he has to obey the rules. We're Academy assassins, respected, feared, outside the law. Where's the fun if you always obey the Academy rules?" *There's another brother.* I had almost forgotten. The middle brother. He took one finger and ran it from my knee to my ankle; I bit my lip to keep it from quivering.

"I don't see why you and Raysh should get to have all the fun anyway." He gripped my arm, pulled me from the saddle, and wrapped my braid around his palm, forcing my head backward. Rylan tightened the string of his bow, taking aim.

"I'm warning you, Rowan. Take your hands off her." His snarl was toxic. The other two men also drew arrows, pointing them at Gen and Rylan. Gen put her hands behind her head; Rylan just glared, not taking his eyes off his brother. *Why does he care?* Rowan tightened his grip on my braid, forcing my head all the way back. With one finger, he drew a line from my chin down my neck, between my breasts, and over my torso, stopping at my waist.

"Queen of Lynnea," he tutted, shaking his head. "Immaculate." My eyes started to water, but I stayed still, trembling slightly.

Out of the corner of my eye, I could see some confusion mixed with the intensity on Rylan's face. "You wouldn't even know what to do if the girl let you touch her, Rowan." He spit in Rowan's direction before he loosed an arrow, hitting his brother right in the side of his stomach. Rowan released me in surprise. He took one step back, looked at the arrow buried in him, and frowned.

"You'll pay for that!" He looked at the other two men and snapped his fingers. One loosed an arrow that buried itself in Gen's ankle, forcing her to the ground; the other turned and loosed an arrow in Lyra's direction. I shouted as it zipped past her, clipping her ear just slightly. She let out a yelp, and the arrow plunged into a tree behind her. She lifted her hand to her ear and, at the sight of the blood, let out a blood-curdling shriek, and the horse she was planted on reared back, throwing her backward onto the ground and taking off toward the river behind our assailants. Rowan snapped off the arrow in his side and straightened himself, wheeling around toward his brother, a sneer plastered on his threatening face. Gen was on the ground, grunting and attempting to pull the arrow from her ankle.

Rylan swapped his bow for his sword and positioned himself defensively, waiting for his brother to approach him. "Just like you always made me pay at the Academy?" Rylan taunted him, shifting his weight back and forth between his two feet. "You might have beaten everyone else there, but you could never beat me. Too distracted to train properly."

That made Rowan snarl. "Don't you dare."

The corner of Rylan's mouth curled up slightly. Like a predatory cat, he circled Rowan, never letting his trained eyes off him. "Cienna was too good for you, anyway. Until Raysh got a hold of her, that is. Pity." I slowly tried to inch away while they were distracted.

"Raysh never would have known about her if it wasn't for you." Rowan spat at him with the last word.

Once I was more than an arm's length from Rowan, I started to run toward Lyra. Something shot out and wrapped around my ankle, dragging me back toward Rowan. I clawed at the ground and forced myself to look behind me, wondering what had grabbed me. It was black, long, and snake-like, covered in obsidian scales; I followed it with my eyes until I realized it had come from Rowan's backside. *A tail.* I screamed and dug my nails firmly into the dirt until it released me, dropping me on the hard ground with a thud.

"Finally figuring out a good use for your little deformity, eh?" Rylan taunted him. Rowan's men came up behind Rylan, but Rowan held up his hand for them to cease and drew his own sword. "It's funny, Ro, you always need your goons with you to carry out your missions. I work alone. And I have a higher kill rate." He licked his lips, hungry for the argument with his brother.

"What do you call that?" He jutted his chin out toward Gen. "Working alone? And that." He gestured toward me. "How's that treating your kill rate, 'God-killer?'" Rylan locked himself in place, keeping his mouth closed.

"There's a good way out of the rules, you know, brother," Rowan hissed. Rylan turned his head to the side and lunged at his brother, sword forward. The familiar clang of metal on metal rang out as they swung back and forth. Their feet moved so fast that I couldn't keep up with them.

"If I kill you, Rylan, she's all mine, along with all the glory and recognition that comes with delivering her. Steele will let me do whatever I want. Maybe our beloved Crown Prince Raysh will even reward me by giving me a crack at her first. You know, before their wedding night." A glimmer of anger flashed across Rylan's face, and he lunged at his brother, swinging harder and faster. They locked themselves together with their swords, temporarily at an impasse, their strength matched. They panted, huffing angrily at each other.

"It's funny, Ro, how you talk a big game, but you and I both know once you step foot in that castle, you'll be running from Raysh with your monster tail between your legs."

"If I didn't know any better, brother, I'd say this Princess might've cracked that hard shell a little bit," Rowan jeered in reply. "Or was it Gen? She put a spring in your step again? Or put a spring somewhere else?"

Rylan growled and forced himself forward, knocking his brother to the ground. He put a foot on his chest and leaned over him. Rowan smiled, and I felt his tail grasp my waist, pulling me over to them. "I guess we will just have to see."

Something sharp stuck into my side, a spike from the tail, maybe. At first, I felt nothing but the sting from the poke, but then I started to feel a tingling sensation spread all over my body. I held my hands up in front of me and watched my veins puff up and turn purple. I opened my mouth to scream, but nothing came out. Rowan's menacing laugh sliced through the ringing in my ears, and I could vaguely hear Rylan shout something at him in a language I couldn't understand. My vision started to blur; blue and red streaks made their way across my eyes. The sky began to darken around us, and a lightning bolt flashed near me, sending them all scattering toward the trees. I started to convulse, and when I looked at my hands again, my fingers had started to twist inwards. I tried to straighten them, but I couldn't. The fear set in as I began to choke on my own saliva, and involuntary tears streaked down my face, down behind my ears, and into the ground behind me. Another bolt flashed, this time even closer. Against the now-black sky, I could only see a shadowy figure outlined. More lightning flashed horizontally out as if from the shadowy figure. I heard the yells of what I assumed were the two men accompanying Rowan, another shriek from Lyra, then dead silence. *Can they see it, too?* The shadowy figure started to step toward me as the pain began to throb through my entire body. I twisted and contorted involuntarily on the ground, then everything went black.

No blade can cut a golden stem. The words rang through my ears louder than I had ever heard them before. Closer. A familiar warmth flowed through my body as it washed away my pain. My fingers untangled from their inhuman twist, and my spine relaxed, the pain subsiding. My shoulders dropped to the ground, and my jaw unclenched, leaving my face throbbing and sore. I opened my eyes and turned my head to where Rylan and Rowan had been. Rowan was on his back, gasping for breath. Rylan was crouched not far from him, eyes locked suspiciously on me. Gen, Lyra, and the two men accompanying Rowan had disappeared completely, and there was no sign of the shadowy figure.

I rubbed my eyes in confusion and looked at my hands; they had returned to normal. An eerie haze had been cast on the ground around us, though the sky had returned to its beautiful blue. Rowan turned slowly on his stomach and pushed himself up, locking eyes with me.

"What are you?" he asked me with a horrified look on his face.

"Excuse me?"

"What. Are. You?"

"I'm Queen of Lynnea."

"But you just—"

"Shut up, Rowan," Rylan glared at him and cut him off. Rowan turned toward him, fully standing now. "All we need to do right now is get the royal brat to Astinia and into the custody of King Rhonan and Raysh, and you can go back to the Academy, forget all of this."

"But she just *hit me with LIGHTNING,*" he whined.

"No, I didn't! That was just a storm!" I shouted; I didn't fully believe that it was 'just a storm', but I was certain I had nothing to do with it. He looked me up and down, eyes narrowed. Rylan stood and grabbed his brother by the shoulder, pulling him a little farther from me and whispering something to him that I couldn't hear.

"Where's Lyra?" I demanded, ignoring their whispering.

"Gen's taking her back to Griddick's. One of my messengers will return her to Lynnea from there," Rylan said to me. His tone was cold and even. He approached me cautiously.

"Why? You know she was the only thing keeping me cooperating with you."

"Astinia is just across the river. Rowan and I will be escorting you. You wouldn't be able to overpower or run from the both of us. We're Academy-trained assassins. Not that you know what that means. Lyra was never going to be safe in Astinia anyway." He took me by the arm, firmly but gently. I looked him up and down.

"Since when do you care about anyone else's safety?" I demanded. He stayed silent. "What just happened here?"

"Honestly, I'm not sure." He cast his eyes across the river, then down to the ground. "I'm sorry," he said. The words took me by surprise. Then I realized what he meant. Rowan had come up behind me and started to tie me up with a tight-knit chord. He took me by my braid again and forced me to my knees, tying my legs up as well.

"How exactly do you expect me to ride with my ankles tied together?" I spat at him. I turned to look at Rylan, but he looked away. Rowan threw me over his shoulder as Rylan had done a few times before, then roughly threw me over the saddle of one of the other men's horses. I looked up from the saddle and glared at Rylan.

"Really? I've cooperated with you all this time, and now we are back to this?" Rowan secured me to the saddle with another rope and secured a lead line on the bridle.

"I like you better tied up like this, anyway. And this way, no lightning," he chided. "...Right?" He looked warily at Rylan, who shrugged, and back at me. I turned my face away from him, ignoring him completely. Leading the horse by the line, he mounted his own horse and moved forward. Rylan rode along silently beside me. The horses splashed through the shallow river and back up onto the bank on the other side. I couldn't tell how long it had been before one of them said something; I felt as if I had looked at the same patch of grass repeatedly for miles until I finally heard Rylan speak.

"Astinia," he said quietly. I turned my head as much as I could, and looming in front of us was a large obsidian black castle covered in beautiful green ivy. Astinian flags adorned each tower, and the crest of house Thorne fluttered proudly in the wind. I let out a heavy sigh. I had failed. We'd arrived. At least Lyra was safe.

The air had turned cold, as if the border of Astinia had sucked all the warmth from the atmosphere. It surely had sucked out all the happiness.

The ground below me turned from lush green grass to dark, worn cobblestone. Small weeds were intricately woven between the pavers. I set my jaw.

"You're going to present a foreign Queen to your King and Crown Prince like this? Tied up and swung over your horse like an animal?" Rylan didn't reply to me.

"Yep, we sure are," Rowan chided. "We aren't royalty. Second and third sons aren't princes in Astinia. We don't have to abide by your special rules, Princess." I looked up at Rylan with pleading eyes. He looked away from me, and I scowled at the ground. It changed again below me, this time to a beautiful dark gray solid marble. A set of doors closed behind us, and I felt myself being pulled from the horse. Rylan turned me around and cut my ropes loose. I found myself face to face with the throne of the Astinian King. In it, the man himself was perched, his large, black, beady eyes sending terror through my body. He was one of the largest men I had ever laid eyes on; he was tall and built with bulging muscles that seemed to stretch even the silver-plated armor he wore. The parts of him I could see were covered in battle scars and black tattoo markings, symbols I didn't recognize. Atop his head sat a large, spiked iron crown with a massive ruby set in the middle. It looked too heavy to be worn by a human, yet here he was.

I glanced around. The servants I could see looked sullen, scared. Most of them wore iron bracelets. A few noble members of the court walked the halls around the throne room, all dressed in black and red, their clothing sheer, loose, and the women's dresses low cut.

"Queen Allanora, how pleased I am to finally make your acquaintance." His voice dripped with raw terror and power, echoing through the throne room. I trembled. He smiled the most menacing smile, sending a sting of fear straight up my spine. His person dripped with the soulless air of someone who enjoyed pain, death, destruction. A thousand fears of his victims swam in his empty black eyes. If this was a man, and I truly wasn't sure, he was not the type I wanted to be associated with. As he grinned at me through perfectly white, bared teeth, I knew I was in trouble, and I knew, at that moment, that there was no diplomatic way out of this.

The ground below me turned from lush green grass to dark, worn cobblestone. Small weeds were intricately woven between the pavers. I set my jaw.

"You're going to present a foreign Queen to your King and Crown Prince like this? Tied up and swung over your horse like an animal?" Rylan didn't reply to me.

"Yep, we sure are," Rowan chided. "We aren't royalty. Second and third sons aren't princes in Astinia. We don't have to abide by your special rules, Princess." I looked up at Rylan with pleading eyes. He looked away from me, and I scowled at the ground. It changed again below me, this time to a beautiful dark gray solid marble. A set of doors closed behind us, and I felt myself being pulled from the horse. Rylan turned me around and cut my ropes loose. I found myself face to face with the throne of the Astinian King. In it, the man himself was perched, his large, black, beady eyes sending terror through my body. He was one of the largest men I had ever laid eyes on; he was tall and built with bulging muscles that seemed to stretch even the silver-plated armor he wore. The parts of him I could see were covered in battle scars and black tattoo markings, symbols I didn't recognize. Atop his head sat a large, spiked iron crown with a massive ruby set in the middle. It looked too heavy to be worn by a human, yet here he was.

I glanced around. The servants I could see looked sullen, scared. Most of them wore iron bracelets. A few noble members of the court walked the halls around the throne room, all dressed in black and red, their clothing sheer, loose, and the women's dresses low cut.

"Queen Allanora, how pleased I am to finally make your acquaintance." His voice dripped with raw terror and power, echoing through the throne room. I trembled. He smiled the most menacing smile, sending a sting of fear straight up my spine. His person dripped with the soulless air of someone who enjoyed pain, death, destruction. A thousand fears of his victims swam in his empty black eyes. If this was a man, and I truly wasn't sure, he was not the type I wanted to be associated with. As he grinned at me through perfectly white, bared teeth, I knew I was in trouble, and I knew, at that moment, that there was no diplomatic way out of this.

Chapter 11

Henrie

I checked the raven's tower day after day, but Aros' raven didn't return. I spent my nights wondering, worrying what his reaction would be to the news of his daughter's death. When I let myself go to bed, I tossed and turned in bed next to my wife. When I couldn't rest, I'd walk through the castle halls so I wouldn't keep her awake. Five days had passed since I had delivered the news, and I had only been met with bitter silence.

One night, I lay in bed staring at the canopy top of our bed, following the intricate etched designs with my eyes and willing myself to fall asleep. I would close my eyes, and Aros' face would appear behind my eyelids, his face twisted in disappointment, a broken promise of his daughter being protected lingering on his trembling lips.

I shook the thought from my head, rose from the bed quietly, and put on my spectacles, careful not to wake my Eleanore. We had gone to bed early; she'd been hit with a wave of exhaustion from my growing child inside her. I kissed her forehead and tiptoed out of the room, ready for another anxious walk through the castle halls. I made my way through my family's wing, passing my older brother's door, which was dark and quiet. Usually, there would be dim lights and the thrilled squeals of my brother's latest catch behind the door. His charm probably wasn't having the desired effect anymore. Considering the disappearance of Allanora's handmaiden in the night, the servants were nervous and more cautious. Most inhabitants of the castle, myself included, assumed that she had simply taken off after Queen Allanora's death, perhaps thinking she no longer had a place here. With Brysa having Julian's favor, the talk amongst the servants was that she would gain a favorable position over Lyra. Though, as long as there was no

Queen, there was no need for a Queen's handmaiden. Lysan had said they'd squabbled over it the night of her disappearance. Aside from whispers among the servants, the rest of the castle's inhabitants weren't much interested in where the girl had gone.

No longer worrying myself with those thoughts, I walked toward my father's room next. Since he was crowned King Regent, he'd moved into a larger room with a study where he spent most of his nights holding meetings or reading books. The door leading into his study was cracked open, and my brother's gravelly voice carried from inside. Curiosity stopped me from announcing my presence, so I stayed outside the door and listened.

"You can't be King in Lynnea like this, with no Queen and no legitimate heir, Julian," I heard my father say and bit back a laugh. The idea of Julian having an honest marriage was a thought that wouldn't cross anyone's mind.

"You can't just marry me off to the first prized horse that struts through here. She at least needs to be pretty, Father, and young because of um— you know, so they're fertile." He stumbled over his words. I'd eavesdropped enough and knocked softly on the door before pushing it open. My father was rubbing his forehead in annoyance, and my brother's face looked like he was going to implode from frustration.

"Henrie. Finally, my intelligent son. Please talk some sense into your brother. He's the heir to the Lynnean throne now. He must marry a woman of noble birth and produce a legitimate heir of his own. No more whoring around, no more funny business." My father's forehead was wrinkled, and his eyebrows were lowered almost over his eyes. "We have to secure our place here, and the way to secure your place in Lynnea is with a Queen and, of course, a little Princess."

"One of Henrie's daughters can be my heir. He has enough children, girls and boys, for both of us," my brother spat out, his voice heavy with sarcasm. "Too bad I didn't get my hands on his wife; we'd have made Lynnea quite a fine heir." Anger flashed through me, my skin prickled with ferocious heat. Heart pounding, I pushed him back against my father's bookcase, holding him by the throat; he smiled, knowing he'd gotten to me, as he always did. He might've been bigger than me, but I'd tear him apart to defend Eleanore. My father's wine cup slammed on the table.

"You don't deserve a woman like Eleanore," I grumbled, releasing him from my grasp.

"Lynnea will be in a state of unrest with no Queen on the horizon. You know how the people feel about their woman leaders. Even my position now is at risk, and I've been the Queen's advisor for years," my father told him, frustration building in his voice. "The Lynnean families are at my throat, wanting to establish a connection to the royal bloodline to put their daughters on the throne. My only choice to establish our rule is to wed you to one of them."

"What, so I get the throne and immediately have to hand my crown over to my wife?" Julian pouted.

"Officially, you'll be King consort, Julian, but we will find you a young, malleable Queen who will settle the people but bend to your will. Your first daughter will be the heir to the throne, and the Lynneans will rejoice again, with house Hawkham at the helm. I just wish you had a legitimate daughter already; it would be easier for the people to accept us that way." Father sighed. "Out of all twelve kingdoms, it had to be this one to favor a Queen over a King," he muttered.

"First daughter? I don't want more than one daughter. Women are so emotional and clingy," Julian said, rolling his eyes.

"Look, Henrie," my father said, ignoring Julian, "I need you to help me find a match for your brother and fast. I'm not a young man, and I need our line to be settled before I'm gone." He spoke of his own death so calmly, not a hint of fear. I wasn't sure that I fully loved my father, but I did admire him, and I wasn't ready to bury him.

"Of course, Father. I'll have a list of eligible, noble women that would be willing to put up with him to you by tomorrow morning." I looked my angry brother up and down and gave him a little smirk.

"Young, Henrie," my brother reminded me.

"Don't worry, Julian, I've seen your type. Where is Brysa anyway?" My father's eyes shot up and contacted Julian's.

"The late Queen's handmaid, Julian?" He looked at him disgusted.

I smiled smugly. "Oh yes, Father, didn't you know? How could you not? Eleanore and I can hear her squeals in all corners of the castle."

"I'm not trying to marry her, Father, just having a little fun." Julian rolled his eyes and glared at me. Father rubbed his temples again vigorously with his fingers.

"Son, you can't do this once you're married. I can't have everyone knowing the heir to the Lynnean throne is sleeping around with servants while his Queen waits in an empty bedchamber with an empty womb. It's improper." I could tell my father's irritation was reaching new peaks; his eyes were burning a hole through Julian's chest, and an angry, purple vein popped out of his forehead.

"Lots of Kings do whatever they want with whoever they want," Julian muttered. Father grabbed a book from the table and hurled it at Julian. It missed his head by a breath and hit the wall behind him.

"Not in a queendom, they don't!" Julian was finally speechless, and I put a hand on my father's shoulder to calm him.

"Look, this conversation isn't going to get us anywhere tonight," I reasoned. "How about we start fresh and meet back here at first light? I think you both need a little bit of sleep. I'll start working on that list of eligible noble women. Both of you need to bring your open minds to the meeting in the morning." I shot a pointed look at each of them while they mulled over what I said. They both nodded curtly to the other and shuffled from the room, heading in opposite directions for their bedchambers. Moving quickly out of sight, I made sure to wait and listen until they both seemed to retire to their rooms. I let out a deep breath; my family was exhausting.

Sleep was calling me, but I was restless and needed to check the raven's tower one more time tonight. In truth, I couldn't stand Aros haunting my dreams any longer. Slowly, I made my way up the winding stone stairs, expecting to see the usual—no raven from Aros, no message. Before I turned the final corner to the top, the soft ruffle of feathers stopped me in my tracks. I dashed up the remaining stairs and was met with the raven I had sent away days ago, a small scroll tied to his foot. A surge of fire and energy—call it hope—pulsed through me with every quickening heartbeat. I unrolled the scroll with my eyes closed, afraid to look, and then peeped with one eye to read what it said. Only two words, and when I read them, my fingers went numb. The scroll feathered to the floor.

I'm coming.

Aros, who hadn't set foot in Lynnea since his disappearance when Princess Allanora was about four years old, was coming. Fear and wonder set in. I had only truly met the man once that I could remember, and I was only a boy then, only a few years older than my oldest son, Lysan. He would want answers, and I had none. The memory of my only meeting with him hit me in the chest like a loose arrow.

"Boy, what are you doing in here?" The tall, powerful, terrifying King glared at thirteen-year-old me over the desk in his study.

"I–I," I stuttered, trying everything to regain my words. Adjusting my spectacles, I took a deep breath and looked him in the face. "I'm sorry, Your Majesty. My brother, he told me I was supposed to meet someone in here." I let my head hang in shame and fear.

"It's all right. What's your name, boy? Who were you supposed to be meeting?" My face flushed, and I looked up at him quickly; he had softened to a look of curiosity and concern.

"Henrie, sir, Your Majesty, I'm... I'm Tobyn's son, Tobyn Hawkham. I just, there was a girl, Eleanore, and Julian said she wanted to meet me in here. I'm sorry, I didn't realize this was your study. I'm so sorry, Your Majesty; please don't tell my father." He let out a chuckle and motioned for me to sit. Quickly, I bowed and scurried over to the leather chair he had pointed to.

"Ah yes, of course, Tobyn's younger boy. You fear your father, Henrie?" I gulped and nodded. "I won't tell him. I promise. But can you

do something for me? It's something very important." I stitched my eyebrows together, confused.

"I don't see what I could do to help a King, Your Majesty. My brother, he's the strong one, I just like to read." He peered at me, sizing me up and considering my words.

"You know the Princess, yes? Allanora?"

"Your—your daughter, of course, Your Majesty. Everyone knows the little Princess."

"I might need to go away for a while, a long while. I don't know how long. I won't be able to connect with all of you in Lynnea as I've done for so long, and I think people might even forget me. But I need you to watch over the Princess and let me know how she's doing as she grows. I fear she will forget me, too. When all this mess is over." He let out a heavy sigh. I nodded my agreement. He stood wearily from his chair and made his way over to a shelf of books. I had never seen books like these; they looked as if they were made of glass, but when he pulled one from the shelf, it opened, and the pages turned just as a regular leather book would.

"The girl's name is Eleanore, yes?" He peered at me from over the book. I nodded while trying to decipher what the cover of the book said.

Suddenly, I felt myself going cold. The memory was fading, changing. Aros' face twisted in my mind, then disappeared completely from view. The strange feeling only lasted a moment before I felt normal again, but when I tried to recall the memory once more, it danced just out of my reach.

How odd. I quickly picked the scroll up and set it aflame on a lit candle, the way I'd done with all his messages over the years. It crackled under the heat and went up in purple flame. A strange color for scroll and ink, but from what I could tell, Aros was a strange man.

Regaining some of my mind back, it flooded with all the possible outcomes of what it would mean for the King to come here. Would Aros come to reclaim his wife's throne in his daughter's name? Would he punish my father, as his wife's protector and advisor all these years, for failing her?

My mind raced, thinking of all the people that this would put in danger, especially if he decided to unleash his wrath on the castle and all the people in it that he thought had wronged his family. I shook my head free of the thoughts. I couldn't worry about the possibilities; I'd simply have to wait and prepare for his return.

It occurred to me that I didn't remember much about the former King Aros. I was young when he disappeared from Lynnea, and I had never really interacted with him before then. There were whispers around the castle, though, calling their marriage unorthodox, although I never truly knew why. My memory of that time was clouded, though not many people ever talked about the late Queen's marriage to the former King, or the former King at all, for that matter, strangely. I peered out the window; it was the middle of the night, dark and still. I should have gone back to bed, but I was wide awake now. Instead, I wandered down to the library where I had spent most of my life. There weren't many books there that I hadn't read, but I knew there must be some information out there about Aros.

I started with a book that kept records of all the Queens of Lynnea and their Kings. I found the final entry—Queen Violet, House Harthope—no King listed. I sighed—no help there. I made a mental note that I'd need to add an entry for Allanora, no matter how short her reign was.

Onto the next book. I skimmed through every text I could think of that would have information regarding Queen Violet, but there was no mention of King Aros anywhere. It was almost as if he never existed. But I remembered him. Others did, too. I'd been corresponding with him all these years, so there had to be something.

By the time the suns had started to kiss the horizon with the first flecks of light, I was surrounded by stacks of books, still looking for any snippet of information. The library was vast, but I knew every book in it, and I couldn't think of any more that would be helpful. Defeated, I slowly started returning the ones I had gathered back to their shelves in the section that was dedicated to Queen Violet, slipping each one into its place. I slid in the last book and took another glance over the organized shelf—so many volumes of useless information. But then, in the far corner, I noticed a book that was out of place.

It was a book about the Old Religion of the twelve kingdoms. I'd read it once when I was younger, but after the war, when the Triini took over, the Old Religion was tossed out, most teachings and histories along with it. Strange that this one had slipped through the cracks. I flipped through the book nostalgically, thumbing through stories of the twelve Deities that ruled and patronized the twelve kingdoms of Cidris, of which Lynnea was one. It must have been one of the last books in existence with these stories. After the Great War and the fall of the Deities, the people of Cidris mainly burned the books and teachings of the Deities upon the direction of the Triini. My father had been one of them, collecting and burning books from the library. It had created a crack in our relationship that could never be repaired. As much as I followed the New Religion, the writings and stories of the old were a significant part of our history, and as a bookkeeper, it was part of my job to maintain our history. I wondered how this one book had made it. My curiosity got the best of me, and I brought it to my desk, losing myself in the old stories I hadn't heard of since I was a young boy. Strangely, I couldn't recall any of them until this moment, as if they'd been erased from my mind.

The Great War had occurred when I was only about eight years old; Queen Violet had been a young woman herself, preparing to become Queen. The Brothers and Sisters of the Triini had created a following of the 'Golden Dawn', a renaissance in the religion of Cidris in favor of a new God, the Unnamed God. They gathered followers from the Great Houses of each kingdom, who all fought among each other until, finally, the Golden Dawn prevailed, forcing the Deities into hiding.

I flipped to a page that wrote out the names of all the twelve Deities.

Elios—God of Fire, Asna—Goddess of the Moon, Rimus— God of the Sun, Brasta— Goddess of Wisdom, Verus— God of Water, Ahena— Goddess of Earth, Phimus— God of Air, Kahtix— Goddess of Death, Yra—

Goddess of Love, Orthar— God of War, Ata— Goddess of Truth, Aros— God of Lightning.

I read over the last name again. Aros, God of Lightning. I guessed that must have been King Aros' namesake. Obviously, he was named before The Great War and the Fall of the Deities, as no one would name their child after a Deity now for fear of being cast out by the Triini. I was puzzled, still wondering why King Aros wasn't mentioned alongside Queen Violet in any of the books. I slammed the book shut and removed my spectacles to rub my eyes.

"Are you looking for something, bookkeeper?" A raspy voice crawled into my ear, and I cringed. "I can't imagine what you think you'd find in that old text."

I turned slowly, and as I suspected, Brother Sol was standing behind me. Something about him had always seemed off, a little creepy. But he had never done anything malicious, so I had no true reason to feel that way.

"I—was looking for other information when I came across this book. I wanted to know what was in it before I brought it to the temple—to you, Your Excellency." The words were acid on my tongue with the thought of handing a book over to him to be destroyed.

His pale, bony hand shot out of his sleeve and snatched the book off my desk. "Being the King Regent's son will not save you from the wrath of the Unnamed God if you go against the following of the faith."

"My wife and I were married in the light of the true God, my children bathed in the protection of His forgiveness upon birth. I have no other allegiances, only mere curiosity in the histories of Cidris, Your Excellency." It was true, though it felt strange to have to say it. I had barely known the faith of the twelve before Cidris accepted the Golden Dawn. It had never occurred to me to question it.

He nodded and turned, silently striding toward the marble staircase that led out of the library. "If you find any more forbidden texts, bookkeeper, bring them to me immediately." He didn't leave me any room to reply before he was up the stairs and out of earshot. It was no matter; I knew this library inside and out. It was enough that one book had slipped past me. There was no way there were two.

The suns were fully above the horizon, and I had not slept at all. Not only that, but I had gotten nowhere regarding Aros, and I had promised to compile a list of eligible noblewomen for my brother's marriage. Determined to keep my word, I forgot about my interaction with Brother Sol and found a newer book with the Great Houses of Lynnea and all their children. Only women from the Great Houses would be eligible to marry Julian, although I didn't think he deserved a single one of them. I quickly skimmed through all twelve Great Houses and scribbled down the names of their young unmarried daughters, then made a second copy to give to a messenger for invitations.

I hurried to put the book away, then hesitated momentarily, a thought crossing my mind. *Only a member of one of the Great Houses is eligible to marry the heir to the throne. Aros must be listed in this book.* I quickly returned to my desk with the large book and, with my finger, skimmed through each line of the twelve Great Houses, looking for the husband of the late Queen. Page by page, I read hundreds of names, none of them Aros. *He must be in here,* I thought; Queen Violet wouldn't have bent the rules. More pages flew by under my searching eyes, and when I reached the end, no child of the Great Houses had been named Aros. He must have been from one of the other kingdoms. I looked out the window and realized I wouldn't have time to skim through the Great Houses of the other eleven kingdoms before meeting back with the King Regent and his new heir. I fought an eye roll and slid the hefty tome back into its place before hurrying up the stairs and back toward my father's study.

Just outside the room, I heard tense voices inside, so I leaned close to the door to listen.

"You're unfortunately mistaken, Sir. The Queen is dead; I closed her coffin myself, and I signed the papers for the crown to pay for the funeral. The entire kingdom of Lynnea watched her be buried. Allanora is not running around the world with some ruffian. Please, allow her to rest in peace," It was my father. His voice was thick with irritation, and I peered slightly inside the door to see who he was talking to. I could tell it was a knight, but his back was to me, and I couldn't tell who he was.

"I danced with her at the choosing ball; I know her eyes, Your Majesty, please. There was another girl she was traveling with. She looked like the handmaid. I also saw her at the ball. Please, I think she's alive and may have been kidnapped. I just want to take a few men with me to Astinia to investigate. Doesn't Lynnea deserve its Queen?" My father slammed his cup on the table; I wondered how much more of my father's rage that desk would take.

"The entire kingdom saw that arrow rip through the Queen's chest, Sir Blackwood. How do you expect she could have survived that? Let alone be wandering around Astinia in the woods. I know you're distraught over these events, as we all are. Allanora was like a daughter to me, but we all must accept that she and Queen Violet are *gone,* and they're not coming back. I'm sure your eyes deceived you. Maybe you'd spent too much time in the tavern, and you just saw what you wanted to see. Please, Sir, we have more important things to attend to than ghosts and false Princesses." My father motioned to the door, and I slipped back behind it before he noticed me. I heard the knight stomping from the room, and I quickly knocked on the door as if I had just arrived.

"Come in," my father growled. I stepped in and saw the scowling knight, Arthur Blackwood, stalking out as I approached. Julian was in the corner of the room, arms folded, and my father was angrily leaning over his desk.

"What's going on with Sir Blackwood?" I inquired, approaching my father and brother.

"Nothing, he's been hitting the taverns, I'm sure of it," my father replied shortly. "Have you compiled a list of the ladies of the kingdom eligible to marry the heir to the throne?" I held out my list with the names scribbled on it. My father took it and glanced it over.

"It seems silly to hold another choosing ball. It's been only two weeks, and the crown has paid for a choosing ball, two funerals, and two coronations already. There will have to be a wedding. I think that's quite enough frivolity and expense." His voice was cold and firm. He didn't look up from the paper once. "Send for these ladies to be brought to the throne room this evening. We will have them introduced, and Julian will be free to choose." My brother rolled his eyes.

"Tonight? I have to choose a wife tonight?" My father eyed him over the piece of paper.

"Every royal Princess in Lynnean history has been given one night to choose her husband at a choosing ball. I think you will be just fine," I told him. He pursed his lips almost in a pout. "Don't be such a child, Julian." I scoffed at him.

"And you have to break up with your servant girl," Father demanded.

"Maybe if you had your own servant girl, you wouldn't be so uptight," Julian grumbled back. I choked on a laugh. My father wasn't amused; he turned red, and the scar on his eye seemed like it was going to pop right off his face.

"I'm doing everything for you, Julian. I've done everything for you. It's high time you show some appreciation and respect for your King!" he yelled. "Now take this list and study it." He shoved the paper at Julian's chest. "I don't need you making me look like a fool tonight! You may be the heir, but I am King, and you'd better not forget it!" Julian snatched the paper from him and stormed out of the room, slamming the door behind him and leaving me alone with our father, seething with rage. I opened my mouth to speak, but he held up his hand. "Please leave me." He dismissed me with a wave, and I slunk out of the room. There was a messenger stationed outside my father's room, no doubt waiting for me to give him the list of women to be invited to the palace to be presented to my brother. I rolled up the second list I had made for the messenger and handed it to him quickly. He nodded and dashed down the hall to prepare the invitations.

Solemn and confused, I returned to my rooms, where my lovely wife waited for me with open arms.

"You never came back to bed last night," she commented, worry in her eyes. She reached up and touched my face, cradling it in the palm of her hand. "You always carry the weight of the world on your shoulders, Henrie."

"I guess there isn't any use lying to you anymore, Eleanore." Her face was confused, and she took a step back from me, waiting for me to continue. I took a deep breath. "I've been communicating with the former King Aros." Eleanore still looked perplexed but released a visible sigh of relief.

"I was afraid you were going to tell me you were having an affair." Her voice was quaking a little. I took her hand and kissed her palm, carefully drawing my lips up her arm before finding her mouth. In one swift movement, I wrapped my arms around her waist and pressed her against me, feeling our growing baby between us.

"Never, my sweet, there are no women in this world besides you I would ever have eyes for," I crooned. "Don't ever worry about that, but—" I sat her down on the bed. "Years ago, before we were married, Aros asked me to watch Princess Allanora, to keep her safe and to communicate with him about anything 'interesting' going on regarding her. For years, I had nothing significant to report, but these last days, I've had to give him a lot of bad news." I could tell she was starting to worry. "I wrote him about the death of the Princess, and his response concerned me."

"He can't blame you! How could you have stopped an arrow from taking her in the chest?" She was angry—my fiery angel, always rushing to defend me. I soothed her and put a hand on her belly.

"I'm not sure he blames me, but he might blame my father or brother," I explained. "If that's the case, we may be directly affected."

"Well, what did he say? You know, when you told him?" Her eyes were searching mine carefully.

"He said he was coming. Nothing more."

"Do you even know where he is? Where he's been all this time?"

"Honestly, dear, I didn't ask many questions. When a King asks something of you, especially something like reporting on his daughter, you just do it..." I trailed off. "You know what's strange, though? I couldn't find him in the history of any of the Great Noble Houses of Lynnea. I looked through every single one, and I found nothing. No Aros." She gave me a questioning look.

"Maybe he wasn't from Lynnea. Maybe he was from one of the other kingdoms?" she reasoned.

"I thought the same thing, but I ran out of time working on the list of women eligible for Julian to marry." She made a face of disgust.

"Poor girl—whoever she is." I thought about the list I had handed off to a messenger before returning to our room. I wondered which of the 'lucky' women it would be.

"They're being gathered in the throne room today for a small choosing ceremony. My father didn't want a ball on top of all the 'events' we've been having lately."

"So, you'll be in the library until then? Even though you haven't had a wink of sleep." She smirked; she knew that when I had something to figure out, I'd spend every waking moment working on it until it was settled. I nodded, gathering myself up to return to the library. If I moved quickly, I might have been able to go through the books of all the kingdoms of Lynnea and find where Aros came from. I hurried down the hallway, and when I reached my brother's door, I could hear him inside—he clearly hadn't ended things with Brysa. I could hear her happy squeals from inside the room, mixed with my brother's amorous grunts. I shuddered in disgust and kept walking. As I passed my father's room, I heard hushed, urgent voices, one of them being my father's.

"It has to be tonight—my son's place needs to be secured!" I could hear my father, but the other voice was muffled; they must have been on the far side of the room. "My son weds in the morning, and you're going to secure the castle tonight. We aren't letting any more fiascos get in the way. *No one is to enter this castle without being brought to me first.*" I shook my head and just kept walking. I couldn't concern myself with his affairs when I had things of my own to worry about. Listening to one side of a conversation wasn't going to do me any good, either. I'd become quite the eavesdropper lately.

I shuffled down the hallway and back into the library. Amongst thousands of books that whispered their stories to me, I had always felt the most comfortable. My thumb ran over the leather bindings of the other eleven kingdom's books of Great Houses, selected the most recent edition of each, and got to reading. Behind my spectacles, my increasingly tired eyes skimmed line by line for what felt like hours. First, I started with the slightly smaller kingdoms of Yoln, Drocia, and Khesan, having no luck. Moving on to the neighboring kingdoms of Mura, Balyra, Gathen, and Astinia—I found nothing there either. Paging through the larger kingdoms of Voludor, Crithia, and Wrilon turned up zero information. My fingers trembled with frustration as I opened the book of the final kingdom of Vreca and slammed that book down the moment it was no help to me either. My head, heavy and throbbing, fell into my hands. No record of Aros in any of the twelve kingdoms in the last 100 years. I looked out the window and realized I was running out of time. I left the stack of books on the table and hurried to the throne room, hoping I wouldn't be late.

Eleanore was standing outside the doors when I arrived, looking as lovely as ever and knowing I would be researching in the library until the very last minute. I offered her my arm, and we entered the throne room together. It was strange to see my father seated where I had seen Queen Violet receive subjects so many times. The throne was golden and etched with intricate flowers, each adorned with a small colored gemstone. It was a beautiful throne, but my father didn't look like he belonged there, and I was sure my brother wouldn't either. Tobyn was a tall and rugged-looking man, especially with that scar carved into his face, dressed like a King and crowned like a King, but he perched uncomfortably like a bird in the wrong nest. He motioned for me to come forward and stand next to my brother. I kissed Eleanore on the cheek and took my place, facing the line of young women ready to be presented. They were of varied ages, from about fifteen to twenty-five years old, with varying looks. There were a total of seventeen of them, and I was antsy to get the ceremony started so I could return to my research. I could hear the books calling my name from the library. Julian, on the other hand, seemed to be antsy for other reasons. I could see him periodically look to the corner of the room where a group of servants was watching. Brysa, of course, was in the mix, looking slightly disheveled, no doubt from their spirited activities earlier in the day. She avoided his glances, her eyes glued to her pretzeled fingers.

Each of the ladies was presented to my brother directly, being given nothing but their name, their house, and who was presenting them. Lady Valeria of House Blackwood was presented by her brother, Arthur, the knight who had met earlier with the King. Arthur scowled at my father as he presented his beautiful young sister; he didn't seem happy about the presentation, but she was particularly giddy. She was young and beautiful, with long, dirty blonde hair and blue eyes. At 16, she was just my brother's type. As Lynnea was a queendom, young women did not grow up thinking they'd ever be given the opportunity to become Queen, so the thought was no doubt exciting for the young lady. Arthur whisked his sister quickly back into the lineup to make way for the next, but it did seem that Lady Valeria had caught Julian's attention. One by one, each lady was presented and returned to their place in the lineup. Excitement filled the room as a servant finally brought Julian the ring that he would present to his lady of choice. I watched him as he walked down the line of young women, looking each of them over as he passed by. He most likely wasn't the dashing prince that all girls dream of when they're young. He had my father's rugged looks, minus the scar on the face, of course. But he was also much older than all of them at 36, going on 37, though none of them seemed to care.

Once he had taken a careful look at all of them, he carried the ring to the young Lady Valeria Blackwood and bowed as he slid it onto her slender finger, to the apparent dismay of her brother. Arthur dutifully bowed his head and guided her hand into Julian's. He swept her onto the dance floor into a waltz commemorating the choosing of his future Queen. His bride-to-be was pink-cheeked with glee, while the cheeks of his servant mistress were blazing red with jealousy. *That'll be fun for him later,* I thought, smiling to myself. The song ended, and his new future bride curtsied to him before returning giddily to the rest of the ladies in the room. A few of them joined her in whispers of excitement before King Regent Tobyn stood and took the floor.

"Congratulations, House Blackwood. Lady Valeria has been chosen to be the next Queen of Lynnea by marriage to the heir and Crown Prince, my son, Julian. The kingdom will share in your joy tomorrow afternoon, where we'll tie your house to the crown in the sacred wedding ceremony! Please, everyone, welcome your future King and Queen, long may they reign!" He announced this with pride, a small smile spreading across his face.

Slowly, everyone started to exit the throne room, greeting and congratulating Julian and Valeria before starting toward home. I hung around, waiting for the opportunity to speak with Arthur, wondering what had been going on between him and my father in the study before I'd shown up. Finally, he was making his way out, and I pulled him aside where no one would see us talking.

"Arthur, may I have a word?"

"If you're about to 'congratulate' me for my sister 'winning' the crown, save it. I wouldn't have even brought her here if I didn't have to. Your brother is a brute, so is your father. I imagine you must be, too." He tried to push past me, but I held my hand out for him to stop.

"I'm not a brute, firstly. Second, I'm not trying to congratulate you. I'm trying to ask you what was going on between you and my father in his study earlier. You think Allanora is still alive?" He seemed surprised and looked over each of his shoulders before answering me.

"I know it was her. Out in the woods on the way to Astinia. She was with a man, his name was Justyn, and two other young women. He originally said she was his sister, that they all were, but then, when I showed interest in the Princess—Queen—he changed his story and said she was his fiancée. It just didn't add up. I knew he had to be a dangerous man, and I'd need help. I didn't want to endanger her by attacking him. Who knows what he would've done to her? I went to your father, asking to take a group of men with me to find her and bring her home. He told me I was crazy and completely dismissed me." He sounded exasperated and almost desperate. Not like someone who'd been having one too many drinks at the tavern, like my father claimed.

"But we buried her, Arthur. We all saw her die by that arrow."

"*No one* saw her body after your brother took her out of the throne room. The casket was closed for her funeral, and a servant told me Julian had sent all the healers out of the room when he took her out of that throne room. He was the last person who saw her. Until I saw her in the woods." I pondered his words; I just couldn't understand how it happened or why. I'd seen the wound from the arrow. There wasn't a way she could have survived that, but Arthur would have nothing to gain from lying about her reappearance. Especially with his sister about to be crowned Queen. My brother, on the other hand, would have everything to gain from making her disappear if she was still alive. Behind Arthur, I saw Julian appear, my beautiful wife hooked uncomfortably on his arm. I nodded my departure to Arthur and walked to her, allowing her to transfer from Julian's arm to mine. She visibly relaxed.

"Congratulating the family of the future Queen, brother?" Julian asked me pointedly.

"Of course, a joyous day in Lynnea." I felt my wife's hand grip my arm tightly, but she didn't waver from her warm smile. My brother strutted back into the throne room, giving my wife a look over his shoulder that I didn't understand. I turned back to Arthur, who seemed to be seething through his teeth.

"Arthur, please meet me in the library at first light tomorrow morning, yes?" I whispered to him so my brother wouldn't hear us from inside. He nodded and strode off in the other direction, disappearing down the hall.

Chapter 12

Henrie

I whisked my wife back into our room, and when the door closed behind us, I took her face gently in my hands.

"My dear, whatever is the matter? You looked like you have seen a ghost. Is it the baby? I'll get you a healer immediately." I reached for our bell, but she shook her head, and I let out a sigh of relief.

"I overheard Julian talking to a guard. But I couldn't understand what they meant from what they were saying." Her hands were shaking a little bit. I led her to our bed and sat her down, offering her a glass of water from our table. "Julian sent him away. He told him to keep anyone that might match Allanora's description out of the castle, but that doesn't make sense because Allanora's dead. When he caught me watching him, he grabbed my arm and shoved me off to the side. I guess he wanted to make sure I didn't hear anything. He said if I was eavesdropping, he'd—" Her voice quivered, and she rubbed her neck. I held her in my arms to calm her.

"I will never let him hurt you. He may be larger than me, but I will tear him limb from limb if he ever tries to touch you, even if it kills me." She nodded, fighting back a tear. When it fell, I wiped it gently from her face. "Eleanore, I spoke with Sir Arthur Blackwood briefly tonight. He said that he saw Allanora in the woods; she was traveling with a strange man and two other young women. Arthur was suspicious and brought it to my father's attention, but he only dismissed him. I think Allanora might be alive, and I think my brother might be behind her disappearance." More tears filled her eyes, though I didn't know what kind of tears they were. "It's going to be okay, Eleanore; no matter what happens with Aros, Allanora, my father, and my brother, *we* are going to be okay." I rubbed her cheek softly. She turned her head up and kissed me gently. Everything else melted away. I laid her down and kissed her neck, her chest, her belly.

I spent the majority of the night comforting her and reminding her how much I loved her. Finally, I was able to sleep soundly. I found myself still sleeping as the suns began to rise in the sky and carefully untangled myself from Eleanore's perfect body and warm touch before making my way down to the library for my meeting with Arthur.

He was already there when I came scrambling down the stairs. I was met with a sigh of relief from him. He shook my hand, and I invited him to sit. I opened my mouth to speak, but he spoke first, quickly.

"I can't let my sister marry a murderer." My mouth dropped open a little bit.

"If she isn't dead, I guess that wouldn't exactly make him a murderer?" I questioned.

"Whoever is behind the death or kidnapping of the Princess is definitely behind the death of the Queen, and if that's him, it makes him a murderer," he reasoned. The wheels in my head started to turn—he wasn't wrong.

"Look, Arthur, where was the Princess? How far away? Do you know where she was headed?" I prodded.

"He said he was taking all the young ladies to be presented to the Astinian King before being matched for marriage. They were less than a day's journey from Astinia when I turned back to Lynnea."

"The Astinian castle is days away from here, even on a fast horse. We'd never make it there and back before the ceremony tonight." Arthur let his head drop into his hands.

"I thought I was doing the right thing coming back here. I thought I could return with a hoard of Lynnean soldiers to rescue the Princess. I never even considered that the person behind it all was right here in our own home, within the castle walls, about to claim the throne, and now I don't know what to do. She could really be dead now for all we know, and my sister is in the meaty, whorish hands of your brutish brother. As long as he's the heir to the throne, I have to let her marry him. I have no choice without committing treason. Of course, my father thinks otherwise. He says all that matters is she's Queen. House Blackwood rises." He grumbled. "It was supposed to be me." He pounded his fist on the table between us, a jealous rage slipping from underneath his ever-noble mask.

I was a little lost for words, scrambling to find good ideas. Sending a raven to Astinia wouldn't do us any good; they would never let her receive a message even if she was alive, and there was no way they'd admit to us that she was alive in the first place.

Arthur's frustration and jealousy were tangible in the air; I felt I could reach out and touch them. Restless and fidgeting, he stood and started to pace back and forth. I thought he might dig a trench with his feet right there in the library.

"Arthur, I understand your frustration. I've never been the biggest fan of my brother, as I think everyone knows. But this marriage would be very advantageous for your family, and I think you know that. Julian can think all he wants that he'd have control over her, but your father and House Blackwood would be very much in play as well. I don't think you're thinking very much about how much this would benefit you all." He hung his head slightly.

"I talked at length with my father before the Queen's choosing ball. We thought that I had a good chance at being chosen." His eyes were far away, back in time. "My father Horst had a good rapport with Queen Violet. Allanora and I, well, I thought that we made a connection." He ran his hands uncomfortably through his hair. "Seeing her out there, with that horrible assassin." He balled his fists. "It's like everything slipped away again. She slipped away again." He sat back down, letting out a huff of frustration.

My hands were curled underneath my chin. I had seen the girl die with my own eyes. The pool of scarlet blood that poured from her shoulder. It was bruised into my memory. I still couldn't believe that she could be alive. Perhaps his story truly was just the ramblings of a heartbroken and jealous man.

"Father!" My son Lysan's voice cut through my thoughts and brought both Arthur and me to our feet abruptly. He flew down the stairs and landed right in front of me, panting for breath.

"There's a—man—outside the—gates—he says he's the—King! He's demanding—to talk to—you!" he panted. Arthur and I exchanged looks, and we raced up the steps and out of the castle toward the gate.

The scene that unfolded before us was quite astonishing. My father and brother, backed with a slew of Lynnean soldiers, were facing off with an inhumanly tall, muscular man sporting the golden rose crest of Queen Violet on his breast. A small crowd of Lynnean subjects had gathered inside and around the gate, staring in wonder at the strange man who had appeared. He had long dark hair, light olive skin, and liquid golden eyes. He wore shiny golden armor that glimmered in the sunlight. He was almost too bright to look at. He turned and addressed the crowd.

"My people! I am King Aros—I have returned to reclaim the throne of Queen Violet in the name of Princess Allanora." A chorus of gasps rang through the crowd; some started to whisper among themselves. Other, braver souls began to approach him curiously. He held a letter above his head and motioned me to take it. It was a small white envelope, sealed in unbroken wax with the crest of Queen Violet. I broke the seal carefully, scanning its contents and reading it aloud, facing the people of Lynnea.

I, Queen Violet of Lynnea, daughter of Cressida of House Harthope, being of sound mind and body, hereby state that in the event of my death and the death of my daughter, Her Royal Highness Princess Allanora of Lynnea, leave the throne and regency of Lynnea to my Husband, King Aros. In the event our deaths leave Lynnea with no heir, Aros will assume the throne as the sole heir and King, naming the next Queen of Lynnea by his own choice in the event of his own death. Should our deaths leave Lynnea with a young heir, King Aros is to assume the throne as King Regent until the heir comes of age. No other words or documents are to secede this will.

The document was signed with the Queen's signature and written in her hand. I had seen her writing a great many times before; it was unmistakable. Everyone was looking on in shock. I looked the man over carefully, trying to recall his face, but it had been so long since my single meeting with him that I just couldn't be sure.

Brother Sol was standing near the back of the crowd, eyes trained with a fiery anger on the claimant to the throne.

"As the rightful King of Lynnea, I call on you, valiant and noble knights of this kingdom, to seize the false King, Tobyn, and his treacherous son. They are to be tried for treason in the murder of Queen Violet, attempted murder of Queen Allanora, and unlawful seizure of the Lynnean throne!" Aros called out to the Lynnean guard surrounding all of them.

"Knights of Lynnea! Seize this man; he is a pretender to the throne and seeks to harm the King and heir!" my father demanded. "Throw him in the dungeon." The knights looked back and forth between the men, unsure of what to do. A few lunged for Tobyn, the rest for Aros. None of them reached him before a lightning bolt flashed in his place, striking the ground and sending everyone falling on their backs, stunned. Everyone but Aros, the God of Lightning.

Chapter 13

Allanora

King Rhonan had sent me out of the throne room to bathe and be made presentable for my "official introduction" to the King. While the handmaid presented to me scrubbed me down in the copper bathtub, my informal meeting with the King played over and over in my mind.

I was disgusted; I hated the lot of them. Rowan and Rylan had dragged me there, thrown over the back of a horse like an animal to cower before their monster of a father. King Rhonan had looked me over as if I were being presented to him as a prized pig instead of a foreign Queen. All of them had a dark, haunting disposition. I had looked at the three of them towering over me; Rowan and Rylan were lean but muscular, with hard exteriors that were somehow still human. Rhonan was a different animal, taller than his younger sons with muscles that couldn't be contained and a beast-like stature that instilled the kind of fear that one feels in their darkest nightmares.

He had dismissed his younger sons and circled me like a predator, his black eyes not leaving me for a moment. He had nodded his approval, his own eyes seeming slightly lustful, though I got the feeling his lust was less for sex and more for something darker. More sadistic. He had trailed one large knuckle down my cheek while declaring to no one in particular that I would be the perfect bride for his son, Crown Prince Raysh.

I had balked at the thought. Once I had cleared my head enough to fathom his words, I asked him how he intended for us to rule both kingdoms at once. The answer was devastating. He had planned to keep me here, perched like a prized bird next to Raysh's throne, and make an alliance with Tobyn, allowing him to rule as regent in our name until my heir was old enough to take the throne. My first daughter's marriage would be overseen by Raysh, making sure that the match would benefit Astinia along with Lynnea. Our first son would be Crown Prince of Astinia and ascend the throne after Raysh. He spun tales of a great alliance and the greatest power Cidris had ever known, all stemming from my marriage to Raysh. My whole life was mapped out for me, all while he circled me with that rapacious gaze, almost drooling at the prospects this marriage would bring forth.

I would never truly rule my own people, stuck under the thumb of the Astinian royal family. The only silver lining was that his son wouldn't be able to ascend my throne after him. Only our daughter would.

Nothing he had said to me had been a question, a proposal. All of it was demands, circled by unspoken threats that I knew hung in the air between us when I remembered his second and third sons, the highly skilled killers.

At least Lyra was safe, so all that was left to worry about was my kingdom. I wasn't sure what was considered appropriate for an official meeting with a man who'd plotted to kill and then eventually kidnapped you. But I had a feeling I would soon find out; Astinians were prideful of their ways. It was a rugged and brutish kingdom that held onto many of the old ways of our ancestors, such as torture chambers, fighting pits, and other ruthless practices that Lynnea and most of the other kingdoms had done away with long ago. For centuries, the Thorne house had bred sons who lived and breathed these traditions. Each King seemed to be more unfeeling, more terrifying than the last, if the whispers were to be believed. They were known for slaying anyone who got in their way, and stories of their methods of torture reached all throughout Cidris. In Astinia, women, even royal women, were expected to be silent, breed sons, and obey the word of their husbands. Women here were considered property, my mother had always told me, and were more valued for wide birthing hips and large breasts than a sharp mind or educated tongue.

Lynnea was a more graceful kingdom. Our armies were vast, but we never went looking for a fight. We never condoned unnecessary bloodshed, and our Queens never ruled by instilling fear; happy and cared-for subjects caused significantly fewer problems than those who lived in fear and oppression. Our vastly different ways of living and ruling had always caused a rift between our two kingdoms and made diplomacy between rulers difficult. I winced as I imagined how far my kingdom would fall should I be forced to marry the Astinian Crown Prince, allowing me to rule only in name, myself and my kingdom under his thumb. How could I rule such a ruthless kingdom? How could I allow myself to rule next to such a man, allow him to be called King of my lands, let alone sleep in my bed? I wouldn't even allow myself to imagine what raising children with him would be like or the vile acts he'd make me commit to conceive them.

The possibilities had put my mind into such a spin that I had stopped paying attention. Suddenly, I stood before a large mirror and was being dressed in a fine gown, with no memory of stepping out of the bath in the first place. If I wasn't already sure of what was expected of women in this kingdom, this dress told me everything I needed to know. It was a deep red and cut tight at the top to show off my waist, and the neckline plunged so deep the dress almost seemed to be in two pieces. I had never felt so exposed. The skirt of the dress, thankfully, was long and flowing, though it was sheer enough to see the shape of my legs underneath. I wondered how the Great Lords of Lynnea would feel, seeing their Queen paraded around in this dress. I paled at the thought.

I sat in front of the mirror of the unfamiliar room while a handmaid went to work on my hair. She was styling it in an Astinian style, with lots of intricate braids woven among locks that hung freely down my back. Astinians were a battle-heavy people—their hairstyles stemmed from how their ancestor warriors wore their hair in ancient times. I felt like a completely different person; I looked like one, too. While the dress was revealing in more ways than I was used to, it was almost comfortable without a corset to secure it.

A sharp knock on the door ripped me from my thoughts. Without waiting for my permission to enter, a guard popped his head in. I blinked, incredulous at the intrusion, which my own guards would never have dared.

"The King asked that you be brought to him as soon as you were considered presentable." The handmaid made no eye contact and kept her eyes fixed on my hair but nodded to the guard, who swiftly made his exit. She would not look at me either; it seemed Astinian royalty was not very friendly towards their servants. She hadn't spoken a single word to me, and in an effort to win over her trust, I opened my mouth to speak to her when there was another knock on the door. First, I felt panic, expecting the guard to come bursting in to haul me away because we'd taken too long. But when the second knock came, I finally found my voice.

"Come in," I said quietly. The door slowly opened, and I held my breath. It was Rylan. He looked me up and down carefully, with his hand under his chin.

"Astinia suits you fairly well, Princess." His eyes dragged over my midriff and up over my breasts before making eye contact.

"Queen," I snarled at him.

He chuckled dryly. "Buried under my tunics, I forgot how ravishing you are." He looked me over again and dismissed the handmaid with a wave of his hand.

Instead of scurrying away, she made a few odd hand gestures and shook her head nervously, avoiding eye contact with either of us. The exchange confused me, but I watched on silently. He seemed to understand what she was trying to say to him.

"You're more than welcome to take it up with my father. I'm sure he'd be thrilled to hear about you disobeying the orders of a member of the royal family." When she didn't move or communicate more, Rylan stepped forward and raised his hand up at her. The handmaid's eyes went wide, and I quickly moved myself in between them, one arm out to stop Rylan, the other grabbing behind me for the servant. It seemed that even my touch frightened her, and she ran off, stifling a sob from behind her small hand. I watched her go and turned back to Rylan with a glare.

"Why are all of you so cruel and unfeeling?" I yelled. He laughed and shrugged, leaning himself carelessly against the wall next to him.

"Some of us aren't soft, pampered Lynneans. And some women aren't as important as you are, Your Majesty," he growled. "You have to have a tough shell to survive in Astinia. Sometimes, people need a little help toughening up." He dragged an overconfident finger down my face, between my nearly exposed breasts, igniting static heat in my skin with his touch, until he landed at my waist, where the dress finally came back together. "Oh, Raysh is going to like this," he chuckled darkly. The heat at my core faded with his words. Raysh, not him.

I took a step back, trying to free myself from his suffocating touch. "Lynnea isn't soft or pampered." I puckered; his green eyes lit with wicked wildfire.

"But you are, Princess," he sneered.

"I am not!"

"We'll see..." He motioned for me to exit the room ahead of him, like some backward chivalry, when I knew he was simply escorting his prisoner. His face changed then, his mask slipping just slightly. "Look, I wanted to say—"

"You are all nothing but monsters," I muttered as I passed him. Suddenly, I felt a tight grip on my arm as Rylan stopped me in my tracks and spun me towards him, the harsh motion almost making me lose my balance.

That slight bit of humanity he'd started to show disappeared and shifted back to his snarky sneer. "The only monster here, Princess, is Raysh. That's who you should be worried about. I guess you could also consider Rowan a monster with that freakish tail of his, but you get used to it," he snickered. I yanked free of his grip, pivoted on my heel, and whirled around, the loose fabric of my skirts swirling around me.

"You're just as much of a monster as either of them!" I shouted over my shoulder as I kept walking, even though I didn't know where to go. "Your fiancée killed my mother, and you tried to kill me. Twice! I don't know how you Astinians define it, but that seems pretty monstrous to me!"

I turned back to look at him, as he'd fallen suspiciously silent. He looked astonished, only briefly. "Despite what you might think, Princess, I don't have many choices in my own actions," he snarled. I looked back for a second, just to make sure Rylan was following behind and to assess the almost soft look on his face, and then turned back around in time to slam into something. Someone.

Before me was a large man with broad shoulders and a chiseled jaw. He was built like Rhonan but had a face structure similar to Rylan's. He'd be handsome if everything about him wasn't absolutely petrifying. Black ink markings, like those of the King's, crawled over every inch of his arms and up his neck. His obsidian eyes were pits of despair, threatening to drown me in my own fear. Like a wolf poised to devour his prey, he leaned over me. *Lynnean Queens fear no one, bow to no one, and rise above.* My mother's voice was so faint in my mind, dwarfed by my own fear.

"Raysh," growled Rylan from behind me, confirming my suspicions that this was the oldest brother, Raysh of House Thorne, Crown Prince of Astinia. I subconsciously tried to take a step back, even into Rylan, but Raysh grabbed my forearms and held me in place to face him, unable to escape. I gulped. He stood about a foot and a half taller than me, just a little taller than Rylan and Rowan, but his presence was significantly more intimidating than the other two.

"Just thought I'd take a look at this foreign Princess everyone is all in a fuss about." He smiled and looked me over, taking me in with his eyes, then let me go. Fear had gripped me so much that I couldn't fathom telling him that I am a Queen, not a Princess. I stumbled back a step, then another, putting as much distance as I could between myself and him. "I can see why you couldn't kill her, Rylan," he mocked. Rylan's nostrils flared out; his cheeks flushed red. He approached Raysh from behind me and stood chest-to-chest with him. Next to each other, Raysh didn't actually look that much bigger than Rylan, but I was pretty sure who'd win in a fight. They stood eye to eye for a moment before Rylan shoved Raysh to the side and stormed down the hall, leaving me with the prince. Suddenly, that familiar terror I had felt so often since my coronation snaked down my spine. Raysh took my face in his hand, pinching my jaw between his fingers, and turned it side to side, looking me over again carefully. He nodded but didn't make any sort of comment. I wasn't sure if I should feel relieved or offended that he had nothing to say.

"King's this way." His voice was deep and raspy, and he pointed down the hallway, the same direction in which Rylan had disappeared moments ago. I gathered my long skirts and slowly started making my way. I could feel Raysh's stare piercing my back. He stayed a few paces behind me, walking slower but taking longer strides to keep time with me. I reached the end of the hallway, where two double doors greeted me, and I turned around slightly to see if this was where I was meant to go. Raysh nodded, a menacing smile crawling across his face. I took a deep breath, determined not to show fear. I was the Queen of a proud kingdom, and I would not let bullies overcome me. Lynnean Queens feared no one, bowed to no one, and always rose above. My plan remained unchanged, regardless of what the King had already said. I would formally meet with Rhonan and come to a diplomatic resolution that would hopefully benefit both of our kingdoms, allowing me to return to Lynnea as its Queen. *Hopefully, without a Thorne husband in tow.*

I reached for the door, and it creaked open before I could even touch the handle. From what I could see, no one had opened it from either side. Was that magic? I furrowed my brows in confusion, which was still plastered on my face as I locked eyes with the King of Astinia, who had a knowing smile ready for me. The room was set up like a council meeting room. A large marble table claimed the center, where the King and his two younger sons were perched. Bookshelves and candelabras lined the walls. There were a few guards peppered around the perimeter of the room.

Looking around, I spotted a woman seated in the corner, the only other woman in the room. She was wearing a tightly wrapped black silk dress with a slit up the side, and her head was adorned with a golden crown dripping with blood-red rubies. Her eyes were cat-like, and her pointed cheeks sat above a thin line of lips that had been painted scarlet and curled into a sinister smile.

"Astinia doesn't shy away from magic as Lynnea does, my dear Queen," the woman crooned. I assumed she was the Astinian Queen based on the crown and her presence with the rest of the royal family. Her hair was jet black, her eyes the same obsidian as the rest of the family, making Rylan's eye color even more astonishing.

"But the Triini—"

"Have learned their place in Astinia, as you will," Raysh's voice cut me off, and he joined his father and brothers at the table. The Queen stood and slowly made her way over to me. She looked young to have sons as old as they were. I bit my lip while she examined me, softly trailing her hand across my shoulders, my face, and my waist. Without saying a word, she returned to her seat beside the King, and I let out my breath as quietly as I could. King Rhonan motioned for me to take a seat across from him. Reluctantly, I did.

"Lynnea doesn't 'shy away' from magic, Your Majesty. It is just not as widely practiced since the fall of the Deities and the Old Religion; the Brothers of the Triini in Lynnea are not fans of magic," I explained, meeting her gaze. She nodded slowly in approval. I took another breath.

"You let the Triini ban magic, purge it from your walls, your lands." She sneered at me.

"Look, I—" King Rhonan held up his large, tattooed hand, and my jaw snapped shut.

"You're not supposed to be here," he said coldly. "Yet here you are." He folded his hands together and leaned forward on the table, locking eyes with me. I felt a chill but refused to let him see me rattled, so I straightened myself, sitting as high as I could. "The golden stem." He tutted.

"The what?" I scoffed.

"The golden stem," he repeated. "That's what you are, isn't it?"

I shook my head at him. "I don't even know what that means."

I keep hearing that phrase, even in my dreams. It sounded like some fancy rose. If they thought it was some sort of nickname, they were wrong. Either way, I had no information on the subject, so I started to try reasoning with him again. "Look, I'm a Queen; you and your sons are holding a monarch against her will. I think we'd both like to avoid a war here, and I think—" He cut me off again.

"Avoid a war?" His feigned ignorance was infuriating.

"Well—yes! Kidnapping a monarch is a treacherous crime. Especially after having one murdered and attempting to murder another. The Lynnean army will be knocking on your door very soon." His face had a look of derision, and he sat back in his chair and folded his hands, pondering my words.

"Well, I guess there's one problem with that, Your Majesty." His tone was mocking, and it took all my willpower to keep my composure. "Your army won't be knocking on my door. They all think you're dead."

"They'll know soon enough, and I—"

"They'll know when I want them to know. Here's the deal, my dear little Queen," he began. It seemed like my time for speaking was up. "I can keep you here, just like this, rotting away in my dungeon. I can give you to my guards as a plaything. Which, from what I can imagine, would be quite an interesting endeavor, considering your particular...abilities. Or you can agree to my terms, which would be wise since I'm the one here holding all the cards." My mouth dropped open just a little bit. I knew I couldn't talk myself out of this one. He was right; I didn't have any bargaining chips, my entire kingdom thought I was dead, and any hope of them coming for me was fading by the second. There was no way for me to let anyone know that I was still alive. I sat back in my chair slightly, struggling to shift this conversation in my favor. I had nothing to offer them but myself.

"What exactly do you want from me?" I mumbled quietly. "You killed my mother, you took me from my throne, what else can you take from me?" I pleaded angrily.

"I didn't order the kill on your mother, Allanora. I didn't order the kill on you, either, as unsuccessful as that was." He glared at his youngest son, Rylan, who shrunk angrily down into his seat, his arms folded over his chest. A shocked expression crossed my face.

"What do you mean it wasn't you? Rylan—"

"Doesn't work for me."

"But he's your son!"

"I didn't hire him to kill you. Someone else did."

"Then why am I here?" A million thoughts were swirling through my head.

"Well, he couldn't very well leave you. You were supposed to be dead. Yet you aren't. Which is incredibly fascinating, don't you think, little Queen?" My eyes darted back and forth between all of them. They were all staring at me, their black eyes—save for Rylan's—studying me, waiting. "Nevertheless, it works out in my favor to have you here now. So, I guess I must thank the person who did order your assassination."

"And you know who that is?" I asked sheepishly.

"Of course I do. That doesn't matter, though; none of it matters now. You're here, and I'm going to make that work out best for Astinia and my family." He smiled, his least sincere smile yet.

"If you are right and my kingdom believes me dead, I am no longer Queen and can do nothing for you. So, what do you want?" I started to twirl my fingers together in my lap, wrenching them until they were almost purple.

"As you know, my dear Queen, Astinia and Lynnea have not always been...allies." He stood from his chair and moved slowly toward me. "Always back and forth, even when we weren't officially at war. My father, diplomatic as he was, sought a marriage between my younger brother and your mother, Violet." That predator-like gaze focused on me. If that was true, we'd come full circle as now he was arranging for me to marry his son. "He arranged the marriage with Queen Cressida, and all was settled. Although, as everyone knows, Violet ignored her mother's orders and chose your father at her ball. I would never have stooped so low as to give your mother a chance to repent for her betrayal by arranging a marriage with one of my sons. That would have shown weakness on my part." He drew one of my hands from my lap and placed it on the table, covering it with his. His hands were cold as ice, as if blood didn't run through his veins, and I started to wonder if it did. He continued, and from across the table, I noticed the Queen looking at me uncomfortably. I swallowed hard. "No, as far as I was concerned, Astinia would be at odds with Lynnea for the rest of time. Now, as new circumstances have risen, things have changed." He released my hand, and the Queen and I both exhaled audibly. He turned toward the large fireplace, and it lit immediately, warm crackles filling the once silent room. He placed his hands on the hearth, took a deep breath, and turned back toward me. "We find ourselves in a particularly peculiar situation. You see, having a Lynnean Queen would provide many benefits to Astinia. Everyone knows the pockets of the Lynnean Great Noble Houses are very large, and the golden vein to the throne runs deep. Then, of course, there's the army, which you yourself have stated is very vast. An Astinian King at the head of the Lynnean army... Cidris will have seen nothing like it." I furrowed my brows; he was laying out a future for me and my kingdom that I just couldn't imagine. "You'll remain here, under our careful watch, while your kingdom is ruled by a regent, Tobyn, of course, if he cooperates. I wouldn't be so daft as to allow you to rule in Lynnea, unchecked, where you could rebel against us," he hissed.

"You said it yourself; my whole kingdom thinks I'm dead. How do you expect to reach into Lynnea's pockets if I'm supposedly dead?" I didn't feel very confident in myself as I spoke, but I wasn't done fighting.

"Oh, don't worry, you'll be making a miraculous return. Just not before you've been married off to my son. I won't be giving another Lynnean Queen the opportunity to disgrace my kingdom again." The smile on his face faded slightly. I swallowed hard, and my eyes drifted to Raysh, who was beaming menacingly at me from across the table. I shrunk down in my chair, wishing to be anywhere but at this table. Every one of them was watching for my reaction, except for Rylan, who sat in brooding silence, staring out the nearest window.

"I'd like our wedding to be as soon as possible." Raysh's deep voice cut through the menacingly quiet moment.

"You automatically assume it'll be you?" Rowan interjected begrudgingly, folding his arms childishly over his chest. The King and Raysh looked at him in confusion, and I remembered he had been sent away when Rhonan had laid out his plan for me.

"I am the Crown Prince." Raysh shot daggers at his younger brother. I crinkled up my nose in disgust at their childish bickering. Rowan sat silently, contemplatively.

"The good news is, she doesn't want to be with either of you. So, I think your arguing is unnecessary here," Rylan broke his silence to snap at his brothers. His beautiful eyes were shining with an emotion I had a hard time reading. If I didn't know any better, I'd think he almost seemed jealous.

"Go back to the Academy, Ry—you're not needed here. We know your only love is for the hunt," Raysh snarled at him.

"You've never loved anything in your life, Raysh. The only thing that makes you happy is to make people suffer. Even your own family." Rowan was seething.

"I don't know what you're talking about," Raysh brushed him off with a scoff.

"Cienna. I'm talking about Cienna," Rowan retorted between gritted teeth.

"Ah, right. Your little high-born Academy plaything," Raysh mused. "She made you soft, I solved the problem. You should thank me. She wasn't even my best lay anyway." Raysh studied his fingers like there was something interesting about them. He flicked his eyes to his still-angry brother, then back down at his hand. "Just remember, I can mess with your playthings, but only I can put hands on mine." He shifted his gaze to me with a sickeningly malicious and lust-filled glare.

"Arrangements will have to be made for your wedding, my dear son," the Astinian Queen interrupted quickly, laying her hand carefully over Raysh's when she spoke to him. She turned her gaze back to me. "A bride deserves a perfect wedding day." She ran her hand through his hair, and he scoffed, rolling his eyes. He leaned back in his chair and folded his arms over his chest. The oversized toddler they had made Crown Prince flushed red, looking like he was about to throw a tantrum. Rylan was glaring daggers at him and had taken a few more steps toward us, his body angled toward me in a protective stance.

Why is he even bothering to protect me? He's the one who tried to take my life. The one who brought me here. Men are so territorial.

"Good luck," Rowan muttered under his breath, catching the attention of the King, Queen, and Crown Prince all at once. They gave him a questioning look.

"She can use lightning. Like, make it come out of her hands." He held his hands up and made his fingers dance mockingly.

"I can't do anything with lighting. I told you that already," I argued, annoyed. The Queen narrowed her eyes and made her way over to me again. She took my hand and held it, palm up, her own hand hovering not far above it. Her fingers were small and dainty but looked worn, showing her age. She wore a large ruby ring on her left hand, a symbol of her marriage to the King. I felt a warm tingle at the center of my palm, starting there before it spread to my wrist and arm.

"What are you doing?" I asked her curiously. She was focused hard on her task, squinting and muttering under her breath. She nodded to her husband, who brushed her off with a wave.

"All you magic types are so strange," Rhonan commented, rubbing his temples with his fingers.

"I don't have magic," I repeated.

"You do, my dear. Ancient magic," the Queen finally said. Both Rhonan and Rylan glared at her from across the table. "Your father must have been something special."

"That's enough of that. There's a wedding to plan," Rhonan cut her off. She nodded thoughtfully and returned to where she had been sitting, delicately folding her hands in her lap.

"But what if I don't—want to marry him?" I whispered. Following through with a wedding required me to agree to the marriage. I didn't, I wouldn't. The familiar, almost evil smile returned to his face.

"Oh, I am so glad you asked. This way." He crooked his finger and motioned for me to follow him as he stood and went through a different door than the one we had entered through. *A secret doorway,* I thought to myself, *how interesting.* Raysh and Rowan exchanged excited glances, and the Queen carried a pale, grave look on her face. Rylan stayed put. Reluctantly, I followed them down a long, dark hallway. There were only a few doors along the hall; some were ornate, some were plain, and all were made of solid wood. We entered the door at the end of the hallway. It opened to a large balcony overlooking an empty pit. There were two guards standing just inside the doors who quickly lit the torches along the walls, lighting up the room. Rhonan leaned on the balcony banister and gestured for me to join him. Concern tugged at the back of my mind, but I wouldn't risk disobeying him. I leaned next to him and, out of the corner of my eyes, peered at the tattoos that painted his skin. Some of the markings seemed to be numbers and letters, ancient Astinian markings that I could barely recognize.

Momentarily, I lost myself, remembering reading of Astinian culture, how tattoos were symbols of battles won, enemies defeated, signs of triumph. In ancient times, the ink was laced with the blood of their enemy, but the practice had slowly died away. Maybe one day, the rest of their brutal traditions would die as well. Shaking my head, I snapped back to attention at the sound of heavy doors being raised. Gears creaked to life, and my stomach tied itself in a knot.

The pit was empty, but from the look of it, it was a well-used fighting pit. There were damaged weapon pieces strewn about the sand, blood stains splattered about, and dents and scratches in the walls. There were doors that more than likely led to cells where prisoners were kept. Rhonan snapped his fingers, and I saw one of the doors open slowly, a shadow beginning to crawl out from behind it. I watched fearfully as a giant reptilian creature appeared, slithering across the floor of the pit. The reptile was covered in black scales and had spikes down its back. It flicked its long tongue out. It was chained, presumably to the wall from its cage, and could only come about one-third of its way into the pit before catching its collar. A high-pitched yell came barreling from it before it stayed still on the ground, positioned to pounce.

Out of a different door, another shadow appeared. The shadow split itself into two figures, slowly making their way out of the cell. I squinted my eyes and watched in horror as the second figure was dragged into the center of the pit, tied up in ropes and chains. It was Lyra; she was being dragged by Gen, who looked up at me smugly from where she had dropped my beloved handmaid. My heart dropped into my stomach. Rhonan turned toward me, a menacing grin on his face.

"You didn't think I was going to let her get away that easily and lose my best leverage over you?" He smiled.

"But Rylan said Gen returned her to Lynnea." Tears filled my eyes.

"And you believed him?" He scoffed. "He tried to kill you twice, he kidnapped you, basically handed your crown over to that oaf, Tobyn. He was the one who kidnapped your precious handmaid in the first place. You thought he was just going to let her go? That's rich. Rylan, God-killer, convinced the Lynnean Queen he might have some good in him." Rhonan was laughing; a chilling, menacing laugh. I despised him; my entire body was quaking anxiously.

Out of the corner of my eye, I saw the lizard creature sizing up Lyra. Her tiny body was trembling beneath her restraints, and she was shaking her head and trying to lean away, looking up at me with pleading eyes, screaming through the gag in her mouth. "You know what's interesting, little Queen?" I turned my attention back toward Rhonan. "From what he told me, he spent a lot of time watching you before your coronation. No one had any idea, of course, but he knew you inside and out. You know what he found? You're alone. No close friends, no family outside of your mother. The only person he could find to hold over your head was this pretty little handmaid. Any of your subjects would've had the same effect since you're a walking bleeding heart, but now that your mother is gone, there really isn't anyone in this world that you love. How sad." He taunted me with his piercing eyes. My lungs started to feel restricted, and it was like someone was slowly crushing my chest. He wasn't wrong; there were so few people in my circle, and besides my mother, there wasn't anyone I was particularly close to. The tears in my eyes threatened to fall, and I shook my head, praying for strength.

"I'll do what you want, Rhonan. Just let her go," I begged him, looking sadly down at Lyra. I couldn't let anything happen to her, just as I couldn't let anything happen to any of my people. What kind of Queen would that make me? Feeling defeated, I hung my head low, the weight of the royal family's eyes on me.

"Raysh, why don't you show the Queen back to her chambers? Planning starts tomorrow." The Queen wrapped her arms around the King when I looked back up from the floor. Raysh was reaching for me to lead me on; briefly, I caught her eyes before she closed them. They changed just as Rowan's had back at the riverbank. Her eyes, though, changed into distinct cat eyes, whereas Rowan's had been lizard-like.

"Wait. What are you? Who are you?" I couldn't help myself; I had heard of people who could change shape and take on different forms, but I had never seen anything like it myself. She smiled a saccharine smile and opened her eyes again, maintaining a feline look.

"If you're wondering if I'm human, of course I am. I've been blessed with a second form that I can use as I please. I guess you could call us shapeshifters." She gestured for Rowan to join her, bringing him into the family embrace. "Only one of my babies was blessed with the same gift. Although the other two are inhuman in their own way." She sighed and withdrew from both men, coming too close for comfort and taking my face in her hands. Her hands were warmer than I expected, almost sweaty. "I can sense your fear, my dear. All of Astinia will. You'll need to work on that since you're going to be Queen here one day. Astinian rulers have no fear. I'm sure my son will show you that soon enough." She kissed me gently on one cheek and tapped the other one with the palm of her hand. *How could two neighboring kingdoms be so vastly different?* Before I could open my mouth, I felt Raysh's rough grip on my arm, pulling me back out of the fighting pit and out into the hallway. He took such long strides that I had to walk quickly to keep up with him, taking at least two steps for each of his. He kept his hand clenched tightly around my arm, pulling me along under his grip.

We came back through the room we had come from, where Rylan was still seated. We locked eyes, and his expression changed briefly, an angry, disdainful look replacing it.

"You lied to me," I spat at him. His face froze with shock.

"Excuse me?" he retorted, his cool calm washing back over him.

"You said you sent Lyra back to Lynnea, you promised she'd be safe!"

He stole an angry look toward Raysh, whose hand was still tense on my forearm. "You took the handmaid?" Raysh shrugged and shoved me forward, sending stinging pain up and down my arm.

"I hate you," I bit out at Rylan, venom on my tongue. For the first time, it seemed I hurt him. Good. He quickly looked away from me, and he was gone once we turned the corner. We made it quickly back to my chamber; the large mahogany door was closed, and a guard was now posted outside the room. I looked at him with a confused expression, but the guard made no eye contact. Raysh grabbed me by the face and turned it toward his, pulling me upward, almost off my feet. I was balanced only on my toes now.

"You're going to be Queen of Astinia. You'll need to be kept safe from anyone who might want to harm you. And we can't have you trying to run away, either. Don't even think about going out the window; you're much too far from the ground, and the castle is surrounded by rocks. No one would survive that fall. Got it, Your Majesty?" I nodded my head slightly under his firm grip, and he released me, allowing me to regain balance on the floor before letting go completely. He led me inside the room, this time allowing me to walk on my own. Shortly after, I heard the door lock behind me. Thinking he had left the room, I took a relieved, deep breath and closed my eyes.

I took a step forward and ran directly into him, my body jumping out of its own skin, and my eyes flew open. He backed me to the wall and held his hands over my head, trapping me. His eyes were lustful and menacing. I shrunk back from him, already feeling small with him towering over me. His warm breath heated my face. He leaned down and rested his nose in the crook of my neck, breathing me in. His jaw locked, and he ground his teeth. Fear set in. I put my hand on his chest, trying to distance myself, but he was solid as a rock, and there was no way I would ever be able to overpower him.

I needed to distract him. "Um, don't you think we need to get to know each other? You know, um, since we are going to be married and everything..." I started to tremble, which seemed to only encourage him. His eyes met mine again, and I tried to hide my fear as the Queen had told me to. He leered at me for a moment before he answered me.

"Oh, you want to get to know each other? I was just toying with you, but hey, you're the Queen. Whatever you wish, Your Majesty." He took my wrists and pinned them above my head, firmly but gently, and then leaned in to kiss me. I managed to turn my head to the side before he could, and his wet lips met my cheek. He was unphased by my movement and leaned down to kiss my neck. He held my wrists with one hand and trailed the other down the exposed skin of my chest. Where I had felt a momentary warmth of electricity when Rylan had done it, the only thing that trailed behind Raysh's fingers now was dread.

"No, um, no, no, no, I meant like—what's your favorite color?" My whole body was shaking now, fear emanating from my soul. Confusion spanned his face, but he released my hands. I breathed a sigh of relief.

"Black. My favorite color is black." He leaned in and planted another claiming kiss on my neck, my cheeks, before finally claiming my lips. Every inch of my body wanted to recoil, to run, but I was held firmly in place by his body on mine. His tongue forced its way into my mouth. I forced myself not to gag, swallowing bile back to my stomach. He tasted like ash and death, and he smelled of tobacco and charcoal. His roaming hand found my breast and squeezed, forcing the contents of my stomach to churn.

He finally released my lips and backed off just an inch, just enough to look me up and down, hunger in his eyes. "It's funny that Rowan thought he could take you from me, that you'd be the trophy of anyone besides me." His tongue found my neck, and a yelp escaped my lips before he covered my mouth with his hand. "Maybe he thought he could spare you. Their minds are so confused, guilty, my little brothers. They go on their missions, and they kill because they're told." He was breathing against my neck, sending terrified chills all through me. "The difference, darling, is that I do it for fun. I do it because I can. I do it so I can see the light leave the eyes of my prey. I bathe in those final moments, the gasps of fear before the life is snuffed out. Rowan's play toy, Cienna, the high-born training at the Academy..." His free hand slipped behind me and gripped my backside, pressing my hips to his. I stiffened, helpless. "I'll never forget how she fought me, fought death. I crushed her neck as I took her body. She was stealthy, stubborn. You look like her. Maybe that's why he stuck up for you." He let out a low, dark laugh. His tongue reached out just slightly and made a trail from my neck down between my breasts. I shuddered at the thought of him torturing the poor Cienna girl just for being with Rowan, just to hurt him. Chills crawled up and down my spine like spiders, and my vision started to blur. I thought I could just die right here. "Just remember, you're mine." Though it was barely a whisper, the words boomed through my mind, echoing in my soul. "You might find that you'd be safer with one of them, but you're mine, Allanora. Mine." My name on his lips was the most terrible sound I had heard since coming here. He planted one final, claiming kiss on my lips before releasing me, leaving me shuddering in his wake while he half-heartedly bowed and left the room.

Finally alone, I let my breath out completely, walked over to the bed, and fell over backward on it, still trembling, still trying to comprehend his words. His scent still filled my nostrils, and there was a phantom feeling of his hands still on me. This was the life I would be resigned to.

It wasn't long before the same handmaid that had done my hair earlier tiptoed in and started preparing me for bed. She tied my hair in loose braids and helped me dress in a silky black nightgown. I ran my hands over the fabric; it was soft and beautiful, very similar to the nightgowns I wore in Lynnea. I sighed sadly and looked up at the girl in the mirror, but she avoided my gaze immediately and kept her lips shut. As soon as she finished, she scurried out the door, and I was alone again. I laid back down on the bed and rolled myself up in the soft sheets, willing myself to sleep. It was the first time I had slept in a real bed since leaving Lynnea. It had been nights of sleeping on the ground and the horrible mattress on the floor at Griddick's with Lyra. As nice as the mattress felt, though, I couldn't get comfortable. I couldn't escape the feeling that Raysh was going to come back and finish what he started. I rolled back and forth for what felt like hours before exhaustion finally won, and I fell asleep.

Chapter 14

Allanora

It seemed as if I had been asleep for only a moment before I felt a hand lightly clasped over my mouth, followed by the feeling of someone sitting over me. I pinched my eyes closed further in fear. *Oh god, it's going to be Raysh wanting more after our uncomfortable encounter earlier.* I peered out slowly from under one eyelid, and shock consumed me when I realized it was Rylan over me. My eyes flew open all the way, and I went to yell out, but he pushed his hand over my mouth harder, holding one finger to his lips, shushing me. *What is he doing? Where did he even come from?* I was uncomfortable, remembering the dream I had had of him kissing me in the woods. I shuddered beneath him.

"What on earth do you want?" I hissed when he finally removed his hand from my mouth. I pulled the blanket over myself as much as I could, feeling exposed and slightly self-conscious. He shifted so he wasn't hurting me or putting too much pressure on me, but he didn't get up from on top of me either.

His face was ice, cold and unfeeling. "I didn't mean for the handmaid to be brought here."

Confusion stitched my brows together. "Right, sure you didn't, Rylan."

"I didn't. I gave you my word. She was supposed to go back to Lynnea."

"And your word is supposed to mean what to me, exactly?"

He rolled his eyes. "Look, I know what you think of me. But we are going to have to deal with each other for a long time now, at least occasionally, when I have to come back to the palace."

"Get to the point, Rylan," I snapped at him.

"Just—Raysh doesn't like a challenge. If you fight back, he'll only make it worse for you. You're going to be better off if you just do what he wants, ok?" He sounded genuine, for once.

"And why exactly are you telling me this?" I became acutely aware that he was still on top of me, his waist pinned to mine.

"I saw what he did to Cienna. I've seen what he's done to all the women he's been with. He's horrible."

"Oh, right... because you and Rowan are so much better." I shifted uncomfortably underneath him, but he still didn't move.

"We are. We are hired killers. We kill for money, not for fun. And I don't... do what he does to women." His sentiment mirrored what Raysh had said earlier about his brothers.

"And who hired you?"

He ignored my question entirely. "Let's just say that you would've been better off if my arrow had actually taken you, Nora." Something arrogant and fiery made his eyes gleam in the moonlight from the window.

"You do not get to call me that," I snapped at him, but the gleam didn't leave his eyes. He leaned over me, inching closer. Recoiling, thoughts of Raysh pinning me to the wall earlier flooded my mind, and tears stung my eyes.

Stunned, he shifted back, sitting on my legs instead of my midsection. I shimmied up from underneath him, pulling myself into a sitting position.

"Come on now, Princess, I was just toying with you."

A sob escaped my lips. "Earlier...when he brought me back here... I thought he was going to force himself on me... and now here with you, I thought that you..." Stifling another sob, I buried my face in my knees.

"I may be a killer, Princess, but I would never do that. No matter how perfect your breasts were in that dress today." I looked up through bleary eyes, and the murderer himself was almost smiling. A twinkle danced in his eye. "You know, I did watch you for a long while before your coronation. And I did find it kind of sad that you didn't have anyone that you loved."

"You felt sad for me?" I forced away the tears and swept my face into a look of incredulity.

"You have to admit. Your life was a little sad."

The comment infuriated me.

"Just you wait. All of you. My army is going to come for me. Arthur is going to come for me." I pouted angrily.

"Arthur, the knight from the woods?" He stifled a laugh.

"Yes, Arthur from the woods. I know he's going to come for me. We had a connection. He couldn't have just forgotten my face. He's going to come and take me home to Lynnea, and I'm going to reward him with a crown." I forced myself to sound absolutely sure of myself, though I wasn't.

He let out a laugh. "Your noble knight won't want you anymore after Astinia chews you up and spits you out. After Raysh gets his hands on you." His eyes darkened, and part of me knew he was right.

"Arthur is the son of a lord, he isn't just a knight. And what's that supposed to mean?"

"If you step out of line, if you do something Raysh doesn't like, or Rhonan, they'll punish you. Once you're married to Raysh, he can do whatever he wants to you; no one in Astinia will stop him." A twinge of pain rippled across his face. "Your army isn't coming, your Arthur isn't coming. And if he does, Raysh will rip him in two before you even know he's here."

"Your countrymen may feel no loyalty to you, but mine are loyal to me. They will come. Arthur will rescue me from you." I couldn't help the slight pout that my lips made. They would come, I knew they would.

"You think I'm the one you need rescuing from, Princess?" A malicious grin began to tug at the corner of his lips, but he didn't smile.

"Of... course..." He raked his eyes over me, a strange fire igniting in his eyes.

"Why's that?" he whispered. "You think I might do something to you?" He almost sounded vulnerable, with just a hint of humanity in his voice.

Of course I feared him; his reputation and his actions were nothing short of malicious, but what I feared most was what I had felt in that dream before

I woke up in his arms in the woods. "Well," I could barely speak, "you might."

"Like ruin you before your lordling comes to rescue you?"

My face flushed, and my skin prickled.

He saw me blush, and by the look on his face, he was reveling in it. "He was too stupid to know who you were in the woods. What makes you think he's going to be smart enough to come for you?" He'd dropped his voice to almost a whisper, and he leaned in closer to me.

"How dare you!" There was more snap in my voice than I even intended. He was so infuriating.

His face was cloaked in mischief. "How dare I what?" He took my face in his hands and looked at me, actually looked at me. I stuttered, confusion clouding my mind. We hung there, so close together, for what felt like an eternity. Then something in his eyes snapped, and he kissed me with a burning and hateful passion. It was different from Raysh's dominating kiss; it was sincere, at least, impassioned. Still, my mind went to Arthur, and allowing Rylan to kiss me felt like a betrayal, especially since part of me was enjoying it. I struggled against his lips, and it was just like it had been in my dream. His lips were soft and inviting. The hate melted away, the guilt starting to follow it. With a sigh, I finally gave in. His hands held my face gently; he wasn't as forceful as Raysh was. I leaned back when my core ignited, and when I gave in, he slid a calloused hand to the back of my neck, holding me.

I tensed at the motion, and he broke the kiss and sat back on the bed.

Out of the corner of my eye, I saw movement behind Rylan. I let my eyes drift just enough to catch what it was, a guard that had opened the door, probably to check on me, and was trying to slip out. Rylan caught the drift in my eye and immediately turned. Swiftly, he pulled a dagger from his belt and threw it, catching the guard in the neck. He dropped to the floor with a thud. Shock took over me, and I froze, unable to process what I was seeing. The guard's body twitched, and blood poured from his neck;

I closed my eyes tightly, unable to look. I heard Rylan making his way over to the other side of the room.

"You're a monster!" I whispered firmly behind closed eyelids, locking everything I had just felt behind an invisible door in my mind.

"If I didn't kill him, we'd both be dead." I peeked out from behind my eyes. Rylan was quickly wrapping the body up in a carpet.

"What are you talking about?"

"You think if a guard saw you in here with me alone that he wouldn't be going right to my father or brother? And what exactly do you think my brother would do with that information? Give us both a slap on the wrists?" He scoffed.

"We weren't doing anything," I insisted, even though he had kissed me, and I enjoyed it. Maybe there was something to tell.

"It doesn't matter. My brother is an actual monster, Princess. So, unless you want to know what would happen if he took that pretty head off with an axe, I'd suggest you thank me for getting rid of him and move on with your life." He brushed his hair to the side of his face before easily swinging the rolled-up guard over his shoulder.

"What are you going to do with that... with him?"

"It's probably best if you don't know." He winked and slipped quietly out the door, closing it softly behind him.

As soon as he was gone, I collapsed back on the bed, my mind whirling and mulling over everything that had just happened. *What was he trying to accomplish, anyway? Swinging in here and kissing me as if he isn't the whole reason that I'm in this predicament in the first place.* I took a deep breath in and absently touched my fingers to my mouth. *Even though he's a monster, I guess he was a pretty good kisser, even good-looking. I guess that's what Gen saw in him this whole time.* I shook the thought out of my head. *A killer, Nora, he's a killer.* My mind kept wandering, thinking about how easily he killed that guard without even hesitating or considering what that meant. He killed him to protect me. I started to wonder if that man had a family or friends who would miss him. My eyes started to well up with tears, and a sob escaped from between my pursed lips.

No matter how hard I tried, I couldn't fall back asleep; memories of Raysh's rough grip, Rylan's soft hands, and the dying guard kept flooding the space behind my eyelids. When I saw the first sun peeking up from the horizon, I couldn't handle lying in bed anymore. I found a silk day robe, tied it around myself, and slipped my feet into the shoes that had been placed there for me before sneaking out of my room. I closed the door behind me and came face to face with King Rhonan standing over me. He gestured to the empty doorway.

"I posted a guard here last night, little Queen. He seems to have slunk away in the night. You didn't see him, did you?" I shook my head slowly back and forth, my wide eyes fixated on him. "I suppose not. What's a mousy thing like you going to do against an Astinian guard, anyway? But don't you worry…" He brushed my cheek with his thumb. "I'll have another guard out here tonight. And that one will be taken care of for abandoning his post." His menacing smile mirrored his sons'. "I need you in one piece for everything to come together." He smiled coldly and turned to walk away without giving me a moment to speak. I shuddered, remembering the guard yet again.

"Excuse me, King Rhonan?" He turned and glared at me; I dropped into a clumsy curtsy, and he raised an eyebrow in question.

"Um—are there, um, gardens? That I could walk around in, perhaps?" I stuttered. He smiled and looked me up and down.

"I'll send Rowan to show you the grounds. Raysh is busy with his mother planning the wedding, and Rylan hasn't been seen since last night. I'd suggest you wear some different clothes. There's a bell in your room for the handmaid." He grinned menacingly and walked away. I looked down at myself and scoffed, knowing I couldn't walk around with a member of the royal family dressed in nightclothes. I quickly shuffled back into my room and rang for the handmaid. She appeared almost immediately. I greeted her, but she only nodded.

"Why won't you speak?" I finally asked her. She was silent a moment, but then she opened her mouth, revealing that she no longer had a tongue; she was mute. The shock was obvious on my face. I couldn't believe what I was seeing; someone had cut out her tongue and silenced her.

"Did they do that?" Confusion filled her face. "The royal family," I clarified. She nodded quickly and busied herself, tying me into a gown. "Why?" She shook her head. "I mean, was it a punishment?" She shook her head again. "It's because you're a servant, isn't it?" She nodded slowly. Servants didn't need to speak in Astinia, apparently. I felt my face flush with anger, and I rolled my eyes. "I'm so sorry. Maybe when I'm Queen, I can try to put an end to some of these inhuman ways."

"That's exactly the attitude that's going to have my brother doing the same to you." I snapped my head in the direction of the door. Rowan was standing in the doorway, leaning nonchalantly against the frame, his hand curled up near his face, watching the handmaid finish styling my hair. It was the first time I saw him in something that wasn't an Academy tunic. It was still black, riding pants and a loose fit shirt and vest. The tone of his muscles in his chest was still obvious, but I found myself noticing the softer look about him. He was fearfully handsome like his brothers and still edgy but had something gentler about him.

"Excuse me," I said, remembering myself, "don't you know how to knock?" He laughed and knocked half-heartedly on the inside of the frame before striding fully into the room. He approached us, and the handmaid quickly bowed, eyes to the floor, and half ran out the door. I sighed, annoyed. "You've all made it so absolutely everyone is terrified of you."

That gentle edge around him hardened. "Of course we have. To rule is to instill fear. Rylan and I are well-known assassins, though everyone fears us; that doesn't have anything to do with the crown." He laughed haughtily.

"My mother didn't rule with an iron fist, neither will I. Love and respect ensure growth and prosperity in a kingdom. That's how Lynnean Queens rule," I stated stubbornly, crossing my arms over my chest.

"I see what good that did both of you." A dark smile spread across his face, and I winced, my nose twitching slightly, the hatred I had for the royal family seeping from my pores. "My father told me you wanted to see the grounds." He offered me his arm. I walked past him, rejecting his chivalry. "It's ok, 'Lightning Queen.' I still think you're pretty, even though you're dangerous and don't know how to rule a kingdom," he joked. I wasn't in the mood for jokes, though. He motioned for me to follow him out of the room into the hallway. I stayed one or two steps behind him as much as I could.

"I know how to rule a kingdom better than your brother," I mumbled. He turned back toward me, and he looked torn. Torn between fear of his brother and acknowledgment of the truth I spoke. "I know what he did to you, to Cienna, and I'm sorry."

His face shifted, almost sad, but he ignored me and kept walking, his shoulders slumped just slightly.

"Tell me about her, please?"

He held open a door to the gardens outside. "Why?"

I walked behind him for a few moments silently, taking in the sights before me. The Astinian gardens were full of red flowers of all kinds, all surrounded by black rocks. They took their kingdom's colors seriously. I stopped and studied a blood-red rose. "I guess it would just be nice to be reminded that there's some humanity left in Astinia. I haven't seen much since I arrived."

His face changed, a shadow of that softness and vulnerability I had seen momentarily before replaced the typical hard and uncaring mask he wore. Rowan sighed but finally broke, his voice barely a whisper, "Cienna was stunning. But she also had a sharp mind, she was strong. She was better than Gen, and everyone knew it." He paused, lost in the memory. "She had perfect hips, breasts, and the face of an angel. Her blue eyes reminded me of the morning sky. When she first arrived at the Academy, she had long cascading brown curls. Steele made her cut her hair short, but even with shorter hair, she was drop-dead gorgeous."

"Raysh said he thought I looked like her."

He winced in response, and I knew that I had misstepped.

He picked the flower I had been studying and handed it to me. I took it warily. "I guess you might look a little bit like her." He studied me for a moment, and I started to feel a little self-conscious. His eyes shifted. "You know, you don't have to be afraid of me," he said as he shot me a glare.

A painful sting had my finger throbbing. I put the stem in my other hand and noticed a small drop of blood where the thorn had pricked me.

"That's a little rich coming from you."

"You're betrothed to my brother now." I shuddered at the thought. "In Astinia, that makes you his, by all rights. Anything having to do with you goes through him. Putting a hand on you, harmful or otherwise, is treason, which is punishable by death."

I kept my eyes trained on the flower, the blood dripping down my thumb, the symbol of my new life here. "Is that supposed to be comforting?"

"Normally, I would say yes, but like I said, you're his by all rights, and that isn't exactly comforting," he mused.

"What's that supposed to mean?" I winced.

"It's treason for me to lay a hand on you, it's treason for Rylan to lay a hand on you." I caught his eye briefly, and he lifted an eyebrow. "Raysh can do whatever he wants, it's not treason. So, like I said, you don't have to be afraid of me. Or Rylan, I guess. Even if you didn't have your—" he gestured up and down at me, confused, "whatever it is that makes you, you know, not die. Rylan still wouldn't be able to kill you now, even though he was hired to. Well, he could try, but Raysh would crush him." He made a crushing motion with his hands to make his point. My mind started spinning again, thinking of what that meant, Rylan laying a hand on me. It made me understand a little better why he killed the guard so quickly.

Rowan was being so genuine, honest, in his own way. It was the perfect moment to take advantage. "Who hired him?" I questioned. I hadn't gotten anywhere with Rylan, let alone the King. Maybe Rowan would finally answer me.

"Oh, you don't know?"

"If I did, I wouldn't be asking you now, would I?" I trained my eyes on him. I hoped he didn't think I was flirting. He shifted uncomfortably.

"Right. Um—I don't think that's for me to say."

"Rowan..." I seethed.

"Um, I guess that would be the King now? Tobyn? He enlisted the services of the Academy. Gen and Rylan were chosen to carry out the task. You know, you and Queen Violet." My heart shattered. Out of all our adversaries and enemies, Tobyn had been my mother's advisor, protector, and close friend. He was like a father figure to me, and all this time, he had planned our deaths to steal the crown. I dropped to the floor. My world spun out of control. All the feelings I had tried to suppress from my mother's death and everything that had happened since came flooding out of me. My throat started to close, and I felt myself struggling to breathe as I sobbed. Rowan knelt next to me on the ground and shouted for guards. I curled my knees to my chest and started to hyperventilate, my face, hands, and feet going numb. Pins and needles made their way up my body, and then my eyes went static before unconsciousness claimed me.

Chapter 15

Henrie

Terror and confusion flooded the throne room when the King Regent and Crown Prince were dragged down the aisle where Princess Allanora had taken her last steps and drawn her final breath. The prisoners were thrown at the feet of her father, King of Lynnea and God of Lightning. He was quite a sight, seated upon Queen Violet's throne, wearing the jeweled King's crown as if he had never left. His eyes were golden and terrifying. He had all the looks of a mundane man in his mid-fortieth year, though being a Deity, he was more likely hundreds of years old. In his hand, he held a solid gold staff, a sapphire lightning bolt adorning the top. He sat, perfectly poised as if he were ready to pounce.

I stood near the back corner of the throne room, not wanting much notice to be taken of me. I had my wife and children placed under the watch and protection of two of my most trusted guards while everything else proceeded. I watched my brother and father thrown at King Aros' feet, both stammering and cowering before him. He stood and addressed the crowd of confused Lynneans; his voice was firm but soothing.

"As you all know, I took leave from being your King after the events of the Great War and the fall of the Deities. I left Lynnea to honor an agreement between the humans and the Deities, but not by my own choice. Queen Violet, my beloved wife, and my daughter, Princess Allanora, were everything to me. As further war threatened, I left to protect them and, by extension, to protect all of you. I had to watch my daughter grow from afar and never see my wife again. Lynnea prospered under the lone reign of Queen Violet; all of you prospered." His gaze swept the room, making sure to lock eyes with every single member present. Slowly, as the words left his lips with authority and benevolence, the cloud of apprehension and fear lifted.

"Lynnea is a wonderful kingdom and has grown and thrived since I last set foot on this land." He took a deep breath before he continued. "As you also know, the deaths of Queen Violet and Princess Allanora have brought devastation, confusion, and loss to this great kingdom. These deaths were not only unnecessary, but they were orchestrated by the very man you crowned King. The man my wife put her trust in to advise her, the man meant to be her friend. Who guided my daughter during her upbringing into the crown. The very women he paid to have slain before the eyes of all of you." A chorus of gasps rang out through the throne room, but in one swift and effortless movement, he held out his hand to silence them. "Lynnea is a queendom, and under a Queen, Lynnea will thrive. Queen Allanora, your Queen, will lead you into a prosperous tomorrow." More astonished voices rippled through the throne room. *Allanora is alive,* I thought. *Arthur was right.* Whirls of thoughts flew through my mind, the gruesome display that was Allanora's body on the ground, yet she lived. I knew what everyone was thinking and whispering. They all saw Queen Allanora die. Aros held up his hand again, and the room fell into a dead silence.

"Queen Allanora has been kidnapped. Queen Violet is dead, and the man responsible must face justice. Tobyn, son of Tygrin of House Hawkham, King Regent of Lynnea, and advisor to the late Queen Violet, you are charged with treason against the crown and sentenced to death." A few small gasps broke the silence, but most were too afraid to make a sound, waiting for him to continue. A pit formed in my stomach. "Julian, son of Tobyn of house Hawkham and Crown Prince of Lynnea, you are charged with treason against the crown and sentenced to death." He returned coolly to the throne and sat, staring into the crowd; people had started chattering amongst themselves, sounding surprised and confused. My father and brother were shaking, kneeling before him. Julian begged for his life, but the treacherous King Regent stayed stone silent.

I had never cared much for my brother, and my father had always acted more of a father to Allanora than to me, but in that moment, my chest constricted, and I found myself wanting all of the accusations not to be true. I longed for Eleanore, her comforting touch. My father and brother were family, no matter how treasonous, but she would remind me that my loyalty should lie with the innocent, our betrayed Queen.

King Aros ignored them. I started to make my way toward the front of the crowd, catching the eye of Arthur along the way, who was looking relieved and triumphant. I reached the front of the crowd and raised my voice so that Aros could hear me.

"King Aros!" I called out. Suddenly, I could feel the glare of hundreds of eyes burning into my back. "You say Queen Allanora lives. Where is she?" I wanted to feel sadness for my father and brother, and I knew that once all the excitement died down, I would start to mourn. For the time being, though, I knew what they had done was wrong; they had committed treason, and there was no way around that. I knew if I argued with Aros, I might secure my spot right next to them at the execution. A warm smile spread across Aros' face as he locked eyes with me. He stood once again, leaning on his staff planted firmly on the ground.

"She has been taken to Astinia, where she is held captive by King Rhonan." Angry shouts started to break out amongst the people; they began to push against the wall of guards that was separating them from the King and the two sentenced prisoners. "Guards—please escort the prisoners to the tower to await execution. Henrie, please." He motioned for me to join him. I stood near him while he addressed the people one last time. "I plan to meet with the Generals of the Lynnean armies to plan the rescue and return of your beloved Queen. If anyone has any information for me, please relay it to Henrie." He clapped me on the shoulder. Arthur made his way forward and nodded to me before taking a knee and holding his sword before Aros.

"King Aros, please accept my sword as yours to help fight for Queen Allanora. I pledge myself to you and would give my life for the Queen."

Aros gave me a questioning look, and I nodded to him, letting him know Arthur was true and trustworthy. Aros nodded to him and motioned for him to rise before shaking his hand firmly. He gestured both of us to follow him out of the throne room.

He had chosen the late Queen Violet's rooms as his chambers. We made our way there in silence, walking past a few who tried to stop and question him, but he waved them off politely. Once we reached the study and the door was closed, I wasted no time in asking him questions.

"Someone needs to explain some things to me. How is Allanora alive? The entire kingdom witnessed her death right in these halls. Then Sir Arthur—"

"Allanora is the daughter of a God," he said simply, cutting me off, and started to unroll a map of the twelve kingdoms, placing markers on Lynnea and Astinia.

"Children of Gods can die, Gods can die, we all know that," I whispered.

"Allanora stays alive because I keep her alive." He spoke so plainly as if the explanation bored him.

Arthur and I exchanged wide-eyed glances. "What? How?"

"I have been transferring my life force to her, healing her wounds and keeping her alive. Every time that measly, worthless thug has tried to kill her, I heal her. No blade can cut a golden stem." He took a stone map marker and easily crushed it to powder in the palm of his hand.

"Golden stem... That's how the Gods used to refer to their half-human children," Arthur interrupted, his eyes wide and searching, as if it was something he just remembered.

"Yes, before we were no longer allowed to have children with humans. It was agreed it was too... messy." Aros shook his head solemnly. "I guess now I understand why we made that agreement."

"You broke the agreement when you had Allanora. You started the war." I spoke before I could think about what I was saying or who I was saying it to. Aros hung his head low.

"I loved Violet. I thought if I married her, it would make things better... I thought if I took on a human role as King and gave up my role as Deity, it would suffice to make up for it. Now, Violet is dead, and Allanora is in the hands of that *Rhonan* and his monstrous sons." Aros balled his fist and slammed it on the large stone table. The table cracked in half under the weight of his rage. Arthur's mouth fell open, watching the two halves of the table collapse.

"I never should have left. Those cowards had me run off and hide and abandon my wife and daughter. We never should have surrendered that war. I would've burned every single one of those humans to the ground." Lightning started to crackle around his palms, sparking off his wrists. His words echoed through the study that seemed to shrink around us. As if he truly meant them. For a moment, I questioned Arthur and my safety in the presence of this vengeful Deity. Raw power pulsed through the room, thrumming like a heartbeat.

"Look, we can rescue her still. We can bring her back, make it right," I told him softly. He ignored me and turned toward Arthur, who was still aghast at the Lightning God's pure strength.

"Arthur, I need you to help me choose the best men for a small mission to Astinia. I want you and the best warriors of Lynnea to go there with a message from your King. When he refuses diplomacy, I want you to attempt to take her by force. I'll be sending the rest of the Lynnean army behind you if necessary." Arthur nodded. "I know what I'm asking of you," he continued, "and when the time comes, you may choose your reward, anything in my power to give, and it will be yours."

Arthur seemed ready with his response, sparing no time in his request. "When the time comes, my King, I would choose Allanora's hand." Aros pursed his lips as he considered Arthur's request. He said nothing but nodded in return. The feeling of discomfort in Aros was palpable in the air, promising his only daughter off to a man he barely knew, knowing that she should have been able to make that decision herself. He knew that it was in her best interest, though, not only because Arthur was offering to rescue her but also because he was a good man who would treat her right, even if it wasn't a union born of love. The thought stung me, imagining if I had an arranged marriage instead of being able to choose my Eleanore. I winced, allowing the thought to slip from my mind. There was always the chance that Arthur would not survive the mission. Nothing was set in stone, but the time to act was now.

I stepped forward, asking for permission to speak with a soft glance in Aros' direction. I was still unsure of how to behave around him or approach him. Sure, we'd been sending ravens to each other these last few years, but it was one thing to scribble a few cryptic lines on parchment. It was another entirely to speak to the God of Lightning in person. A God scorned and angry, at that. Still, I hoped he had at least some respect for me, even if I'd failed my secret duty and my father and brother were the reason.

"There may be some... unrest among the people of Lynnea and the ranks of the armies about the sudden change in leadership, Your Majesty." I bowed my head when I spoke and felt his eyes burning into my skull at first. But when I looked up to meet his eyes, his gaze softened, and his own head dropped. "Not to mention that the Triini leaders who reside here may not be happy about a Deity of the Old Religion taking the crown. They won't even allow us to read the old texts or learn your stories as part of our histories."

"I understand, there's been a lot of change for the people and the soldiers of late." He completely ignored the mention of the Triini. I expected nothing less; he was here for his wife and daughter, not power. "Who is the head of the army?" He rubbed his forehead with his thumb and index finger, small sparks flowing between the places where his skin touched.

"My father, Your Majesty. Tobyn." I couldn't dance around the truth. My father had overseen the Queen's protection and, therefore, was the General of the entire Lynnean army. Aros winced and sighed.

"I can't give clemency to Tobyn to give the people comfort. He's responsible for the death of Violet, and he—" He stopped himself as the sparks became more urgent, almost flying from his face. Curiosity had me urging to reach out and see if his skin would shock me or electrocute me, but fear held me back. No one alive truly knew the extent of the power of the Deities, since in the final years of the war and for a little while before, they had been more secluded, keeping from humans as much as they could.

"Perhaps if you appointed a new leader, one of their own and a face they know, that would show them that you truly have their best interests at heart." Both Aros and I looked toward Arthur, who looked between both of us, shock drawn across his face.

"What, me?"

"It makes sense. If you are to lead the mission and marry Allanora in the end anyway, a position of power would suit you well, prepare you for your new position as King," I coaxed him. He drew his lips together into a line but nodded, fully realizing the extent of what it had meant to ask for Allanora's hand. He looked down at his feet almost sadly.

"My sister thought she was to be Queen; she was so excited. I didn't think about what it would mean for her when I went after Julian," he said quietly. He laced his fingers together in resolve. "It doesn't matter. She will see what I did in the end is best for her. Your brother is a monster, as is your father. She deserves better." He nodded to himself.

"Arthur, you have two days to organize the troops of the Lynnean Army. During that time, you will carefully choose your men for your mission, no more than ten. You'll need finesse, not numbers, to carry this part out quickly. While you're gone, appoint someone to lead the army to the gates of Astinia in case it comes to a full battle, and I will ride with whoever you appoint." Aros' fingers twisted around themselves as he spoke. His words were cold, and he seemed to be holding back, his focused eyes completely inhuman as he stared down at the broken table before him. His powerful presence was unnerving.

"My King," I interrupted quietly, "if you'll ride with the army, who is to be here, sitting the throne and tending to the kingdom while you bring back the Queen?" They both looked at me with shocked expressions on their faces.

"Why, you, Henrie," Aros said, irritation laced his tongue.

"Me?" I couldn't hide the surprise on my face. I was a bookkeeper, a writer... Certainly not King Regent.

"Of course, Henrie. I trusted you to keep an eye on my daughter, and I trusted you to keep my secret and keep me informed. I now trust you to maintain the kingdom while I bring her back."

"I'm not a leader, Your Majesty. I'm a reader, a scholar... I'm a librarian, for God— uh—goodness sake." I stumbled over my words, wary of enraging him further. He was unphased, so I continued. "My father... My brother, they were leaders, not me," I pleaded.

"That's exactly why I chose you from the very beginning. I knew I could trust someone who wouldn't want to overthrow Violet, who would look out for Allanora's best interests. Someone who holds his wife over money or power. I can feel it from you, Henrie; you're not selfish, and you're not ambitious. You only need to stand in for me for a few days. Then Allanora will reclaim her seat, as she was always meant to, and you can go back to your beloved books." His words were concrete, final. They hung in the air between us. I knew there was no arguing with him, so I only nodded.

Chapter 16

Henrie

I hadn't slept at all, knowing both my father and brother were due to be executed in the morning, and very soon, Arthur would be setting off with his small band of warriors to carry out their mission. It would be a trying day for the kingdom of Lynnea. There hadn't been many public executions during the reign of Queen Violet. She had been a forgiving Queen, sparing the sword as often as she could. Though, no one had gone as far as treason in a very long time. The thickness of betrayal hung in the air and settled throughout the castle. I went for a walk down the hallway so my constant tossing and turning would not bother Eleanore. I encountered Aros on my way to the library, speaking quietly with Arthur, who quickly bowed and left him when I approached. Aros approached me with open arms, pulling me in for an awkward hug. I furrowed my brows when he released me, looking at him confused.

"I'm sure this must be hard for you today, knowing that I must execute your father and brother. I'm sorry that it has come to this. It's hard to separate yourself from family sometimes," he said to me coolly. I noticed a longsword strapped to his hip that he didn't have yesterday. I couldn't see the blade, but the hilt was magnificent. It looked to be pure gold inset with endless jewels. I could tell it was old, but it was meticulously maintained; each jewel seemed to have been individually polished. An incredible instrument for such a dark purpose. "You can go see them, you know. There are a few hours before the execution is scheduled. I wouldn't deny you your right to say goodbye." His words were heavy in his mouth, but he was being sincere.

"I wouldn't know what to say. I knew my brother was a dark and cruel man, and I knew my father had his own edge to him, a chip on his shoulder since the death of my mother. I just never imagined that he would be capable of something like this. He never seemed to have anything but love and respect for Violet and Allanora. I always thought he saw her as a daughter—" I snapped my mouth shut quickly. It was obvious that Aros was biting back frustration at the thought of this other man—this betrayer—being remotely fatherly to his only daughter. "I guess it wouldn't hurt to say goodbye," I said quietly before I turned and headed in the direction of the tower where prisoners were kept. It was a long walk there, and as I got closer, the castle got emptier. There were never very many prisoners in the tower, so maintaining that part of the castle was not much of a priority for the servants. The stairs were stone, like the ones to the raven's tower, but they were hardly worn, almost new, despite being hundreds of years old. I counted the steps to the top as I went, keeping my mind from thinking too much about what I would say to my father when I got to the top. *Two hundred twenty-three, two hundred twenty-four, two hundred twenty-five*, and the steps plateaued off to the landing. There they were: the prisoners' cells. I had expected the corridor to be quiet, but I could hear distinct voices. *Someone else has come to see the treasonous monsters on execution day, how kind of them,* I thought sarcastically. As I got closer to the cell where the voices were coming from, I realized it was not speaking I was hearing; it was moaning, the amorous shrieks of a woman mid-pleasure. I rolled my eyes, approaching slowly. Each of the cells had a small window at the top of the door. There were enough bars that not even a hand could fit through; it was more of a way to keep an eye on any prisoners who were a flight risk without needing to open the door. I peeked into the cell from which I thought the noise was coming. The door was locked from the outside, but I looked through the small opening and saw Brysa completely naked and straddled on top of my brother, who was slumped back in ecstasy on the prison mattress with one hand on her waist and the other kneading her breast. I shook my head, turning away and looking around for a guard, but I saw no one. I moved to the side so I wouldn't be seen and rapped on the door. Brysa gasped, and my brother muttered something under his breath before the squeals continued. I sighed. *Disgusting, he's disgusting, he's always been disgusting.* Finally, an out-of-breath guard tumbled from one of the open doors; a small servant girl, about sixteen, scrawled out after him and darted down the stairs after glancing at me. The guard looked at me and gasped, straightening himself and nodding to me.

"The girl just, uh, she just wanted to see 'im before they'd be takin' off 'is head." The words rolled awkwardly off his tongue. "I locked 'em in there before takin' me...break," he stuttered. I just rolled my eyes.

"I'm not interested in my brother's extracurricular activities, nor yours, for that matter," I said shortly, glancing once more time at the door and shaking my head in disappointment. "Check him and the room before you let her leave, make sure she didn't bring him any weapons or anything else suspicious." The guard nodded hurriedly. "Show me where my father's cell is." The guard scurried off a couple of doors down and rapped on the door to his left. He ducked away quickly, and my father's face appeared at the window. *Great guard,* I thought, *afraid of a locked-up prisoner.* He opened the door slowly and let me in before locking it behind me, shifting to the side to wait. My father's room was quiet, as I had expected, with no sultry handmaids to keep him company. He had a mattress similar to my brother's cell, but he also had a small desk. He stayed seated in the desk chair and lifted an eyebrow at me.

"Why'd you do it? How could you do it? How *did* you do it?" I asked him. My questions were repetitive; I knew they only needed to be answered once, but I couldn't help myself. We hadn't been close as father and son, but I had always looked up to him. I had considered him a virtuous man who thought of the betterment of the kingdom and would never resort to killing just to give himself power. He half-smiled at me, the same malicious face he had made once when he had first taken a seat on Violet's throne. I had thought he had been drunk with unexpected power, but in fact, he was just enjoying the fruits of his schemes, poisoning the virtuous vines of Lynnea along with him.

"I don't have to explain myself to you, boy." He wasn't even looking me in the eyes; he was focused on something underneath his fingernail, paying more attention to getting it out than the presence of his son.

I didn't know why, but his nonchalance and calling me 'boy' had made my blood boil. "It's funny, Father—you've been looking out for yourself and Julian all this time, including him in your plans, your schemes... You've never included me in anything."

"You wanted to be privy to the murder of the Queens?" He smiled menacingly down at his fingers; he knew the answer to his own question.

"Of course not!" I was seething, shaking with anger.

"Then why do you care so much?" He taunted me with his tone, and he knew it, too.

"It was always you and Julian or you and Allanora. Your whole life revolved around your oldest son, your pretend daughter, and your beloved Queen. You barely even showed your face at my wedding to Eleanore, all because you were too busy doting on Violet and Allanora. I just don't understand why you wanted to have them killed. They were your life. I thought you loved them." He scoffed, finally meeting my eyes. His gaze burned me, the window to his soul flickering with hatred and disdain without even a hint of regret.

He slammed his fist on the little desk. "I never wanted to settle for being the Queen's advisor, son," he hissed at me. He stood from his chair and strode over to me, malice his only emotion, with his hands pressed behind his back. "I had proposed to Queen Cressida all those years ago at her choosing ball. She didn't accept me. I married your mother a while after and finally had your brother after years of no children." He looked distantly out the window. Speaking of my mother had allowed a flicker of humanity back into his expression. "In fact, I had it all laid out when Violet was younger. She was to be assassinated on the road by the Astinian soldier that I 'protected' her from. It was unsuccessful, and I had to kill him to keep my cover. After that, it became a waiting game. Julian was too young for me to present him to Violet, but I had thought of marrying you to Allanora when she came of age. But then you had other plans, didn't you." I tensed at the mention of my wife and felt my teeth biting into my cheek; the taste of blood settled on my tongue.

"Sorry to ruin your power grab with my love match," I hissed at him.

He continued, ignoring my discomfort, "I settled for offering Julian to Allanora in a conversation with Violet. Allanora refused. Violet was never interested in the idea, anyway. Everyone knows how Julian is. Listen to him over there. A bloodthirsty whore, that one is." He rubbed his eyes with his fingers, still frustrated. "I've spent my whole life trying to better our family. I tried the diplomatic way of befriending the crown, thinking we could marry our way up. But the truth is, they always looked down on us." He kicked the small desk, and it clattered on the ground. The guard peeked through the window, but I waved him off.

"Allanora doesn't look down on us, and she treated you like a father. You were presented in court along with them both. Everyone in Lynnea knows who you are. You were the head of the army. You commanded respect because, even though you weren't from one of the Great Houses, you had the ear and respect of the Queen. Three Queens, Father. Three Queens you had the ear of. They listened to and trusted you. You're a hateful man for spurning their respect this way. How will our house look now? I'll be lucky if my family can stay here in the castle after this." I couldn't help my sour tone. He and Julian may have been executed that day, but I would have to live on with their black mark on my life and my family forever. "You're a coward. You're a coward and an imbecile for thinking you could ever pull this off without consequences." The words left my mouth before I could even think about what I was saying. He lunged toward me and slapped me across the cheek, the sting and shock of it searing my skin like a brand. It was a feeling I had grown accustomed to as the younger and lesser son of Tobyn Hawkham, but it still somehow always hurt.

He shoved his finger in my face as I rubbed my cheek in shock. "I had Astinia backing me at first when I planned the attack with the soldier all those years ago; Violet had snubbed King Rhonan's younger brother, so they were thirsty for her blood as it was. When that failed, they abandoned me. It looks like they have their own plans now. I knew that, with Allanora coming of age and refusing Julian, she would choose someone from another noble family to be her husband. Their family would advise her, and I'd be cut out entirely. So, I hired assassins. One for Violet and one for Allanora. I knew it had to be public, and I knew I had to be present to absolve myself from blame. That bitch Steele screwed me. Her golden boy, her 'God-killer,' couldn't even hit her heart." He dropped his head in his hands, his body shaking with rage.

He had laid everything out for me, and I still couldn't feel sympathy for him. Everything he had done had been selfish. I couldn't absolve him of that guilt. I turned silently from him and headed for the door. The truth was all the closure it seemed I would get. Silence hung in the air as I left him to his own guilt, to be executed for his crimes against the crown. I rapped angrily on my brother's door. The horrendous gasps and grunts stopped abruptly. I opened my mouth to say something to my brother, but nothing came to mind. So, I just left, feeling unsatisfied. Feeling like I shouldn't have come in the first place. I returned quietly to my bedroom, where Eleanore was sitting up on our bed, taking breakfast. I said nothing but sat down next to her, burying my face in the crook of her neck and drinking her in. She was my safety, my solace, my family. She leaned her head on mine. She knew what she was to me; nothing needed to be said.

"Sometimes I really hate them," I groaned.

She took my face in her delicate hands, and our eyes met. "Henrie Hawkham, you are the most noble, most intelligent, kind, and handsome man to have ever set foot in Cidris." Her words thawed the ice that my father had placed on my heart. "There will never be another man like you, and you are everything to me, your children, your actual family. Forget those treasonous bastards." She slid a hand over my chest, unbuttoned my shirt, and slid it off. Leaning me back on the bed, she slipped her dress over her head and let me drink in her beauty, her perfection. I took the rest of my clothes off and let my hands wander over her, periodically letting them fall on her pregnant belly.

I spent the next two hours kissing her, holding her, burying myself in her, and letting myself forget about what this day meant for my family. And I knew as we were entwined, and I didn't know where she began and I ended, that there was no way that my brother would've ever understood love with how he treated his partners. And here I was, surrounded by it. I would not let myself cry for my treasonous father and brother; all I would let myself care about were my wife, my children, and my Queen. When we finally resolved that we must get ready, we got dressed in silence. She knew I didn't want to talk about any of it.

"We don't have to go, you know," she finally said. "We could make an excuse." Her voice was soft and sweet. I hesitated for a moment, letting her words wash through my mind.

"Yes, we do. If we don't go, the people will think I sympathize with them, and I don't. What they did was wrong, and they deserve the punishment they're being given." She nodded quietly, and I put my hands on her shoulders to comfort her. She was shaking just slightly under my touch. I put my hand under her chin and tipped her head up, her watery eyes locking with mine.

"I never liked your father." She sobbed softly. "And I definitely never liked your brother. I just know how lonely it can be when your parents are gone." She let herself breathe and wiped her tears away quickly. I swept a tear that she had missed from under her eyelid, studying her perfect face. She smiled softly.

"We should go. We shouldn't just be walking in when the heads roll," I joked. She tried to force a laugh; she was obviously nervous. We made our way through the gardens in silence and out to a gathering area where executions had been held, on the rare occasion they were held, that is. There were two chopping blocks that had been dragged up the steps. They had marks and divots in them, but not as many as would have been expected from an executioner's block. I had hoped that there would be few in our future as well. Dread hung in the air as more people gathered to witness the event. Out of the corner of my eye, I saw Brysa sobbing into the shoulder of the other servant girl I had seen that morning, the one that had been entertaining the guard. She was making quite a spectacle of herself, drawing the attention of many others around her. I glared at her but then noticed my brother and father being led out to the blocks and turned my attention to them. When I saw them, my heart clenched.

My brother looked emotional; I wasn't sure if it was anger, disdain, fear, sadness, or some mixture of them all. My father, on the other hand, looked like stone, his face fearsome and cruel, even in his last moments. They were led to their blocks, each kneeling beside them. Aros appeared almost out of nowhere behind them, clutching his glittering deadly sword. He was poised, and his expression was dangerous, like that of a cat about to feast on its prey. He had seemed almost human to me before, except for the sparks, of course. Today, I couldn't see anything human about him. He radiated power; it thrummed through the once-empty air around us. His expression was dark, and his eyes shone gold in the light. The calculated and cold anger on his face was chilling. Silence swept through the crowd of people.

My brother was prepared first. He was laid neatly over the block as words were read to him from the book of the New Religion, preparing him for death. Aros winced when he heard the sacrilegious words. The New Religion had replaced the old, of which he was a patron God. There had been much discomfort amongst the Triini leaders since his arrival, but he had made it clear he wouldn't be staying once Allanora was returned to her throne. The Triini were a strange, cold, and even a little disconcerting group, but even they could not deny a father the chance to save his daughter, especially when restoring Allanora meant peace in the kingdom again.

Julian was asked if he had any final words to say, and he shook his head slightly. The man reading nodded slowly and backed away to make room for Aros, who intended to execute them himself. It was an odd practice for Lynnea, as we had always been ruled by Queens, none of whom carried out their own executions. There had always been an executioner on retainer, though his services were rarely needed. Aros had resolved to carry the sentence out for the death of his wife himself to show his true power to the people, and to show that he was a just King who knew what it meant to hold someone's life in his hands. It was a beautiful and dark sentiment for him to hold.

I held my breath; Aros had taken another step toward Julian. My ears were ringing so much I couldn't hear the words. He was undoubtedly listing his crime and sentence. Finally, he raised the sword over his head and brought it down—one smooth swing—and my brother's head rolled. A clean cut. No one moved. No one made a sound except for Brysa; her shrill scream cut through the silence like a knife. Julian's body slumped and fell to the side. A couple of men quickly busied themselves, moving him to a box in which he'd be buried. Aros was not so cruel as to deny them Lynnean burial rites, and Lynnea still allowed prisoners to have final rites as anyone else did. There was nothing barbaric in the way we viewed death, even for criminals.

Once my brother's body was cleared away, Aros stepped toward my father. I saw Aros' jaw clench as he maintained his composure in front of the man who'd plotted his wife and daughter's deaths. For a being who had immeasurable power, he had a significant amount of restraint, too. His knuckles were white around the hilt of his sword. He handed it to one of the men to wipe clean, preparing it for fresh blood. He stared at my father with such disdain I thought my father's head might just explode under his gaze. I felt my wife clutch my chest and turn her head into my shoulder. My son, Lysan, appeared next to me, folding himself in my robes. I curled my arm protectively around my boy and returned my eyes to the scene unfolding before us. Aros sentenced Tobyn, and as the sword was returned to his outstretched hand, he put it over my father's head. He paused then, thoughtfully, as if he had more to say. But I saw his knuckles turn white again when he brought the sword down with all his might, and with another clean cut, he took my father's life. What was left of the light in his eyes went cold, his body slumping just as my brothers had. My wife sobbed into my shoulder with the pure shock of it, and my son held his hand over his one exposed eye. I felt oddly numb, removing any emotion from what was happening before me, resolving myself to know that justice had been served to those who had done wrong. The feelings I would've had were locked beneath the knowledge that they'd committed treason. I pursed my lips and willed myself to keep my hardened expression as my father's body was dragged to its own box. I let out my breath, knowing it was finally over and there was no going back.

The crowd had remained quiet, taking in the sheer power of their new King. Many had looked over at me to see my reaction, to see if I was going to lash out or do something irrational. I hadn't, I wouldn't. Aros handed his sword to be cleaned once more, and he turned to address the crowd, a more human-like expression on his face.

"Justice has been done today, justice for the death of your beloved Queen, Violet, the love of my life." He hung his head just slightly before raising it again. "Tomorrow, some of our best will be departing on a special mission to recover Queen Allanora, led by the new General of your army, Arthur Blackwood." He held his hand out to where Arthur had been standing, and a small applause broke out as he was acknowledged. House Blackwood was well-loved. "Queen Allanora is being held hostage at the castle of Astinia. This small force will try to handle the situation diplomatically with the King of Astinia. In the case that this is not enough, our army, accompanied by me, will march on Astinia and reclaim our Queen. Please send your hearts on with our men, and hope that we can bring her back safely, with minimal bloodshed. In my absence, Henrie, loyal to the crown even through his family's execution, will sit in my place until I have returned with Allanora." He bowed low to the people, showing them a sign of respect, and left the square, leaving them murmuring in approval as he stepped away. Some looked at me, sizing me up, seeing if there was any inkling of alignment with my father or brother. I looked on, holding my head high and not giving in to any speculation. I wouldn't allow for any leeway that would tarnish my wife or children.

Slowly, Brysa approached me, wiping hot tears from her eyes and shaking violently, traumatized from the scene that had unfolded just moments ago.

"He wasn't as bad as everyone thinks, you know. He loved me, and I loved him." Her voice was small and mousy. I didn't want to ruin the moment, but I knew that my brother had no love for this poor girl.

"Love of one doesn't absolve crimes against another." I shut her down, my voice cold and unfeeling. I wouldn't allow myself to feel sympathy for my brother's little play toy; she'd move on soon enough, as she would've had to when he would have married anyway.

"We were going to be together forever." I rolled my eyes, and she skittered off, sobbing, her skirts billowing around in the wind. As I watched her leave, Aros appeared behind me, and I turned.

I shuddered at the sheer size of him and the power that emanated from his being. "How did you know? I mean, how did you know what they did?" I asked him quietly.

The crowd had mostly dispersed, leaving us and a few others. My wife had reluctantly peeled herself from my shoulder and whisked Lysan back toward the castle.

"As a Deity, I was able to know everything going on in the kingdom I was patron of, the kingdom of Vreca. I was able to hear all their thoughts and see everything that went on. When I married Violet, I tied myself instead to Lynnea. When I left, it would have been unbearable to be able to hear everything going on in my wife's and daughter's minds and not be there to help them, celebrate with them, be with them. I resolved to bind the power that was tying me to all of Lynnea when the rest of the Deities and I went into hiding. I only allowed myself the knowledge of whether

Allanora was alive. The others cut ties completely. When I received your message, I broke the bind that had cut off my ties to Lynnea, allowing the return of information to my mind. I saw it all. I knew what he'd done, and I came for him." He shrugged. I knew in that moment that I truly knew almost nothing about this man, but he had put his trust in me, his wife and daughter's kingdom in my hands. I nodded slowly and made my way, alone, to return to my wife and the family I had left.

Chapter 17

Allanora

My head was spinning, and bile gathered in my stomach. I couldn't tell if I was lying down or standing up, and I could feel nothing around me. I tried to open my eyes, but letting even a small amount of light in brought only blinding pain, so I squeezed them shut. My heart was pounding quicker than I had ever felt before. When it finally slowed and I started to feel again, I recognized the soft wood of a table beneath me. A cold shiver spread from the top of my head all the way down to my toes, and I slowly peeked out from under one eyelid, allowing just a little light in. My brain objected but not as strongly as before; I allowed my eyes to open fully, slowly.

I adjusted, took in my surroundings, but I didn't recognize the room I was in. My neck wouldn't budge when I tried to swivel to see more. What I could see of the room was full of what looked like medical equipment, potions, and lots of vials of things I couldn't name. I took another calculated look around with my eyes, and my gaze flashed to a still figure in the corner, watching me with predatory cat eyes. Squinting, I realized it was a woman. She had dark hair and a thin figure and was dressed in loose black clothing. It hit me quickly. *The Queen of Astinia.* As the realization inevitably spread across my face, I tried to sit up and address her, but I couldn't. Confused, I looked down at myself; I wasn't restrained, but I couldn't lift myself. I looked back at her with questions in my eyes.

"It seems you had some sort of panic attack in the gardens, my dear," she hissed at me. "Rowan brought you to the castle healers. He was so sweet, carrying you in here like that. I think if it had been either of my other two, they probably would have watched you seize." She sighed, glossing over the severity of what she just said as if it were a completely normal thing for them to enjoy. "Of course, the healers got you fixed up right away. I just figured I would take the opportunity to take a closer look at that exceptional blood of yours." She smiled a mawkish smile while she waved her hand over my body. I held my breath as if breathing was going to provoke her in some way. We hadn't spoken much, but she had been a mysterious and intimidating figure to be face-to-face with in our few meetings. I kept my lips pursed into a line. "It's curious, such an exceptional magical signature you have, yet your power seems almost completely untapped. Almost dormant, like a fiery volcano lying in wait for the right moment to just—let go." Her eyes lit up with fierce interest, and she brought her hands over my face. Over my head, endless webs of spinning gold twinkled in the bright light of the room. I watched with interest as she studied them. She squinted, eyes glazed, lost in the curiosity before her. "Your power is connected to his, connected to him. Your magical signatures are nearly identical, save for the human factors. Normally, I'd say that these parts wouldn't allow you the immortality that a Deity is blessed with, yet somehow, you don't seem to be killable." It was as if she was talking to the web, but I knew she was talking to me. All I could do was lie there in astonishment and confusion. I had never known I had a magical signature or any power. There weren't many in Lynnea that had magic; it was rarely even talked about. Brother Sol kept a tight cap on magic in Lynnea.

"My power is connected to whose?" I asked her slowly. Her eyes flicked down toward me, but she ignored my question, focusing harder on the golden threads spinning before her. She seemed to be looking for something. "What exactly are you doing?" She flicked her eyes toward me again and sighed.

"You're betrothed to my son. I'd like to know exactly what he will be getting into, what kind of grandchildren you'll be bringing forth." I snorted. It was funny to think that *I* was the concern in the marriage. Her eyes darted to me, a slight flash of anger as if she could read my mind.

"How are you even doing that?" I asked, trying my hardest to avoid her flaming gaze.

"Your magic surrounds you. It's always there, I just made it visible so I can study it," she said quietly, refocusing her eyes on another part of the golden web.

"What are you?" I asked her quietly. She smiled at that, bright and menacing shook hands like old friends on the corners of her lips.

"I'm a witch, my dear. And a shapeshifter, of course, as I already told you. I spent years studying the magical arts. There isn't much for a Queen to do around here except attend executions, events, and bear children. So, I studied. I occupied my time learning something that would give me power of my own right." Her smile faded, and she almost looked sad, lost momentarily in a memory. Her eyes flicked to me again. "Your magical signature is connected to your father's, of course. Where do you think you got your magic from?"

"I didn't even know I had magic until you all told me," I said defensively. "Are you saying my father had magic?"

She looked at me through narrowed eyes. "You really don't know, do you?"

I shook my head slowly. She made the web around me disappear and lifted whatever magic had been holding me to the table. I sat up straight, letting my body shift back into place.

"Your Father is a Deity. One of the twelve patron Gods of our world, of the Old Religion that is." Her face was grave. There was an unknown fear laced between her words. *She is afraid of me,* I realized.

"He was a *what?*" My world started to rattle around me. I had never known my father, and I had never imagined he was anyone important. He had left me and my mother. That had been the only thing that mattered; I was the unwanted daughter of an abdicated King, that's what they always said about me. Never in my wildest dreams would I have thought he was a God.

"A Deity of the Old Religion, before the fall, before the war. You really don't know anything, do you?" She said it as if she were disgusted. As if I was pathetic. All I could do was shake my head. "Your magic is of one of the oldest existing bloodlines. Your magic, while being an almost identical signature to your father's, runs through the core of this world, through the very veins of the twelve kingdoms. All magic is connected to the world around us, and that makes yours, well, special." Her eyes were wide with fascination, or perhaps it was fear. I couldn't tell. She heard footsteps outside the door and immediately went to leave the room, retreating to the shadows.

"Wait, please!" I called after her, but she had already disappeared, and I was alone. My whole world had come crashing down around me. Everything I thought I knew, everyone I thought I knew... It was all a lie, or at least not the whole truth. Even my mother had hidden the truth from me. Not just about my father but also the truth about myself. It all made me so angry I didn't even know how to contain it. I threw myself off the table furiously and stalked out of the healer's room, slamming the door behind me. I turned the corner in hopes that I would be able to find my bedroom and ran right into Rylan, whose solid, unwavering form sent me flying backward. He quietly offered me his hand to help me up. I warmed at the thought, but I refused, pulling myself up and dusting myself off. In complete silence, he turned to walk in the other direction.

"You knew, too, didn't you?" I saw him cringe; his shoulders tensed, and he slowly turned back toward me.

"Knew what, Princess?" he hissed at me. He edged closer to me, and his green eyes narrowed to dark slits as they locked in on mine.

"Don't play dumb with me. You knew who my father was, didn't you, *God-killer.*" I spat at him. He was seething through his teeth; his nostrils flared out wide. I didn't care. I needed someone to be angry at, and I had more reasons to lash out at him than anyone else.

"Of course I knew!" he shouted. "I used a special arrow for you and everything. You shouldn't have survived. But you just—" He cut himself off.

"I don't have to explain myself to you." He turned to leave again, but I caught him by his arm and pulled him back; I wasn't done. He spun back and forced me away with his palm, the blow so strong that I hit the wall behind me, sending a shot of pain through my spine. He balled his fists and stepped back, opening his mouth to say more to me, when Raysh appeared from around the corner. My skin prickled, and my stomach tied itself in a sickly knot as he drew closer, eyes locked on me, occasionally darting toward Rylan. I felt the familiar yet thoroughly unwanted rough hand grasp my forearm. Rylan glared at his older brother through still-gritted teeth. Raysh's fingertips dug into my arm, and I bit my tongue, trying to stay aware of myself to keep from flinching.

"Have I interrupted something, brother?" His sneer was audible, almost a hiss toward Rylan. Rylan returned his glare with a snarl of his own. I was trapped in a cage with a bear and a wolf, and I was a mouse. I looked between the two of them.

"Well, either way, I would think you'd be happy for me to take this problematic Princess out of your hair," Raysh continued to taunt. He faced me toward him, and his hand crept up my spine. Chills seized my bones. It made its way to my hair, and his fingers twisted themselves into my long locks, tugging downward just slightly. Fear gripped me, an icy cold hand holding me frozen in place.

"I'm not interested in *her*," Rylan said coldly, looking me up and down with derision. "I just hate *you*."

Raysh's face drew into a suspicious smile as he took a step back from me and faced his brother again.

"You wound me, baby brother," he said sarcastically, his absurdly large hand curled over his chest. He released my hair and shoved me out in front of him down the hallway. I planted my feet when he tried to walk me forward. He didn't flinch and just took a step in front of me, not letting my arm out of his iron grip. I couldn't keep my feet rooted when he pulled me forward. We left Rylan behind us, seething. Although I wasn't sure if he was upset about me or his brother, I didn't have the mind or space to worry about it. Raysh shuffled me along down the hallway. Once again, I was almost running to keep up with his pace.

"Could you just slow down a little while you're dragging me?" I pleaded, pawing at his hand with my own, trying to loosen his grip. He looked down at me indignantly but slowed his pace slightly. The tattoos on his arm seemed to ripple as he flexed his muscles, not giving me an ounce of relief from his grasp.

"What were you doing in the hallway with him?" he growled at me, his dark eyes peering into mine. I scrunched up my nose defiantly.

"First of all, he literally ran into me in the hallway. It was an accident. Second, I don't think you get to dictate—" He rounded on me and wrenched my wrist, twisted it behind my back, and came face to face with me. His hot breath steamed my cheeks, his black eyes burning into my soul.

"You're in *my* castle, Princess, you're *my* betrothed. Anything having to do with you in this castle is dictated by me. I know in that sweet little candy-coated kingdom you've been nestled in all your life, no one ever told you what to do, but hear me because I will only say this once more. You're mine now." His hold on me was so tight I thought my arm might snap or crumble beneath his grasp. I averted my eyes and turned my face to the side, but he grabbed my chin with his other hand, forcing me to look at him. My breath caught in my throat, and terror rose in me, knowing that this was the life I was resigned to, married to this monster who would spend all his time making sure I stayed well under his foot. I thought of what the Queen had said about being a figurehead, paraded around for events and bearing children for the King. I thought of the sadness in her face and how maybe she felt trapped as well.

"Tell me you understand," he fumed. I felt a tear burn my eye, but I refused to let it fall; I refused to give myself away like that. I bit the inside of my cheek.

"I—understand," I choked out. His snarl melted into a devious smile.

"Good girl," he said quietly. He leaned down and kissed my neck with feverish desire, his lips burning a brand into my skin. Using my own arm against me, he pulled my hips into his, one of his legs forced between mine. I heard footsteps approaching, and I squirmed, but he kept me pinned and removed his lips from my neck. I let out a relieved breath when I saw Rowan had approached. He bowed uncomfortably; Raysh reluctantly turned his harsh smile toward his middle sibling.

"Do you need something, brother?" he murmured before miming a bite at me with his mouth.

"I just... I was showing Her Highness the grounds when she fell unconscious. When I went to the healer to see how she was doing, she was gone. I just wanted to make sure she was alright. I knew what you would do to me if something happened to her on my watch." He looked as if he was struggling to breathe. He was terrified of Raysh. They all were. Rowan seemed a completely different person than the one I had met at the riverbank. His lizard-like tail flicked uncomfortably back and forth behind him.

"She's fine," Raysh spat shortly. "Anything else?" Rowan's eyes drifted quickly to me. I pleaded to him with my own eyes for the split second they were locked on mine. He snapped back to attention on his brother.

"I—um—" he stuttered. Raysh shot him a glare that could've killed him on the spot. "Uh—no—" He quickly bowed again and took off in the other direction. I let my breath out in frustration.

Raysh returned his attention back to me, released my wrist, and squeezed my hip. I used my now free hands to push him back by the shoulder. His mouth curled into a frown, and his nostrils flared out, similar to how Rylan's nostrils had flared during our altercation in the hallway. Besides being tall and having that dark handsomeness about him, it was the only physical similarity I could see between the two.

He wrenched my hands down to my sides, pinning them there. He pushed me in front of him and guided me forward, locking my hands where they were. I tried to dig my heels in the ground, but he was significantly stronger than I was; something I intended to work on. We reached my room, and the guard hurriedly opened the door for us to shuffle through, and it clicked shut behind us. He picked me up quickly and tossed me on my bed. I whimpered a little when I hit the mattress and scrambled backward toward the headboard, curling my knees up to my chest.

"You're mine," he growled.

"Please, I don't want to." My head was shaking violently, and the room around me started to quake. "I always wanted my wedding night to be special. Don't you want to wait?" I begged. He ignored me. Instead, he pried my legs from my chest and flattened me on the bed with the crushing weight of his own body. He smelled like sweat. His eyes burned with desire. Forcefully, he pressed his lips on mine and then ripped my dress down from the sleeve, tearing the delicate fabric. I felt his rough and calloused hands all over me. His lips bit at my flesh like I was some sort of chew toy. I sobbed beneath him, willing myself to disappear, to be anywhere but here, but he didn't care. He pawed at my dress again, and it ripped further, exposing my breast. His hand went to my mouth and covered it, and he bent his head down, letting his tongue roam the exposed skin of my chest. No sound escaped my mouth as I tried to squeal, salty tears welling up in my eyes.

Suddenly, mercifully, the door behind him opened; it was Rylan. He walked in with his head down and started talking.

"Look, Allanora, I—" He stopped abruptly as he looked up and realized what was happening. Anger flashed behind his eyes, but he kept composed, drawing himself up and folding his arms over his chest. Raysh ignored him at first. His lips were still locked on my breast, and his free hand roamed my midsection, then my leg, and he slid his hand up the hem of my dress. I thought I'd die pinned underneath the Crown Prince of Astinia, half-naked now, with his younger brother watching.

The hand covering my mouth finally shifted. I stifled a sob, and Rylan started to take a couple of steps toward us, eyes blazing. In that moment, I could almost see a golden halo around the head of my original captor.

"Rylan," I squeaked out. Raysh flung himself inhumanly fast out of the bed and approached his brother, grabbing at his throat. Rylan didn't even flinch. His eyes burned just as menacingly as his brothers, but he kept his composure and didn't show any weakness or give himself away.

I let out another sob and scrambled up into a sitting position, trying to cover myself with the shreds of my dress and the bed sheet. Quietly, I thanked the Unnamed God and any other God that may have existed for sending Rylan just in time. It was only a stay of execution. I knew that once my wedding was over, I wouldn't be able to avoid Raysh anymore.

"What are you doing here?" Raysh snorted at him. Rylan's face drew itself into a taunting smile.

"Did I interrupt your fun, brother? Need I remind you what Father told you?" Rylan sneered at him. Raysh pursed his lips together. "He said you weren't to treat her like one of your little playthings that you keep around here." My mouth dropped open just a little. *Disgusting pig.* "She holds the key to Lynnea, to a large boost of power for our family, our kingdom. He wants her well and intact. Nothing is to compromise her before you're married. Remember?" Rylan's smile widened. Flames danced in his emerald eyes, his face triumphant. Raysh looked annoyed. Rylan reached out and patted him lightly on the shoulder as his brother released him. "Go find one of your little playthings if you need something to stick that badly. You have one around every corner if I remember correctly." I made another face of disgust. What a stand-up man I was to marry. Raysh turned back to me. Rylan was still poised coolly, arms folded over his chest as if his brother wasn't just dangling him by the throat; he was completely unphased.

"Your wedding night is going to be special, all right," Raysh snarled at me. Icy terror flooded my whole body, an angry tidal wave of dread. The blood rushed from my face, and I immediately felt dizzy at the thought of him keeping his word. He walked out, almost as if he had forgotten Rylan was still there, and slammed the door angrily behind him. A small painting crashed to the floor when the door bit into the wall. I cringed and let myself collapse on the bed, sobbing, my face buried in my hands.

I felt a hand on my shoulder and jumped out of my skin; it was only Rylan. I relaxed slightly. At least he was the evil that I knew.

"Look, I—I heard something today that I thought you should know," he said softly. I lifted my head and looked at him in wonder. "The Lynnean King, the new one, he uh—he was sentenced to death for your mother's murder and your um—attempted murder." My eyes narrowed, and I studied him carefully.

"My *attempted* murder? They know I'm alive?" I asked hurriedly, thinking of Arthur. He shook his head.

"I don't know. The person who informed me knows who you are and that you're alive. So, they could have just put it that way for accuracy. I didn't ask any questions. I just thought you should know." He brushed my hair off my face gently; it had stuck to the tears that streamed down my cheeks.

Instinctively, I grabbed his shirt and started to wrap the fabric around my hands, pulling him closer, looking for any sort of comfort, familiarity. I didn't know why I did it. He pushed me away immediately, and the force made me hit the frame of my bed. The quick shift in the air between us stunned me.

"Don't be stupid, Princess," he said dryly as he left the room, slamming the door behind him. He was right; it was stupid. I was clinging to the only familiar thing here in this castle. I didn't even know if Lyra was still alive. They could have killed her without telling me; I wouldn't even know.

I grabbed a pillow from my bed and screamed into it. With my eyes closed tightly, I pictured her, probably still tied up and confused, and hoped they weren't hurting her. She was surely trembling, probably twisting her hair around her finger if her arms weren't chained to their sides. Tears streamed from my eyes, drawing wet lines down my face. Everything was out of control. Once the tears started again, I couldn't get them to stop. My chest began to shudder beneath my sobs, and my whole body followed suit. Outside, thunder rumbled low and deep, a solemn growl of a wolf who'd lost its pack, followed by the sound of heavy rain hitting the walls and roofs of the castle. I let out a shrieking sob, and a flash of lightning cracked outside my window, lighting up the walls of my room. I ignored the growing storm outside, gripping the pillow in front of me, and I screamed again, louder and without the buffer of the pillow. As I did, another bolt of lightning flashed, this time breaking my window and hitting the floor beside me. I flew across the bedroom out of fear. I had never seen a lightning bolt so close before. My body shook, and the scare snapped me out of my tears. I surveyed the room around me; much of the furniture had gone flying with the force of the lightning bolt. I looked around in confusion.

The door to my room swung open as if it had been kicked. I spun around and saw the new guard that was posted outside my door, followed by the Queen and my betrothed, Raysh. Raysh was wild-eyed. I couldn't tell if it was fear or anger, and the Queen looked less than astonished, looking around the floor as I had been, taking it all in. Raysh opened his mouth wide to speak, but the Queen held her hand out in front of his mouth. She stepped carefully toward me, watching me intently with her eyes. She turned her head back and forth, studying me, never allowing her eyes to leave me. I became aware of the storm outside; the pounding rain had become pitter-patter, the thunder choked by silence. The Queen approached me quietly, taking my face in her hand and turning me back and forth. She was peering into my soul, peeling back my layers one by one to see what was at my core. Her black eyes twitched into varying shapes; it seemed like it had been hours since she entered my room.

"Incredible," she said finally. I felt a release of pressure as she took her eyes away as if she'd had some sort of hold on me. I looked at her curiously, afraid to speak. "It seems that your unharnessed power, while dormant, has grown wild, like a dog that has grown into a wolf, an untamed wildfire." Her eyes glinted. "Your magic is, well, it's almost feral. Uncontrolled magic is very dangerous. You'll need to learn to control it." She said it simply, as if learning to control magic was the same as learning how to sweep a floor.

"I don't know how to control something I didn't even know I had." I cast my eyes onto the floor, feeling her burning gaze now on the top of my head. Raysh was shifting uncomfortably back and forth, the corners of his mouth twitching.

"You'll see Sinric. He's a mage that helped me to control my magic when I was a girl." Her voice softened, almost motherly sounding. I couldn't quite figure out if the Queen was kind, unlike her husband and sons, or if she just had more finesse to her cruelty. She was like a cat, and not even just her eyes. Everything about her was feline: the way she walked, the way her mouth curled, the way she watched me...

"I don't want her to spend all her time with some crackpot mage. She's mine. I have—plans for her," Raysh growled from behind her. She snapped her head back toward him, snarling and looking at him with disgust.

"Don't be foolish. Would you prefer your new bride disintegrate you with lightning during your wedding night, my darling boy?" Her voice dripped with derision. It was all I could do not to smile at the thought of him sizzling underneath the force of a lightning bolt. He cast his head down angrily, defeated. It hadn't occurred to me that I could possibly use my new power to get myself out of this situation. Perhaps spending some time with a mage to help me harness it would work out to my advantage. I looked down at the ground, at the scattered furniture and burn marks, and allowed myself the tiniest kernel of hope. Keeping Raysh at bay seemed to be proving exceptionally difficult. I eyed him up and down. He was vile, dripping poison from his very pores. I trembled at the thought of sitting on the throne next to him, laying in a bed next to him, underneath him, bearing his children... What kind of monsters would they be?

"Where can I find Sinric?" I asked meekly, shrinking myself back from Raysh as much as I could. The Queen opened her mouth to speak and was interrupted by a guard opening the door slowly.

"My apologies, Your Majesties. There's a messenger here. He's uh—" He gazed at me, unsure of what to say next. The Queen saw his hesitation, gestured for him to step out, and followed him. Raysh stepped toward me, caressed my cheek with his large and rough fingers, and sneered. I remembered where those rough fingers had been roaming not long ago and shook violently. Without saying anything more, he smirked and followed his mother out the door, closing it behind him. I could hear their muffled voices outside and down the hall, but couldn't make out what they were saying. I leaned back against my door and took in a heavy breath.

Chapter 18

Allanora

I stayed alone in my room for what felt like hours after they had left, trying to allow my mind to go blank. I changed out of the dress that Raysh had torn without the help of a handmaid. I didn't want to be touched by anyone else. I was unsure of the time, and I couldn't remember when I had last eaten. Feeling a hunger pang in my stomach, I resolved to walk the castle, looking for the kitchens in a hopeful search for food.

Easing my door open, I peered into the hallway. Only my guard was at the door. He nodded but said nothing as I left the room, making myself look like I knew where I was going. I wandered the halls, taking a couple of staircases downward, assuming the kitchen was lower down than my bedroom, which seemed to be nestled in the clouds. I saw a few servants along my way. None of them spoke, but they all bowed or curtsied as I passed. I asked one man where the kitchens were, and he pointed down another flight of stairs. I blew a piece of hair out of my face in frustration. The Astinian castle was huge and winding, and the smell of suffering hung in the air all around me. It was a scent I couldn't fully explain. I ran my hands along the stone walls; the wall was as cold as its décor.

The castle was dark and bleak. Everything was black and red, the colors of Astinia. The servants all wore black, and the tapestries were all red. My head started to hurt from the two stark colors that surrounded me. I longed for a nice blue, yellow, or purple. I looked down at the red dress I had slipped on. It was a simple, soft fabric that draped down to the ground. Soft, glittering rhinestones were sewn into the hem. I hated it. I had been given a whole wardrobe of gowns, nothing but red and black. I stopped at the top of the staircase the man had pointed to and considered my bleak surroundings, missing Lynnea terribly. Wishful thinking had me dreaming of Arthur, wondering if he and I would be getting married by now if I hadn't been abducted. With my eyes closed, I imagined his soft brown locks, his cerulean eyes, the way his smile was so warm and protective. I wondered if he would be gentle. He had to be. I couldn't imagine him being anything like Raysh.

My eyes snapped back open when I heard footsteps coming from the staircase, and I narrowed my gaze to see who it was. An unfortunately familiar face looked up at me.

"Ah, the little *Princess*," Gen sneered at me, meeting my eyes and sweeping her long blonde hair behind her back. My shoulders dropped, and I scowled. She was the last person I wanted to see right now. Maybe second to last, behind Raysh.

"Queen. Shouldn't you be busy tormenting my handmaid?" She smiled and took a bite out of the apple she had in her hand, making my stomach grumble in envy.

"Well, I think Raysh is responsible for that now," she said, her voice dripping with sarcasm. I wasn't sure what she meant by that, but I was so hungry that I didn't care. She tossed the apple up in the air and caught it a couple of times, keeping her eyes locked on mine. "I guess we are going to be sisters-in-law." She smiled a wicked smile. My blood ran cold, thinking of her getting married to Rylan and all of us living unhappily ever after together in this dreary castle. "Don't worry, I'm sure Raysh will keep you so busy, you'll hardly have time for the extended family anyway," she taunted. I felt my face flush with anger, and the hair on the back of my neck prickled.

"Rylan isn't going to marry you. And if I'm going to be Queen, I'm going to send you far away," I snapped back. I felt like a child, threatening to banish her. I loathed the Thorne family, but I truly hated Gen.

"He doesn't have a choice. His father has already made the arrangements with mine. I don't even know why you care. Per the law, we are supposed to wait for *your* wedding to be over anyway," she bristled, crossing her arms over her chest. I shrugged and pushed past her, remembering how hungry I had been before I encountered her. Normally, the sight of her would make me lose my appetite, but I was too famished to allow her to ruin that, too. I skipped a few steps to get away from her quickly, but I could feel her eyes burning through the back of my neck.

At the bottom of the steps, I finally found the kitchen. It was well-stocked and smelled wonderful. I started to look over the fresh fruits and warm bread. My eyes landed on a small block of cheese, which I picked up and put on a plate. I picked out a few fruits and a couple of rolls, adding them to my small plate. *I should've gotten a bigger plate.*

I snapped to attention when I heard dishes clatter and hit the floor. A gaping woman stood across from me, her eyes wide and a pile of mostly broken dishes now at her feet. She took in a sharp breath and curtsied low, almost to the floor.

"No, no, it's ok, I'm so sorry, I didn't mean to alarm you." I rushed in front of her and started picking up the dishes that had fallen. The woman knelt to help and started to tremble, her hands shaking so much she could barely hold them. I took them gently from her grasp and set them on the table. Leaning down, I helped her up and had her sit down in a chair nearby. She sat for a moment, then shot back up.

"Your Highness, I do apologize." I was shocked that she was speaking. Most of the servants I had encountered so far were mute. She bowed again, still visibly shaking.

"It's all right, dear. Please, sit." She shook her head violently.

"If anyone were to see me sitting in your presence..." She clutched her throat. I looked down the corridor to both sides, listening intently. I heard nothing.

"No one is around. Please, sit, I apologize." I led her back to the chair and offered her some water from a pitcher. She looked at me suspiciously, analyzing for a trap, but took the water from me.

"I wasn't expecting to see you here, Your Majesty." Her head dropped shamefully; I placed a hand on her shoulder.

"I should have rung for someone. I just thought I would explore the castle on my way here; I didn't mean to cause you any trouble. Is it all right if I take this food with me?" I gestured to my plate of things I had gathered. She nodded slightly. I took my plate and made my way to leave. As I reached the bottom of the stairs, I heard her speak again.

"Thank you for your kindness. Perhaps you might be exactly what Astinia needs." Her words dug into my chest. I had never considered anything except Lynnea. It didn't occur to me that the Astinians might have been craving a ruler with a softer hand. Sorrow bit into me as I took a final glance at her, pale as a ghost and terribly frightened. She was probably wondering if I was about to run to the royal family and sell her out. That's how things seemed to go around here. I sighed deeply and started up the steps, feeling even more down than I had been before I went to the kitchens.

I wound my way back through the halls and staircases until I reached the wing where my bedroom was nestled. Lost in thought, I opened the door that I thought was to my bedroom, oblivious to the fact my guard was not posted outside. The scene I came into made me drop my plate of food. Raysh was completely naked, with a woman pressed up against the wall. He had her held by the back of her head, and she was making pained sounds. My stomach filled with horror; I couldn't help but twist my face in disgust. My atrocious betrothed.

At the sound of the clatter, Raysh turned his head to look, his eyes wild. Before I could cover my eyes, the woman turned around, and I saw her face. Lyra. I screamed. Something in me finally snapped, and I made a mad dash for the door. Somehow, Raysh made his way over and yanked on my braid, knocking me backward onto the floor. I covered my face with my hands, convincing myself that it wasn't Lyra, that my mind had been playing tricks on me.

I stayed still, and the two started to shuffle around quietly. I peeked out from behind my fingers and saw Raysh towering over me in a loose robe, his face twisted in a terrifying scowl. Looking over, I saw Lyra on the bed, trembling and covering herself with a sheet. My mind hadn't been playing tricks on me. My fear turned to anger, and I scrambled up from the floor.

"What the hell?" I shouted, directing my anger at her. She shrunk backward on the bed, pulling the covers up over herself. The bruises on her face and shoulders were enough to make my blood boil. "Why were you doing that with him?" I shuddered, the scene replaying involuntarily in my head. She opened her mouth to speak, but he held his hand up to her, rounding on me. He brought his face right up to mine, holding himself over me so my surroundings were completely overwhelmed by him.

"What are you doing in here," he bellowed in my face. I winced slightly. My face was covered in little flecks of his saliva.

"I—thought this was my bedroom. Clearly, I was mistaken." I mustered up as much venom as I could into my voice, willing myself to be acid under his touch.

"Your bedroom is on the other side of this wing. You do not belong here," he shouted. I turned my attention back to Lyra, opening my mouth to speak again. He grabbed me by the neck, and instantly, I felt the oxygen leaving my lungs. Lyra screamed, and he held his hand out to silence her again. She stifled her sobs frantically. He started lifting me in the air, and I felt my toes leave the ground. I kicked as I dangled, clawing at his large hand with my nails. He was unphased and seemed almost entertained by my attempts. "Everyone in this castle belongs to me, Princess. *You, her,*" he pointed with his free hand to Lyra, who was now trembling violently, "*anybody I want.*" He pressed me back against the wall, gripping my neck tighter as I gasped desperately for air. "I like you like this. My helpless little Queen. I'll take you next."

The door flung open, and the King appeared. Raysh dropped me instantly. I fell to the ground in a heap, the oxygen urgently filling my lungs. Gasp after gasp, I forced myself to breathe, my neck inflamed from his touch.

Rhonan regarded his son murderously, silently digging into him with his eyes and looking like he was deciding on what way to kill him.

"I gave you a very clear, very simple order." His voice was quiet but chilling. "You were not to touch her, you were not to harm her, you were not to leave a MARK on her before your wedding day." He pointed at me, indicating the inevitable bruises that I was sure graced my delicate neck. "What part of my orders was not clear? Are you ignorant, or are you an imbecile? Apparently, my son, you need to be reminded exactly who is King." Raysh did not respond, but his face twitched repetitively, and his anger simmered just below the surface. Rhonan's attention turned to Lyra, who squeaked and backed herself off the bed, curtsying low and clutching the sheet to cover her naked, bruised body.

"Your Majesty, I—" He cut her off, his cold eyes looking her up and down. She bit her lip and backed into the corner of the room.

"Whoring yourself to a member of the royal family is against the law in Astinia." He scowled at her. "The punishment for this is—"

"Please—" I croaked, trying to bring myself up into a sitting position. "Don't harm her, I beg you." My breaths were coming in short, painful bursts, but I couldn't let him harm Lyra.

"You beg for mercy for this servant, this *whore*? You found her in the bed of your betrothed, and you're asking for her clemency?" He regarded me curiously. I pushed myself off the floor, standing straight as I felt waves of healing relief wash over me.

"I ask that you don't harm her. She disgraces your kingdom, please, send her home," I begged him. Raysh looked between me and the King in disbelief as Rhonan mulled over my words.

"All right, little Queen. As my son has gone against my word in my order not to harm you, I'll give you two choices." His dark smile returned to his face, and I gulped. "The little whore can go back to her chains, never to be released as long as she lives." I winced slightly, trying to keep my composure. "Or she can go back to Lynnea with no tongue. The choice is yours." I cast my eyes on Lyra, who had gone white as the sheet she clutched desperately to her chest. "I'll give you one hour to decide. If I don't hear from you, I'll go through with the original sentence," he said casually.

He gripped Raysh by the shoulder and shoved him out the door ahead of him. "Now, it's time to deal with you." Raysh scowled under his father's hand as he was pushed out of the door, which slammed behind them. As soon as the door closed, Lyra crumpled on the floor in tears. Hesitantly, I made my way over to her.

"Lyra, I don't understand," I whispered. A sob escaped her lips when she tried to speak.

"He—told me—he—was letting me—go—" she said between sobs. She took in a deep breath and tried to gather herself. "He brought me here, and he forced me to—to—" I put my hand over her mouth gently; I didn't need her to say it.

I whispered as if the very walls were listening, "Lyra, I don't have much of a choice here. Please tell me what you want. Neither of the choices is death, but if I try to let you escape, I know they will kill you," I said gravely to her. She nodded slowly. "I'm sorry for what he did to you."

"I've—been in here for days. Since the first day you were here. The only time I've left was when they brought me back down to the prison to show you that I was alive." She whimpered. "I don't want to go back to that prison. I don't want to be here for him to—" She shuddered, cutting herself off. "I just want to go home. He can cut out my tongue, please, just send me home." Her eyes were begging. I nodded, dropping my head a little bit. Even though I hadn't spent any actual time with Lyra while in the castle, I had been comforted by the fact she was here and thought maybe one day I'd be able to free her, and we could be together again, as we had been in Lynnea. It would be selfish of me to keep her here now, after what she had been through.

"I will speak to the King," I whispered to her, wrapping a blanket from the bed around her trembling shoulders. Her hand went to her throat, surely thinking of what that would mean for her. Her eyes welled up with tears, and she started to sob again. I left her there, knowing I had little time. I found my way through what seemed like endless hallways back to the King's study, where I found him towering over a kneeling Raysh with a leather whip in his hand. Raysh's back was bare, and he had fresh bleeding whip marks carved into his already scarred skin. I felt myself getting dizzy at the sight of all the blood, but I kept my composure and cleared my throat to alert them to my presence.

"Little Queen," Rhonan greeted me with his cold stare. "I imagine you are here to let me know your decision in regard to the fate of the whore."

"Please do not refer to her as a whore. Your son dragged her out of imprisonment and forced her into his bed. She's no more a whore than I am," I said sternly. He scoffed and flashed his wicked smile at me but said nothing in return. "I wish for my servant to be returned safely to Lynnea."

"As you wish, little Queen. She will return to Lynnea a mute. I can't have her telling any tales of what she has seen here. Or spreading any messages about you to anyone there. But know that I will also be sending someone along, someone that, with a single message from me, will kill her and anyone else you hold dear if you misstep here. Have I made myself very clear?" I nodded slowly. Looking down, I absently twirled the fabric of the glittering red dress around my fingers. "Red is a lovely color on you, my dear. I imagine you'd prefer to wear that for the wedding, as opposed to black, I mean." He was taunting me. I sighed and nodded. I was defeated, my soul crushed. Everything I had in the world was taken from me by this family, this family that I'd be marrying into very soon. I felt my happiness drain from me, my hope, my soul...leaving me a husk of whoever I had been, whoever I might have become. I bowed slowly, no longer allowing the sight of the scarlet blood pooling around Raysh to turn my stomach.

Chapter 19

Henrie

The castle buzzed about with hope. The shock and horror of my father and brother's execution passed quickly. It was as if a suffocating weight had been lifted off everyone's shoulders, and we were reunited with purpose and drive. For the first time since Queen Violet's death, the people were cheerful. Arthur was preparing his small group of men for their voyage to Astinia, each one of them prepared to go down in history as a hero who rescued the endangered Princess. It was a lovely sentiment, surely, though I couldn't help but worry that these men might not even survive stepping through the gates of Astinia. Aros had thought of everything we could offer to them in exchange for Allanora, and every tradeable good Lynnea had to spare was brought into the throne room, with bits of each loaded into a carriage to prove to the Astinian King that Aros' word was true and that his offer would be honored. Drawings of eligible women to be presented for marriage pacts were prepared, weapons were forged... Aros was willing to give anything to retrieve his daughter without bloodshed and war.

I busied myself skimming through some old texts in the library; I was meant to be researching the preferences of marriage pacts of Astinia, but my mind was elsewhere. I knew that Astinia would not easily be bought; house Thorne was an old house with three strong sons ready for the throne. They had little concern for marriage pacts that wouldn't involve merging with another kingdom. Our offer of goods wouldn't outweigh the value of our only Princess. Holding her kept our kingdom unstable, which was what Astinia would need in order to bring us down. Aros knew this; for every weapon he had forged to trade to Astinia, he had another made to arm a

Lynnean soldier. He could sense war was coming, no matter how much peace was the priority; I could see it in his eyes when he spoke. I shook my head, trying to rid myself of the negative thoughts clouding my mind. The rest of the castle was bustling with optimism, which was all good and well, but I just couldn't feel it.

My son, Lysan, appeared in front of me, his eyes glittering, clutching a small sword in his hand.

"I want to fight, Father. I want to fight for Princess Allanora." He held the sword clumsily and playfully in front of himself, swinging it about.

"Queen Allanora," I corrected. "Where did you get that, Lysan? Why do you have that?" I took it from his hands and set it on my desk. Immediately, he popped out his lower lip.

"King Aros gave it to me! He said it was special. He said I could be a warrior one day!" He pouted, keeping his eyes locked on the sword. *That day might come sooner than I hoped if we are about to go to war...*

"You have a long time to wait before you can be a soldier, my boy. Shouldn't you be busy?"

"King Aros doesn't drink like grandfather did," he said softly. "There's not as much for me to do..." A flash of sadness clouded his young, innocent gaze. Lysan knew his grandfather did something bad but still felt the sting of him being gone, and I knew watching him die before his own eyes had been difficult for him. I outstretched my arm to encircle him.

"Your grandfather and uncle were not good men, my boy," I whispered to him.

"Are you a good man, Father?" I thought about it. I had been the one to let Aros know what had happened; I kept connected to him, even though he could find any of these things out on his own. Perhaps, if we went to war, I would carry some of the blame, for I had a part to play in all of this. I let my father and brother be executed without protest, my own flesh and blood. If I had allowed myself to be offered for a marriage pact to Princess Allanora instead of marrying Eleanore for love, perhaps my father would not have gone down such a path. I stopped myself there and shook the thoughts from my mind. I couldn't put the weight of his choices on myself. I loved my wife and my children and wouldn't give them up for the world.

"I consider myself a good man, my dear boy. All we can do is what we think is right and best every day. Sometimes, we all make mistakes, and that's all right." Lysan looked down, his face twisted as if he were thinking hard about what I had said.

"Did Grandfather make mistakes?" he pondered.

"Grandfather made bad choices, son. He made the decision to end someone's life. Grandfather left our kingdom without a Queen; he left us unstable and open to this war. What he did was dangerous and unforgivable." I knew I couldn't lie to him; he needed to know the truth, needed to know the difference between right and wrong, forgivable and unforgivable. Lysan looked satisfied with my answers and reached out for the sword.

"Can I have it back, please? I promise I'll be careful." I shook my head.

"Your mother would never forgive me if you took your eye out with that thing. Go back to work; I'm sure there's someone in this castle in need of some wine." He pouted for a second but quickly took off back up the stairs. I followed him with my eyes; my gaze met Aros, standing ponderously at the top of the staircase leading to the library. I brushed the dust from the old books off myself, straightening up as he approached me, and slipped the small sword between my desk and the wall, where I knew it would be safe.

"It's not going to work, is it, Henrie?" he asked, rubbing his forehead with his static fingers.

"Well—Your Majesty—I," I stuttered. "I think it could, possibly... If we catch the Astinians on a good day, that is." *Do Astinians have good days?* "I just fear that without any true royal blood to offer for a marriage pact, they may insist on one of their sons being married off to Allanora and sitting on the Lynnean throne." His eyes narrowed, considering my words. "I think they're looking for blood. They're an awful royal family, I'm sure you know." He winced, surely remembering.

"I could never forget. My baby sister, Ata, was the Goddess of Truth, the purest of heart. She was their patron Deity, and they snuffed her out just like that. Not a shred of remorse. It should've been me. That damned arrow was meant for me..." He trailed off, his voice angry. His humanity was shining through his emotions. His fists were balled at his sides, and I admired his restraint, knowing he could destroy this entire library with a flick of his wrist.

"We can still get Allanora back." I tried to sound reassuring.

He ignored me, inhuman flames engulfing the flicker of humanity I had seen. "I started the war. I started it when Violet and I had Allanora. We had said we wouldn't have any more children with humans. And then Allanora was born. The humans rose against us with the Triini whispering in their ears. The war raged on, so many died." He pounded on the table. "We bound her powers; she never would have known anything other than being their human Queen. But it wasn't enough. The Triini had their talons so deep in the humans. That Astinian rat, Rhonan... He never forgave Violet for not marrying his brother. His bloodthirsty son came for me in Astinia, and when he loosed that arrow..." His eyes were distant, as if he was reliving the entire event; they glinted with gold.

"I still don't understand why the Astinians wanted to kill a Deity?"

"The Triini got their hooks in Astinia pretty easily," he snarled. "Rhonan, like all Astinian Kings, is thirsty for power. The Triini painted them a picture of human Kings and Queens being symbols of absolute power, with no one above them except for the Unnamed God." The thought shook him, a tremble crawling visibly across his body. "Everyone said the boy was aiming for me. I was the target because I started the war, but I think Rhonan secretly whispered to the boy to take Ata instead and make it look like an accident." His nails were biting into his palms, and outside, thunder rumbled, shaking the walls of the castle.

I didn't know what to do except stand there and stare at him. I had barely remembered what happened when Ata died. I had only been a boy myself, and it had all happened so fast. "Henrie, I'm going to Astinia with

Arthur's men." My mouth fell open slightly. He had promised to wait until a show of force was needed.

"Sir, you can't!" I pleaded. "You're needed here, you give the people hope. We agreed you'd stay until you were needed." He cleared the table of my books with one swift motion, sending them flying to the floor from my desk. I grimaced. He leaned on the table with both hands, then removed a scroll from his pocket, holding it out to me. I unrolled it slowly.

The Astinian King plans to marry his oldest son to Queen Allanora. The writing was scrawled so clearly across the paper. My fear had been correct; they did plan to marry a son off to Allanora, but the son being the oldest means they were planning to sit her on *their* throne, weakening our kingdom and keeping her prisoner forever.

"Nothing we can offer them is going to outweigh the marriage of our Queen to their Crown Prince," he said gravely. He looked defeated, but his eyes were wild. I knew he was right; all our preparations would be for nothing if this message was true.

"Who sent you this?" I searched his eyes with mine; he pursed his lips. He shook his head.

"It doesn't matter. It's a trusted source of information." His words crackled like the lightning he controlled. I nodded.

"So, if you know that nothing we have to offer is going to work, what's your plan now?"

"I'm going to kill them, Henrie. I'm going to kill them all." His tone was final. Cold.

"We don't know what weapons they have. That arrow that killed Ata... They could have more. What was it made of?"

"Onyx, an incredibly rare stone in our world. It neutralizes magic completely and is the only thing that can render a Deity's power useless so that we can be killed. Our ancestors used Onyx to forge weapons and build fortresses against the dark magical creatures that used to roam and rule our world. Longer ago than even the Deities have lived. From what I gathered from your father's memories, there are very few of those weapons, and they're kept in a place called the Academy, led by a woman named Steele. After the old war, they agreed not to make more, though there isn't a way for me to know if they've upheld that promise," he reasoned. "Either way, they don't keep those weapons in the Astinian castle. Plus, if they're receiving a Lynnean envoy, they're not going to expect me to be a part of it." He clapped me on the shoulder. "I'd give my life for hers, Henrie. I'm sure you can understand that." I could; I'd give my own life for any of my children or my wife without a second thought.

"What if you don't succeed? What about Lynnea?" I pleaded.

"Lynnea's only chance is me succeeding. They won't stop when Allanora is married off to one of them. They'll use Lynnea against her. They'll strip Lynnea for parts." He growled, angrily gripping the desk in front of him. With a scrunched nose, he concentrated deeply as the redness left his face. He held his hands together, and without touching them, a ball of light began to glow between his palms, growing and growing until it filled the space between them. His eyes closed, and the ball started to disappear slowly until it was a puff of smoke. I was dazzled and confused by the sight. I narrowed my eyes in question.

"We Deities have a tendency to, well, explode, for lack of a better word." He chuckled slightly. "I've found that concentrating that excess energy into a ball and making it disappear helps to channel my feelings so that the outbursts don't cause me any *problems.*"

"Do the other Deities do that as well, then?" I asked quietly, stunned.

"Well, I think we all have our ways of doing things. Allanora will have to learn her own way as well. Another reason why we must bring her back. Her powers are untapped." He sighed and looked out the large window to the side of us.

"I don't understand what you mean..."

"When I left and disconnected myself from Lynnea, I bound her powers, just as I had agreed to do when I broke my promise to not sire human children—golden stems, as they'd been called. To herself and everyone else around her, she would've seemed completely ordinary, which is far from true. Allanora has many of the powers I have, her very own magic. She may not even know it yet, but when I reinstated my connection to Lynnea, her powers were also unbound. Violet never told her, I assume, because I was never going to unbind her magic. I was never going to return. We wanted her to live a normal life, not constantly be under the scrutiny of the Triini. Now, though, she's walking around there with completely untrained, completely untapped magic just pent up inside her. It can be very dangerous for everyone around her and for herself. I need to bring her back, teach her how to control it, and use it for good." The glow in his eyes flickered with lightning of their own, sparking across the beautiful liquid gold of his irises.

"So, basically, Allanora is like that ball of energy that you just made disappear? Except there's no one controlling it, and it could...explode at any moment?" As if she hadn't been through enough, she had one more thing on her plate.

"Don't be so dramatic, Henrie." He brushed me off. "She's not a ball of lightning." My mouth dropped open, and I snapped it shut, seeing Arthur approach out of the corner of my eye.

"Your Majesty, excuse me, my apologies." He strode confidently in our direction. Aros nodded to me and turned to him, receiving him with a strong handshake. I started to step away, but Arthur stopped me.

"Henrie, please stay." I stopped where I was, listening intently. "Your Majesty, I understand you plan to join our escort to Astinia." His face was hard and concerned.

"I do, Arthur. I received a very troubling message this morning from an associate of mine who has eyes in Astinia. I fear that we do not have time only for diplomacy, and I plan to take matters into my own hands, should it go the way I expect."

"A message, sir?" Arthur prodded. Aros looked at me, and I held the message out to Arthur, forgetting I had even had it. Hurriedly, he took it from me, scanning it carefully. He paled and crumpled up the message angrily.

"Sir, perhaps we just ready the entire army. Bring the full force of Lynnea down on them, forget diplomacy entirely." He sounded enraged, determined.

"I had considered the same, Arthur, only I fear that with an entire army at our backs, it will take us two or three times as long to travel to Astinia. As of right now, I don't think we have the time to waste. We don't know when they plan to hold this wedding. And with an entire army traveling together, they'd know we were coming for them, and who knows what they'd do to Allanora in the meantime." Aros' face was dark and cold but icy calm.

"How can we be sure she hasn't already been married off to that—that—beast they call a prince?" Arthur bristled. Aros landed a strong hand on his shoulder.

"I received the message only this morning, Arthur. It would have only taken a day, maybe two, to get here. I don't think the Astinians would move that fast. It would be a grand event they're planning, a show of force as well as grandeur. Events like that don't happen overnight."

"What if they kill her? What if they kill her before we get there?" Arthur's concerned face twisted in fear.

"It doesn't benefit them to kill her, boy; at least, not until they're married and have an heir to sit on our throne," Aros replied coldly, fire burning behind his eyes. "Marrying her forever ties the Lynnean kingdom to theirs, something they've been trying to accomplish for years. Lynnea is a fruitful, rich, and proud queendom. A Lynnean Queen would be a perfect jewel on the crown of any kingdom. Since we have always allowed our Queens the final choice in their own marriage, few succeed in this sort of endeavor. Killing her would throw away a chance they'd never have again." He didn't give Arthur any more room to respond as he trod to the staircase to leave the library, leaving me and Arthur behind in his wake. "Make sure your men are ready, Arthur. We leave tonight." He turned his head down, eyes narrowed, deep in thought, as if he were listening to something in the cold silence surrounding us. Before our eyes, he snapped his fingers and disappeared in a flash of lightning, his body replaced by a small burn mark on the floor, leaving both of us gaping at the empty space where he had been.

"That's not something you see every day," I whispered. Arthur still had his mouth open, and his eyes were wide with disbelief. "That's the sort of thing we—well, more you—are going to have to get used to, I reckon." I patted him on the shoulder, bringing him out of his trance.

"Get used to? Why me?"

"Well, we are both working with him, but you'll be marrying her, right?" All the color drained from his face, and he questioned me with his eyes. "Apparently, she's got his powers, and they were unlocked when he came back." I smirked as realization spread across his eyes.

"You mean she..." He looked cautiously at the burn mark on the floor.

"Can do that? Well, I'd assume." I smiled at him and clapped him on the shoulder again. "That might be fun for you. A magical wife and father-in-law. I'll let you ponder that." I could hear him swallow hard as he hooked his finger in his collar, pulling it away from his neck.

"I guess I should, uh—I should finish preparing to leave." He straightened himself, tightening his sword belt around his waist. I turned to immerse myself again in my books, beginning to pick them off the floor where Aros had thrown them, when I felt his hand reach out and grab my shoulder.

"Henrie, do you think she'll uh—do you think she'll even accept me?" He ran his fingers absently through his hair. I looked him up and down carefully. I hadn't fully realized until this moment how young he was. He looked to only be in his twentieth or twenty-first year. He was well built, had the perfect stature for a knight, and came from a very well-known Lynnean noble family.

"I don't see why not, Arthur. She's a Queen in need of a husband. You're from a noble family, you aren't 100 years older than she is, her father likes you. And you're one of the reasons we are all preparing to rescue her. She owes you her life, should we all survive. I don't really see what she wouldn't like about you." He nodded, not looking entirely satisfied with my answer.

"There's not much exciting about me, Henrie. My life isn't full of adventure." I gave him a reassuring smile.

"I think adventure might be the last thing she's looking for right now. She's been through enough. When she comes home, she's going to be ready for safety and stability, someone who's reliable. I think you can give her that, right?" He half smiled back at me, nodding slightly.

"I can give her that. I just hadn't really thought about anything past getting Aros to even agree to let me have her hand. Talking about her having...powers...really made things a little real." He looked past me, thinking distantly. His smile faded, and his eyes suddenly looked tired.

"What are you worried about? Marriage is only the rest of your life." I chuckled.

"Yeah, I guess that's true." His smile widened, and his eyes brightened slightly, cheered up by my joke.

"If you're leaving tonight, I'm going to need to get back to this research. There's still a slight chance that diplomacy might get us what we need." He nodded, and I turned back into the library, losing myself among hundreds of years of history and stories where I truly belonged.

Chapter 20

Allanora

Neither of the suns had begun to break the horizon, but the alarming rapping on my door was enough to bring me out of sleep. I tied my robe tightly around myself and dragged myself to the door, peeking out into the dimly lit hall. Rowan, the shortest of the Thorne brothers, though he still towered over me, was looking down at me with wide eyes, a bright torch caught in his white-knuckled grip.

"Rowan?" I rubbed the sleep from my eyes, wondering if he was actually standing there or if I was just imagining things.

"Your Majesty," he bowed awkwardly, "my father, the King, has requested your presence downstairs." He gripped the torch with his other hand.

"Downstairs? Rowan, everything is downstairs from here." I was so tired; I didn't even know if I was getting proper sleep anymore. I glanced out the window, seeing what felt like the entire kingdom of Astinia spanning underneath a dark sky. I was irritated, partially from exhaustion but mostly because I was tired of seeing a Thorne every single time I opened my eyes—or closed them, for that matter.

"Yes, he's asked me to escort you to the dungeon." He took in a sharp breath and held it there, studying my face.

"Excuse me?" I tore into him with my eyes.

"He's asked me to escort you to the dungeon. He—he plans to carry out the girl's sentence. Now," he stuttered. I rolled my eyes.

"I don't want to watch that, Rowan, but thank you for the invitation. And if you're wondering, I'm not going to hit you with lightning." I started to close my door, but he stopped it with a heavy boot, pushing it open all the way. His hesitant expression darkened to the malicious glare I was used to.

"It wasn't an invitation, it's a demand." My face shifted from tired irritation to red-hot anger. I moved to push the door closed again, but he forced it open easily. "He wants you to be there, and then he plans to send the girl off immediately, back to Lynnea." He stood over me, nostrils flaring.

"I'm not going down there." I folded my arms over my chest. Saying nothing, he let out an irritated breath and reached out, grabbing my arm and pulling me forward.

"Rowan! I'm not dressed!" I squealed angrily, stomping my foot and trying to pull my arm from his grip. He sighed.

"Dress quickly," he said, shoving me back into my room, "the King doesn't like to be kept waiting. He's not patient."

"None of you are." I huffed at him and slammed the door in his face. Despite not wanting to, I did dress quickly in a simple black gown to match the Thorne family's black souls. I knew if I wasn't quick, he might make Lyra's punishment more severe or punish me as well. I winced as the image of Raysh's mangled, whipped skin pushed its way to the front of my mind. I shook my head, trying to free myself from the thought. Raysh was cruel, and he deserved his punishment. Their way of life was just entirely too difficult for me to stomach. I opened the door and stepped outside, holding my head high. Rowan reached out to grab my arm again, but I avoided his hand, stepping to the side of him.

"You don't need to grab me. I don't understand you people. I dressed, and I'm coming willingly, there's no reason for brute force." I turned my face up and away from him, holding my head high.

"Tiny and feisty." He tutted. I rolled my eyes and gestured for him to walk ahead of me. He stepped forward and snapped at the guard outside my door, motioning for him to follow us.

He led me silently down many flights of stairs, each hall getting darker than the last. Each corridor was hung with portraits of many Kings and

Queens I didn't recognize. A few, I did. I stopped at each of their paintings in turn. King Salemon, father of Rhonan, was said to have been killed by a wolf while hunting, but whispers said that Rhonan's patience ran thin, and he killed his father himself. A rumor that would not have surprised me. King Sevar, poisoned by a handmaid who he had taken to bed. King Olaf fought a war against Mura and died ceremoniously in battle. His son, Roman, took his army to obliterate Mura's, winning the war in his father's name. The histories I had read came swimming back to me, the brutal Kings of the past. Astinian blood ran deep. The family was easily recognizable by their raven-black hair, and every single one of them had black or brown eyes. *Except for Rylan.* I paused at the thought. Rylan's eyes were a beautiful emerald green. I found myself pausing at a painting of a woman poised alone with a snake coiled around her arm. Rowan kept walking ahead of me until he realized I wasn't behind him. Huffing, he returned to my side, exasperated.

"What are you doing?" he begged, his eyes darting back and forth between me and the descending stairs.

"Who is she?" I mused, entranced by the painting.

"What? She's Princess Thalia. She's dead. King Sevar beheaded her and her mother, Queen Miriam, when he found out Thalia was not his child. Look, there's like a thousand portraits hanging in this castle, are you going to ask me about all of them? We don't have time for this, my father is probably angry enough as it is," he grumbled.

"She has green eyes," I marveled.

"So? Lots of people have green eyes. Can we go now?" he urged.

"You people don't." I gestured to all the other portraits.

"I guess that's because she's a bastard. I don't have time for this." He grabbed my elbow and started stomping off into the darkness.

"What is your problem, Rowan?"

He clenched his jaw and kept walking, dragging me behind him. "I don't like this kind of thing, believe it or not."

"What kind of thing?"

"Torture, Allanora, I don't like torture." He dragged in a deep breath. "I've done it, of course, we all have. This is the Astinian way, after all. I prefer when my assignments are quick deaths. I've had to witness a lot of horrifying things during my training and being brought up here. It didn't used to bother me. When Raysh... When he took Cienna the way he did, killing her while he raped her, just because she was with me, it made me look at all of this differently. The Academy... It changes people. It changed me, but after what he did to Cienna, I've fought tooth and nail to try to keep even the slightest shred of humanity." I didn't know what to say. I didn't know how to feel badly for someone that I knew had killed so many people. Tortured them. But I was learning that there was much more to the Thorne men than I had expected.

We approached a large wooden door at what I presumed was finally the bottom floor of the castle. The door had intricate locks all down the side. I imagined not many people tried to break into a dungeon. I felt like I had walked a thousand hallways and staircases, and the not-so-sensible shoes I was wearing were making me pay for it. When I finally had the chance to catch my breath, I was almost gasping for air, my lungs agitated by all the steps. "Was it really necessary to come *all* the way down here?" I stammered.

"The King prefers to make his sentences a show of force. The dungeon is far below the surface of the earth, which is why you might be feeling like you're getting a little less air than usual. You'll probably get used to it." He set to work unlocking the door, starting with a small silver lock at the top. The rusted keychain he held jingled as he moved down to the next lock. "The King who built the castle did it on purpose, of course. The lack of oxygen in the lungs makes torturing prisoners even more, well, painful. We all get brought down here occasionally to 'work' on prisoners. Learn the different 'methods' of inflicting pain. Whenever Rylan and I are in the castle, that is. But I always try to get out of here as quickly as I can."

He glanced over at me; I felt the color drain from my face as he continued. "I remember the first time my father brought me down here; it was before he sent me to the Academy. There was a man down here, probably in his late twenties. A servant. Apparently, he had lingered too long in a room looking at my mother. My father, of course, didn't take kindly to that. That's when I learned that the flesh beneath the nailbed is some of the most sensitive. I will never forget the man's screams, like a small child wailing for its mother. It was just the tiniest tool, inserted underneath the nail. It's still one of my father's favorite methods to this day." He flashed me the classic Thorne smile, dashing and full of such toxic darkness. He stopped fiddling with the locks long enough to pull a small tool from his belt. It glinted in the dim light of the dungeon hall, the tiniest blade. My chest tightened as I imagined him pressing the sharp blade underneath my fingernails, the biting pain that would inflict. He flashed me another smile as he finished working the last lock and pushed the door open. The hallway ahead was completely black, lit only by the bit of light from his torch. "After you, Your Majesty."

I swallowed hard and stepped ahead of him, the heel of my shoe clicking against old stone floors. I could hear running water dripping slowly but couldn't tell where it was coming from. My eyes were straining to adjust to the darkness, but all I could see was the slight outline of stone walls that seemed to stretch an eternity ahead of me, snaking like a maze. I felt Rowan's hand between my shoulder blades, gently guiding me through the twisted hall. The creepy, dreary dungeon halls made me thankful that the Lynnean castle had a tower for its prisoners; it felt much more humane to allow prisoners light than to force them to suffer in the dark, not that Lynnea ever had many prisoners.

"Is this where you've been keeping her? Lyra would never hurt anyone; I don't understand why she'd have to stay in an awful place like this. She wasn't going to fight any of you."

"It's where she was meant to be kept. I think she only ended up down here a few hours before my brother took her to his bed." I winced. Everyone here was so nonchalant about everything that Lynneans held sacred. "Well, doesn't that at least make you feel better? It's just a different type of imprisonment." He snorted at his own joke; I was not amused.

"No. It doesn't make me feel better. You all remind me daily how absolutely disgusting I find your way of life. None of you have any respect for humanity, for my kingdom, for me. You're just a bunch of selfish, evil bastards." We turned the corner into an open room, and I ran directly into the King, who was standing in the doorway. I drew in a sharp breath, knowing he had heard everything I said. I felt Rowan's hand drop away from my back, and he took a couple of steps away from his father.

"You wound me, little Queen." A smile spread across Rhonan's face; I couldn't tell if it was humor or sadism. "I like to think that our way of life does value humanity in its own way. See, we value law, order, loyalty. Those who can't fall in line need to be punished, you see. Fear is what keeps people in line. There is no disorder in my kingdom because my people know what I am capable of. They have seen my power and know that very power will keep them safe or be used against them should they disobey me. No one dares breach the walls of my castle. Anyone who does—well, see for yourself." He motioned around the room. On the walls hung all kinds of weapons and devices that I assumed were meant for torture, almost all of which were completely foreign to me. There was a bar that had two prongs on either side. I gagged at the sight of the dried blood on them. A large rack with rollers that looked like someone might get strapped to. A pair of tongs with forks that looked like they'd clamp down into skin—bits of dried flesh hung from them. I forced down another gag. Lynnea had never had a need for such devices. This room was much better lit. I could see everyone else in the room clearly. The entire Thorne family was standing before me, dressed completely in black. Raysh was bare-chested, presumably because of the wounds that were still fresh on his back. I looked him up and down carefully until we locked eyes.

"Not all of us can heal our wounds so quickly, Your Majesty." He sneered at me; I felt a chill down my spine. "The same can be said for your sweet little handmaid." I shivered again as he stepped to the side, revealing

Lyra completely strapped to a chair, looking helpless, a table full of tools laid out next to her. She was visibly shaking; her grey eyes were flickering back and forth between everyone in the room. Tears were streaming down her face, but she couldn't make a sound; her mouth was pried open and held there with some sort of mask. I rushed to her side and slowly patted her head, allowing a few tears to fall from my own eyes. Trembling, I looked over to Rylan, who immediately cast his eyes aside. I turned to whisper in Lyra's ear.

"It's going to be ok. It's going to be over soon, and you can go home. You'll be safe at home, I promise, Lyra." I hugged her tightly around the shoulders and took a deep breath, calming myself so that I could be strong for her. I turned back to face the Thornes. The Queen was in the opposite corner of the room, completely disinterested in what was going on around her. Her boys were all gathered near their father, whispering amongst themselves. Another figure appeared, shadowed in the darkness of the entryway. I let out an audible groan and wiped a couple of tears from my cheeks.

"Gen, why is it you're always around when I *really* don't want to see you?" The exasperation seeped from my trembling lips. She cast her blond waves back over her shoulder and draped herself on Rylan, who tried shrugging her off, but she held tight.

"I'm as much a part of this family as you are, *Your Majesty*." The sarcasm was thick as it rolled off her tongue. The thought of this even being considered a family sent chills down my spine. I couldn't take it anymore; blind rage took over. I lunged at her, flinging myself toward her, allowing the anger to take control of me. Rylan instinctively caught me around the waist, pushing me backward and pinning my arms down to my sides. I let out a high-pitched yell. I couldn't think of anything to say to her, so I just screamed at her. She smiled at me, which only made me angrier. I gathered all my anguish and willed it to force Rylan away, trying to feel any ounce of the magic that the Queen had said laid dormant just beneath the surface of my skin, but nothing happened. I only felt exhausted and weak on shaky legs. My lungs were out of oxygen as if I had just run laps around the castle. Defeated once again and out of energy, I let myself slump against Rylan, who leaned me against the wall before backing off and into the corner of the room near his mother. Gen blew me a kiss and left. Rhonan, Raysh, and Rowan were all fixated on me, poised like they were ready to jump at me, but also with eyes filled with fascination. Only Rhonan spoke.

"Your magic isn't any good here, little Queen." He disparaged me with his eyes. "The King who built this castle made sure that magic wouldn't work in the dungeon. He had a fascination with mages and witches. He liked to have them pulled apart. He wanted to know what was going on in there. Of course, it made it more difficult when they were fighting back with their magic, so when he had the dungeon built, he had the magic blocked. Bricks of onyx line the inner walls, and in front of them, layers and layers of brick and iron. There's no way to get to the Onyx. Onyx, of course, neutralizes all magic. Most of it is gone now, used up in ancient wars and even the last bits used in the Great War of the Deities. But occasionally, we can find some in some long-forgotten corners of Cidris." I hadn't even known about Onyx. With the near extinction of magic in Lynnea, the Triini had removed all the rules and secrets of magic from our teachings, our books. I wondered how much vast knowledge my mother had allowed to be destroyed. Rhonan walked over to me and then behind me, tracing his hand along the back of my shoulders. "I could keep you down here, you know. I could see what makes you tick." He whispered it so quietly that I wasn't sure he even said it. Slowly, he moved to the table beside Lyra, fingering a few of the tools that lay there. A sob escaped my lips as he turned his attention to her. I instinctively stepped toward him, but strong arms wrapped around me from behind, pulling me back and locking my hands behind me. I threw my head forward; I figured if I had any chance of freeing myself, I could probably stun them by biting their arm, but before I could, I felt my braid pulled, tilting my head back. Raysh had me completely locked in his grip. He'd twisted my braid around his hand enough to keep me from pulling, but not so much that I couldn't see what the King was doing to Lyra. He studied the tools on the table next to her carefully before selecting a blade. He heated it leisurely over a torch before he slowly approached Lyra. His movements and demeanor were so comfortable, as if he was simply about to carve up a pig for dinner. Lyra began to shake even harder as he drew near her, and I wrenched myself forward, trying to get free to comfort her, but it was no use. I was trapped in Raysh's firm hold. He sneered down at me, lust gleaming in his eyes. *Pig.*

"It'll only be a moment, girl," King Rhonan said, twirling the hilt around between his fingers. He paused a moment and pondered before pointing to Rylan. "Rylan, my boy. I think you shouldn't have much of a problem doing this, would you?" Rylan rolled his eyes promptly but didn't object. I watched as he took the red-hot dagger from his father's outstretched hand. Unexpectedly, I felt the tiniest sense of comfort at the thought that Rylan would carry out the punishment. Somehow, I knew that if it was Rhonan, he would enjoy the torture and draw it out as much as he could. I'd watched him whip his eldest son without a hint of remorse. A part of me hoped that Rylan would be swift and quick. Get it done so Lyra could go home. If not for her, then maybe for me. It was only a small comfort, and I held onto it desperately; it was the only thing that was keeping me sane. Lyra was a panicked mess by the time he approached. She tried to shake her head and fought her restraints, but Rhonan took her head and held it while Rylan brought the knife to her mouth. I closed my eyes tightly; I couldn't watch.

"Look, or you'll be next, that's how it works here," Raysh whispered menacingly into my ear. Tears flowed freely down my cheeks as I forced my eyes open. I couldn't bear to see Lyra thrash and panic, especially because I saw how it excited Rhonan to watch the fear exuded by his victim. *Sadistic bastard.* I couldn't let him win.

I took a deep, steadying breath and called Lyra's name sharply. Her wide eyes found mine. The horror in them was heartbreaking. I wanted nothing more than to look away. But there was no stopping what was about to happen, and all I could hope for was that it would truly end in Lyra's release. "Look at me, Lyra," I spoke to her as her Queen, as her protector and matriarch. This situation was impossible and horrible, but we would see it through together. Lyra's eyes never left mine, and I held her gaze, willing her to take this punishment with whatever dignity she had left. It was as if Lyra understood, and she nodded to me gently, recognizing that we both needed to endure this together. I gave her a weak, broken smile, sending all my love and care her way, praying we would both survive this torture. None of the men took notice of our silent communication. Rhonan and Rylan were too high on adrenaline, focused on the torture ahead. Raysh gripped me tighter, crushing my body, but I kept my eyes on Lyra, who was still straining but had settled. Her fingers dug into the chair as Rylan leaned forward slowly. It all happened quickly, the way I hoped it would. Rhonan held onto Lyra's tongue with metal tongs, pulling it out to give Rylan a clear space to cut. I could hear a mangled scream that turned into a gargle of blood coming from Lyra as he touched the hot blade to her tongue, swiftly slicing through the thick muscle like butter. The inhuman wail that came from her was horrific. Blood pooled and ran down the sides of her mouth as Rhonan held her severed tongue up like some trophy. Quickly, Rylan pressed the side of the searing blade to cauterize the open wound, pulling another torturous scream from Lyra's trembling, bleeding lips. My knees gave out from under me, but Raysh held me fast, keeping me in place. My wails mixed with Lyra's, and Rylan backed off. I fought the nausea and dizziness that was racing through me. Lyra was writhing in pain, covered in tears, blood, and sweat, but she was keeping her wits about her. I could see her fighting the urge to slip into unconsciousness, and my heart swelled with pride. Lynnea was not weak. My people were strong, determined, and it would take so much more to even try to break us. It was a small comfort, but a comfort, nonetheless.

"I'm so sorry, Lyra, I'm so sorry," I yelled over and over, knowing that nothing I could say to her would help ease her pain. All I could hope for was that this was over. Rhonan held a hand up to Rylan as he turned away.

"Are servants in Lynnea taught to write?" Rhonan asked him thoughtfully, studying Lyra's slender hands as he pondered. Rylan tensed and turned back to his father. My eyes went wide.

"I'm not sure, sir," he said simply.

"Take her hands, Rylan. Both of them." Lyra's eyes shot open, huge tears falling from them as she tried to yell and free herself from the bondage. Panic shot through me at the realization of what the King was demanding. A disgustingly wicked smile spread across Rhonan's lips, sending fury through me I'd never felt the likes of. Raysh's grip on me tightened once more as I thrashed in his arms.

"No! No, please! We don't teach our servants to write! I swear it on my life, I am telling you the truth. Please, she's been through enough!" The desperation dripped from my voice, I barely recognized myself. Rhonan studied me carefully. His black eyes sunk into mine, tearing through my soul with his darkness. He pondered momentarily, then waved to Rylan again. He nodded at his father and cut Lyra from her bonds, releasing her from the chair; she immediately collapsed on the floor. I lunged for Lyra, but Raysh wouldn't let me go. There was no longer a need to hold me in place save for his own amusement. I'd had enough of the torture and the games. Without thinking, I smacked my head back hard, feeling it collide with Raysh's face. There was a satisfying crunch as my skull bashed his nose, and Raysh's arms instantly fell from my body, dropping me to the ground. I heard him swear behind me, saw Rylan cover up a snicker, and Rhonan eyed me with bemusement, but I didn't care. Raysh had it coming; that and so much more. My legs felt like jelly, and I crawled on my hands and knees over to Lyra, pulling her into my embrace. I held her to my chest, her blood seeping through my dress. She smelled of sweat and burning flesh, but I didn't care.

"I'm so sorry, Lyra, I'm so sorry. It's over now, you did it. You can go home; they promised you could go home," I soothed, stroking her soaking hair. Her skin was cold, and she was shivering. I wrapped her tightly in my grasp, trying to warm her, sobbing into the top of her head. Everything that she had to endure had been my fault. She didn't deserve to be maimed, used, tortured. My heart was solid stone in my chest, hatred ripping through my body. I shook and cried as I held her, and they all just stood there, staring at us.

Eventually, Rhonan sighed and rolled his eyes. "Oh, come now, Allanora, you're making a scene. The girl can go now. I'll be sending her home when the suns come up. She won't ever set foot in Astinia again." The King spoke with such a cold calmness, I couldn't stand it. I stared daggers at him, the fire burning inside me. My furious gaze turned to Rylan, then Raysh, who was covering his nose with a bloody hand. I felt a tiny sense of joy, of justice, at the sight. Rowan handed him a wet rag to clean himself up. The Queen watched from the shadows, not a single emotion readable on her face. King Rhonan snapped his fingers, and Rylan stepped forward toward Lyra. Without thinking, I covered her with my body and snapped at him. "Don't touch her! Don't you dare touch her! You did this!" I shouted desperately, getting up, ready to fight him. "You did ALL of this! You tried to kill me; you brought her here! This is all your fault." I landed one hit right in the center of his shoulder, and Rowan was on top of me in a second, pinning my arms behind me as I continued yelling. Lyra had slumped down to lie on the floor, all the color drained from her face. I kicked and screamed, trying to free myself from Rowan, but it was no use; he was much stronger. Rylan stared at me with his cunning cold glare, ever the emotionless enigma.

"The Queen is distraught. Rowan, Rylan, please escort her to her room. One of you is to always be outside her door until I give you the word. Keep the posted guard as well. No one is to go in or out of that room without my permission," the King ordered, his eyes like black wildfire, drunk with the power he had over me. Rylan caught my face in his hands as I continued flailing within Rowan's grasp.

"Are you going to walk, or do we have to carry you?" My face twitched as he held it in place, locking me in with his emerald eyes. Lyra was not out yet; she was not safe yet. My mistakes could still cost her, and I'd taken enough from her already. I let my body relax enough that Rowan loosened his grip.

"I'll walk." I scowled. "I don't need you monster Princes putting your hands on me," I spat at him, yanking my arms away from Rowan and smoothing my dress with my hands.

"Well, that's no fun." Rowan pouted sarcastically. "I thought we'd get to carry your spoiled butt all the way up a million flights of stairs. I was going to enjoy that." He rolled his eyes and shoved me toward the door.

"They aren't Princes, don't you forget that," Raysh said from the other side of me. I looked him up and down with disgust before exiting the room, not gracing anything he had to say with an answer.

We had gone up a couple of floors before I felt courageous enough to speak again, feeling confident that the others were not around to hear.

"They are going to send Lyra home, right? He gave me his word that she'd go home."

"She'll go home all right. Perfect excuse for Father to get some boots on the ground in Lynnea," grumbled Rylan behind me. I stopped dead in my tracks and pivoted on my heel.

"What do you mean? Boots on the ground?" He turned his face away from me, but I clapped my hands together in front of his face. His arm shot out, and he caught my hand in his grasp, his nose twitching in frustration.

"I think you've forgotten exactly how it is you got here, Princess. Maybe the King is being too soft on you, after all." His dark gaze peered into my eyes, searching. "My father is going to put a few men inside the walls of your precious little kingdom to make sure no one there plans anything funny." He brought his face so menacingly close to mine that our noses were nearly touching. "Once you're married to my brother, your sweet little queendom will be under his control. Just like he wants."

"I'll never allow it." I let the venom slide into my voice once more, and the corners of his mouth turned up just slightly.

"You can't stop Rhonan. Not when you're nothing more than Raysh's pet."

I gaped at him in disbelief. *How dare he?*

"I'll have every traitor that sets foot in my kingdom executed. Every. Single. One," I spat back and darkened my own gaze to match his. "I'll burn Astinia to the ground with your brother in it. And your father. All of you," I whispered the words as the anger boiled inside my chest. Rylan grabbed my face with one hand under my chin. I braced myself to fight back, but he brought my face to his and crashed his lips into mine. My defenses dropped, and I relaxed momentarily in his grip. I felt his hatred burning me while he kissed me, like angry wildfire tearing through both of us. My own hatred met his, a powerful force meeting an immovable object, and we collided. Reality came rushing back at me, and I went to push him away, but before I could, I felt him be pulled away. Rowan had him by the chest and flung him backward into the wall.

"What the hell do you think you're doing, Ry? What's wrong with you?" he yelled, then, looking around quickly, he dropped his voice to a whisper and grabbed Rylan by the collar. "You're going to get us all killed, Ry. I thought you were smart. Could you imagine what would've happened if Father or Raysh saw?" He pulled him close to his face and snarled. "I don't know what's gotten into you, but you'd better snap out of it. You can only hide in here for so long. Steele is coming for you, and you know what's going to happen if she thinks you've gone soft." Rylan shoved his brother's hand away, freeing himself from Rowan's grasp.

"Only one of us is hiding, Rowan, and I think we both know it's not me," Rylan growled, placing the palms of his hands on Rowan's chest and pushing him back forcefully. Rowan's hands balled into fists.

"At least I'm not stupid enough to *kiss* my brother's betrothed. The Crown Prince of Astinia forgives nothing, and you know that. Not to mention Rhonan." Rowan shuddered. Frustrated, I looked back and forth between them, reeling from the last couple of moments.

"I don't belong to Raysh, and I certainly don't belong to Rhonan," I said stubbornly, folding my arms over my chest. They both turned toward me as if they had forgotten I was there. My heart pounded, and my face flushed red from the burning sensation in my cheeks.

"This isn't Lynnea, Princess, you're promised to Raysh, and you belong to him." Rylan bristled visibly. "I shouldn't have kissed you; you just make me so angry."

"If I went around kissing everyone who made me angry, I'd have been executed years ago," Rowan half-joked. He wrapped his hand around my forearm and started leading me down the hallway, away from Rylan.

"I'll walk her back," Rylan said, irritated.

"I don't think so." Rowan scoffed. "I'm not stupid. And I'm not stupid enough to let you do something that is going to get us all whipped. You know Rhonan loves his cat o' nine tails."

"I'm not going to touch her, Ro. I'll take her back. Just go." Rowan looked back and forth between me and his brother for a moment before shrugging and taking off in another direction. He stopped thoughtfully after a couple of steps and turned on his heel, striding back toward us. Rylan squared up, preparing for a fight.

"I'm not going to lie to protect you. If anything happens and I get questioned, I'll rat you out. I'll rat you out to Father, to Raysh, to Steele. Don't you forget that. We may be brothers, but we've never been friends. You made sure of that at the Academy." He gave Rylan one more hard shove, but Rylan didn't budge. He was rooted, a stone standing against a tidal wave. The two of them exchanged a glare before Rowan took off again, more quickly this time, disappearing up a flight of steps.

Chapter 21

Aros

I hadn't slept since the execution, not that I had really slept in what felt like a lifetime, anyway. The energy pulsing through my veins was too much. The voices in my head were overwhelming, a constant headache. I knew I should turn them off, tune them out as I had always done. But if I did, I would be left with fear. If I turned it all off, I could miss something, something important that might cause me to lose Allanora. I couldn't risk that. Allanora was everything. I wish I could connect with her as I could with the rest of Lynnea, but as she had Goddess blood and her powers were unbound now, I couldn't. None of us Deities were able to hear each other's thoughts. Knowing that she was at least safe and unharmed would have made setting off on this journey significantly easier. I paced around my study in the castle, waiting for Arthur to send word that he had his men ready to go. The suns were setting in the sky, and I was becoming restless.

Arthur knew what he was doing, had everything prepared to bargain for Allanora's exchange. He was a determined young man, surely. I had to admire him for having the courage to ask a King and Deity for his only daughter's hand in marriage. I imagined that must have been terrifying for the boy. I chuckled to myself, imagining what it would have been like to ask Violet's father for her hand.

Violet had always been strong-willed and independent. I thought of her quite often and missed her dearly. She chose to marry me without permission or even telling her parents her plan. Of course, Queen Cressida was mortified, but Violet was to be crowned Queen, and by the law of Lynnea, she could choose who she wished to marry, regardless of what her mother wanted. She had told me she didn't care what anyone else thought, that she loved me and didn't care about the repercussions.

I looked out the window into the darkening sky. It saddened me to think of her, even though she filled me with such joy. I wondered what she would be doing right now if it was her in this predicament instead of me.

I turned to a small table in my study, where I had placed a quartz bowl filled with water. Holding either side of the bowl, I closed my eyes, muttering a communication spell under my breath. Finally, the face I was looking for appeared. Ice blue eyes, dark blue hair, and rigid cut features, my sister, Kahtix, appeared in the quartz bowl, looking as irritated and terrifying as ever.

"Aros? What on earth are you summoning me for?" she barked quietly. Her already narrow eyes squinted at me.

"Kahtix, I just want to talk to her, please. Let me talk to Violet," I pleaded with her. Her face turned from irritated to rageful instantly—a reaction I had been expecting.

"I am not summoning your dead wife's soul, Aros. In case you haven't forgotten, the rest of us are in *hiding*. Using our powers to connect us with the human world puts all of us in danger. They could find us. You're insane. Steele and her mercenaries are still out there, and you know they're still looking for us, even though we agreed to step back. You chose to leave here; you chose to put yourself in danger. Don't try to drag the rest of us down with you like you did Ata!"

If she hadn't been an image in a bowl of water, I was sure her icy stare would have taken me out right then. Her words cut me deep, reminding me of my baby sister. I puckered in frustration and sadness but refused to give up so easily.

"It's about our daughter. Please, Kahtix. If it wasn't important, I wouldn't ask you. You're the Goddess of Death, the only one that can connect me to her. Please." She shook her head and disappeared from the bowl before I could try any more persuading. Frustrated, I kicked the table out from under the bowl, sending the water flying and the bowl clattering to the floor.

"Your Majesty." I turned to see a guard peeking in from outside my door. I sighed heavily and waved for him to continue. "Arthur 'as sent word that the party is ready to move out for Astinia." I nodded and sent him away.

"Wait!" I called after him. He came scurrying back into the room, immediately standing at attention.

"My horse, Aelarion, he is still in the stables?" The guard returned my question with a look of puzzlement.

"Aelarion is one of Queen Allanora's, Your Majesty. I imagine, though, that she'd allow for her father to borrow 'im. I'll 'ave the stable boy saddle 'im up." I smiled at the thought of my daughter growing up riding the horse I had so cherished during my few years at the palace.

"Oh, and please send for Henrie." The guard nodded and left the room quickly. I looked at the quartz bowl once again, thinking maybe I could try to summon Kahtix one more time, but I pushed the thought from my mind. It was time to move out.

I readied myself in my armor; I hadn't worn proper battle armor since the war, before my siblings and I went into hiding. Just as I tightened my sword around my waist, Henrie appeared in the doorway behind me. He had dark, tired circles under his eyes, and his hands were trembling slightly. He didn't stand as tall as he usually did.

"Henrie." I grasped his hand in my own, shaking it firmly. "You don't look well." I peered at him curiously.

"I just haven't been sleeping well, Your Majesty. I imagine I'll sleep much better when you and the Queen return, and I can go back to my quiet life studying books," he said quietly. I nodded slowly at him.

"You can just call me Aros, Henrie. I know you'll do well for the kingdom while I'm gone. You're a good man, and I'll see to it that you're taken care of, and your family, of course." I clapped him carefully on the back; he looked as if he were going to turn to dust beneath my touch. "It won't be long, Henrie, I promise. I'll bring her back, and everything will be normal."

"I'll uh—I'll walk with you to meet Arthur, Your Majesty—Aros." He shook his head like he was forcing a thought out of it. We walked silently for the first few moments; I could tell he was holding something back.

"Sir, I—I have a favor to ask," he finally said as we approached the exit to the grounds where Arthur would be waiting for us.

"You can ask anything of me, Henrie, except my daughter's hand, of course." He chuckled uncomfortably.

"Sir, my family has served the royal family in this castle for quite a few generations, and I've been happy to do so, of course. Overseeing the crown right now will cast some light on me that wasn't there before. If our efforts turn to war, I'd like to ask that my family be protected along with the royal family. I fear that my children, my wife, will be targets as I've so willingly aligned myself with you. Which I would do again, of course, I—" I cut him off by raising a hand.

"Henrie, you've been endlessly faithful to the crown, even stood with me when your family was executed. You looked after my daughter for many years, even when you were still young yourself. Your wife and your children will be safe as long as I'm alive. I swear that to you." I extended my hand to give him my word, and when he took it, I pulled him into an embrace. "Thank you for watching over my daughter." I released him, and he nodded, looking relieved. I hoped this reassurance would help him sleep a little better.

The next face I saw appear at the door to the castle grounds was a Brother of the Triini, Sol, the Lynnean castle leader. It wasn't wholly unexpected.

"King Aros," the words slid from Brother Sol's lips like sludge. "I have to admit, I never thought I'd see you here again. I didn't think you'd have the courage after what we did to your sister." His face was a mix of arrogance and a just hint of fear.

Shuffling some papers around on the desk, I looked up at him, "Can I help you with something? I have much to attend to, not the least of which is trying to rescue my daughter from the monster you unleashed on this world."

"The Unnamed God does what he needs to do for order, for peace. He is unhappy with your arrival, which I'm sure you understand. I have for you a message." Narrowing my eyes at him, I motioned for him to continue. "He wishes to tell you that he is running out of patience for your games, and if you do not go back into hiding soon, he will make you pay, he will make Allanora pay. He does wish to see her safe return, for she is a large part of his plan for the ultimate order in Cidris."

The smile he flashed was triumphant and eerie. All I did was nod. I wouldn't take empty threats from the follower of a God who had never shown his face. I circled him, and he shrunk away from me.

After giving him a satisfied smile, I turned, exited the door, and was met with the proud and motivated faces of Arthur's party of knights. They were lined up perfectly, already mounted on horseback, armed and waiting for me.

I followed behind Arthur, listening as he named off all the knights: Roland, Tristan, Alaric, Cedric, Oliver, Hecter, Geoffrey, Peter, Victor, and Brendon. He had chosen ten of the best knights of Lynnea. Together, we made a strong and hopefully unbeatable group of twelve.

"Twelve men on a mission to rescue a Queen." I chuckled. "Very fitting, twelve kingdoms, twelve Deities, twelve brave champions of Queen Allanora."

"Alla-knights," one of the younger men chortled to the group. Arthur glared at him, and he straightened himself up, snapping his mouth shut.

"Oliver, of house Hawkend. He's young but one of the most promising knights we have. My apologies, Your Majesty, such insubordination won't happen again." Arthur's voice was low and embarrassed. He mounted his horse and gestured to mine, Aelarion. My steed looked as if he hadn't aged. He was still black as night and taller than all the others. He held his head high and swished his tail back and forth at the sight of me. My heart swelled. Aelarion still remembered his rider after all these years. I patted his nose, and he knickered, allowing me to swing into the saddle. Gathering the reins in my hands, it was as if I had never left the saddle, and the last 14 years melted away.

Arthur led the way into the woods in the direction of Astinia. I fell in behind him, just a couple of paces back, and the others made a line behind me. I could feel our energy rising as we rode, and it brought me some much-needed resilience. Silent and hell-bent on achieving our objective, we ventured on.

Chapter 22

Allanora

Rylan was pulling me up the flight of steps by my forearm. It seemed as if my arm would always bear the red mark of a Thorne hand. Halfway through, I shoved his hand off me and planted myself where I stood, forcing him to turn around and look at me.

"Look, I don't know what game you're all playing here, but I've had enough. I'm not being manhandled anymore; I'm not being pushed around, and I'm done dealing with all of you," I said defiantly. He strode down a couple of steps until he was face-to-face with me again. I felt a rush to my cheeks when he came close to me. My eyes widened, which he seemed to find amusing, a smirk scrawling across his lips.

"No one is playing games with you, Princess."

"Queen." I didn't feel as strongly about my title as I had before. I was weak, reeling, and he was relishing it. He moved toward me, his eyes unreadable. I stepped backward, my heel slipped on the stair, and Rylan caught me before I could fall. He spun me quickly until I was up against the wall of the staircase, backed into one of the portraits hanging there. He trapped me there by putting his arms on either side of me. Heartbeat racing, I shrank back against the cold bricks. He wasn't moving, but I felt as if he were closing in on me, filling my vision only with him. For a few moments, we stared at each other, breathing hard. Slowly, he lowered one hand, waiting for me to protest or shove him away. But I didn't. He bunched my dress at the hip and pulled me to him, kissing me again, more softly, more slowly. A tear spilled from one of my eyes, filled with confusion, anger, sadness, frustration, and guilt, as I let myself lean into the kiss. Memories of the mysterious suitor that had stunned me and filled me with excitement at my choosing ball flooded through my mind. The beautiful, emerald-green eyes, the way he moved me across the dance floor... He had melted me like butter, and here I was again, forgetting what a monster he truly was. He broke away from me gently, and for the first time, I saw him genuinely smile. His eyes lit up like a warm and comforting hearth, and the smile had my heart skip a beat. Without the smile, he was devilishly handsome like the rest of them, but smiling, he was downright perfect.

"Apologies, my Queen." He winked, backing away from me and kissing the back of my hand, leaving me reeling. I couldn't respond. I didn't understand what was happening. My heart was in my throat. He was unphased. He simply turned and started back up the stairs as if nothing had happened. I knew he was toying with me, testing me.

"What are you doing?" I demanded.

"I don't know what you mean," he said nonchalantly, not even turning around to look at me.

"What was all that?" I pointed at the stairs where he just had me pinned against the wall, but still, he refused to stop or look.

"I don't know what you're talking about." My mouth dropped open in frustration. I followed him silently until we reached my room, where a dutiful guard was posted as usual. I nodded to the guard and stomped into my room, slamming the door behind me and leaving Rylan on the other side of it. With my back to the door, I slid to the floor in a heap as my emotions overcame me, and I burst into tears. I allowed them to flow freely down my cheeks. My anger at Gen, at Raysh, at the whole Astinian family, the horror I had watched Lyra endure, the fear of what was to become of my kingdom, the confusion and heat I felt toward Rylan... It all poured from me until I had nothing left.

Once there were no tears left to cry, and I was drained of all my energy, I continued to lay on the floor in a miserable heap. Overwhelmed, I succumbed to just lying there.

"Too many tears will snuff out a candle." I heard the voice from the corner of my room. I yelped and scrambled to my feet, my hands searching the wall behind me for the door handle. "No need to fear me, I'm here to help you." I peered into the corner where I thought the voice had come from, trying to make out a shape. A man appeared directly in front of me, dressed in dark, rich purple robes embroidered with gold. His skin was dark, his eyes were golden, and he stood tall. An unwelcomed sight in what was supposed to be the safety of my room, but his gaze felt weighted with centuries of wisdom, though he himself seemed just under middle-aged. Something about him made me reconsider screaming for help. He hovered in front of me, waiting, his eyes shimmering.

"Who are you?" I squeaked out.

"Sinric, Your Majesty." He sized me up and bowed low. I hadn't encountered such formality in a while. Before I could forget myself, I returned the bow with a curtsy. He smiled wide and reached out for my hand. I gave it cautiously, and he kissed the back of it. "The Queen has informed me of your particular...predicament, and I would like to offer my services to train you to control your magic." His smile was kind and genuine, something that had seemed to be particularly absent from Astinia.

"I don't think I've quite met an Astinian that wasn't trying to kill me... or was at least considering it," I said half-heartedly.

"Oh, I'm no Astinian, my dear."

"My apologies, I just assumed—" He held up his hand.

"I visit here from time to time at the request of Queen Eudora. But I am from Drocia. You see, the Drocians have a much more sophisticated approach to utilizing magic. I intend to teach you." He closed his eyes for a moment as if he were taking in the air around him through his skin, breathing slowly and carefully. Finally, he opened his eyes and refocused on me. "Yes, Eudie was right, a very ancient magic runs through your veins. Your blood connects to the very soul of the earth beneath our feet. Your father... He is a Deity." I nodded cautiously.

"I'm sorry," I interrupted. "Did you say Eudie? How do you know the Queen?" I scoffed.

"I did. I've known Eudora since she was a child. Her lovely mother always referred to her as 'little Eudie.' It stuck. Eudora was a high-born Drocian, promised to the King of Astinia almost from birth. She never wanted to come here, as I imagine you didn't either. The terrors she's survived from the King, I'm sure, are similar to what you are experiencing or expecting from your own betrothed. I taught her everything she knows about magic. When she moved to Astinia, I came when she called on me, but I refuse to stay here in this dreary place."

"It is dreary..."

"You are from Lynnea. Of course Astinia would seem dreary." He chuckled.

"Why are you here?" If he was indeed close to the Queen, he may not be a trustworthy friend to me.

"Well," he considered. "Eudora told me that you were here, that your magic needed controlling. I wanted to see the extent for myself." He snorted a little through his nose, flaring out his nostrils.

"What exactly did she tell you about me?" I twirled my thumbs around each other nervously.

"She said that you were brought here, you're betrothed to Raysh, and she's concerned about the extent of your magic, and you need to be trained. Unfortunately, Astinian royalty tends to shy away from power that isn't attained through brutality. The King wasn't particularly thrilled at the Queen's study of magic, but he has her well under his foot. I think she's fought hard to keep her kind Drocian soul intact...but sometimes I think she's let it slip away. Maybe with you here, she will have someone else to help keep her human side whole."

"Rylan brought me here," I said simply. He furrowed his brows and pursed his lips.

"Eudie said you were to marry Raysh."

"Yes, that's true."

"And Rylan brought you here?"

"Also true."

"Why?" I shrugged. It wasn't a lie; I truly wasn't sure why all this was happening to me. "I see. You're not here willingly, are you, Your Majesty? Eudie made it sound like you agreed to be here, but I don't sense that at all." An involuntary tear slipped from the corner of my eye and down my cheek. "All right," he comforted.

I started to lose control of my emotions. Something about Sinric's presence comforted me and gave me a sense of safety. "My mother was killed at my choosing ball. There was an attempt on my life at my coronation, and when I woke up, I was being brought here by Rylan. When I arrived, the King told me I'd have to marry Raysh. I don't have any more control; my kingdom thinks I'm dead. This dreary castle and its depressing inhabitants are my new home, and I have no say in it." The tears started to fall from the corners of my eyes freely. "I should've been marrying a gallant lord of Lynnea, someone who respects me as a Queen and would rule by my side and...have a gentler approach." I balled my fists, Arthur coming to the forefront of my mind, and a few crackles of lightning sparked around my knuckles. "But here I am, betrothed unwillingly to the most...petrifyingly horrid man I've ever known. They will probably never let me go back to my own kingdom, and who knows if I'll ever really get a hold of these dumb powers."

"It'll be ok." He placed his hands gently on my shoulders. "Let's start small, get a bearing on those emotions, hey?" Taking my hands in his, he held them facing each other, "Hold your hands like this. Keep them about an inch or two apart." I did as he said, and warmth started to brew between my palms. It was instantly calming, and I felt more grounded.

"Good, now imagine sparks between your palms, visualize them until you can see them there." Squinting, I focused hard on the visualization until I saw a few sparks fly from my palms. I gasped in shock, dropping my hands. Immediately, my concentration was broken, and I stared up at Sinric in disbelief.

"Good, Your Majesty," he encouraged. "Let's try that again." I took a breath and repeated the steps. This time, when the sparks zapped between my palms, I kept them there.

"That's it," Sinric praised. "Now will the sparks to form together into a ball, a simple ball of energy pressed between your palms." I focused harder on the sparks, shaping them with my mind until they took the form I wanted. The tiniest ball of static formed perfectly between my hands.

"I'm doing this?" I whispered in surprise, staring at the glowing energy.

"You are, my dear. This is the first step to controlling, visualizing." He watched me as I stretched and pushed the ball between my hands playfully, like a cat playing with a ball of yarn, mesmerized by what I was capable of.

"Be careful, Allanora. It may be small, but your magic is powerful, as you've already seen. Keep practicing this, and I'll teach you more when I return." He bowed and disappeared before I could even protest, leaving me alone once again. My palms dropped, and I felt a little empty. The interaction had been surprisingly pleasant, and his sudden departure just reminded me I was still stuck in a place I hated against my will. I was happier now, though. I had something to focus on, something besides Rylan. I laid down on my bed and practiced forming the balls of energy, making them disappear and reappear, playing with them between my fingers.

What seemed like hours flew by, but I didn't care; there wasn't anyone else in this castle I wanted to see. I was content on my own. The suns set on the horizon. I had spent much of my day in here, a glimmer of hope dancing on my fingertips. Suddenly, there came a tiny knock from the window, and I almost jumped out of my skin. I looked over to see Rylan on the other side of the glass. Reluctantly, I unlocked the window, and he climbed through easily, a mischievous grin painted between his cheeks.

"Rylan, what do you want?" My tone came across sour and indifferent. At least, that's how I hoped I had come across. My whole body was trembling—that, I hoped he wouldn't notice.

"I forgot something," he said simply, shrugging his broad shoulders.

"What could you have—" He grabbed me by the back of the neck and placed his other hand on my cheek, pulling me in for a kiss, deeper and more passionate than before. His hand slid behind my head, and I was reminded how strong he was. Instinctively, my arms wrapped around his waist. When he pulled away, he smiled, which I returned with a scowl. I hated him for confusing my feelings and making me not hate him. "You're marrying Gen!" I groaned. "And I have to marry your monster of a brother. What are you doing?"

"I'm kissing you. Because I can." He looked into my eyes for a moment, and I studied his incredibly handsome face. He was twenty-eight, ten years older than me, but he had such a young face. His jaw was chiseled, and he had just one dimple on the right side. I was lost in his endlessly beautiful green eyes until he kissed me again. This one was more hungry, more desperate, more powerful against my lips. He wrapped both hands in my dress, pulling me closer to him by the fabric. His lips brushed against my neck, and my breath caught. Instinctively, I put my hand to his chest to push him away, but I couldn't bring myself to do it.

He backed me toward the edge of my bed, and I leaned on it. He slid his hand into my hair and gripped it, using the leverage to pull my head back slightly while he leaned over me. One hand gently slipped down my back, and heat boiled in my core. It hit me then, as my body betrayed me, that I wanted the assassin. Without breaking my lips from his, I leaned back, and he came with me, sliding his other hand out of my hair and down my back as well so he could lift me up enough to set me on the bed. He broke the kiss, and I gasped as if the oxygen was knocked out of my lungs. There was fight in his eyes, an internal struggle I couldn't quite comprehend.

"Rylan..." I breathed out, and his eyes ignited in green flame.

"Nora."

I didn't correct him.

"If we get caught..." His expression sobered slightly.

"I don't care. I'm already a prisoner. Raysh is my death sentence." I was panting, his hands were clasped around my waist, his hips pressed into mine.

"I can't give you what you need. I'm not a knight in shining armor." He leaned ever closer, waiting on my answer, waiting for permission. I expected him to just claim me, overpower me like I knew he could. But he remained leashed, patient.

"I don't need to be rescued." It was a lie. All I'd done since I'd gotten here was pray to be let out, for someone, anyone, to get me out of here. But, in this moment, all I wanted was him.

Something feral took over his expression, and he crushed his lips to mine again. If I truly was to be Raysh's Queen, eternally his prisoner, I'd have Rylan first. I swept my hands into his hair and wrapped one leg around him, pulling him closer.

A knock sent us both hurtling to separate corners of the room, panting and coming back to reality. He grunted and dashed for my closet, and I smoothed myself over to answer the door. I opened it, not knowing who I should be expecting in the late evening. I hoped I didn't look too flushed with excitement. It was the King. Any color that had been in my face drained immediately.

"Little Queen. May I come in?" I bit my lip and nodded quickly, gesturing to the table for him to sit. I prayed to anyone who would listen that he didn't know Rylan was there. Warily, I sat down across from him. "I come bearing good news." His menacing smile spread across his face. "Your handmaid has been released. She's on her way to Lynnea as we speak. I am sure she will be just fine there and will find someone new to serve," he taunted. I nodded slowly, unsure of where this was going. "In even more exciting news, I've chosen a date for your wedding." There it was. I gulped and nodded, trying to look excited. "You'll be married tomorrow. It's been decided. All the preparations are being made." His sneer was so sickeningly violent, I couldn't stand it. I stood from my seat, immediately feeling dizzy, and placed my hand over my stomach for balance, quietly panting for air.

"I—um—yes, Your Majesty. I am glad all is going well." I tried to catch my breath, but I couldn't; my world was spinning around me. I didn't even know what I was saying. All I knew was that I had to keep the King happy.

"First thing in the morning, you'll be fitted for your wedding gown. Don't worry; the royal seamstress is the best. Everything will be perfect for tomorrow night. I know how important this night is to you women." He smiled again, kissed the back of my clammy hand, stood, and left my room without another word. I crashed to the ground, and Rylan was at my side as I burst into tears.

"I don't want to marry him." I sobbed. "He's awful and cruel, and I don't love him." My breath caught between every word, and I began hiccupping between sobs. "Please help me, Rylan, you have to get me out of here," I whispered.

"Nora—it's the law. The King made a choice, there's nothing I can do to change that. Out there, I'm beyond the law, but here, in the castle, I'm bound by my father's word."

"Please, I wouldn't be here if it weren't for you," I pleaded. He looked wounded, but he knew I was right; this was all because of him. His look of hurt surprised me. It wasn't even that long ago he'd tried to kill me multiple times, threatened to kill me, drugged me with Dragonshade, kidnapped my handmaid, and cut out her tongue. It was all too much. "Rylan, I don't understand what's going on. You kill people, you tried to kill me, your fiancée killed my mother, you brought me here to be married off to your horrible brother, and now you—" I paused. I couldn't bring myself to talk about kissing him... wanting him out loud. The guilt made my gut wrench.

"I was hired to do a job, Nora. None of it was personal, it never is. I never expected to be attracted to you, not like this, anyway. You're just—" He sighed. "Look, I never wanted you to marry Raysh either, he's awful. I told you that at the very beginning. *He* should've been sent away to the Academy. He's exactly what they want." His face twitched angrily.

My eyes drifted to his slightly tousled hair that my hands had just been wrapped up in. I wanted to push all of this out of my mind and just kiss him again, but the news from Rhonan had sobered my mind, and my body.

I took the opportunity to press Rylan. "Sent away to the Academy? What even is the Academy?"

"That's just what they call it. 'Torture dungeon' doesn't quite sound appealing to royal families sending off their 'spare sons'. Not that my father would've cared anyway. In fact, that would've made it better." He shook his head. "They recruit young boys for an army of sorts. Most of them end up as soldiers, an army-for-hire, for lack of a better term. High-born boys are recruited as assassins, specially trained for hire-to-kill. Steele developed the program to recruit highborns. Most 'higher up' families weren't keen to allow their sons to be part of an army-for-hire where they'd die nameless. Apparently, there's less shame in having your son be a specially-trained assassin. Of course, becoming this way wasn't easy. I spent the first year of my time there being broken in." He paused, looking at my face. I figured I looked speechless.

"I don't understand, who just agrees to that for their son? Why is anyone okay with that?"

"Well, most of them do it to pay off a gambling debt or a debt of their kingdom. Astinia is a little different. As you say, 'brutish'. They find a lot of value in the abilities taught by the Academy. Torture, killing, secrecy, mind games, etcetera. Being sent to the Academy is considered an honor."

"But you don't—you don't see it that way?" He furrowed his brows and pursed his lips.

"How could I?" He slowly drew his shirt over his head, exposing his arms and torso. He was covered in scars of all kinds. Burns, cuts, whip lashes. Some of them had been carefully tattooed over, but most were left alone. I gasped and instinctively reached out to touch his chest, putting my hand on a cluster of burn marks. He winced, turning his head to the side, ashamed.

"But—why?"

"They say that once you know you can survive incredible pain, it doesn't bother you to inflict it. To a point, I guess they're right. It does make it easier." His hand balled into a fist, and his knuckles turned white. I traced a long whip scar up his shoulder and over to his back. He breathed in and out heavily. "I was fourteen. It was only my second assignment."

"What was?" I asked. His hand went to the front of the scar where my hand had been.

"I was supposed to kill Aros. Your—your father. I was supposed to kill him, but Ata... She pushed him out of the way. My arrow hit her instead and killed her instantly. The patron Goddess of my own kingdom. Steele punished me. I was whipped each day for a month. The final day, I was brought into a cell, but it wasn't Steele waiting for me. It was my father. He took one of my arrows and cut me from my shoulder blade to my chest. Ata's death... It left a mark on Astinia and my father. Eventually, when the war came to an end and the Deities left, he managed to turn it into a good thing. I got the nickname God-killer, and everyone was asking for me. That man—your advisor, Tobyn—he asked for me. He knew who Aros was, what you were, and even though you aren't a full Deity, he wanted to be sure." I listened to him intently, tracing the scars on his body with my fingers.

"You were—meant to kill my father? Why?" He nodded; his eyes were full of shame.

"The war wasn't ending. The Triini had the majority of the kingdoms on their side, but the few kingdoms that held out in the end combined with the power of the Deities... People were dying, so many people." He entwined his fingers in his hair; frustration turned his knuckles white against his dark brown locks. "Steele had a meeting with a Triini leader. They agreed the Deities needed to be weakened. The Triini had developed an elixir with onyx. They had coated a few weapons with it. They believed it would be able to kill Deities. I was her shiny new toy; I'd spent the better part of two years training to be a weapon. They sent me after him. He was to be here in Astinia, something that hadn't happened in a long time, considering your mother wasn't particularly fond of our family. He was the one who started everything, and they were going to use him to finish it. Astinia had been one of the last kingdoms to turn against the Deities. My father wasn't thrilled about aligning with the Triini. His father had a soft spot for Ata, and he had always worked well with her. I think watching her die solidified something in him; he didn't want Cidris to fall to the Triini, but then it was too late. The rest of the Deities went into hiding, and the Triini took over. They're against magic for the most part, but they used magic to erase most memories of the Deities from Cidris."

"What do you mean he started everything?"

"The Deities—they had agreed no more stems, no more children with humans. Your father, when he married your mother and had you, gave the humans—us—reason to side with the Triini, who had been trying to raise forces against the Deities. The stems had become too powerful, and the destructive nature of Deity power in a human body was causing too much chaos in Cidris. Your father, he went back on his word when he had you."

The wind was knocked out of me. I tried to catch my breath, but my lungs constricted, and I couldn't get any air. Salty tears dripped from my eyes down to my lips. I forced air into my lungs. "The war—they fought the war because of me. Ata died because of me. He left my mother because of me."

"I'm sorry, Nora. I'm so sorry. It's all my fault." *It started because of me, but it ended because of him.* I cut him off, taking his face in my hands and pressing my lips to his. He removed my hand from his face and pulled away from me. "Please forgive me," he pleaded. I twisted my hand from his grasp, returning it to his face. I held his gaze with my eyes, looking into his soul.

"I guess we are both prisoners." I captured his lips once more, leaning into him and bringing myself closer. Finally, he relaxed and leaned into me, holding my hips gently.

I felt so free. For the first time in my life, I made a decision that wasn't best for my kingdom or dictated by my mother, by Astinia. I knew that it couldn't last. I knew tomorrow was opening the door to a life I didn't want, a life dictated by everyone else. So, I allowed myself this one moment of selfishness, to be engulfed in a passion that was entirely mine. I traced my hands over his chest, committing him to memory by touch. His skin was so warm beneath my fingers; I had always imagined he would be cold. He drew me closer to him, pulling me into his lap and into a tight, devouring embrace. We were closer now that his shirt was gone. I wondered how his skin would feel against mine.

"I have to go, Nora," he whispered in my ear. My mind crashed back to earth, realizing suddenly how entangled we were, and I immediately felt self-conscious.

"Right, you should probably get to your fiancée," I said shortly, breaking away from him. He touched my face gently.

"I'm not marrying Gen," he said softly.

"Your father's word is law, you said it yourself." He nodded, flashing me a knowing smile.

"I have my ways." He disappeared out the window he had come through, leaving me with a whirlwind of emotions in his wake.

Chapter 23

Aros

I hadn't set foot in Astinia since Ata's death. The desolation in the air was thick, just as it was on the night she was murdered. A land of fear, misery, and suppression. The men became visibly more uncomfortable, more alert, and less joyous as we crossed into Astinian territory. The castle stood not far from the border between the two kingdoms. We were close. Arthur was determined to get there as quickly as possible; he was a driven young man.

"Arthur, I need to speak with you, quickly." We rode off to the side. He maneuvered his horse around so he could face me, poised proudly atop his white steed.

"Yes, sir?"

"I just—I need to make sure you understand. The Lynnean law is very clear. The Queen can choose her own husband, regardless of any political agreements made. I just want you to know that even though I give you my blessing, Nora—Allanora still must choose you."

"I know, Your Majesty. When I saw her out in the woods, I felt, well, I felt like she and I had a moment. I think, well, I hope that when I ask her for her hand, she will say yes. And I promise you, sir, I promise I'll do everything in my power to make her happy. I know that I can." I nodded, gathering the reins back in my hands and returning to the group of men waiting for us.

The Astinian castle was peeking out over the horizon, and the suns were rising in the sky. The castle would be waking.

"The Astinian King is not a kind or forgiving man. I want you all to remember that. Let Arthur speak, let me speak. These people, they—well, you'll see," I told them, each man nodding in turn.

We approached the castle quickly. The grounds outside were bustling, preparing for a sort of event.

"Arthur, I think we might have gotten here just in time." He looked around, noticing all the flowers and decorations. His face flushed red, visibly angered. "Don't forget, we are here for diplomacy. Don't do anything irrational." His eyes flicked toward me and back to the castle. I couldn't tell if he was going along with what I was saying or ignoring me. I didn't have time to figure it out. Two guards stopped us at the gate. I gathered myself up while Arthur spoke to them.

"What is your business here?" the guard barked at him.

"We are here to see the King."

"Is the King expecting you?"

"If he isn't, he should be. I am Sir Arthur Blackwood of Lynnea. I am here on behalf of King Aros. Your King is holding a monarch hostage, which is against the law. We are here for the release of Queen Allanora of Lynnea." The two guards locked eyes before nodding to each other. If they were shocked, surprised, or worried, I couldn't tell.

"Wait here," the first one said while the other took off for the castle. Arthur looked warily at me, and I gave him a reassuring nod. King Rhonan was a powerful brute, but if I had to, I'd take him out. I'd take them all out. I felt the power, the emotions, building up inside me, but I suppressed them, keeping control. I breathed in heavily.

"What, exactly, is going on here?" Arthur asked the remaining guard, who shifted around uncomfortably.

"Well, it's um—it's a wedding," the man stuttered uncomfortably.

Arthur's lips pursed angrily. I held my hand up, signaling him to stay calm and stick to what we were here for. He nodded, staying still.

"Who's getting married?" one of the knights behind me asked. The guard looked between them all, eyes narrowed in suspicion. He opened his mouth to speak when the other guard returned, out of breath. He stopped next to us, hands on his knees, trying to catch his breath. I watched him curiously.

"We are to—bring them to—the King's study—immediately," he huffed. The other guard nodded and motioned for some more men to join them. They surrounded us and waited while we dismounted our horses and left them outside before being escorted inside the castle. The castle was exactly as I remembered. Dark walls, dimly lit, portraits of menacing past Kings and Queens hanging drearily on the walls, black and red tapestries draped from the rafters.

Inside, we were greeted by an angry-looking young man, possibly in his late twenties or early thirties. He was tall, built like a fighter, and dressed fully in black. His eyes were black as well; he was the epitome of an Astinian. He cast a menacing smile in our direction as he took the lead in front of the guards.

"And who are you?" Arthur growled at him. I reached out and put my hand on his shoulder to keep him calm.

"I am Raysh. Crown Prince of Astinia. And you are?" he sneered over his shoulder. His voice was deep and dripping with condescension. His back was turned to us, but I could tell he was smiling to himself.

"Arthur of House Blackwood, General of the knights and armies of Lynnea." Arthur drew himself up tall. He already was a tall man, but Raysh was still taller and larger.

"And the rest of you?" He cast his eyes back suspiciously at me. I did not meet his gaze.

"My trusted knights." Arthur folded his arms over his chest, and Raysh huffed in reply. He led us into another dark room, most definitely a study. Bookshelves lined the walls, and the King sat at a large stone table in its center. He was a big man with black eyes and bulging muscles. *Strong, but no match for a Deity.* He had aged significantly, of course, since the last time I saw him. I wondered if he would recognize me. I hoped he wouldn't.

"You Astinians hate light," one of our knights exclaimed.

"And any color that isn't black," another chimed in.

"Or red," the other added.

I bit back the urge to lash out at them, but I didn't want to draw too much attention to myself. Arthur turned and glared at them instead. The King had his hands folded together in front of him, his fingers pointed upwards, and his chin resting atop them thoughtfully. He was a terrifying-looking man with sharp features, tattooed all over, in contrast to his son, who must have had all of his covered beneath his clothing. Astinians were always covered in tattoos; they always thought it made them look more intimidating and tough. I looked down at the tattoo on my hand, a blue violet against a starry night sky. The King wore no sleeves and a lower neckline, showing off the menacing art that covered his body. There were symbols, old Astinian runes, and intricate drawings of battles, most likely his victories. If I were any other man, I'd have been terrified of him. But I was no man. I gripped the hilt of my sword subconsciously. The King motioned for Arthur and me to sit, and we took our places across from him. In the corner of the study, I noticed the Queen seated in a chair looking thoroughly anxious. It had been a long time since I had seen her. I couldn't remember exactly when that was. Though I knew that she was from Drocia originally, she looked thoroughly Astinian now. Beside her sat another young man, presumably another one of their sons; he had a long tail that curled around his chair, and he looked disinterested in anything going on around him, focused mostly on his mother. The men were studying the swishing tail carefully, trying not to look too horrified. I'd seen all kinds of shapeshifters in my hundreds of years; though there weren't many left, nothing surprised me anymore. I refocused on the King, who was studying both of us thoroughly.

"I understand you're here to negotiate the release of Queen Allanora. I am Rhonan, King of Astinia. I have agreed to hear your terms as a show of courtesy, considering you traveled all this way, though I don't think you will have anything of value that would convince me to return her to you." He grinned and folded his hands in his lap, leaning back into his chair.

A Dance of Storms and Shadows

"We are," Arthur said shortly. The Crown Prince snorted and joined his father at the table.

"And on whose authority do you have to negotiate terms of release of a held monarch?" Rhonan's eyes shot daggers into Arthur.

"I am here on behalf of King Aros."

Rhonan drew his lips together in a tight line at hearing my name.

"I'm sorry, I think I misheard you. I thought you said *King* Aros?" His eyes didn't show even a hint of surprise. He knew I had returned, but he wanted to taunt Arthur.

"That's correct. Aros, King of Lynnea, husband of the late Queen Violet, father of Queen Allanora." Arthur was impressively collected and handled himself well. The King and his son were harsh, intimidating men.

"Aros is gone. He and all the other Deities fled their kingdoms years ago like cowards." *Cowards? The Triini are the cowards. Burning humans for worshipping us instead of their 'Unnamed God'... Pathetic.* My eyes flicked back over to the Queen, who was studying me intently. I shifted slightly, uncomfortable under her gaze.

"Aros returned to reclaim his throne in the name of his daughter and late wife. He executed the traitors who orchestrated the murder of Queen Violet. I am here to negotiate on his behalf for the return of his daughter. We are prepared with many offerings in exchange for the Queen." Arthur leaned forward in his chair, meeting the King's wicked glare.

"Allanora is to be wed to my son, Raysh." He gestured to the son by his side, who smiled proudly.

"The Lynnean law states the Queen is to choose her husband. I can't imagine our beautiful, gentle, kind Queen would choose such a brutish man, or kingdom, to align herself with." Arthur's voice was licked with anger. He regarded Crown Prince Raysh with a look of burning envy and disdain. I willed him silently to keep his emotions in check. Though he was keeping his composure, his lips were pursed, and his sword hand was clenched around the hilt of his weapon.

"The Lynnean law does not matter here. This is Astinia, she is my prisoner, and I have decided that she is to marry my son. I can't imagine you have much to offer that would outweigh a Queen, you understand. I suggest you go home and tell your 'King' that he will be gaining a son-in-law, a King-to-be, at that. He should be proud. And tell him to leave, go back to wherever he's been hiding. Cidris is now ruled by human Kings and Queens and is led by the religion of the Golden Dawn. His return will not go over well." My attention was drawn to a shadowed corner of the room. A hooded figure stood in the unmistakable cloak of the Triini, watching us with two piercing eyes from under his hood.

"He doesn't have to tell him. Aros is here." The Queen rose from her seat, her deadly eyes locked on me. The hooded figure took one step forward, toward me, then hesitated. Rhonan and Raysh looked at each other, then at us. Arthur and I both stood quickly. Rhonan snapped his fingers, and the guards took hold of each of our knights, forcing them to the floor behind us. Rhonan came chest to chest with me, looking me dead in the eyes.

"So—it's you, is it? It's been quite a while." He studied me carefully, trying to read behind my eyes. "You finally came out of hiding, did you?" My nose twitched. Static danced on my fingertips, begging to be set free. I quelled the pull of my power. The Queen approached us, gently placing herself between her husband and me, studying me carefully.

"Her magical signature is almost identical to yours. Almost." I narrowed my eyes at her. "The girl shouldn't have the power of invincibility as a full-blooded Deity does, and yet, my son can't kill her." She stepped back from me, though her eyes never left mine. "I couldn't put my finger on it. I couldn't figure it out. But now, I see you. I understand. You're pouring your magic into her, you let that haze around you slip. I can feel your magical signature. You're giving her your life force to heal her. I've never seen anything like it. I didn't know it was possible. It shouldn't be possible." She reached out to touch my face, no malice, only curiosity in her expression, and Rhonan grabbed her by the wrist and threw her backward onto the table.

"None of this concerns you, woman." She turned her face away as he lifted his hand to strike her. I grabbed his hand and turned him around, smashing a sizzling knuckled fist to his face with my other hand. He was stricken with surprise, but only for a moment. I drew my sword, and he drew his. Sparks flew from mine as they clanged against each other, metal on metal. I feared unleashing my full power, knowing I'd take out Arthur and his men as well. Allanora would never forgive me. Out of the corner of my eye, I could see Arthur grappling with Raysh back and forth. He was holding his own very well against the grisly Crown Prince. Rhonan knocked my sword from my grip, but I replaced it with a lightning bolt. Everyone else in the room froze as sparks flew. I guessed none of them had seen a Deity fight with a bolt of lightning before. Rhonan was sweating, but I was gaining momentum. Every blow he tried to land, I dodged. I finally knocked him to his knees, holding the bolt across his chest, both of us panting. He held his hands above his head as far away from the bolt as he could.

I felt the rush of victory I hadn't felt in quite a long time, the excitement of even such a small battle had my heart racing. The thrill of the fight. I raised the bolt above his head to strike. Suddenly, I was washed over with a chilling cold I'd never felt before. A hand clasped around mine—no, a cuff. The lightning disappeared, and I dropped to the ground. Above me, the Queen was standing, her eyes wide with shock as if she hadn't expected it to work. The King scrambled to his feet, looking to his men.

"Seize them!" he shouted; his eyes were wild with anger. In a flash, Raysh had Arthur pinned to the ground, the guards having already disarmed the knights. "Take the Lynnean King to the dungeon. His powers are no good there. And bring Queen Allanora immediately." Two guards brought me to my feet. I had never felt this before. Powerless, human. I looked the Queen in the eye, and she looked down, ashamed.

"I was defending you," I spat at her. She refused to meet my eyes.

"Your daughter will understand one day when she's in my shoes. This is the life I live. I'm loyal to my husband, always." Her eyes were wide, fearful, and sad. Angrily, I fought against the guards, trying to free myself, but I couldn't.

"What did you do to me?"

"I bound your powers with a cuffing spell. Only temporarily. My magic is powerful, but I can't hold the powers of a Deity for long. Our dungeon will do the rest for me. It's completely magic-proof down there. Not mine, not yours..." She trailed off, flushed with guilt. "Take him away, we don't want the young Queen to know he is here." They dragged me off.

A couple of guards took off in the other direction, I assumed to look for Allanora. I made sure to note which staircase they were taking to get to her chamber; I would take any opportunity I could to release her from here.

All the way down into the dungeon, I kicked and fought against the guards, almost forgetting what it felt like to be human. I hadn't gotten free, but both were visibly tired by the time we reached the ground floor of the large Astinian castle. They brought me into a cell, where they chained me on my knees to the floor, and large metal bolts kept my shackles in place. I yelled out to no one, releasing my rage out into the silence and darkness.

I'd make them pay, every last one of them.

Chapter 24

Allanora

I had been getting ready, as ordered, trembling from head to toe while I prepared for the wedding I had always dreamed of to a man I was absolutely terrified of. A handmaid had brought me a scarlet gown adorned with diamonds and rubies in the stitching. It was beautiful, but I hated it. I hated it for everything it stood for, my imprisonment in Astinia and my marriage to the Monster Prince.

My mind wandered to Rylan. My lips still tasted his. My expectation would've been that he'd taste like tar and brimstone, but it was more like rain; I closed my eyes, and I could feel his soft touch still. Even though I knew my fate was sealed, I still held out a little bit of hope that he would find a way to get me out of this or that I could find out how to get out of it myself. I sighed, knowing it was a pipe dream. As strong and powerful as I knew Rylan was, one look at Raysh told me Ry couldn't overpower him; it just wasn't possible. Suddenly, my door burst open, and two guards forced themselves in. I turned around quickly. They both averted their eyes immediately when they realized I was still only in undergarments.

"Your Majesty, our deepest apologies," one said from behind his hands, keeping his eyes covered. "If you wouldn't mind, we were told to escort you immediately to the King's study. He has urgent business for you there."

"Excuse me, I am not dressed, and I was told to be getting ready for the wedding. I am a bride-to-be, you know." I felt a mixture of relief and irritation as I spoke to them. The one that had been speaking nodded hurriedly. "I don't think the Crown Prince would take kindly to you bursting into my room and seeing me like this." They both tensed and shrunk back. I'd gone too far; these people were already fearful of the royal family. I didn't need to double down on it. I'd be just as bad as they were. The guilt gripped my chest.

"Yes, Your Majesty, it's just that something has come up."

"I don't have a handmaid here to lace me into my gown. It'll have to wait." I continued brushing my hair, pretending not to be bothered by their sudden intrusion.

"You'll have to put on a robe, Your Highness. The King won't wait. It's very important." I rolled my eyes and slipped into a long dressing robe. *Very important... He probably just wants to make me wear a black gown instead of a red one.* They uncovered their eyes, and I tossed my hair back behind my shoulders. Astinian hairstyles were so difficult to maintain; everything was free and all over the place. I stepped behind them and out the doors, not waiting for them to escort me. I stomped into the King's study, where he was sitting, his hands folded on the table in front of him and a smug grin spread across his face. *Here comes the black dress.*

"Well, well, little Queen, do I have a wedding gift for you..." The sarcasm in his voice was unnerving as he gestured across the room. I surveyed the scene in front of me and let out an audible gasp.

Eleven men were lined up on their knees, ten of them held down by guards and the eleventh locked in the deadly grip of Raysh, my betrothed. Tears immediately welled up in my eyes when I studied their armor, the crest of Lynnea proudly emblazoned on their chests. My eyes landed on the man trapped by Raysh, and I dropped to my knees when I realized it was Arthur Blackwood. He had recognized me after all, and he had come for me. The knight in shining armor I'd been begging for was here, and Raysh was going to kill him. My heart sank into my feet. Raysh studied me, watching the unmistakable swell of emotion when I locked eyes with Arthur.

"No—No, please, I don't understand." My voice trembled. I tried to make eye contact with each man, memorizing their faces and reciting their names and titles, biting back a sob.

"This band of treasonous vagabonds broke into my castle, attacked my son, attacked my Queen," the King announced smugly, not taking his eyes from me.

"You lying, disgusting, son of a—" Arthur started, but Raysh gripped him around the neck from behind, silencing him in a chokehold. I watched as he shook under Raysh's grasp, gasping for air.

"Please, please, I'll do anything. Please let them go. I've done everything you've asked. I—I—" I felt myself going numb, felt helpless, knowing I had nothing left to offer the King. I was already their prisoner, I had already promised myself to their son... I had nothing more to give.

"They say they are here on behalf of the *King* of Lynnea. They said they were here to make terms to negotiate your release. Then, they attacked Raysh and Queen Eudora. This cannot be stood for. These men must be punished."

"I'll bear their punishment, please," I begged. "These are good men, loyal men, soldiers, sons. Spare them, please." Rhonan reached around me and pulled me up from the ground, grabbing my face with his hand and watching the tears stream from my face. I could tell from his smile he was enjoying my pain, enjoying hearing me beg for their lives.

"Raysh is going to be your husband in a couple of hours, so I think you should ask *him*." He threw me at Raysh's feet, and I gathered my strength, forcing the sobs down, as I looked up at him, trying my best to avoid Arthur's pained and panicked gaze. Swallowing my pride, I bowed my head. I knew this was what my life would be like from now on, bowing before Raysh, bending to his will.

"Please, my beloved future husband, I beg for the lives of these loyal men, spare them and let them go, and I'll be yours truly, forever obedient. I'll do whatever you ask without question. Without defiance." Rhonan took over restraining Arthur so that Raysh could crouch before me, his hands behind his back and that familiar evil grin smeared on his darkly handsome face. He grabbed me by the neck and dragged me to my feet just as his father had, squeezing me in his grip. Fear, hatred, and disgust all pulsed through me as I locked in on his black eyes.

"Tell me you love me," he taunted. He knew I didn't, but he was going to squeeze every last bit of humiliation that he could out of me.

"I–I love you–" The words were so sour I could barely utter them. Raysh snapped his fingers, and the guard farthest from me plunged a sword into the shoulder of one of the Lynnean knights. He let out a groan as he fell to the ground, blood spurting from his deadly wound as the light left his eyes. An angry, earth-shattering scream found its way out from between my lips, and suddenly, I felt cold and weak as something clasped around my wrist. I turned around to see the Queen casting a spell. All my power drained from my body. It was a strange rush of darkness, emptiness; I wavered, but Raysh kept me on my feet, staring wildly into my eyes.

"Hmmm... Somehow, I just don't believe you. Especially after that stunt you pulled in the dungeon. Try again, *Your Highness,*" he jeered. "Or I'll kill the next one. I'll kill every single one of them until this entire room is covered in Lynnean blood." I sobbed; Arthur was fighting violently against the King's hold.

"I love you, ok? I love your eyes, and your strength, and your handsome face," I exclaimed. I couldn't stop the tears; they dripped down to my mouth, down my neck... My whole face was wet with them. He smiled, but he didn't release me. Arthur's expression was even more pained, and Raysh took notice.

"Kiss me," he sneered. Instinctively, I recoiled, and he lifted his hand to give another signal.

"No!" I shouted, my eyes unable to leave the sight of the poor young knight in the pool of blood before me. I leaned forward and touched my lips to his. He grabbed the back of my head with his other hand, holding me in place as he violated my mouth with his. I tried not to sob as his tongue forced its way past my lips, but I couldn't help it. He snapped his fingers again, and I watched the next guard take off the head of the next knight with his sword in one swift movement. I screamed again, and Raysh dropped me to the floor. More inhuman sounds clawed their way from my mouth as I knelt in the pool of blood, helpless.

"Stay down there and beg, Your Majesty." He stood over me, eyes wild and drunk with power. He knew he had me exactly where he wanted me, broken and begging for the lives of my people. I said please about a hundred more times between sobs, my dress robes soaked in the blood of my loyal knights.

"Stop this, Raysh, it's getting out of hand." Rowan emerged from the shadows, standing in front of his brother. "You're torturing your Queen on your wedding day. I wouldn't say that's the best way to start your partnership," Raysh growled, but Rowan held firm.

"She needs to know her place."

"I think you've shown her enough. If anything, you're just showing her you're exactly the monster she thinks you are. Now send her back to her chambers to get cleaned up and ready unless you want to present a bride dripping in the blood of other men to your people as their Queen." Raysh was angry but stepped back from me. Rowan put his hand on my back and helped me to my feet, holding me up.

"Take these men to the pit," he grumbled. "We will hold them there until after the wedding." My eyes locked with Arthur's momentarily, both of us trying to apologize without words. The nine of them were led out of the room, past the bodies of the other slain men. *Hecter, Peter, you won't be forgotten.*

"Can you walk?" Shaking, I tried to take a step and collapsed, so Rowan carefully lifted me to my feet and then picked me up, holding me in his arms. "I'm going to return the Queen to her chambers. I'll send for a couple of handmaids to clean and dress her," he told Raysh, trying to push past him to get to the door. Raysh held his hand out to stop him.

"I'll take my own betrothed to her chamber. You shouldn't even have your hands on her." He grabbed for me, but Rowan dodged him.

"With all due respect, brother, I think you've done enough damage today. Rylan and I might be paid to do evil things. You do it by choice. I'll never forget the things you've done." Raysh bristled but surprisingly allowed him to pass.

Silently, he carried me back to my room. He laid me down on the bed before ringing for a handmaid to attend to me. He sat at the table in my room, picking at his fingernails while he waited uncomfortably.

"Are—are you all right, Your Majesty?" I shook my head violently, curling my blood-soaked knees into my chest. He sat down on the bed next to me and gently stroked my hair. "Sorry," he said, "I'm not sure exactly what to do in situations like this." I nodded slightly, and he continued to stroke my hair.

"Tell me about Cienna..." I muttered.

He went pale and ran his fingers uncomfortably through his own hair. "Cienna was from Wrilon, a high-born daughter of one of the Lords. Her father had racked up a tremendous debt and was given the choice to sell her to a brothel or send her to the Academy. Her father gave her the choice, and she chose the Academy." He gulped. "She caught on quickly, only the second girl to attend. The first was Gen, of course. I trained her for a while. I'd been there for 5 years."

"Why did he kill her?"

"My father comes to 'inspect' the 'students' occasionally. Raysh came with him once. Rylan swears he didn't tell them about us, but I know he did. Raysh took her back with him. I never saw her again." I reached out to put a comforting hand on him when I heard a loud clatter behind me. My head whipped around, and I saw that Rylan had come through the window in a hurry. He was out of breath and rushed to the bed. Rowan's face scrunched up.

"The hell are you doing?" Rowan asked him.

"Well, what the hell are *you* doing?"

Rowan didn't reply. Rylan turned to me and studied my face carefully. "I heard what happened from one of the servants. I'm so sorry, I had no idea they were even here, Nora."

"Nora?" Rowan questioned him. Rylan waved him off, taking me into an embrace. I sobbed into his shoulder.

"It was awful, Ry." I swiped at the tears that wouldn't stop falling. "They were good men. Young men. Loyal men. The rest of them are imprisoned. Who knows what will even happen to them now? I can't protect them. I'm their Queen and completely useless." My lips trembled. Rylan looked between me and Rowan.

"Rowan, could you give us a minute? Please?"

"Uh. No. I just got her out of one mess, I'm not letting you get her into another one." Rylan rounded on him, throwing him up against the wall by the window.

"Please, stop," I begged, crumbling underneath the pressure and emotions. "Please, I can't take any more fighting." I clutched my head between my hands, tucking my face into my knees. My breaths were coming fast and shallow, my face going numb. My hands started to shake, and I felt like I was going to vomit. The two brothers laid me down carefully, trying to help me relax. Footsteps clacked outside the door, and Rowan rushed to lock it. The handle turned back and forth, but the door didn't open. Frantic knocking started from the other side.

"The Queen isn't feeling well, give me a moment." Rowan looked desperately at Rylan, who was stroking my hair and holding my hand. I was shaking violently as all the moments that had darkened my life recently flashed before my eyes.

"Rylan, if I keep this door locked any longer, Raysh is going to kill me. He's going to think I'm defiling his wife." Rylan shot him an angry glare.

"If you don't shut up and give me a minute with her, Rowan, *I'm* going to kill you." Rowan's jaw snapped shut, and he turned back to the locked door, talking to the guard through it.

"Hey, hey, Nora? Look at me, focus on me, just me. It's going to be ok. I promise you. I swear to you, it's going to be ok." He knelt next to the bed, locking those beautiful eyes with mine. With the back of his hand, he stroked my cheek. "Just breathe, it's ok, please, just breathe." I nodded frantically, trying to slow my breaths. I felt pain in my chest as the shallow breathing continued. Terrified, I tried to calm my mind with happy thoughts.

Riding through the forest with my mother, the wind whipping through my hair, galloping freely through the trees. My first ball, surrounded by happy faces and beautiful gowns. My mother's face lighting up as I stepped into my choosing ball. Dancing, being twirled around by handsome men, all hoping I'd choose them. Rylan, his touch, his kiss, his eyes.

My breathing slowed, and I forced myself to sit up. Quickly, Rowan let the handmaid waiting outside into the room. The guard followed.

"What's going on in here?" he demanded.

"The Queen was unwell after the shock, as I'm sure you can imagine. Please leave the room, she has to get ready for her wedding," Rylan said forcefully, dismissing the guard quickly. The maid looked between both men before turning to attend to me. She wiped my face clean quickly, then turned around to start hot water for a bath. She looked at them pointedly, trying to shoo them from the room with her hands. They both looked at me, unsure of what they should do. I waved them off.

She busied herself washing me up, washing my hair, cleaning all the dried blood off me, and getting me ready. I felt like my hair took hours while she detangled, combed, and styled it like an Astinian Queen. She pulled me into a strange corset, tying it so tight that I could hardly breathe, and slipped my red wedding dress over my head. I knew then why the corset felt so odd. It had to accommodate the plunging neckline of the gown that went down almost to my waist. My breasts were almost completely exposed, yet I was drowning in silk layers from the glistening ballgown. The train extended the length of the room. The sleeves were see-through and sewn with tiny gemstones. The dress was gorgeous. I would've loved it if it didn't remind me of the blood of my fallen knights, or the monster I would be sleeping beside for the rest of my life, or the cruel kingdom I was meant to rule. A sob caught in my throat, and tears threatened to fall from my eyes.

No more tears, I told myself.

The handmaid decorated my face in the Astinian fashion, sticking red rhinestones to the skin underneath my eyes. When she finally turned me toward the mirror, I could barely recognize myself. My usual regal braid had been replaced with tumbling curls woven with tiny braids throughout. Some locks had been pulled and twisted behind my head and fastened into place. My face was painted and decorated with rhinestones. I had been transformed into an Astinian. The thought terrified me, but then I remembered all the knights who were still being held captive, who depended on me being complacent. I drew myself up as tall as I could in my seat, holding my head high as I always had to. No matter what kingdom I was in, I was a Queen. Lastly, the handmaid placed a golden tiara atop my head. It was covered in hundreds of flawless rubies. They caught the light and cast drops of blood-red around the room. *Fitting, always surrounded by blood.* She fastened it carefully on my head. I stood silently from where I had been sitting.

She opened the door for me and gathered as much of my train as she could in her arms. Stepping from the room, I was greeted by two guards and both Rylan and Rowan. The Thorne brothers each gasped and smiled. Their eyes lit up but were filled with sadness. The guards helped the handmaid with my train, spreading it out and carrying it behind me. Each of the Thornes held out an arm for me to take.

"My lady, we've been asked to escort you to the throne room to be wed." Rylan's eyes were twinkling. I was lost in them momentarily, but I nodded solemnly and let them lead me on either side to the throne room, to my new life.

Entering the throne room felt different. During my coronation, I felt so much hope for my kingdom, for myself, even though it had been one of my darkest days. Stepping into this life, surrounded by hundreds of Astinian subjects staring at me, only filled me with gut-wrenching dread. Raysh was dressed in full wedding attire. He looked almost handsome, and the thought haunted and terrified me. His black dress clothes trickled with rubies to match my gown. I began to shake when I came closer to him. Both Rylan and Rowan gripped me tightly, holding me steady, and I was grateful for them in that moment. In the front of the crowd, I saw Rhonan, flanked on each side by Eudora and Gen. The sight of her made me feel ill, and I faltered again, but the brothers kept me steady. I noticed another woman, dressed entirely in black, her blonde hair pulled back tightly, standing next to Gen, but I didn't recognize her.

Reaching the large altar at the front, I stood across from Raysh and in front of a Brother of the Triini holding a large dusty book. Rowan and Rylan released me gently, only returning to the King and Queen once they were sure I wouldn't collapse without their support. Gen reached out to hold Rylan's hand, but he pushed her away and moved to the other side of his mother. If I wasn't so afraid, I would have smirked. Rhonan was smiling smugly up at me. Raysh clasped my small, sweaty hands in his, gripping me tightly. I avoided his gaze as much as I could. I could barely listen to anything that was being read to us. I was so overwhelmed with fear and hatred of Raysh that my mind was blurring. Every once in a while, I stole a glance over to Rylan, who was ever glaring and looking angry but didn't move a muscle.

Chapter 25

Rylan

Letting her go at that altar was one of the most difficult things I'd ever had to do. Turning her over to my brother, the man who killed animals for fun when he was a child, who tortured and killed people for amusement, was nearly impossible. I hated him, hated everything he stood for. He was violent by choice; I was forced to be. He'd have her now, and I couldn't. I saw her small body shaking visibly, even underneath her wedding gown. She was stunning; every curve was accentuated perfectly, and the tiara looked as if it belonged atop her head. She was perfect. He didn't deserve her. I didn't deserve her.

An unfamiliar pang wrenched in my gut when I thought of the knight that was trapped in Raysh's fighting pit. He deserved her.

I returned to my spot in the crowd but kept my focus on her, only her. Gen reached out to touch my hand, and disgust shot through my body. I moved my hand away and slipped over to the other side of my mother, away from her.

Gen was a reminder of everything I had become, everything I didn't want to be. Being with her in the past had been a mistake, a mistake I couldn't get away from. Gen was a beautiful woman, surely, but she was a killer inside and out, with no desire to be anything better, anything more. She was the daughter of Steele, the leader of the Academy, the bloodthirsty group of assassins that I'd been given to, alongside my brother at the age of 12. Steele was here, of course. She had arrived in the early morning with the intent to bring me and Rowan back to the Academy after the wedding. I looked over at her momentarily. She was a petrifying snake of a woman dressed entirely in black, her hair pulled back tightly behind her. She could kill a man with barely a flick of her wrist, and she had taught me to do the same.

Allanora hesitated a couple of times at the altar. It took all my willpower not to rush to her side, tell her everything was going to be ok. I hated my brother for torturing her, and I hated him for being able to stand across from her now and claim her as his wife. My blood boiled at the thought he'd claim her tonight. He wouldn't worship her body like she deserved on her wedding night. Before I even knew it, the ceremony had ended. My face flushed with anger as he pulled her into him, claiming her hungrily with his lips. The way her lips had melted into mine when I kissed her... the thought enraged me. I groaned and looked away.

All the people started filing away to the ballroom, where a huge feast was being served in honor of the marriage of the Lynnean Queen and the Crown Prince of Astinia. No Lynneans had been invited, of course—too risky for my father. He planned to announce they were wed after it had happened, although it seemed the Lynneans had found out anyway and sent their envoy to rescue her. Part of me had hoped they would have succeeded for her sake, but another, more selfish part of me was glad that she was still going to be here in the castle. A castle I didn't intend to leave as long as Nora drew breath in its halls. No matter what tricks Steele had up her sleeves, I wouldn't leave her.

The ballroom was decorated grander than it had ever been—in my lifetime, anyway. People were happily chatting away at tables, greeting the new Queen, and enjoying the lavish spread of food before them. A suckling pig graced the center of the table, the apple in its mouth only another reminder of how Nora would be treated here. Alongside it, roasted quail, swan, and game hens, and each table was littered with more potatoes and side dishes than I could count. A grand feast in honor of lifelong imprisonment. It was disgusting, the whole thing. Once the food had all been devoured, Raysh and Allanora were welcomed to the dance floor. He twirled her clumsily around the floor; Raysh was significantly less than graceful, while Allanora was the picture of poise and beauty. I watched the crowd around them staring, some in awe, others in discomfort. Raysh's prowess and ferocity were well-known amongst the subjects of the kingdom. Many fathers around Astinia had let out a sigh of relief, knowing it wouldn't be their daughter on his arm, in his bed. Others started making their way to the dance floor to join them, and soon, a sea of black and red glittered around the married couple. I felt a tap on my shoulder and turned around.

"Care to dance, my beloved?" Gen asked softly. Her eyes were sincere, but her words did not seem to be. She held her hand out to me. I took it reluctantly, and she sighed with relief. I danced with her for a moment, moving us closer and closer to Allanora. A few men had asked to cut into their dance, as was customary at a wedding, but Raysh brushed them all off with an irritated huff. Territorial ass, as if anyone would dare try to take her from him. When we made our way next to them, I offered my hand to Allanora and Gen's to Raysh.

"My Queen." I bowed to her, and her blue eyes lit up, dazzling blue sapphires in this sea of black souls. Raysh made the switch grudgingly, watching as I whisked Allanora away to the center of the floor, twirling her gracefully the way she deserved. It felt like muscle memory; my hands rested on her just as they had at her ball, but her eyes were so much more knowing now. She knew me, yet her eyes were still soft, joyful at my presence. For the first time, I realized she made me feel human, something I hadn't felt in a long time, if ever. She had broken through my walls. She rested her head on my chest and took a deep breath.

"I'm scared, Ry," she whispered, her voice shaking. I came crashing back down to reality, remembering that she had just vowed to spend her life with my brother, the beast.

"I know." It hurt me to know she was afraid, and I couldn't help her. *How can I help her?*

"Please, can you convince them to release my knights? It's over now, I married him, they can let them go home."

I sighed heavily. "I will do my best, Nora. My father doesn't always listen to me, you know." She nodded slowly. I could feel her heartbeat in her chest slow as we danced, relaxing against me. I wanted to tell her that I wouldn't leave her here alone, that I'd do my best to protect her. Rowan would too, in his own way. But I couldn't ruin this moment, I wanted her to have this peace. Raysh came up behind me and tapped me on the shoulder. She immediately tensed, and her heart started pounding so hard I thought it would pop out of her chest.

"I'll have my wife back now." He offered her his hand. She shook her head, terrified, as tears welled up in her eyes. He glanced around quickly, then grabbed her by the wrist, pulling her up to him. Everything in my body screamed at me to take her back, to fight him. My fists balled at my sides.

"I'm going to make something very clear to you, Allanora. You are mine now, for as long as you live. You can make it painless for yourself, or you can make it very painful. The decisions you make will dictate how it goes for you. No matter what, though. You. Are. Mine. Do you understand?" She nodded quickly, drawing in a deep breath and letting him lead her away roughly. I made a pointed glance at my mother, who was seated just off the dance floor, watching the two of them. Her face reddened when our eyes met, and she turned her eyes away from me. Raysh sat Allanora down at the table with a firm hand on her shoulder. She hadn't touched any of her food, so she began pushing it around the plate absently, staring at it, her mind seemingly miles away. He grabbed the side of her neck and pulled her to him, roughly kissing her down to her collarbone. She winced, but he didn't stop; he was marking his territory in front of the entire kingdom. In front of me. I looked away and saw Rowan was doing the same. He motioned for me to come over to his table.

"You know what he's going to do to her, right?" he whispered to me. My hand gripped the fork in front of me, digging it into the table. I nodded. "Steele wants both of us to return, Ry. Neither of us is going to be here to protect her. You know that, right?" There was no use in explaining to him that I didn't intend to leave. I glanced over at Steele; she had been joined by about eight men. Rowan was looking, too. "Others," he said through gritted teeth. I grimaced. 'Others' were the soldiers that were trained at the

Academy, the army-for-hire. They did whatever she told them whenever she told them to do it, and she had brought some of them with her. Inevitably, if we tried to resist going with her, it wouldn't go well for anyone. I sighed.

"When is she planning on this?"

"After your wedding to Gen..." I winced. The thought stung me. I couldn't marry her. I hated her and everything that came with her.

"Oh, good, so never," I joked, but Rowan's voice was grave.

"Father's word is law, and he agreed, Ry."

"I don't care what Father says."

"Then why'd you let her marry Raysh?"

I stared at him, not knowing what to say. I glanced back over at Allanora. He was groping her roughly in front of everyone while she was beet red and trying to keep her composure.

"I didn't know how to stop it, Ro," I confessed, defeated.

"Look. I know it's a little different, what happened with Cienna. But there's not a day that goes by that I don't wish that I had killed him." He gripped his fork tightly and bent it in half.

"It is different. Cienna wasn't promised to him, he just took her to get at you. This is political, this involves the kingdom, it involves Father." My own blood boiled at the truth behind my words. I hadn't cared about anyone in a long time, if ever. I hadn't even realized that I hadn't truly felt anything for more years than I could count. But Allanora awakened something in me, something that had been buried so deep in the dark pit of my soul I didn't think it was still there.

Rowan shrugged. "After what he did this evening, I wanted to kill him. I imagine you would, too."

"You want to kill him?" I didn't mean to sound as surprised as I did, but like me, Rowan had spent so much time at the Academy that I didn't think he had a soul.

"I hate him too. Just a hair more than I hate you." He elbowed me. "But I hate what he's going to do to Nora. She doesn't deserve it. Just like Cienna didn't."

"I guess you're not that bad yourself, Ro," I mused.

The night passed by slowly. People greeted Allanora, congratulating her on becoming Queen of Astinia and creating such a strong political alliance between our two kingdoms. She handled every moment with such dignity. She was a perfect Queen. Rowan was drowning himself in wine, surely out of anxiety about returning to the Academy. Rowan was never meant for this life; he was soft, even if he tried hard not to show it. I could still remember him burying the animals Raysh had tortured and killed when we were children. He had adapted to survive, but Rowan hated killing and feared death. I kept my eyes trained on Allanora, watching her every moment until Raysh picked her up to carry her out of the throne room. She paled and tensed; fear struck through her entire body.

"Ro, cover for me." I tapped him on the shoulder and stood, making headway toward a different staircase than the one Raysh was carrying Allanora up.

"Ok, when I said that about wanting to kill him, I didn't think you were going to act on it. You're going to get yourself killed. And her. And me. Sit down." He grabbed at my arm and shoved me back into my seat. Sometimes, I forgot how strong he was. "Even if you stopped him tonight, he's married to her. He can have her any time he wants. You can't do anything about it now."

"I swear, if he harms her..." I gritted my teeth, forcing my mouth closed.

"Rylan. You and I both know he's not a gentle man. In any way. We've seen the state of his mistresses and the aftermath of what happens when people try to interfere. Allanora is a strong girl, she will survive this. Who knows, maybe she will get smart and try to enjoy it." I gripped him on the shoulder, digging my fingers into him. He twitched but made no sound. Instead, he pushed a cup of wine towards me. "Here, drink. Maybe you'll forget." I downed it in one gulp. "There you go. You keep doing that. I'm going to go find a woman, so maybe I can enjoy the rest of my night in someone's company a little more pleasant than yours."

"Please, take Gen off my hands." He rolled his eyes, choked down the rest of his drink, and made his way over to a table of women, trying a few charming lines on them.

After an hour of watching Rowan hit on the eligible Astinian women in attendance, I grew tired and slipped away to bed. I was hoping I wouldn't have to say goodbye and give excuses to everyone along the way. I made my way to my own chambers with every intention of sleeping off my anger. I reached the floor where my brothers' and my rooms were, and as I turned the corner, her scream ripped through the hallway. I held my hands over my ears, but I couldn't stand it. I drifted toward Raysh's room without even thinking. Her screams were pained and terrified, not the kind you'd expect from a woman on her wedding night. Angrily, I stood outside the door, knowing that any decision I made here was going to change everything.

"No, no, please, no!" I heard her shout and start to sob. I couldn't take it. I cracked the door just enough to look inside the room without alerting them to my presence. Her dress was in a tattered heap on the floor, and he had her pinned to the bed, his hand around her throat, forcing himself on her. She was screaming and crying, and there was a significant amount of blood on the bed around her. Anger ripped through me. I saw red, and I moved as quickly as I ever had. I kicked the door open, drew the dagger from my belt, and flung it at him, hitting him square in the back but missing his heart. He crumpled and fell on top of her. She screamed in shock and forced his limp body off her, flinging herself off the bed and gathering her shredded dress around herself. I stalked into the room and kicked Raysh over. He was still breathing.

His eyes flew open, and he launched himself at me, completely naked, and started swinging. *This is new for me.* He snatched a sword from his wall and came after me again. I caught it with my bow and drew my own sword. His movements were slow but strong, and he reeked of alcohol. I glanced over at Allanora. She was sobbing wildly, trying to regain composure. She held her palms close together, sparks flying between them. *It can't be her; it has to be me.* I shoved Raysh backward, giving me enough room to kick him square in the chest, knocking him on his back. My dagger was still lodged in him, and it was starting to tear through to the front of him. We locked eyes, and I stepped on his chest; blood oozed from his mouth. More pooled around his back from where my dagger had struck him. He growled weakly.

"You'll never hurt her again." I pushed down on his chest with my foot, driving my dagger forcefully up from his back. Blood gurgled from his mouth in thick gushes, and his eyes drained of color. I felt no remorse for my monster of a brother; the Academy had made sure of that. His body thudded on the ground when I rolled him over and covered him with a blanket so she wouldn't have to look at him anymore. Quickly, I rushed to her side and picked her up, holding her dress over her. I ran her down the hall to my own room and locked the door behind us, barricading the door with as much furniture as I could. She tried to speak, and she couldn't. I shushed her and, removing the dress from around her, studied her body, looking for injuries. She was covered in bruises, had multiple burn marks, a couple of whip marks, and a cut down her arm that was bleeding significantly. I ripped off my shirt and tied it around her arm. I shuffled around in my clothes and found a shirt and pants to slip onto her. She was bleeding significantly between her legs, so I did my best to help her dress and lay her down on my bed.

"We can't stay here long, Nora, but I want you to rest. I'm not going to leave your side." She shook her head back and forth violently. "What, what is it?" She pointed to the carafe of water, and I poured her a cup and waited for her to drink it.

She coughed dryly, some of the water sputtering back out of her mouth. "You have to free my knights, please. They'll kill them when they see what happened," she begged.

"Nora, he raped you, he beat you, he cut you. I have to take care of you right now. I can't leave you like this," I argued with her.

"Please," she begged again, clasping her shaking hands together. "Please. Everyone will be distracted right now; you have to free them. They don't deserve to be punished because of me." I leaned over her and kissed her gently. She winced as she tried to kiss me back.

"Okay, Nora. Don't strain yourself. I'm going to be right back, ok? I promise. I'm going to free them, and I'm going to get you out of here. Do not move." Not that I really thought she could. I slung my bow over my shoulder and grabbed my quiver of arrows. Grabbing a couple of extra daggers, I slipped out my window and scaled down the wall to the pit.

"I can't believe I'm doing this," I whispered to myself. But I knew I couldn't think too much about it. I'd killed my brother, the Crown Prince. There was only one way out for me now, and that was with Nora, away from the wretched palace. I slipped into the window of the pit. Allanora's knights were all chained to the floor in the center. Perched above them, in the rafters, I surveyed everything below me. Nine men in chains, a pile of their weapons, three guards, possibly more outside. I rolled my eyes.

Too easy, I thought to myself wryly before drawing my bow and arrow. I knocked three arrows and drew the bowstring back to my cheek. On my exhale, I let the string go, letting all three arrows fly and find their unknowing marks. All three guards dropped to the ground with nothing but weighty thuds and the clatter of armor on the pit floor. I smiled to myself, *and they thought I lost my edge.* Allanora's knights looked shocked as I dropped to the ground in front of them, studying them intently. I approached them slowly, tossing my dagger up in the air and twirling it between my fingers, contemplating what should come next. I sighed deeply and took the keys off one of the guards. As I was unlocking them from the ground, I recognized the man that we had spent some time with in the woods. The annoying one who'd stared a little too eagerly at Nora. So it was him. The man who deserved her love, the one who she probably would have married if I hadn't interfered in her life. It felt like such a long time ago. I freed him last, and he immediately lunged at me, knocking me to the floor. I put my hands up above my head.

"This is the thanks I get for letting you and your men go?"

"You're the one who kidnapped her! You're the one who tried to kill her!" He tried to throw a fist at my face, but I rolled him onto the ground below me, pinning him down.

"I know! I'm sorry. Look, I just killed my own brother for what he did to her. I'm trying to make things right, and I'm trying to get her out of here, but she insisted that I had to come free you because she knew they'd kill you. She's not wrong, of course. Without her, you're all meaningless to my father." I shrugged. The shocked expression on his face stayed pasted there.

"Where's Aros?" Arthur demanded.

"Who?"

"Aros! King of Lynnea? Allanora's father? They said they were taking him to the dungeon." I rubbed my brows with my fingers, exasperated. It wouldn't look good on me to leave the girl's father here, powerless and chained up in the dungeon. I let out a deep breath.

"Do you know how to climb?" I asked him quietly.

"What?"

"Do. You. Know. How. To. Climb?" The irritation in my voice was thick. All I wanted was to get back to Nora, get her out of here, and run off with her, but I knew if I didn't get all of her men out of this, she'd never forgive me. She wasn't selfish like me. She cared about everyone; all I cared about was her.

"Yes, I can climb. Why?"

"Great. Go out this window here, climb up 27 stories, and through the window, into my bedroom, you'll find Allanora there. She's in bad shape. You'll need to get her out of there as soon as possible. They might be looking for her already." His eyes were wide, and he looked shocked, casting his eyes between me and the window. He pursed his lips decisively and made way. He turned back toward me when he reached the wall.

"What is the Queen doing in your bedroom?"

"How about you spend less time questioning the man who just freed all of you and more time worrying about scaling that wall to rescue your damsel in distress." I rolled my eyes. "All you knights love that shit."

He bristled, stiff with agitation, "What about my men?"

"I'll show them where to go to get out of here. Just go. Finish what I started. If you don't get her out of there before my father gets to her, I'll rip you open and tear you limb from limb, understand?" He looked confused but nodded before starting to scale the wall. Satisfied that he'd make it to the window, I ran off in the other direction, toward one of the tunnels in the pit, motioning for the men to follow me. "I'll show you all where to go to escape from here, and I'll make way for the dungeon to free Aros." One of the knights grabbed me by the shoulder and turned me around. His eyes were fierce.

"We aren't leaving before the Queen is safe. This is our mission. We will help you to free the King. Lynnean men don't run from danger, we will die for our Queen." They all nodded in agreement with him. I rubbed my brows with my thumb and forefinger, contemplating.

"All right, all right, fine. You come with me to the dungeon to free the King, but we are going to have to fight our way back out of the castle. It won't be easy; my father has this place crawling with guards and soldiers. And if you get in my way of getting Allanora out of here, I'll kill you myself. Be prepared to hold true to your promise to die for her." The man who had been speaking nodded quickly. I wasn't going to bother learning their names, it didn't matter. I turned toward another tunnel, one that would lead us down to the dungeon. They gathered their weapons and followed behind me.

The stairs from the pit to the dungeon were narrow and winding. It was one of the oldest parts of the castle. I had only been this way a few times myself. Once we reached the dungeon, there were hallways filled with hundreds of cells, and I had no idea which one they put him in.

"Fan out. Go in twos so you don't get lost alone. He will be in a closed cell with an iron bolt. Iron is more resistant to magic than silver, keep an eye out for that. Yell if you find him, there won't be many guards down here right now." They nodded and paired off, the thump of their boots echoing down the halls. The dungeon was vast but looped around. Eventually, they'd end up back here if they didn't find his cell. I took the fifth hall, peeking through all the closed cell windows. I didn't realize how many prisoners my father had stashed down here, or maybe it was Raysh...

I looked in about a hundred cells, and none of them seemed to be containing a Deity. There were servants, imprisoned knights, and convicted traitors. Some of them I recognized, and some I didn't. Aros would be chained to the floor. Most of these prisoners were not chained but just curled up in a corner of the room, seemingly wishing for death. I circled back around to where I had started and kicked a large wooden door fastened with an iron handle.

"Damn it, Aros, where are you?" I shouted to no one in particular. "I'm trying to get your daughter out of here."

"Hey! Hey! I got him! It's the King!" I heard from down one of the halls. I took off in the direction of the voice, my feet pounding against the stone floor.

His cell was at the end of the first hallway. I peeked in through the window. There he was, bolted to the ground in heavy iron chains. He locked eyes with me immediately and snarled, tugging at his restraints.

"Murderer! I know who you are! You killed my wife, you tried to kill my daughter! You brought her here!" His booming voice echoed through the halls.

"I'm touched at such high praise, but you can just call me Rylan."

He wasn't amused, and I was sure from the burning hatred in his eyes that, if the onyx wasn't blocking his powers, I'd be dead on the spot. "I'll kill you! I'll rip your limbs from your body. You don't know fear, you don't know pain!" I picked the lock open and swung the door in. It creaked deeply and eerily when I pushed it. He yelled something inaudible, possibly in another language. I approached him cautiously, unsure of how to begin to explain. As I got closer, I could see his liquid golden eyes hadn't lost their light; they shone in the darkness. He was ravenous with anger; I could see it in his gaze. Even without his magic active in the onyx-lined dungeon, he exuded power. I could almost feel it pulsating through the air. I kept my hands up by my head as I approached him and motioned for the two knights to come in after me. He looked between them and me, momentarily confused. "Traitors! Aligning with the enemy! I'll have all your heads!" He spat at them, rattling his chains, trying to force them from the floor, but they didn't budge.

"Aros, please. I'm going to free you, and then we are going to get Nora out of here." He paused thoughtfully, looking me up and down cautiously. I got closer to him, my hands still lifted in surrender. "I know what you think, I know what you saw, but I'm not going to hurt Nora. I'm trying to save her." His feral eyes studied me suspiciously. "Arthur sent me here for you. He should be with her now." *If he isn't, I'm going to kill him,* I thought quietly to myself. The knights nodded to him in agreement with me. I took one of the knights' swords and broke both chains connecting the Deity to the floor. He immediately jumped me, wrapping his hands around my neck, shaking me violently. But after a moment, he released me, confused. The rest of their knights had made their way to where we were, filing behind us into the cell.

"You're all here with *him*?" Aros asked them. They nodded in response. They were clearly respectful of him but also entirely terrified. I could see why.

"Arthur went after Allanora when he set us all free. He knew his way to the dungeon," one of the younger men told him, pointing at me. Aros furrowed his brows sternly but nodded to them.

"I don't understand, you tried to kill her. You're the assassin. I saw it."

"Look, I know there's probably a lot of explaining to do here, but I really don't think now is the time to do it. Allanora is in bad shape, and I'm just trying to get her out of here." He pursed his lips in frustration but nodded in agreement. I nodded back and led them out of the cell, back into the darkness of the hallway, and started running for the stairs.

"What did you mean, she's in bad shape?" I stopped running, the men coming to a clattering halt behind me, one running directly into me.

"She has some—injuries."

"From when?"

"Just—an hour or two ago." His expression darkened, and I saw anger boiling in his cheeks. His fists were clenched, and he looked down at them in frustration.

"How much further until my magic isn't blocked anymore?" he growled at me through gritted teeth.

"Um, I think just up the steps." He started stalking angrily toward them. "But look—" I paused thoughtfully, choosing my words very carefully. "I already took care of the problem." He shot me a glare. "I killed him—the man who—the man who hurt her." There were so few things left that I was afraid of, but an all-powerful Deity looking for vengeance was on that shortlist. He huffed angrily and made off for the stairs. We ran after him, but he was significantly faster. He reached the top of the steps quickly, and with a loud *crack* and a flash of light, he was gone.

Slowly, I crept up the stairs behind him. I heard crack after crack of sound reverberating through the walls of the castle; he was looking for her. As the sounds continued, I could hear guards and servants starting to frantically run about in confusion, trying to figure out what was happening. Sighing heavily, I motioned for the knights to slip out the doors while I took off into the chaos, my mind only on Allanora. Traveling alone was much quicker. I knew this castle like the back of my hand and easily slipped through the halls and stairwells without being noticed. The higher I got, the louder I could hear Aros' movement.

Peeking into Raysh's room, I saw his body was gone, and a chill went down my spine. What I'd done wasn't a secret anymore, and everyone would be looking for the Crown Prince's killer. They'd probably come for Allanora first. The room was still in disarray, Allanora's blood splattered all over the bed, Raysh's smeared on the floor. It was a gruesome sight. I rushed to my chamber, where I hoped Arthur had already arrived.

The door had been opened, and all the furniture I had piled up was flung to the side. I swallowed hard. The room was empty of life, with no sign of Nora or Arthur. I picked up a chair and, yelling loudly, threw it violently against the wall. It shattered under the pressure. Frustrated, I kicked over a nightstand. I heard a loud *crack* across the hall and went dashing across to Raysh's room again. I found Aros, in full Deity form, standing at almost the height of the ceiling, lightning sparking all over his body, fuming at the sight of his daughter's blood. His shirt was tattered around the arms, more than likely from the lightning bolts. His muscles were bulging, and veins through his body were popping out angrily from beneath his skin. His face was red with rage, and his golden eyes had turned fully black, reminding me of how inhuman he truly was. In his hand, he held a golden lightning bolt, crackling under the pressure of his grip. He whipped his head around violently, making direct eye contact with me and raising the bolt. I held my hands up instinctively to protect myself.

"Where. Is. She?" he demanded, his voice booming and shaking everything in the bedroom and hallways outside.

"I don't know. I sent Arthur after her. I checked where I left her, and she's gone, no sign of Arthur, either. I'm looking for her, too. I promised her I'd get her to safety." I felt despair and desperation rising in my chest, feelings that I hadn't felt in a long time. In fact, I hadn't felt much of anything in a long time. I pushed the feelings aside, focusing only on Allanora. "How much of the castle have you checked already?" His nostrils were flaring out to the side like an angry bull.

"I've checked it all. Every room. She isn't here."

"Can't you sense her?"

"I can only sense when she's dying. That's when I can heal her. Other than that, I can't find her."

"That explains a lot." He turned his head to the side, confused.

"Why she—why the arrow didn't—well, you know," I stuttered. For once, I was having a hard time thinking about my moments of violent weakness, where I had tried to take her life. It filled me with shame. He placed a large, strong hand on my shoulder. I heard a loud crack, like it was inside my skull and body, and suddenly, we were outside. I tumbled to the ground out of shock. I had never done *that* before. Aros was standing not far from me, eyes closed, concentrating. He was speaking in a tongue I did not understand and reaching out into the air in front of him as if he were touching something I couldn't see. I leaned down on the ground and tried to catch my breath.

"If you've been healing Allanora this whole time, why couldn't you heal Violet?" I mumbled just loud enough for him to hear.

"Violet is human... was human... her body wouldn't be able to handle such a flood of magic required to heal the body the way I've healed Allanora. From your brutality, I might add." The venomous truth of his words stung me. He wasn't just saving her, he was saving her from what I'd done. One day, I'd have to find a way to repay him for that.

When I finally stood, I was face to face with a large, dark man dressed in purple robes. His arms were folded over his chest, and his face carried a menacing look. Aros pushed me out of the way and stood chest-to-chest with the mysterious man. Behind him, I drew my bow and an arrow from my quiver, standing ready.

"Aros." The man snorted.

"Sinric. This is a less than pleasant surprise."

The men lunged at each other, Aros' lightning bolt smacking against Sinric's golden staff, sparks flying. My eyes narrowed; *a mage strong enough to fight a Deity?*

"I'm looking for my daughter, and I'm not going to let you get in the way," Aros shouted as he lunged at him again.

The mage drew a sword of flames from nowhere and swung it to his own defense but never made a move to attack Aros. "I'm trying to help her, too. I don't want to fight you, Aros." I watched with curious fascination as Aros lowered his bolt just enough to look into Sinric's eyes and narrow his own.

"Why are you trying to help her? Aren't you the Queen's personal mage now?"

Sinric shuddered. "I've turned a blind eye to Astinia's way of life for too long because of my connection to Eudora, thinking that there was still some good that the King hadn't beaten out of her yet. But when I heard that she had bound Allanora's powers and left them bound long enough for her to be so thoroughly brutalized by the Crown Prince... I couldn't align with her—with them— anymore." The sword of flames disappeared in a puff of smoke, and the mage held up his hands.

"How did you even know Allanora? I declined your offer to train her. You never even met." Aros looked as if he was trying to peer into the other man's soul.

"Eudora brought me here to train her. Though, it seemed more like she wanted me to tame her in order to protect her son from Allanora's powers. I could understand that. As you and I both know, untapped power in the stems can be...unruly."

Aros was considering his words for far too long. Allanora's life was at stake.

"Um—excuse me? Magical...beings?" I couldn't hide my irritation. I just wanted to get back to Allanora, and these two were going at it like children. "I'm not sure if you forgot, but Allanora is out there somewhere, and she's hurt badly. So, if you two could just... I don't know, save this for later? Whatever this is..." Aros bristled, and Sinric bowed, taking in a deep breath.

A flood of guards came rushing out of the castle then, spears and swords drawn, coming for Aros. He pursed his lips and brought his hands together, releasing a wave of lightning bolts that went hurtling toward the guards. They disintegrated instantly. I blinked my eyes in shock and looked up at Aros, taking an involuntary step backward.

"Oh, and the way *I* used magic is what was forbidden," Sinric commented with a chuckle, surveying the charred ground before us.

"You used *forbidden* magic." Aros squared up to him again, and Sinric braced himself for a fight.

"*Save it!*" I shouted at them. Aros' nose twitched, but he stood down and relaxed his stance. "The King is going to realize Raysh is dead, and he's going to be hunting Allanora. We have to get to her first. We don't have time for your weird magical quarrel. Work together now. Fight each other later." They nodded; they knew I was right.

"We should split up; we will find her faster that way," Sinric added. Aros' face still twitched, but he agreed.

All that matters is Allanora, I thought, taking back off into the castle.

Chapter 26

Allanora

No blade can cut a golden stem. The unfamiliar yet strangely familiar voice rang through my mind. My eyes filled with golden light until it was so bright I had to open them. Engulfed in what seemed like a golden shroud before me stood Arthur Blackwood. I felt the pain wash away from my body, and my chest rose fully for the first time since before the wedding.

The wedding. I winced, remembering. I touched my left hand, where a large ruby sat atop my ring finger. I twirled it around carefully, feeling the cold golden band against my skin.

"Your Majesty." I looked up, and Arthur was bent in a deep bow on one knee. I motioned for him to rise. I didn't have the energy to stand and curtsy. He approached me carefully, studying the parts of my body that weren't covered by Rylan's clothes. He touched a burn mark on my arm, and I recoiled in pain. "You're hurt. Did *he* do this to you? The assassin?" He gritted his teeth, looking around him cautiously. I surveyed the area where I was, just inside the tree line of a forest. I could see the castle not far away but far enough to breathe a sigh of relief. I looked back to Arthur and shook my head, confused at how I'd finally made it out and away from the castle of nightmares.

"No, Arthur, he rescued me from my assailant. I was dying." I looked off into the distance again at the large, looming castle where I had been kept prisoner. "Where is he, Arthur? Where is the assassin?" He pursed his lips, his jaw set angrily.

"He went to free your father." My face was a mixture of shock and confusion.

"My father? My father is here?" My voice was shaking, I still felt so weak.

"Yes, my Queen. King Aros and I led an envoy here to negotiate your return to Lynnea. Only, it went a little sideways. They imprisoned him in the dungeon. They said his powers would be bound there." I looked down at my hands, remembering my own powers being bound by the dark dungeon. I shuddered.

"*King* Aros?"

"Yes, um—he came to Lynnea after you um—died? He took the throne in your name and imprisoned Tobyn. Before he killed him anyway."

"*Killed* him?"

"Yes, well executed. He, well, he sentenced Tobyn and his eldest son to death for treason, for the death of your mother, and the attempted murder of, well, you. He carried out the sentence himself. Shortly after that, we gathered the envoy to come here. For you." He wrung his hands uncomfortably, looking me up and down for a reaction.

"I see. And Rylan—the assassin— was freeing him from the dungeon?"

"Yes."

"And where are my knights, then? I don't see them."

"Well, they, uh, they went with him." She dropped her head into her hands.

"To the dungeon? In a castle crawling with Astinian soldiers and guards?"

"He told me to get to you, to get you out of the castle. He said that you, well, that you were injured. I just didn't expect you to be like *this*. I got you out as fast as I could, Your Majesty. You lost so much blood. I didn't think you'd survive."

"We have to go back."

"No, Your Majesty. My duty was to get you out, I got you out. The rest can manage for themselves. I must get you back to Lynnea, I have to get you home," he pleaded. I shook my head.

"Aros is still in there. My knights. Rylan…" I trailed off.

"The assassin?"

I nodded. He set his jaw and drew in a breath, looking me up and down. "You stay here, I'll go. You're far enough out that they won't come looking here while Aros is still inside."

"No, Arthur. I'm going." I stomped my foot stubbornly, sending pain from one of my bruises shooting up my leg. I ignored it, trying to look strong. I didn't feel strong. I felt weak, defeated, helpless. "All of you have been putting your lives, your homes, your families, everything, on the line for me. Those are my men in there. I have to go. Please, Arthur, take me back to the castle. That's an order from your Queen." He sighed deeply, defeated. I held my head up triumphantly. Arthur helped me up. Limping, I set off toward the castle. Arthur huffed behind me and quickly lifted me from the ground. "I can walk, Arthur."

He smiled a valiant smile. "You're hurt, you walk slow. If I carry you, we will get there faster." I smiled back and let my head rest on his chest. His silver-plated armor was cold against my bruised face, but it felt good.

The Astinian grounds surrounding the castle were vast, dark, and beautiful. Ivies crawled up the trunks of the trees, wrapping them in their deep green stems. Red poppies were sprinkled through the lush green grasses, and dark clouds were cast in the sky. The black stone castle loomed above us, taunting me with its mystery, its secrets, the menacing people within. Across the fields in the distance, I saw movement. I tensed and looked, trying to focus on what it was.

"Arthur, what is that?" He cast his eyes in the direction I was pointing. I could see a flag flying, but I couldn't make it out; my head was still throbbing.

"Your Majesty. It's Lynnea." He sounded just as surprised as I was.

"What?"

"Henrie, he brought the army." My eyes widened and I shook myself from his grip, wheeling toward the direction of the army.

The realization punched me in the chest; the war I had fought so hard to prevent now towered over me, and the shadow was so large and desolate that it threatened to crush me. My eyes filled with tears and immediately began spilling down my cheeks. My heart ached. I couldn't take it, a war looming over me. War meant death, starvation, tearing apart families, *all because of me.* I couldn't stand it. My head spun, and I felt dizzy, my breath catching in my chest. I couldn't draw in oxygen. I watched as countless lines of foot soldiers marched in perfect rhythm, coming closer and closer to the castle. Panting, I fell to the ground. My vision started to blur. The dark clouds above me released a blue crack of lightning, thundering to the ground and obliterating the patch of grass right beside us. Arthur flew backward, trying to drag me with him, but I stayed put.

"We have to go, Arthur!" I shouted. He was stunned, staring at the charred ground. "We have to go; they're going to know where I am now."

"Did... Did you do that?"

"Well, um, not on purpose."

He took my hand in his, holding it gently, though I could see the wariness in his face. He picked me up, more urgently this time, and started walking at a brisk pace toward the castle.

We reached it quickly, more quickly than I would have expected, considering he carried me the entire way. He set me down at a side door, bowing before me.

"My Queen. It has been an honor to have served you. Should I die here, I want you to know that I am happy to have given my life for yours, and I do it willingly." He kissed my hand and then looked into my eyes. Straightening himself, he touched his hand to my face gently, and I felt myself blush. "Allanora—you're worth every sacrifice." He smiled his gallant smile once again, opening the door, not knowing what we would be stepping into.

Chapter 27

Allanora

When the door opened, the hallway was empty. I didn't recognize this area of the castle, but I heard voices not far away and started walking toward them. Arthur grabbed me by the arm, pulling me backward.

"Your Majesty, please, let me go first. Let me protect you." His eyes were pleading. I wanted to storm in front of him, do as I wished, but the look in his eyes reminded me I was a Queen. I couldn't do whatever I wanted. He was sworn to protect me, and I had to let him. I bowed my head and let him pass. Drawing his sword, he crept carefully down the hallway toward the voices. I walked behind him slowly and carefully. Suddenly, I felt a hand cup my mouth. I looked down to see a blade at my throat, the slightest glint in the dim light of the castle hall. I tried to struggle, but the arm held me fast. Arthur disappeared around a corner, not noticing that I wasn't following.

"I've had about enough of you, little Queen." Rhonan's voice was a deep chill in my ear. "You came into the castle to wreak havoc on my life. My kingdom, my son," he growled in my ear. "You'll be answering to me. Your marriage to my son is binding by law. You're a citizen of Astinia, and you will be punished as an Astinian. You may be immortal somehow, but I don't have to kill you to make you feel pain." My heart dropped into my feet, pounding wildly against my skin so hard I thought it would burst right out of my body. My hands started to tremble, and with my mind, I begged Arthur to notice I was gone, to turn around and come back. Rhonan dragged me in that direction anyway; I sank to my knees, dropping my weight, trying to slow him, but he lifted me off the ground, keeping the hand around my mouth firm. I forced my mouth open, hoping to draw even the shallowest breath, and was not surprised that his very skin tasted of ashes.

He dragged me into the middle of a large open room where it seemed the Lynnean knights had been in an altercation with a large group of Astinian soldiers. Arthur had just arrived to join the fight, realizing just a little too late that I was gone. Rhonan threw me to the floor, and I lifted my head up, surveying the full scene before me. There were about twenty soldiers to my eight knights plus Arthur, neither of the living Thorne brothers nor Aros to be seen. Rhonan picked me up by my hair, twisted it around his hand, and held the blade to my neck.

"Enough! One more move from any of you, and I'll cut her pretty little neck." I shivered as the cold blade touched my skin, as chilling and terrifying as Raysh's ring that encircled my finger. The men dropped their weapons immediately, kneeling and holding their hands above their heads, each of their eyes locked on me.

"You killed my son, you miserable wretch of a Queen!" he shouted at me. Angrily, I pulled myself forward, trying to free myself from his grip, but he held on tight. I yelped as he yanked me back.

"Your son was beating me! Forcing himself on me! You're a kingdom full of masochists!" I cried out, tears streaming down my face, remembering too vividly the details of the night. Raysh's hands on my throat, his branding iron on my torso, how I'd torn when he was inside me. I forced back a gag. "I didn't want to come here," I sobbed. "I didn't want to marry him; I didn't want any of this. Your son was a monster, an awful monster. He was no King, and neither are you!" I spat at the ground in front of me, showing him that I meant full disrespect. He roared and ripped me up off the ground by my hair. Arthur stood, grabbing the sword that he had thrown to the side, holding it up. Rhonan smiled, taunting him.

"I might not be able to kill you, little Queen, but I'm going to kill every single one of your knights while you watch. Then I'm going to take my full army to your sweet little kingdom, and I'm going to tear it apart. My soldiers will kill every man, woman, and child of Lynnea and burn everything to the ground. I'll make you pay the price for my son's life." His words were furious and wild, his voice bouncing off the walls of the castle. "If that's not enough," he whispered, barely loud enough for me to hear, "I'll take you for my own, remind you that I am the nightmare from which Raysh was born."

Crack. A bolt of lightning sent everyone in the room flying. Everyone but me and the King. He held me steady in place, bracing himself against the force of the bolt. Before my eyes stood an incredibly intense-looking man who would've terrified me if I hadn't spent the last couple of weeks trapped in Astinia with the Thorne family. He was middle-aged but incredibly muscular, with liquid gold eyes that looked like they'd seen a hundred wars. He looked at me with a mixture of fear and relief. I had been so focused on the strange man that I hadn't noticed Rylan, wild-eyed and bow drawn with an arrow fixed and pointed at his father. Rhonan tightened his grip on me and pushed the blade onto my neck, making a small and painful incision. I cried out; the sting sent a burning sensation down into my chest.

"Don't take another step, Aros, I'll spill her blood. I'll drain her of every last drop. We'll see if you can heal her then."

It hit me like a ton of bricks. The intense-looking man was my father. He smiled, a warm smile that I never thought I'd see in my life, as I stared at him in realization. I wanted to hate him, hate him for abandoning me, abandoning my mother, but in this moment, I only felt relief. He flicked his wrist, and a sparking bolt appeared in his hand. His eyes burning with anger, he raised it above his head, poised to strike.

"Aros, you'll hit her!" Rylan shouted at him. "Let me do it." He drew back the string of his bow, aiming the arrow directly at his father's heart. Out of the corner of my eye, I saw Arthur grab a spear from the floor and lunge forward toward me and Rhonan. I heard Rhonan yell out behind me. His hand moved, and I felt the ripping sensation of my skin coming apart at my neck. He released me as he and I fell to the floor, my own blood pooling around me. It had all happened so fast I didn't have time to react. I heard Rylan shout out and Aros say something in a foreign language, but I couldn't comprehend either of them.

My ears rang, and my heart slowed to a crawl, begging for each beat as the life spilled out of me. My vision blurred into a myriad of colors. I saw Arthur, Aros, and Rylan all make a mad dash for me or Rhonan; I couldn't tell. Blinking slowly, I let myself slip into the inviting warmth of death.

I opened my eyes and was greeted by an unfamiliar and stunningly beautiful woman with liquid gold eyes like Aros'. She was wearing a white floor-length dress, and her whole being seemed to glow. She smiled a warm and comforting smile and offered me her hand. I took it without thinking. Her hand was small and delicate, almost exactly like mine. Looking at her, I realized she bore quite a resemblance to me.

"Who are you?" I asked her softly. "Where am I?" *Is this the everlife?*

"You're nowhere, sweet girl. It's all right, I'm here to help you. I am Ata." Her sweet smile was so inviting.

"Ata? The Goddess?"

She nodded. "It's all right, we're family." She giggled softly. She looked like she couldn't have been much older than me, but like Aros, her eyes were worn with lifetimes. She reached out and touched my face. Her hands were strangely warm.

"I thought you were—well, I thought you were dead?" I looked around. There was nothing but green grass and blue skies for miles around. I couldn't see anything else, no signs of life, no structures, nothing. It was beautiful and vast but also lonely and terrifying.

"Well—I am, but I live here now, waiting for my family." She looked into the distance sadly, like she knew she wouldn't see what she was looking for. Her voice was wistful and detached.

"Why am I here?"

"Well, my dear, you died, too. We are here together, me and you." Her sickly-sweet voice couldn't mask the gravity of her statement. I had failed.

I was never going to stand in front of my people again. I didn't go back to them like I swore I would. I abandoned my knights, Arthur, Rylan, my army, all to fight a battle over me when I was already gone. A war would be fought in my name because I had failed. Failed to live when they needed me. I felt like crying, but my eyes wouldn't shed any tears. The sadness boiled in me and fizzled out in an endless cycle of hopeless emotions. I'd never get to know my father, thank Arthur and the knights for everything they did for me... I'd never see Rylan again.

"I don't understand. I kept being healed. I was hit with the same kind of arrow you were, and I didn't die then. Why now?" My breaths were coming short and fast, but I still couldn't produce a tear.

"You gave up, sweet girl. It's ok. You fought hard; you did everything you could."

"No, I—I didn't give up. I couldn't have. I don't want this. I need to go back, I have to go back." I fell to the ground in a heap, hitting my fist angrily against the soft grass. I looked up, and the girl, my aunt, was gone. I looked around me and saw nothing, nothing but the lonely plains of the afterlife. I put my head into my hands and screamed.

"My flower. It's all right." I looked up and felt the weight of the world lift off my shoulders. Suddenly, she appeared before me. I flung myself into her arms, and she held me tight, my heart and hers beating as one.

"Mother!" I sobbed tearlessly into her shoulder. "Mother, I'm so sorry, I'm so sorry."

"Shh—there now, my dear, you don't have to be sorry. You're so brave, so very brave. You're here, we are together now, that's all that matters," she crooned into the top of my head as she stroked the back of my hair with her hand. She looked over my head and tensed her grip around me. Tucked safely in her arms, I turned my head around just enough to see what she was looking at.

Behind me, a trail of shimmering apparitions hovered as far as I could see. Their forms faded as they went back, but when I studied the first few, I realized that they were the Queens of Lynnea. Just a few back, I saw a familiar face. The face of the woman who had come to me in that vision in Lynnea, which felt like so long ago. The middle-aged woman with the lavender eyes, she was my great-great grandmother. Allanora. We locked eyes, and she smiled. She'd been watching over me, my mother must have been too. They all were. My chest constricted, not from anxiety as I'd gotten used to, but from joy, love, and the comfort of knowing that I wasn't alone.

I came back to reality when I realized that another woman, her presence immediately chilling, with icy blue eyes and electric blue hair, was standing directly behind my mother. She reached out to touch my face, a curious expression about her. I shied away, turning my head back to my mother's shoulder for comfort. When I looked up again, the apparitions of past Queens had gone.

"Queen Allanora," the woman addressed me, her voice as icy and uncomfortable as her presence. "You don't belong here." My mother hugged me protectively. I turned slightly to face her at her words, releasing my mother.

"I don't understand. I died. Ata said so." The strange woman reached out and took my hand, turning it over to look at my palm. A mark had appeared; a circle with a lightning bolt struck right down the center. I looked back up at her, meeting her chilling stare. She shook her head no.

"Who are you?" I asked her curiously.

"Kahtix, Goddess of death." She bent herself into an uncomfortable-looking curtsy. My eyes widened; the Goddess of Death was not someone you wanted to meet. I gulped.

"What do you want with her?" My mother drew me back to her, putting herself between me and Kahtix. Kahtix hissed at her.

"She bears the mark of a God. He calls her to return, she has to go back." Kahtix held her hand out to me. It was illuminated with a soft blue light, entrancing to look at. My mother turned me around to look directly at her.

"My sweet, you don't have to do this, you don't have to go with her. You don't have to fight anymore; you don't have to be brave anymore. You and I, we would be together for eternity, just us, right here." She pleaded with me, pulling me into her warm embrace. I could feel her shaky breath on the top of my head as she held me. "Hasn't she suffered enough? You'd have her go back to that place? They tortured her, harmed her, they took everything from her! She needs *me!*"

Kahtix ignored my mother's sentiments. "This is not your time, Queen Allanora, my brother needs you." I wailed into my mother's chest. I didn't want to leave her; she had been my whole world for all of my life. She was my comfort, my safety, my home. She had been for as long as I could remember. But so much had changed since her death. I, too, had changed. She stroked my hair, and I thought of Aros, a man I barely knew but who had fought so hard to keep me alive, to restore me to my throne. Arthur, who traveled so far to bring me home, who rescued me, who fought for me. I thought of my people who had put all their hopes into my return, who would suffer the most loss in the event a war would be fought over my death. The Lynnean army, marching to liberate us all from the hell I'd so suddenly left behind. Lastly, I thought of Rylan, the most confusing and difficult relationship I had to consider. I thought of all the harm he'd caused me, all the times he'd insulted me or put me in harm's way. Yet I couldn't stop thinking about everything he'd done since to redeem himself. All the things he didn't have to do but did anyway. I sighed heavily, breathing in my mother before releasing her. She looked as if she had just had her heart broken for the first time.

"I'll come back, Mother." She nodded, biting her lip and wiping an invisible tear from her eye. Ata reappeared next to her, and as they embraced, they both waved goodbye to me. Kahtix took me by the hand, and a cold sensation crept through my entire body. Mother pulled me back to her, embracing me once last time and taking my face in her hands.

"You're more powerful than you know. You don't have to do anything you don't want to do. I'm so sorry I never told you who you truly were. I was so afraid of losing you, of having you be hunted just for who you are." Her eyes filled with glittering tears. "Don't let *anyone* make you forget who you are. You're *my* daughter, Queen of Lynnea." She locked eyes with me, and I memorized her face, taking in every detail as she vanished, leaving me alone in the darkness.

I opened my eyes to see Aros and Arthur hovering over me. I looked around for my mother, knowing inside that she wouldn't be there, but I found myself feeling inclined to look for her anyway.

"My Queen." Arthur helped me to sit up. I rubbed my neck where the knife had sliced me; the skin had completely smoothed over, the blood gone. It was strange. I focused on my surroundings. Rylan had his father tied up on the floor in a seated position. The Astinian guards were rounded up in the middle of the room. The Lynnean knights were standing in the entry to each hallway and door, weapons drawn.

"What's happening? What happened?" I asked them hurriedly, trying to scramble quickly to my feet. I got dizzy and leaned back. Arthur rushed to catch me.

"One of the guards ran off when you and the Astinian King went down. We are expecting more soldiers to appear any moment now. We did strike the King." I looked over at Rhonan. He was awake and breathing, blood slowly dripping from his shoulder where the spear had hit him.

"I told you to get her out of here, that they're going to come for her. Why did you even bring her here?!" Rylan was visibly angry, tightening his grip on his father. I started to come to, and everything in my mind snapped back into place.

"I asked to come here, Ry," I said groggily. Aros' eyes moved between me and Rylan. He kept his hand firmly on my back. Rylan's face twitched with fury. "I wasn't going to leave everyone behind just to save myself," I said softly. How could he understand? Everything he'd ever done had been for himself. *Except killing Raysh, he did that for me.* I immediately felt guilty for thinking of him as selfish. I felt my face flush. Arthur was looking at me through narrowed eyes, eyeing the spot on my neck where the cut had been, now replaced only with smooth skin. He opened his mouth to speak at the exact moment a group of Astinian soldiers burst through one of the entrances to the hallway, led by Rowan. His nostrils flared out, and he was poised with an arrow pointed at his brother across the room. Rylan drew his own arrow. Arthur stood in front of me, sword drawn and ready.

"Rowan, please." I clambered to my feet. "This has to stop; the bloodshed has to end." I stepped in between them all. Arthur and Rylan immediately put their weapons down. Rowan didn't move.

"You killed my brother, Allanora. Our King is your hostage." He nodded his head toward Rhonan, tied up on the floor. "You have to pay for what you've done." His voice was shaky but stern. He took a step forward, and Arthur grabbed me by the arm, pulling me backward and drawing his sword again. "And who are you?" Rowan asked Arthur. Arthur gave him an indignant look.

"Arthur Blackwood, sworn protector of the Queen of Lynnea," he stated proudly. Rowan scoffed. "We were only here to bring her home, we never intended on bloodshed."

"Oh, I understand. No bloodshed? That's why there's an entire army that just crossed our border." He spat in Arthur's direction and looked back at me. "Why did you kill him, Allanora? Do you know what you've done? I would've done everything I could to keep you safe while you were here, but now—"

"She didn't kill him." Ry's voice echoed through the throne room, a harsh, demanding growl.

"I saw the body, Rylan. She stabbed our brother in the back."

"I did it. I killed him. I did it because I love her, and I'll kill you too if you even think about touching her." Rylan lifted his bow again with a deadly stillness. "You may not have had the courage to defend Cienna, but I'll never let anyone hurt Nora. You've always been a coward, Rowan. Too scared to even defend what you love. I may be a lot of things, but I'm not a coward." The hurt in Rowan's eyes flashed quickly before melting into deadly, ravenous anger.

Rowan lunged, but not for Rylan. His eyes were trained on me, and he let out an otherworldly howl as his arms and legs turned scaly, a long set of teeth descended from his mouth, and two large horns came out on top of his skull. Not lizard-like... Dragon-like.

Before Rowan could reach me, Aros disappeared and reappeared between us, taller and glowing with a deadly golden light. Aros drew his own sword, standing only feet away from Rowan, holding it out to him, challenging him. Rowan nodded, slung his bow around his shoulders, and put the arrow back in its sheath. He drew a sword from his belt and held it comfortably in his two hands, his tail swishing steadily behind him. Aros rushed him, swinging with an expert fury. Their swords clashed and clanged together, echoing through the hallways; sparks flew with the friction of the two swords. I realized as I watched them that I had never really seen Rowan fight, except briefly against Rylan. He was the thinnest of the Thorne brothers, but he moved fluidly, holding his own against a Deity. Aros got him locked against a wall, pushing his sword against him, both of them dripping sweat.

"Did you have a hand in killing my wife?" Aros demanded, using his whole body to put pressure on Rowan. Rowan shook his head indignantly. "Did you harm my daughter?" Rowan's eyes flashed over to me, then he shook his head again. My father's eyes drifted to me. "Did he harm you?" I shook my head no. "Did he touch you?"

"No. Aros. Father. Rowan didn't harm me, he helped me. He's angry. Rowan's as much of a prisoner as I am. Please let him go. I don't want any more bloodshed over me." Aros let out a low growl but released Rowan from his hold. Rowan took in a deep breath, casting his eyes angrily toward his father; he walked toward him and threw his sword at his feet.

"I'm tired of fighting for you." He looked up at Rylan. "I don't know what happened to you, but I'm not fighting for you either. You let Raysh go on the way he did for years, torturing, fighting, killing for fun. You never once stood up to him. You always said you'd never beat him in a fight. You were there the night he took Cienna, and you didn't even bat an eye when you knew what happened to her. You wouldn't even do anything to help me, your own brother who suffered alongside you for years. Yet this Princess walks into your life and you turn everything we've ever known upside down for her. You killed him for her. You can dig your own grave. You're not my brother." Rylan's eyes narrowed, but he didn't reply. His lips were curled into a half smile, watching his brother walk away.

"Coward," Rylan murmured under his breath. In a swift motion, Rowan whipped around, swinging out his bow and arrow and letting one loose in Rylan's direction; it zipped through the air and landed in the wall behind his head, cutting his ear along the way. Rylan was steaming, his face flushed red. Rowan didn't care. He turned around to leave.

"Sir?" A soldier stopped him, taking him by the shoulder.

"I don't care what you do. I'm not in charge of you anymore. I'm returning to the Academy. By choice." He bristled and left, shrugging the soldier off. Immediately, the soldiers looked to Rylan, confused and unsure of what to do next; Rylan ignored them, focusing his attention on me. I tried not to quake at the thought that I had ripped the two of them apart forever.

"I'm going to keep my father here. I can give you a head start. Arthur, Aros, please get Nora out of here. You all need to go. Tell the army to turn around, please, and leave with them." His voice was stern, but he was pleading with them not to fight. Aros and Arthur were poised, war in their eyes, gleaming swords drawn, standing protectively around me. They looked at each other, exchanging glances I couldn't understand. "Stand down," Rylan told the Astinian soldiers. They looked at one another, confused by the order. "Stand down or answer to the Astinian throne for treason," he demanded. Their swords and weapons clattered to the floor, a clash of metal on stone ringing off the walls. Rhonan let out a roar from underneath the gag in his mouth, thrashing back and forth, trying to free himself. Rylan drew a dagger from his belt and hit him on the head with the hilt, jarring him and making him slump to the floor, eyes closed and unconscious. "Go—take the west wing doors, they'll get you closest to the army. Tell them to turn around and go back to Lynnea. Please. This is your chance," he begged.

"I can't leave you behind, he will kill you." Tears filled my eyes, knowing that Rylan wouldn't listen to me, no matter what I said. He smiled at me half-heartedly.

"Turns out I'm not that easy to kill either, Princess."

Arthur pointed his sword angrily at Rylan. "She's the Queen. You will address her as such," he growled in a low tone.

I held my hand out to Arthur. "It's all right. It's just something he says."

"Well, he shouldn't."

I glared at him, and he closed his mouth.

"He's right, the assassin shouldn't address you that way," Aros muttered, shifting uncomfortably. I rolled my eyes.

"Lead the way out. I need a minute with him, please." Shock and horror filled Arthur and Aros' faces, but they both reluctantly led themselves and the others from the room, leaving me with Rylan, Rhonan, and the Astinian soldiers. I stepped into the hall where Rhonan had dragged me initially, Rylan following closely behind.

"I don't want to leave without you, Ry."

"You know this is your best chance. Their best chance. Even if you fight this battle and win, there will be bloodshed, a lot of it. You must go now. Once my father isn't tied up anymore, he will come for you. I need you to be as far away as possible." The sad but determined look in his eyes tore into my heart. He kissed my lips softly. I leaned into him, grabbing him tightly. I didn't want to let go, but he pushed me away. "I'm sorry, Nora. I'm sorry for causing all of this." He hung his head. Gently, I pulled his face to mine again, a tear slipping down my cheek, dripping past where our lips met. "Raysh is dead. You're free. Go back to Lynnea, where you belong."

"Will I ever see you again?" I let out a small sob as he embraced me.

"I'll make sure of it." He caressed my cheek, looking deep into my eyes. I memorized the beautiful green in his eyes, the dimple on his cheek, the way his mouth curled into the smallest smile. I turned back in the direction where the rest had gone. When I looked back, he had already disappeared.

Chapter 28

Allanora

My heart ached as I approached my brave envoy. Eight gallant knights, their fearless leader Arthur, and their Deity-King Aros. I was proud to call every one of them my subjects. I started down the steps of the castle toward them when a body landed on me, tumbling both of us to the ground. I opened my eyes and was face to face once again with Gen, her dagger drawn. Her eyes were crazy with anger, and she was flushed red. She held her dagger above my head. I flailed my arms out at her, but she had me straddled, pinned to the ground.

"He will never be mine as long as you're alive!" she shouted at me as she brought the dagger down. I closed my eyes and braced myself but felt nothing. I opened my eyes and saw Arthur over her, holding her dagger hand in his fist and her other arm behind her back. He yanked her off me harshly, disarming her and throwing her to the ground, placing his foot on her back to hold her down.

"Your Majesty, are you all right?" His voice was a mix of nervousness and frustration.

"I am fine, thank you, Arthur. This woman was a tool in the murder of Queen Violet. She is the one who poisoned her. I want her imprisoned. Tie her up and bring her with us," I ordered. He nodded. It felt good to be in control again, to be the Queen again. Gen wailed angrily as he tied her up and threw her on the back of one of the knights' horses. The memories of being tied up myself flooded my mind, but I pushed them away, feeling satisfied that Gen was finally getting what she deserved.

"My Queen." Arthur had his hand held out to me. I took it, and he pulled me up in front of him on his horse. I looked back and forth between all of them, beaming with pride. My father pulled his horse alongside Arthur and me, his smile unwavering. He looked at home atop Aelarion, a stallion I had ridden my entire life. My mother had said he was my father's horse, which made sense now; he was probably the only horse in the stables large enough for a Deity.

"My beautiful daughter. Queen of Lynnea. You are just like your mother." He reached out and touched my cheek. We started forward when a shape appeared in front of me, taking the form of a man. Sinric. He bowed low. I took in a sharp breath, and I felt Arthur's hand squeeze my hip.

"Your Majesty. I wish to bid you farewell," his deep voice bellowed up at me.

"Sinric. I would have loved to continue our learning journey. Perhaps, if you ever find your way to Lynnea, we could continue our lessons? I should be happy to give you welcome accommodations while you visit." Sinric's eyes darted between me and Aros. I followed his gaze to my father, whose nostrils were flaring out to the side, and he had a tight grip on his reins. "I'm sorry—do you two know each other?"

"Sinric offered to teach you to use your powers when you were a girl. Your mother and I had—well, we had other plans. Sinric and I fought," Aros said through gritted teeth. "We fought again; he wasn't supposed to come here."

"And yet, here I am," Sinric sneered. The tension between them was palpable; I could've cut through it with a knife.

"I don't understand why Sinric can't teach me magic. He's already started teaching me while I was trapped here in the castle." Aros snapped a cold glare in his direction.

"I think the Queen deserves the ability to learn from someone who understands her power," Sinric seethed.

"I think the Queen deserves to learn from someone who uses light magic only and has never been tainted by dark magic," Aros snapped back. Sinric smiled a half smile.

"Dark magic? You use dark magic?"

"I used dark magic once. To save a life. Almighty Aros never let me hear the end of it." *Dark magic to save a life.* I could understand that. Giving your soul for the life of a loved one.

"What do you mean? You understand my power..." I asked him thoughtfully. Sinric grinned. Aros drew his sword and held it to his throat, silencing him. Sinric held his hands up and took a step back. "Let him speak," I demanded. Reluctantly, Aros withdrew his sword and slid it back into its sheath.

"I understand your powers because I, too, have inherited my powers from my father. Rimus, God of the Sun, Patron Deity of my home, Drocia." *Another child of a God, like me,* I thought. *Another Golden Stem.* "I know what you're going through, Your Majesty. What you will go through as your powers grow and form. I'd like the chance to teach you if I'm allowed." He bowed low to me again. My father was seething in his saddle but stayed silent.

"With my father's blessing, I'd be honored if you traveled with us to Lynnea. I'm sure I have a lot that I could learn from you, Sinric of Drocia, son of Rimus." I cast an urgent look at my father, pleading with him. Reluctantly, he nodded, and I nodded once again to Sinric.

"I shall be honored as well, Your Majesty. Send for me when you return to Lynnea. I shall be awaiting your raven." Before I could respond, he vanished in a puff of smoke. My father let out an irritated sigh once he was gone.

"I understand your displeasure, Aros. But I need to learn to control my powers. He understands me in ways even you can't. He can help me. I won't use dark magic, I promise. But I would like to learn how to disappear and reappear like that." I smiled at him, a reassuring smile. He nodded, defeated.

"It's called pulsing. And I'm sure you'll learn it in time. All Deities and some witches and mages can do it. But Allanora, your mother and I agreed that this was not the best path for you. The presiding brothers of the Triini in Lynnea won't approve of you using your Goddess powers."

I sighed. "I'm tired of all my decisions being made for me. I'm tired of being helpless, I'm tired of being out of control. I'm taking my decisions, my power, my life, into my own hands. I want to learn from Sinric. I know why you did what you did, Father. I know why you bound my powers. This is my decision, and with all due respect, I don't need your permission," I snapped at him. I felt guilty but powerful. I wasn't going to let anyone make my decisions for me anymore. Not my father or mother, not Tobyn, or Raysh, or Rhonan.

I looked on the horizon and saw the entire army waiting where they had been commanded to stop. We met them on the field. I recognized the leader, Henrie, Tobyn's younger son. I felt anxiety rushing through me.

"Arthur, what is he doing here?" I whispered. "His father ordered my death and my mother's," I told him urgently. He squeezed my hip gently.

"Henrie is a close ally of Aros. He's been instrumental in helping us plan your rescue, my Queen. You need not worry, he's nothing like his father or brother." I shuddered, remembering Julian. Compared to Raysh, Julian was nothing. Julian was a pig, from what I remembered. Not a pig I would have ever wanted to be married to. All of that felt like a lifetime ago.

"Henrie," Aros greeted him. He looked out of place, dressed awkwardly in too-large armor. Henrie had never been a warrior. He was a bookkeeper, a peaceful and quiet man. Henrie bowed low to Aros and me from atop his horse.

"My Queen, how relieved I am to see you again." I nodded.

"Henrie, our army is not needed. We will be returning to our home. There will be no battle today. The Crown Prince of Astinia is dead, and the King subdued, if only temporarily. We have detained the woman responsible for the death of Queen Violet, too." Aros choked on his last words. "Your loyalty has had the utmost value to all of us. Whatever you ask of us, it shall be yours." Henrie nodded dutifully.

"As of now, I only wish to return home; my wife is with child, and I prefer to be with her at this time, as much as I can be." He swelled with pride.

Arthur led our horse forward, clasping Henrie's hand as he passed before continuing. The sea of soldiers parted, holding their swords out and bowing to me. My heart sang, feeling at home amongst the dutiful soldiers of Lynnea, proud to be sending them home to their families, where both they and I belonged.

Chapter 29

Rylan

I kept my father tied up in my room for hours. I'd leave him there for days if I had to. The castle was in shambles, drowning in the aftermath of the wedding and the feverish battles afterward. More men had died during Aros' search for Allanora than I had realized. Our halls were painted with blood spatters that servants were frantically trying to clean. My father's eyes stared daggers at me as if wanting to burn a hole in my soul. A futile attempt. Truth was, he meant nothing to me; he never had.

A couple of guards had followed me here, lingering around and waiting for something to do. "I don't need you here. Escort any guests left around the castle off the grounds, set up a perimeter around the entrance. Make sure the servants are getting everything put back in order. And find my mother." The demands slid strangely off my tongue. With Raysh dead and Rowan gone, they were treating me as Crown Prince, not a title I desired, but it served my purpose for the moment, no matter how uncomfortable it made me. I had moved my father to my room, hoping to buy myself some time while I decided what to do with him. I wanted to keep him locked up here, let him rot alone in his own prison like he'd done to so many before. Carefully, I had weighed the decision whether or not to kill him. He didn't deserve to live, I was sure of that, but I also didn't want to take on his kingdom or deal with the consequences of killing him. I resolved to release him and escape, knowing he'd probably hunt me to the end of his days. Perhaps I'd hide out in Lynnea, keep an eye on Nora. I pushed away the thought; I didn't want to endanger her any further. I was sure my father would declare war, but her soldiers would protect her, whereas if she were entangled with me, he'd be even more likely to come after her directly, and she'd been through enough.

We stared at each other in dead silence. I relished the sight of him too much. He finally looked every bit the way I always saw him; a sweaty, destructive monster that needed to be restrained. Eventually, I removed his gag with one of my daggers. The blade sliced his skin when I cut through the cloth.

"You—you atrocious son," he spat the moment his mouth was free. "How dare you betray Astinia. Your *King.*" I sat perched across from him, absently sharpening the arrows from my quiver and returning them to their place. "All for what? For *what?* Raysh is dead, Rowan is gone. And where was my youngest son? My trained killer, the *pride* of the Academy?" I scoffed at him. "You let that wretched Princess kill him. On their wedding night..." He trailed off as I slowly made my way over to him. He looked afraid, as if he was unsure whether I was going to beat him or torture him. Gods know I'd learned how to from the man himself. I savored his moment of fear, crouching down so we were at eye level.

"I killed him," I said plainly and watched the color drain from his face. "I stabbed him with my dagger and stood on his chest as he died. He fought me. Fought me hard. But I'm faster, I'm stronger, despite what you all seem to think, and *I killed him.* I watched the life drain from your precious heir," I whispered. The realization hit him, and he lashed out, trying to throw his body at me. I quickly stepped back, letting him thrash out at nothing. The door to my room burst open, and my mother entered. Her eyes were red and puffy, and her makeup was smeared. I felt a sting of guilt, knowing that I'd brought this upon her.

"Rylan. I don't understand, what are you doing?"

"Eudora," my father interjected before I had the chance to speak. "He murdered our son; he tied me up and let the foreign wench and her soldiers go. He's committed treason, Eudora." The sting of betrayal was apparent on my mother's face as she absorbed his words.

"Ro—Rowan, too?" She locked eyes with me. I shook my head. She sighed with relief; Rowan had always been special to my mother. They were most alike in ways Raysh and I never could be. Between Raysh, my father's heir, and Rowan, my mother's golden child, I was an orphan in my own family. Yet I was the only one left standing here.

"Rowan left of his own choice. He said he was returning to the Academy. Rowan is a coward; he'd rather run than fight for what he believes in. Or fight for anything." She dropped her head into her hands and continued to cry.

"It seems I bred two cowards!" Rhonan roared. My mouth twitched into a smile. "And the only strong one of your litter is dead." He snarled. I grabbed a sword from my wall, balancing it on my fingers.

"Are you challenging me, Father?"

His eyes gleamed. I cut him loose, and he drew his sword, scrambling nimbly to his feet.

"No!" My mother yelped, trying to stand in front of me. She faced him, bracing herself for his blow, as I'd seen her do so many times before. She was a loyal and obedient Queen, but she had always put her sons before her husband. He threw her to the side, slashing at me with his sword. I sidestepped him easily. He kept swinging, his brutish slashes coming one after the other. I moved defensively, bobbing and dodging him, forcing him into an angry rage. He hacked his sword at me again. This time, I raised my sword to meet his. Sparks flew from the metal on metal. I smiled at him, shoving him backward to the floor. He stood quickly, hauling himself up and lunging at me again.

"You. Treasonous. Bastard." He roared with each slash of his sword but stepped forward too far. I leaped to the side, sending him crashing to the ground, and kicked his sword from his hand with one foot. With the other, I held him down, planting the foot firmly on his back. "You're no son of mine," he let out with a heavy breath. I leaned forward over him.

"I wish nothing more than to not be your son." I plunged a dagger into his shoulder where Arthur's spear had hit him, disabling him entirely. My mother's scream echoed through the room. In one swift turn, I shot an arrow from my quiver through my window and vaulted myself out from the sill.

"Rylan!" I heard my mother shout from above me, but I wasn't going back. I didn't care. I was already scaling down the wall of the palace. When I dropped to the ground, I hoped I'd never have to see it or set foot in Astinia again.

I stepped forward into my unknown future as a lone wolf, free of my father, and felt a familiar sting in my shoulder from behind. My head snapped around, and I came face to face with Rowan, guilt and triumph written on his face. I dropped to the ground, unable to move. *Dragonshade.* Rowan laid me down carefully, facing me upward, flat on my back. *Oh, Rowan, when I come to, I'm going to murder you for this one,* I thought angrily. From behind him, I saw a figure step from the shadow on the sides of the castle. *Steele.*

The tall, menacing woman stood over me, an eerie smile spanning her lips. Her pale blond hair, almost white against the darkness of the castle, was pulled back in her signature bun. She had changed from her wedding attire back into her uniform, the one we all wore at the Academy. All black and form-fitting, leaving no extra fabric to grab onto in a fight.

"I've been looking for you, God-killer. It's time for you to come home. You have much to answer for." I couldn't speak, but I knew my eyes were still showing my emotions; enraged at her appearance, betrayed by my brother, and questioning what she intended to make me answer for. "Your precious Queen has run off to her kingdom with my daughter, intending to make her answer for the death of her mother. My Academy is being questioned for your failure to kill the Princess. And my two best assassins have gone soft at the hands of one woman. But don't worry, I intend to make you pay for Gen's capture. In the meantime, I'll be bringing you back up to your former glory. I always promised you'd do great things." She glared at me with some type of sick amusement before snapping her fingers at Rowan. He tied me up and strapped me to a board. Once I was secured, he started dragging the board behind him. He followed Steele north toward the mountains, toward the Academy.

Chapter 30

Allanora

I could barely remember the last time I had felt this much hope for the future. My choosing ball felt like a lifetime ago, and so much had happened since. I took in the beauty around me, the sun, the colors of the grass, the sky, the trees... Everything seemed so warm and joyful compared to the bleak, dark Astinian palace. I closed my eyes, feeling the sunlight on my face, casting its warmth throughout my entire body. I felt at peace, finally. Henrie had joined us, leaving the army in the charge of one of the generals. He had expressed his wishes to return to the library once all of this was over; he was not an army leader or a soldier and preferred his quiet life in the background.

We had ridden all through the night. Our party had continued well ahead of the army, which would take much longer to march back to Lynnea. With no impending battle on the horizon, there was no hurry for them save the desire to be back in their own homes with their wives and families. I, however, shared Henrie's pull to return as quickly as possible.

I hadn't even realized I had fallen asleep sometime in the early morning when the suns were just rising in the sky. My eyes opened to see a fully bright sky; midday had already arrived. I had slumped back against Arthur; he'd held me steady with one hand while holding the horse's reins with the other. I sat up uncomfortably, feeling guilty for being so invasive of his space.

"Your Majesty," he greeted me with a soft voice. "We are almost to the Lynnean border, it's right up ahead. He pointed to where the unclaimed land between our two kingdoms met the Lynnean border. Excitement jostled me fully awake, and I sat straight up. I could see the peaks of my castle in the distance, bright and inviting, nestled in a warm and lush forest that I never thought I'd see again. My eyes filled with happy tears; I was finally home.

"Oh, it's so beautiful. I had almost forgotten how beautiful it is." We got close enough that I could see the whole castle in the distance. I stopped the horse abruptly and slid down from the saddle, taking it all in. Arthur dismounted behind me, holding his hand out to make sure I stayed steady. "Arthur, I don't know how to thank you. I knew you recognized me. You came for me, even though it was dangerous. I wouldn't be here without you." He turned me to face him, and his baby-blue eyes met mine.

"I knew it was you the whole time. I couldn't stand seeing you held hostage by that—that ruffian." He bristled. I winced, the weight of how he felt toward Rylan hitting me like a bolt of lightning. He noticed my apprehension and gave an apologetic smile. "I'm sorry. I know he helped get you out of that situation. Your marriage…"

"It's all right, Arthur, it's all just been a lot for me, everything that's happened." Solemnly, I looked at the castle again, my resolve still intact. All that was behind me now. He took my hand gingerly and kissed it, making me blush slightly.

"My Queen," he lifted me back into the saddle, "we should get you back to your palace. You need to rest." I nodded as he swung himself back into the saddle behind me. He wrapped one arm around my waist protectively. I knew part of the reason I was still weak was from my close encounter with death and all the injuries I had sustained, but my exhaustion went beyond that. I was weak in my heart and in my spirit, not just my body. Back when Arthur first found me with Rylan and Gen, I would have been thrilled to have held his affection like this. But now, with Rylan tucked safely in my heart and Raysh held firmly in the forefront of my nightmares, the thought of anyone's affection only made me feel ill. Even with his arm held around me for protection, the physical touch was too near a reminder of Raysh's own harsh brutalization.

The last short leg of our journey passed quickly. In what felt like the blink of an eye, we approached the castle, the massive wooden drawbridge dropping triumphantly for our party. I slid down from the horse, my soul igniting with renewed hope as I stepped foot on the castle grounds for the first time since I had been kidnapped. Every servant, guard, and soldier bowed or curtsied as I walked past them. I sent two of the knights to the tower with Gen, telling them she needed to be bound and locked in a cell. No one was to come in or go out except to bring her meals. I'd let her rot in a cell if I needed to for the murder of my mother. The satisfaction of knowing that she'd never be able to harm anyone else again was fulfilling. *Not to mention, she won't be able to marry Rylan while she's locked up in my prison cell.*

"Your Majesty," a young boy bowed before me, I remembered him to be Tobyn's grandson, Henrie's oldest, by the name of Lysan. I nodded to him, and he pointed at Gen as the guards dragged her away, kicking and screaming. "Who is that?"

How can I explain Gen? I touched his shoulder gently with my hand, "She's a very bad woman; she killed Queen Violet." I figured he must be old enough to know the truth. The people of Lynnea had seen so much since my choosing ball.

"She looks..." he trailed off, searching for words. "There was a woman here, with my grandfather... before... well you know," his young eyes gleamed with sadness, "she looks like her. Except the other woman was older."

I nodded and pursed my lips. Steele. She'd been here in my own castle, plotting against my mother and me the whole time.

I hadn't even realized I was still walking down the hallway. Lysan had disappeared down a different hallway. The doors to my bedroom swung open for me. I had asked for servants to be sent up there with hot water for a bath. *Servants. Lyra!*

"Did Lyra arrive safely? Is she well?" I asked the nearest servant. She simply nodded but said nothing. I breathed out a relieved sigh. Now that I knew she was at least well, the first thing I needed was to completely wash Astinia off me, wash Raysh off me, before I could do anything else.

"Your Majesty," six handmaids greeted, ready to receive me, all smiling and curtsying when I entered. I hugged them each, thanking them for everything they did for me and for the kingdom. I never wanted anyone who worked in my castle to feel the way the Astinian servants were made to feel. I reached the sixth, and she turned her head up to me, greeting me with as much of a smile as she could muster, and curtsied almost to the floor. I lifted her chin with my finger, bringing her to stand fully.

"Lyra." I embraced her longer than any of the others. The weight of what the two of us had been through together lifted from us. We bore scars we couldn't get rid of, but we had both returned safely when we had not known if we ever would. "Lyra, I'm so sorry. For everything that happened to you. Please know that you will always have a home here, and I will protect you for as long as I live." She nodded her head silently, and I was painfully reminded of her inability to speak. I wiped the tears from her face.

All the fear from my time spent in captivity was washed off me with hot water. My body cringed at the feel of one of the handmaid's hands on me while she helped me wash. *Raysh is dead, Raysh is dead,* I reminded myself over and over, cringing under the touch. Tears stung my eyes, and I fought off a shudder. *Raysh is dead, Astinia is behind me, it's over. I'm home, I'm safe, and I have a kingdom to run.* The tears still flowed; I couldn't stop them. My heart thudded as the water washed me, trying to cleanse away my mother's death, my kidnapping, and my short time with Raysh. Aros' magic wouldn't be able to heal the bruises those memories left on my heart, my soul. I took a deep breath, in and out, and allowed myself to soak until my skin started to wrinkle from the moisture, and the water had gone cold. When I finally arose, I was toweled off, my hair was styled in my favorite regal braid, and I was dressed in a beautiful cerulean gown. I never imagined I'd miss color so much in my life.

The doors opened, and a guard peered in. One of the handmaids waved him in, but he stood respectfully at the door.

"Your Majesty, when you are ready, your father has requested your presence in the throne room." He bowed to me and straightened back up.

"Thank you, sir, you may go," I said softly. He nodded and left the room. I let out a content sigh and stood, moving a couple of strands of hair back into place. Then I reached for the door handle to leave.

"Wait, Your Majesty!" one of the handmaids called out quickly. I turned to see her holding my mother's tiara, the one I had worn for my choosing ball. I knelt, allowing her to place it on my head. Standing back up, I felt whole again. I'd been given another chance to do it right, and I wouldn't waste it.

The guards escorted me to the throne room, where I was awaited by Aros, Arthur, and Henrie, accompanied by his wife, Eleanore. I greeted the men each in turn, returning their bows with a curtsy. Eleanore started to curtsy, but I caught her, bringing her back up straight.

"Please, there's no need in your condition."

She bowed her head. "Thank you, Your Majesty." Her hand touched her swollen belly absently as she turned her head back to look me in the eye, and I felt a twinge of sadness, or perhaps slight jealousy, as she leaned back into Henrie, who caught her in a loving and protective embrace.

"Your Majesty." Arthur held his hand out, guiding me to my throne. I forced back a wince. The last time I had been led down an aisle like this, it had been Rylan at my side and Raysh standing in front of me. The thought brought bile up my throat, but I fought it down. Now, three other men stood before me, Aros in the center, flanked by Henric and Arthur.

"Allanora," Aros started. "The time has come that I must return to hiding with my siblings." His voice was thick with urgency. I felt myself tense up, confronted by the fear of losing him when I had only just met him. I still had so many questions, and there was a certain safety I felt knowing here was here to protect me.

"I don't understand, you just got here. I haven't spent any time with you. I thought you'd stay."

"The agreement that was made with the Trinii at the end of the war still stands, my daughter. The Deities are to remain in hiding, not participating in the affairs of the twelve kingdoms. If I stay any longer, they're going to come for me, and Lynnea would pay the price. I left to spare you and your mother, the kingdom. I can't risk all of that now." His eyes welled up with tears. "Besides, I fear a war might be coming anyway. We may have won this battle, but there will be consequences for what happened in Astinia. With the Crown Prince dead and two traitorous sons, we can only hope Astinia destroys itself. But we shouldn't underestimate them. Should they come for Lynnea, I need to be with my siblings to convince them to fight. I don't know if I can, but I have to try." He approached me and touched my cheek gently with the back of his hand. "You truly are your mother's daughter; she did a wonderful job with you. I only wish that I'd been there to see it all." I nodded, not allowing myself to feel sad. "But, my dear, Your Majesty, I did make a few agreements that I would ask you to honor."

"Agreements?" I asked him and glanced at Henrie and Arthur, who were waiting eagerly by his side.

"Henrie has asked that in the event of a war, his family be treated as your own. Henrie has been loyal to you and this kingdom his whole life. He promised me he'd look after you from afar when I was forced to leave, and he upheld his end of the bargain. When his father and brother were put on trial for your mother's murder and your attempted murder, his loyalty did not waver. He has looked out for your best interest and that of the kingdom his entire life, and I agreed that, when the time comes, his family would be under the protection of the throne." I nodded vigorously and made sure to acknowledge Henrie. Out of the corner of my eye, I saw Eleanore breathe a sigh of relief.

"Yes, of course," I said diplomatically.

"There's one more thing," Aros continued, lacing his fingers together uncomfortably. He gestured to Arthur, who dropped to one knee before me. I studied them both carefully. "Arthur, of House Blackwood, has asked my blessing for your hand, should you choose him to be your husband. Arthur alerted us to your whereabouts and led the envoy to your rescue. He put his own life and interests on the line to protect you and your kingdom. He has only asked for a chance to be considered as your King Consort whenever you feel inclined to choose one."

I wasn't sure why I felt so shocked. This was how I imagined it would go at my choosing ball. I'd look into the eyes of a man I barely knew and accept a proposal for marriage. But that felt like it had been a lifetime ago, and everything had changed so much. I had changed so much. My mind was in a whirlwind of emotions. All I could think of was Rylan. Which was silly. Rylan never wanted to be married, and I was sure he never wanted to be a King, *let alone a father.* Absently, I touched my lips, thinking of our last kiss when we had parted, and he had promised to see me again. But I still had a duty to fulfill. I was Queen, after all. I stood, walking toward Arthur, and placed a hand on his shoulder.

"Arthur of House Blackwood. You honor me with your proposal." He looked up at me; he was truly handsome, and his heart was pure gold. Gently, he took my hand in his; it was warm, and his touch was comforting.

"The honor is mine, Your Majesty."

"I cannot, however, in good conscience, make a decision like this at the moment." His face fell slightly, wounded. "I have been through a great many trials of late, and my heart and mind have grown weary. I would just ask for some time to right myself and make this decision with a clear head." He kissed my hand and rose, meeting me face to face.

"You take all the time you need, Your Majesty. I'm not going anywhere." His hand swept a lock of my hair behind my ear, and before I realized what he was doing, he brought my face to his, catching me in a soft kiss. I stiffened and felt my heart jump slightly, but I didn't allow myself to lean in, even though I felt drawn to do so. The sensation was too much, the fear too fresh. I reminded myself that though Raysh had been demanding and rough, Arthur was being loving and spontaneous. His lips felt softer and less experienced than Rylan's, but I felt the familiar warmth of desire as he drew himself back from me. Without thinking, I let out a breath. I snapped my eyes open and saw Henrie and Aros standing open-mouthed. Eleanore was blushing and holding back a giggle. My face flushed, embarrassed. He smiled triumphantly. "I'll court you for as long as it takes until you're ready to make your decision." I held my hand up to speak, but he turned and strode confidently from the throne room, leaving me with the others, all with questioning looks on their faces.

"I think we'd best be going, my dear," Henrie whispered to Eleanore.

"Hang on one second," she said to him, freeing herself and approaching me, taking my hands in hers. "Your Majesty," she started. "I wanted to speak to you after your coronation, and I'm so glad to finally have this opportunity. My mother died when I was very young, and I was forced to grow up without her, get married without her, bear children without her. I know how lonely that can be, how confusing that can be. I know that no one can replace your mother, of course, but I hope that maybe you and I can become friends; perhaps I can bring you comfort, knowing you don't have to go through all this alone. Or even if you just need someone to talk to, you know, about other things." She cast her eyes toward where Arthur had just exited the room, giggling a little bit again. I leaned in and hugged her gently, being careful not to squeeze her belly.

"Nothing would make me happier than having a friend in this lonely castle," I said softly, returning her giggle as I thought about Arthur and Rylan. It would be nice to have someone to share all that with. She squeezed my hands and returned to her husband, who kissed her softly before turning around to lead her out of the throne room, leaving me alone with just my father. I let out a heavy breath, turning my attention back to him.

"So, you're going to leave again?"

"Well, yes. But first, I'd like to have a ceremony."

"A ceremony?"

"Yes, when I came to Lynnea to reclaim the throne in your mother's name and put those men to death, I made myself King of your people. I think it would be nice for Lynnea to see their Queen crowned again, properly this time, and give some closure to my time with them. It's unfair that you were robbed of your choosing ball and your coronation. I want to try to give that back to you. If you'll allow me." I nodded, throwing my arms around him and hugging him for the first time. He was tall and muscular; I had to stand on my tiptoes to even be able to embrace him properly. His hands drifted to my head, holding me in a protective embrace as I always imagined a father would.

"Allanora?"

"Yes?"

"What happened to you in that castle?" His face was quizzical, and he was studying me carefully.

"Do you really want to know?" I cautioned. He shook his head after a moment of thought.

"Just tell me one thing."

"What's that?"

"Do you love him? The assassin?" I froze. Did I love Rylan? My heart pounded with anxiety and excitement as I thought of him.

"Honestly, Father? I don't think I know." He nodded and, without a word, exited the room, leaving me alone with my thoughts and my throne.

I sat on my mother's throne, my throne, considering everything that had happened. In such a short time, I had gone from being almost completely isolated, without a real friend or much family in the world, to being surrounded by love. My mother had been my only family, but now I had a father. I had Henrie, Eleanore, Arthur, and I still had Lyra, of course. Then there was Rylan. Someone who had caused me so much pain but also made me feel things I never had before. I felt guilty, pining for his touch, his kiss, his warmth, when I had a proposal to consider from a good Lynnean man. A knight who would be a Great Lord when he succeeded his father. Arthur wanted to marry me, run the kingdom with me, father my children. He was handsome, kind, brave, valiant; everything I could want in my husband. It would be a union blessed by my father and all of Lynnea, but I couldn't get

Rylan out of my mind. I just needed some time to process and get my mind straight. Maybe I wasn't the same woman who'd been ripped from Lynnea. The same lost and frail girl who'd just lost her mother and wasn't ready for anything. *A lot has changed.* I sighed again; it had been a lot.

Chapter 31

Allanora

The morning light of the suns broke through my window shades, casting small, golden beams into my bedroom. I opened one eye, surveying the room to make sure it was really my bedroom in my home, making sure that it hadn't all been a dream. A couple of days had gone by since I'd been home, but I still couldn't believe everything that had happened. Excited and impatient, I had sent for Sinric right away, with slight protest from my father. We had our first official lesson yesterday. I couldn't believe Sinric's power; his control over flames and light was astounding. I had much to learn, but my magic was strong, and I knew, with his direction, I'd manage to control it properly. I relished the thought that with my powers, no one would ever be able to harm me the way Raysh did again, and I wouldn't have to watch helplessly when my soldiers rode to battle.

This morning was to be the day of the ceremony that my father had planned to honor me by stepping down from the throne and returning it to me in front of all of Lynnea. An ordeal that filled me with excitement and dread. Every ceremony I had attended of late had ended badly, and anxiety filled me, wondering if this one would be any different.

I had sent for a new dress to be made specially for this ceremony. A beautiful purple silk ballgown embroidered with hundreds of tiny stones of all colors. It was hanging on a partition, and the light was bouncing off the stones, casting beautiful colors all through the room.

I heard a tiny knock on the door, and I bid them to enter. Lyra and a few other handmaids entered the room, curtsying to me before busying themselves, helping me get ready. After I had washed and dressed,

Eleanore entered the room, looking very pregnant and tired. She held her hand on her stomach as a handmaid helped her to sit down next to me. Even in her tired state, she glowed, motherhood becoming her.

"Are you ready, Your Majesty?"

"Eleanore, please, just call me Nora."

"Sorry, I keep forgetting." She blushed and nodded.

"Are you feeling very well?" I asked her. She nodded again but shifted uncomfortably in her chair.

"Oh, yes, I'm well, just ready for him or her to grace us with their presence. The end is the worst." She smiled through her discomfort. "I'm told Arthur will be escorting you today?" I blushed a deep red.

"I can't very well hold him at arm's length forever. He's so kind and handsome, well-mannered, and did I mention handsome?" She giggled and nodded. "I guess I'm not sure what I'm holding on to, but he asked if he could be my escort today, and I couldn't turn him down."

"So—" Eleanor paused and frowned, seeming to choose her next words carefully. She turned around, surveying the faces of the handmaids, and leaned in to whisper, "Is it the Astinian husband? Did you love him?"

"The Crown Prince? Raysh? Heavens, no," I shrieked.

"Then, what is it? What's holding you back?" I looked around at the handmaids, all tuned into our conversation, though they pretended to busy themselves. I waved for them to be dismissed, and they filed silently out of the room, a couple of them looking thoroughly disappointed.

"Can you keep a secret?" I whispered.

"Of course, Your—Nora." She smiled her bright, inviting smile.

"I might've had…a little thing with the Crown Prince's younger brother." She covered her mouth with her hand. "The assassin? The one who kidnapped you?" She gasped, her eyes wide.

"Well, yeah, I guess." I blushed hard, feeling stupid hearing it out loud.

"Did you—well, you know?" Eleanor was locked in, and for a moment, I didn't feel like a Queen with a mountain of responsibility and expectations on my shoulders.

"No, no, no." I beamed. "Not like that, but I did kiss him. Well, I kissed him a lot," I gushed.

"You like a dangerous one, huh?" she teased.

"I guess... There was just something about him, something that lit a fire in me. At first, it was hatred, definitely hatred. But he never hurt me." I started to feel hot and fanned myself with my hand, the familiar heat I felt when I was near him burning in me. "And I don't know, it just turned into desire. One day, we were in an argument about, I don't even know, and he kissed me, albeit angrily, and we both just... We felt it." I sighed heavily. Eleanore's eyes were wide with wonder.

"Nora, this is straight out of a fantasy! Well, I guess I never realized that Queens were allowed to have passion," she jested. "I thought it was all advantageous marriages to old men." She giggled. "That Arthur, though, he's a handsome man, young, from a good family, heavy roots in Lynnea," she prodded.

"I know, I know. At my choosing ball, and when I saw him out in the woods after I had been kidnapped, he would've been my immediate choice. I don't know, I guess I'm just having a hard time letting Rylan go."

She nodded, taking my hands in hers. "I understand. The 'good' and the 'safe' and the 'right' choice can feel boring or restricting. And to experience passion and love are a blessing in this life. Follow your heart. That's all you can do. Sometimes, other people will try to guide you in one direction, but in the end, you're still a Queen." She waited a moment, studying my expression. "It's funny, one of our kingdom's most important traditions is the choosing ball, your ability to choose an advantageous marriage or one of love, and yet seems to be one of the largest burdens you must have to carry. Your mother made her choice, a strange match based solely on love. Their marriage had its advantages, sure, but also its difficulties—" A knock on my door interrupted our conversation.

"Come in," I called. Arthur entered, dressed in full pale blue ceremony attire, a shin-length dress coat over a vest and suit pants. A large oak tree with a sapphire embedded in its trunk, the emblem of House Blackwood, adorned his broad chest. Eleanore stood, touching my shoulder before leaving the room quietly. Arthur's smile was warm and brilliant. He bowed and rose, offering me his arm to take. I blushed slightly, thinking of my conversation with Eleanore, and took his arm. It was hard and strong, yet he had such a soft and gentle grip on me.

"Are you ready, Your Majesty?" I nodded, allowing him to lead me down into the ballroom. The doors opened for us, revealing hundreds of Lynneans dressed in full ceremony attire, smiling at me. The men all wore similar garb to Arthur, with varying colors, embroidery, and house emblems gracing their chests. The women wore magnificent ballgowns that dripped with jewels, all colors except for purple, which was reserved solely for the Queen. As the new reigning monarch, I could have chosen a different color to represent my reign, but keeping purple was my way of honoring my mother, the beautiful Queen Violet. I was starting to feel as if I had never left, as if I was back to the night of my ball. All that was missing was my mother and the mystery man waiting to twirl me across the room. I hesitated in the doorway, suddenly feeling anxious.

"It's all right, Allanora. Nothing is going to happen to you here. We doubled the patrol; the castle is completely secure," Arthur reassured. I found myself clutching him tightly, digging my nails into his arm. He was unphased. I nodded, taking in a deep, shaky breath.

Arthur escorted me down the stairs as a footman announced us. The people below us clapped as we descended; some even cheered. As we reached the bottom of the steps, the sea of people parted for us as we made our way to be seated. Before we reached the table, Arthur surprised me by twirling me around, showing me off in front of everyone. My dress sparkled in the light as I spun, and I flashed him a smile before he brought me into his arms. I felt my cheeks color and saw Eleanore smiling at me from our table; she gave me a wink when I caught her eye. I waved at everyone around me and took my seat at the table.

Aros stood, greeting everyone by raising his glass.

"Good evening, fine people of Lynnea. On behalf of my late wife, Queen Violet, I'd like to welcome you all to our celebration here. As you all know, after the death of Queen Violet and the kidnapping of Queen Allanora, I came here to rid this beautiful kingdom of the reign of King Tobyn, who orchestrated the atrocities. I came here with a purpose: to bring justice to those who played their part in the death of my wife and to bring Allanora back from Astinia, where she was being held hostage. As justice has been served and your rightful Queen has returned, it is my time to leave Lynnea once more." The room was quiet as everyone hung on every word Aros said. He had such a way of commanding his space and demanding attention and respect without forcing it. I hoped to emulate that one day. "Tonight is my official transfer of power back to my daughter, your loving and devoted Queen of Lynnea, Allanora." He raised his glass to me, as did everyone in the room. Light bounced off the shimmering glasses, creating a rainbow that cascaded throughout the room.

I stood from my seat at the table as two footmen came and placed the crown on my head, and the entire room erupted in a cheer.

"Long live the Queen!" Arthur shouted from the seat next to me, resulting in an echo of the chant rippling through the ballroom.

I looked around, seeing how everything in my life had turned out. I was back on my throne, surrounded by good and kind people, feeling an outpouring of love. I had real friends for the first time in my life and an unwavering support system. This image before me was what had kept me alive in Astinia, and now, I was standing before it. This was all I needed, and everything else would fall into place.

Arthur reached out and took my hand in his. His touch was warm and gentle. He smiled at me and kissed the back of my hand as he looked deep into my eyes and smiled.

A Dance of Storms and Shadows

"My beautiful Queen," he whispered. His eyes were locked on mine, and my heart skipped a beat. I had found my new beginning, my new path, and I was ready to take it.

The End

About the Author

S. L. Green has been writing since she started school, she either had her nose in a book or a pencil in her hand. In addition to writing, S. L. Green is also a Reiki Master, a teacher, and makes jam for members of her community at the local farmer's market. S. L. lives on an island in Michigan with her husband, two young children, and deceptively cute dogs, Arlo and Ein. Despite living in a generally cold state, S. L. loathes winter. Though she loves astrology, went to school for creative writing and photography, and enjoys pineapple on her pizza.

Acknowledgements

Scott, my biggest cheerleader, my soulmate, who always reminded me how important it was to just keep going, even when I was feeling discouraged.
Hudson and Elinor, who are the reason I breathe, and who inspire me to make the best of myself every day and challenge me to show what I'm capable of.
My parents and in-laws, who supported me in pursuing my passions.
Ashley and Pauline, my fellow booklovers, and the only people I know who truly understand the love I have for reading and writing. Ever may we reign as the true Book Club Queens.
Lani, who loved these characters from the very beginning, and always believed in me.
Hannah, who taught me the true meaning of friendship and reminds me daily that it's ok to follow your dreams.
Natasha, Emma, and Amy, who walked me through this whole amazing endeavor, answered every silly email, and worked tirelessly to help make this book as perfect as it could be.
Ivan and Katia at MiBlart for designing the beautiful cover and map to frame my world.
Rebecca at Purely You Photography, for taking such wonderful author portraits for me.
And to Mrs. Dusute, sorry I wrote this so poorly the first time in seventh grade, I did it better this time I promise. You always cheered me on and understood that writing was my passion. I finally reignited that dream.